An Unlikely Hero

(Book #3 in the 4-book The Cutteridge series)

Cindy Nord

cindy@cindynord.com

I love to receive emails from readers who share their 'book thoughts' with me...let's connect!

DCT Associates

Copyright 2016

Cover by Lyn Taylor

ISBN: 978-0-9976573-1-9

Praise for Cindy Nord's Cutteridge Family Series

"You'll savor every ounce of passion, adventure, and transformation in Cindy Nord's exquisite debut novel. I didn't want it to end."

~ *Cynthia Wright, Romantic Times and Affaire de Coeur multiple award winner on No Greater Glory*

"The love stories are fantastic, and the research done by this author is minutely perfect – right down to the clothing worn by her characters.

~ *Katherine Boyer, Midwest Book Review*

"Cindy Nord writes powerful, well-crafted novels of complex emotions and beautifully drawn characters that explores the inherent risks of falling in love with one's enemy."

~ *Laura Taylor, multiple Romantic Times Award winner.*

"The love scenes are steamy yet tender. Recommended for anyone who enjoys historical romance, as well as those who would find appeal in a steamier Gone with the Wind."

~ *Library Journal on No Greater Glory*

DEDICATIONS

For Tom, the love of my life ... ALWAYS.

For mom and dad ... Who gave me wings to fly.

For Tex ... Evermore, my bridge.

For Di ... Writing made Delightful.

And, for Louise ... Agent Extraordinaire

CHAPTER ONE

Washington D.C.,
May 1873

Who in the hell came up with this asinine plan?

Dillon Reed grimaced at the stench of burning coal as he jammed the colonel's telegram into his coat pocket. He cut his gaze across the station platform to the nearby locomotive. In a deluge of color, passengers descended the railcar's iron steps; he kept his attention riveted on the opening.

An exasperated sigh escaped from between clenched teeth. He'd delivered the governor's territorial reports to Washington in just under three weeks, a remarkable time, and he looked forward to a swift, unencumbered return home. But, when he'd checked the telegraph office for messages before heading out, this newest malarkey of an assignment waited. He'd also been instructed to shave and freshen-up prior to meeting this train from Boston, but Hell's chambers would freeze solid before Dillon would make the effort.

I'm an army scout, for Christ's sake, not some damn nanny.

A grating responsibility rolled into focus when a peach-colored parasol, the signal he'd been awaiting, popped open to fill the train's doorway. Dillon shoved from the depot's wall and straightened, the crown of his slouch hat bumping a sign that read *Washington, District of Columbia – The*

Capitol of Your Country. The plank swung back and forth on squeaky hinges.

Heat fused with anger when his contact's traveling boot glided to the first iron step. Good God, her entire foot could fit in his right hand.

His gaze climbed a dark-green dress rigged with a ridiculous bustled contraption, raked over a fur encircling slender shoulders like a buffalo mane, then finally came to a stop on golden curls swirling upward into a tarnished knot. Atop the silken mass, a scrap of hat perched at a cockeyed angle. A dozen blue and green ribbons fluttered in the afternoon breeze with all the spectacle of a peahen.

Dillon's throat tightened as the woman descended to the platform, radiant among the other travelers. Her ability to stand out in a crowd added another sting to the onerous assignment. For a full minute, he waited while she scanned the throng, anxiousness shadowing her face. Narrow of waist, she stood barely five feet tall…a good stiff wind would blow her over.

Another curse welled inside him.

The urge to walk away warred against every ounce of military commitment he possessed. What did he do to the colonel to deserve such wretched torment? Dillon straightened, then stepped from the shadows of the depot to collect his damnable…*assignment.*

Boots thumped against weathered wood as each stride echoed his resentment. How could this slip of lace endure the miles they'd have to travel, or the harsh sun of the desert? Christ Almighty, she'd end up sick or dead and slung over his saddle in no time. As his shadow darkened the woman's diminutive form, he retrieved the telegram from his coat pocket, then tightened his jaw.

"Alma Talmadge?" he snapped.

She swung to face him, her eyes widening.

Dillon thrust the telegram forward, his words cleaving the air. "Per these instructions from your uncle, I've been assigned as your escort on the trip westward to Fort Lowell."

A well-shaped brow arched with suspicion. Her mouth tightened as she abruptly scanned the words, her golden-tipped eyelashes raising and lowering with each haughty sweep. A moment later, her gaze lanced back to his. "I was told to expect a proper attendant."

"Proper?" he snorted. "I'm as proper as you're gonna get."

Her attention riveted on his sweat-stained Stetson, then slid all the way down him to his scuffed-up cavalry boots. When their gazes reconnected, disgust dulled the spark in her indigo eyes. "But ... you're no gentleman."

"Where we're going, lady the last thing you'll need is one of those dupes who can't find his ass with both hands."

Repulsion cascaded scarlet across her face. She pressed a dainty, lace-edged hankie to the column of her throat. "I cannot possibly travel with the unkempt likes of you. Y-You're not even clean."

The insistent urge to walk away blistered deeper. "The job is to deliver you safely to the fort...which I intend to do. Cleanliness does not increase my skill."

Her gloved hand clenched the ivory handle of her parasol.

And a streak of hope shot straight through Dillon.

With God's own luck, maybe she'd turn tail and scurry back aboard the train.

Instead, her chin rose. Along with his disgruntlement.

"When I left Boston, Father assured me I would be comfortable with the arrangements." If she'd carved her words into a block of ice and handed them over, her obvious loathing of him could not have been colder.

Dillon scanned her smooth forehead, the silken hollows beneath her cheekbones, her pale and polished skin. He leaned down, his body dwarfing hers. "Did he also mention we're not going on some afternoon jaunt here? And there's no changing your mind once you start missing the lavish amenities of home."

He bumped the brim of his hat against the parasol's silk ruching. "And once we're past Fort Hays, there's no more trains. No embroidered cushions. No luxuries of any kind. In fact, it'll just be me and you and an unforgiving trail back to Tucson." He narrowed his gaze. "We'll be moving fast -- by stagecoach, if we're lucky, by horseback, or on foot, if we're not. And the last quarter of the trip will be through desert, where the heat can kill even able-bodied men."

Confident he'd made his point, Dillon eased back. In fact, he'd surrender a full month's pay without a moment's hesitation to decline this idiotic assignment. "Now I'm not sugarcoatin' this one damn bit so you still have time to reconsider."

He crumpled the colonel's telegram into a tight wad, then jammed the paper into his coat pocket.

The woman merely jutted her chin. "Lord Green assured me it would be an easy journ--"

"Lord Green should've told you the damn truth," he cut in. Whoever the bastard was, he needed his ass kicked clean into next week. Dillon grimaced. He just couldn't keep his damn mouth shut. "And to spare any woman from realism is neither admirable nor honest. I'll be sure to remind the sonofabitch of this fact should we ever meet."

She starched her spine, straightening. "Lord Henry Smyth Green is the Earl of Lochnor. He is every inch a gentleman, Mister..."

"Reed," he growled, pulling his hat brim lower. His eyes narrowed. "Dillon Reed."

She lowered her hankie, and the fluttering pulse in the hollow of her throat caught his attention.

"Well...Mister Reed, my father insists it's safe, and others support his assessment. In fact, Lord Green, *my fiancé*, awaits my arrival. I've little to say in this matter, but if I did, I certainly would not have chosen the likes of you to act as my shield of protection westward." She tilted her parasol to block the sun's glare and scanned the crowd before reconnecting her gaze with his. "Regardless, if my family believes I am safe shackled with... you, then I shall sally forth in my adventure."

Dillon glared across the top of her hat, straight through the green and blue strands of ribbons that fluttered in the afternoon breeze. *Good God, the obnoxious chit views our two-thousand-mile trek as nothing more than an inconsequential hitch in her otherwise lark of a life.*

"And in the future, Mister Reed…"

His glare collided with hers.

"You will do well to remember it is not your place to tell me where I can--or where I cannot go." Her clipped words dripped with censure. "Your task is simply to get me there."

The muscle beneath his eye twitched. The desire to tell this arrogant, bustled-up sugartit exactly where she could go chaffed at him like a tick on a horse's ass. But, he stifled the urge. After all, she was right: He wasn't a gentleman.

Gentlemen didn't kill people.

Anxiety uncoiled from the pit of his stomach. Miss Alma Talmadge embodied everything he despised in this world. *Every. Damn. Thing.* But he owed her uncle, which was the God's truth. Without the colonel, he'd have no job. By now, he'd most likely be in jail.

Or dead.

Habits were hard to break. With an exaggerated bow, Dillon stepped back and motioned for her to proceed to the station house. Head high, parasol aloft, she walked across the wooden deck. As she passed, an elusive fragrance wafted from her person and reached out to stroke his senses. The scent blocked the stench of the locomotive and the crowd milling around him.

And rolled back the pain-filled years.

Roses?

The redolence whirled through him, bouncing off his sanity. *Jeezus.* Did she have to smell like roses? He hadn't relished anything quite so inexplicably woman in years, and he wanted to lose himself in the intoxicating pull. The aroma whispered of long-ago memories of contentment and happiness and love.

He inhaled, deeply…just once, to quench the hellish thirst inside his heart.

On a rough groan, he tightened his jaw. Christ Almighty, he'd rather track a mess of Apache any damn day than babysit this spoiled rotten debutant all the way to Fort Lowell.

***

"Hell no, you can't take them all. Good God, woman, have you no idea where you're going?"

Alma fought to ignore the sheer size of the man while she held her ground behind the eleven steamer trunks that lined the weathered walkway. She could scarcely tolerate him these past three minutes, how could she possibly be expected to endure him for the three-week journey? She swept her gaze over him. A long, mud-colored jacket topped an equally dark shirt and neither had seen soap and water in weeks. Beneath a wide-brimmed hat, dark hair tumbled well below his shoulders. And the thick, tangled strands hadn't met a comb or a brush in at least as long. Stubble shadowed his angular face and upper lip, only adding a wicked distinction to his features.

Worse, a disparaging glare radiated from his eyes.

Dangerous and intimidating -- both words perfectly described this filthy beast. Yet, Alma swallowed fast in an attempt to hold her emotions at bay.

Fear was too strong a word for the feelings coursing through her. This man didn't frighten her. *Did he?* A sense of isolation loomed ever closer as anger at this newest circumstance ripened inside her. Worse, she must now face all of these life changes in the companionship of someone completely unsuited with her station in life.

"Mister Reed," she snapped, praying the bite in her words masked her growing frustration, "these trunks contain everything I'll need in this adventure westward. I certainly don't intend to stand here in the blinding sun and squabble with you about this as if we're common dockhands." She waved him off with a flutter of her hand. "Just move along and make the proper arrangements for putting my belongings onto the correct train westward."

The heathen veered closer, dark brows slamming together. Again, the muscle beneath his eye twitched. With all the force of a raging storm rolling in off the sea, his voice rumbled over her, "Lady, we won't be taking all of these."

Alma fought back another rush of tears as tightness pulled fresh across her chest.

She blinked fast, several times, to staunch the ludicrous urge to weep. These trunks contained her Worth day gowns, her pantalets, petticoats, corsets, bustles and dressing robes, everything sewn exclusively for her by a half dozen exacting seamstresses. And this…this looming imbecile expected her to just leave them all behind?

She swallowed back the bile as she caught the fan suspended from a pale pink ribbon around her wrist. Dropping open the slats, she fluttered the fragrant sandalwood before her in an attempt to catch her breath. What if someone she knew saw her speaking with this lummox? Her gaze dropped to the revolver strapped low around his lean hips.

He probably shot people to death in their sleep.

The soothing image of her diminutive Lord Green flashed through her mind. Her fiancé smelled of limes, not livestock. And in the seven months she'd known the man, she'd never once seen the Earl angry. Nor would he dare to curse in her presence. In fact, he indulged her every whim.

Alma stared up at the heathen. The entire two-day trip from Boston to this Washington D.C. train station she'd envisioned a portly, white-haired escort greeting her. One of her uncle's retired soldiers, perhaps. At the very least, a mannered companion to keep her well amused while she traveled westward to her new beginning. The moment this rawboned toad materialized before her, his eyes squinting in the sun like a madman's, all those agreeable images shattered.

He shifted slightly and crossed his arms. "Your behavior is not the cooperation the colonel's telegram promised. Perhaps, I should wire him back and mention your defiance."

Her approach toward this ungainly reprobate, along with the idea of hiring a more suitable attendant, evaporated as quickly as they had breathed to life. Her father would not approve of her disobliging behavior, and Uncle Thaddeus, the colonel at the fort in Tucson and the destination where she now traveled, might think her a reckless malcontent.

Alma pressed her lips together and inhaled, drawing in much needed air.

When her traveling companion had fallen ill shortly before the train departed Boston, her father still insisted Alma continue onward. The fact that she'd never traveled anywhere without Mrs. Butterfield obviously mattered little to her father, and his strange behavior confused her. The promise that he'd arranged a suitable escort through Uncle Thaddeus to meet her here in Washington consoled her so she agreed to continue. *Think, Alma. Think!*

Surely a lifetime of garden soirees, society balls, and the finest of finishing schools that Talmadge money could buy would help her in this dreadful circumstance. After all, she'd honed her womanly skills to perfection.

Alma again studied the lanky-haired man. Afternoon light played across his chiseled features and obnoxious stand. However, if she looked close enough, beneath all the grime, she could almost see a handsome countenance.

Her lips curved into a soft smile.

Oh yes, she knew full well how to manipulate even a grubby, gun-toting troll such as him. After all, he was only a man.

"Mister Reed," she said, her words dripping with sweetness. "There are many things a woman requires to attain a level of modesty." She ignored his scowl. "Proper etiquette forbids me to speak of personal items, but even in your dangerous part of the country, women surely must have… unmentionable requirements. You know, essential feminine belongings men don't quite understand." She paused to press the hankie to her throat again, taking note of his downward glance. *Perfect.* "I'm to be married soon after arriving at your fort, and everything in these trunks is vital to my trousseau." She gave a soft sigh as she twirled her parasol above her shoulder. "Even you can't deny me my unmentionable womanly requirements, can you?"

Instead of the stammering apology she expected, a heavy silence followed.

His gaze darkened as he stepped closer, dwarfing her beneath his shadow. "Allow me to enlighten you, Miss Talmadge. I'm in charge of things now, so you won't be doling out the marching orders." He thumped his thumb against the center of his wide chest. "I will. And while you're assigned to me, we'll be doin' things a bit different from here on out. Starting with you saving your womanly guile for the sonsofbitches who let you spoon-feed them."

Alma's mouth dropped open.

An ache unfurled in the pit of her stomach as she glared at the pewter buttons riding the front of his shirt.

He pulled back just enough to allow in a bit of sunlight. "But I'm not a heartless bastard either, so I'll allow you one traveling case on the train. I'll freight the remaining trunks to the fort."

Her parasol dropped to her shoulder with an unladylike plunk as a rush of heat bathed her cheeks. "One? That is absolutely preposterous! How am I to manage with one?"

"Trust me. You'll learn."

She'd learn?

With a resounding whoosh, she closed her parasol.

What an arrogant pig!

"Surely you have the decency to allow me time to choose the items I'll need for my immediate journey?" She glared up at him with an arched brow. A heartbeat later, he withdrew a key-wound watch. He flipped open the elegant cover, and an eighteen-karat-gold Brequet with black enameled Roman numerals glinted in the late-afternoon sun. Why would this man possess such a splendid timepiece?

"I suggest you decide quickly while I make the necessary shipping arrangement, " he growled. His detestable smile widened as he slipped the watch into his pocket. "Or these trunks can stay right here on the platform. Matters little to me. In exactly thirty-four minutes, you and

I will be on that westbound train, with or without your unmentionable requirements."

***

Simon Bell stepped from the shadows of the station house and watched Alma Talmadge and her male traveling companion board the train. A smile curved his lips. Revenge had never felt so sweet.

He signaled to the three men standing near the railcar. They acknowledged with quick nods, then boarded the train behind the couple.

All too easy...

Simon shoved his hands into the pockets of his woolen overcoat, sauntering onto the platform. Sunlight fell over him in a wash of warmth. He'd lived in darkness for so long, but now...now he possessed the power to change his life.

His excitement grew.

Payback awaited...within easy reach.

A blast from the locomotive drew him from his thoughts. With a smile, he strolled toward the ticket office, the worn, wooden planks creaking beneath his black hessians. Charles Talmadge's daughter or her companion would never reach their destination. But first, he must head to Boston and kill the man responsible for every damned thing wrong with his life.

CHAPTER TWO

Fort Lowell, Arizona Territory…that same day…

"Shall I wait for a reply, sir?"

Colonel Thaddeus Talmadge shook his head. "No. That'll be all, private."

The soldier offered a quick salute, then closed the door.

Thaddeus picked up the just-delivered telegram from his desk. He leaned back, the squeak of the wooden chair momentarily drowning the tick of the mantel clock across the room. Sunshine filtered in through the narrow window and draped a warm beam across his shoulder. He angled the envelope into its paltry stream and squinted. Hell's fire, he'd half a mind to requisition a whole damn bank of glass. That way he could see something. A mocking snort fell from his lips. If he did manage to work new windows into his military budget, he'd roast to death from the heat of the summer sun blazing through the panes.

Maybe he'd just order a fancy new oil lamp from San Francisco. Something bright and ornate and worthy of a colonel's office. Thaddeus glanced around the sparsely appointed room, the frown on his lips shifting into a lop-sided smirk. Despite his ongoing efforts to bring the fort up-to-date, the high brass back East belittled those who spent money fancifying any of the outposts that hugged civilization's western edge.

He squinted again and sighed. Sooner or later, he knew he'd have to break down and buy spectacles for his aging eyes.

From the parade ground in the center of the fort, a bugler's sharp trill heralded early morning troop formation. In a few minutes, he'd be required outside for the daily review of his men. He flipped open the envelope and withdrew the crisp velum.

Thank you for ensuring safe passage for my daughter. If she were to remain in Boston she would be in grave danger. I trust the army scout you assigned to accompany her is a competent soul. Suffice to say my philandering has caught up with me. I promise answers to your questions soon. Your grateful brother, Charles Talmadge

Thaddeus dropped the telegram to the desktop. Beyond the window, the bugler beckoned once more. *Damnit Charles, what've you gotten yourself into now? And why mention your indiscretions so openly?* He slipped morning-stiff fingers around the handle of his favorite coffee mug. Raising the chipped porcelain, he swallowed the last of his liquid breakfast with a grimace. Good God. His only sibling had built one of the largest shipping empires in the world from practically nothing, yet he'd never been able to control his male urges worth a damn.

Thaddeus thumped the empty cup beside a stack of requisitions. The last time he'd seen Alma, she'd been a young child at her mother's funeral. He'd promised Charles he'd visit again soon, but time always got away.

Tunneling fingers through his thinning hair, he stared down at the words. Charles' correspondence two days' before had been pleasant when he'd requested the chaperoning arrangements. Thaddeus agreed, since her fiancé was currently at the fort anyway, and it would be good to see his niece again before the Earl and Alma sailed for England after their wedding. Besides, it was fortuitous that Dillon also just happened to be available.

But now, intuition's disconcerting chill ignited a heavy sigh.

Something wasn't right. Meshed between the lines of this message lurked a startling tone. Almost frantic, even for his promiscuous brother.

Alma's in grave danger?

Thaddeus leaned across the desk, snapped free a clean slip of paper, then reached for the inkwell and pen. He had enough to worry about with Apache uprisings, raiding Mescalero, and the added responsibilities during General Crook's absence to corral Sioux up north. He sure as hell didn't want additional trouble visiting Fort Lowell. Dipping the pen into the indigo liquid, he thanked the Lord he'd had the good sense to press Reed into this god-awful assignment. His best scout would find a *warning* telegram waiting when he checked for messages at Fort Riley.

***

Two days on the westbound train and they'd crossed into Indiana at midmorning. Alma ached from hours sitting properly poised. A raincloud of tension engulfed her as she shifted once more to relieve the pressure where her corset pinched tender flesh. She stared at the tatting shuttle resting in her hand. After battling the idea for hours, she finally conceded. Conversation with the filthy beast sitting opposite her was better than no conversation at all.

She lifted her head and glared at the man, his large body slumped in the seat where he'd been lounging all morning.

"Mister Reed," she said. "Are you going to sleep away this entire journey?"

A full ten seconds passed before he unfolded his arms from across his chest. Another five seconds were lost before he lifted the hat from his face. He peered at her from behind half-closed lids. "I'd like too," he said, then resettled the Stetson over his eyes.

Behind her someone coughed, and the sound scraped against Alma's fraying nerves.

She tossed aside her handiwork. "I have not uttered a single word since we left the Cincinnati train station early this morning."

His mouth tightened beneath the wide brim. "So how 'bout we keep it that way."

He stretched one long leg, and Alma lost sight of his boot as his foot slipped beneath her seat.

Soft chuckles floated from the elderly couple sitting across the aisle.

Alma's throat squeezed. Had they heard the unpleasant exchange? She glanced at them, an icy smile plastered across her lips.

Relief enveloped her – they'd paid her no mind. All morning the white-haired lady had been diligently knitting while her companion read from a periodical. Several times, he'd stopped to share the latest news. And together the couple would comment on the foolishness of politics or some other trivial slice of life.

Alma swallowed, as another sigh slipped out.

She continued glancing around the railcar. Dozens of people travelled the strip of iron to faraway destinations. Were they all embarking on new lives as well? She scanned the plush drapery embracing the train's windows. Gold-colored cords held back blue velvet, allowing sunshine to pour inside. An intricate pattern of hammered tin hugged the ceiling. Since leaving Washington, she'd twice-counted the one hundred-and-fifty-two shiny square panels, as well as the brown leather benches, one facing the other, paired up in twenty individual groupings – ten on each side of the railcar.

A smartly-dressed steward moved up and down the aisle, ready to assist with the passengers' needs. A newspaper? Cigars? A glass of port or sherry? All were produced with a smile as he pocketed his hard-earned gratuity. Could he as easily supply an end to this madness? Somewhere behind Alma, a baby began to cry. The shushing from the mother hissed through the enclosure with all the intensity of a steaming tea kettle.

Alma pressed her lips together to stifle a scream. The Baltimore & Ohio had spared no expense in artful decorations, yet no amount of money could make this kind of torture bearable.

The noonday sun penetrated the window, and a trickle of perspiration inched down the back of her neck. She ached again for the people who loved and supported her and for those who found joy in her smile. *Coward*, she thought, struggling to ignore the suffocating isolation. At any other time, such distress would be forbidden. She pulled her shoulders back, shrugging off the ill-contented mood.

Her gaze resettled upon her escort. Why had her uncle assigned such a despicable man? And why had her father agreed? More importantly, why had he changed her wedding plans and instead sent her away with such short notice?

Alma shoved aside her disappointment, more determined than ever to strike up some kind of conversation with the recalcitrant toad. Anything to take her mind off her intolerable discomfort. "As disagreeable as this arrangement might be, Mister Reed," she said, stopping short of prodding him on the filthy, denim-covered shin resting much too close to her traveling dress, "ignoring each other will not change the fact we are bound together. So I have decided we must make the best of this situation."

Silence. Not even a grunt. Alma linked her fingers, and pressed, "I would like to chat."

He pushed back his hat. Like two dark wings, his eyebrows rose over equally dark eyes. "Chat?"

At the edge in his voice, Alma stiffened. "Yes, chat. 'Tis a pleasant activity civilized people do to communicate."

He refolded his arms. "In your refined world perhaps, but where we vulgar men live, we prefer sleeping over empty words any damn day of the week."

Empty words? A few choice ones rumbled through her brain to match the unending profanity that tumbled from his. She subdued another shudder. Bluntness seemed Dillon Reed's strong suit. She would try that route. "Could you at least try to be courteous?" She held his gaze for a long moment, then stared out the window.

Unmarred by even one cloud, the sky's vastness stretched before her – a blue so brilliant her eyes ached. Endless waves of rolling hills and forests spread from horizon to horizon as the leafy canopies of massive trees fluttered beneath the whim of the Indiana wind. Clacking train wheels vibrated beneath her, each revolution carrying her farther and farther away from the familiarity of her world.

The baby's hiccupping sobs punctured the stale air.

Cigar smoke plumed around her.

I will not scream. Alma shifted, readjusting the corset's pinch. She glanced toward Dillon Reed, and tightened her lips. Torn between holding back tears and whacking him with her reticule, she mustered a tolerant smile. "You have information about where I'm going. Things I'd like to know. Don't you think this is as good a time as any to share them?"

Someone kicked the back of her bench. Alma fought to contain her shriek. She reached up, pulled out her hat pin, and re-speared the Fanchon into a firmer position atop her head. Never in her life had she shared such little space with so many disheveled individuals. And the dreadful breakfast she'd consumed at their morning stop still churned in her stomach. If she retched on the callous brute, it would serve him right.

A heavy sigh rolled from the man as he pushed himself into a sitting position. He glanced out the window for several seconds before looking back. Sunlight streamed through the pane enveloping him in a patch of brightness. The hat's wide brim laid a butter soft shadow across his face. "What do you want to know?"

Pleased with his compliance, Alma leaned forward, yet her attention flicked downward. He flexed his fingers around the tarnished buckle of the gunbelt at his waist. Dry-throated, she met his gaze once more. "Tell me what it's like...o-out west, I mean."

A smirk touched his lips. "It's big and it's dangerous."

"Be more precise, Mister Reed. Please." She'd received only one letter from her fiancé in the time he'd been in Tucson, but the flowery descriptions were more annoying than informative.

"It's no place for a woman like you."

Alma ignored the gauntlet he kept slapping down between them. "Are there many women in the territory?"

"A few. But they're accustomed to hardship and have learned to settle for less. They need neither coddling, nor maids to do for them."

The brute obviously liked sparing. She indulged him. "But women are women, Mister Reed, and each one brings a certain sense of propriety. Would you not agree?"

"I'll agree women change men."

Even this cockeyed discussion was better than glaring at him as he slumbered for hours on end. "Now see, we've managed to string several sentences together into a conversation. And, in fact, we have even succeeded in remaining civil to one another. As I may, or may not have mentioned, I'm to be married out west upon my arrival, although the thought does upset me. You see, I was hoping to marry in my mother's rose garden." She was rambling and she knew it, yet hopeful excitement laced each word. "I was simply waiting on Lord Green to return. He's currently on assignment out west to study American military protocols at the request of the Queen herself."

"I see," he mumbled, his gaze drifting over her shoulder.

"Yes, and he is quite important. Why, he's even entertained your territorial governor." He kept staring, seemingly ignoring her. Frustration plucked at the chord stringing together Alma's displeasure. "What in the world are you looking at, Mister Reed?"

His eyes narrowed. "Nothing you need to worry about."

She tilted sideways to block his view. "Well then, perhaps you might know this governor? Or where his yearly cotillion will be held?"

"His what?"

Bolstered by the success in recapturing his gaze, Alma pushed onward, "Yes, Lord Green says your governor is quite a colorful character. And he hosts a cotillion in his mansion every summer. I certainly hope we're not too late to attend."

Her escort swiped his hand across his face and inhaled, the sound long and pained. "I'm not sure where your lord gets his information, but there's no mansions in Tucson. I don't even know what a damn cotillion is, and the governor doesn't confer with me about his entertainment schedule."

A hesitant smile tucked into the corner of her mouth. "A cotillion is the social event of the season." Well-versed in the subject, she was more than willing to share. "It's where everyone dances until dawn to a stringed orchestra, and champagne is served in the finest of fluted stemware. Everyone dresses in their best attire." She adored waltzing and for a split second wondered if this lumbering ox even knew how.

"I hate to disappoint you, Miss Talmadge, but the closest thing Fort Lowell has to an orchestra is an odd collection of brass instruments and a few Mexican mariachis." He flipped the gold tassel on the curtain cord. "You see, it's rough out west, and stemware, fluted or otherwise, eventually breaks. And between Indian uprisings, their consequent slaughtering and Mescalero banditos kidnapping and raping of our women, well...," he paused, his gaze tracking back to hers, "...I'm afraid there's little time left for dancing."

Alma's breath tripped into a soft gasp as her mouth formed a tight *O*. Slaughters involved blood. And rape ... rape involved ... Visions of the horrid brutality smeared the enchanting images of flickering candlelight and the gaiety of dancing couples.

Painful seconds passed.

And then, the shadowed hint of a days' old mustache riding the curve of his upper lip shifted as a smug grin tipped his mouth. "You're not a whore, a senorita, or a squaw, therefore you have no damn business being in my territory." He leaned back against the seat and once more pushed his hat over his eyes. His words were barely audible from beneath the brim. "But thanks for the chat. I'll be going back to sleep now."

Anger welled up with all the force of a gale storm to vapor Alma's momentary horror. How dare he toy with her emotions in such a vulgar manner?

"'Scuse me, ma'am," the train steward asked, drawing her instant glare. He hovered near her elbow, a tray of empty shot glasses clutched in his battered hands. "Can I fetch you somethin' to make the journey more enjoyable?"

"Yes," she snapped. "I would like an immediate passage from this nightmare."

"Sorry, but we ain't stoppin' again 'til we reach Vincennes." He issued a sympathetic smile, then moved off down the aisle.

The baby behind her wailed.

The persistent cigar smoke swirled.

No escape ... Alma's frustrations grew.

A throaty chuckle rolled from beneath the wide brim of his hat and she glared at her companion.

The beast had the audacity to laugh?

CHAPTER THREE

"So I gather this trip wasn't your idea?"

The deep voice startled Alma. She pried open her eyes and focused on her companion.

Dillon stared out the window into the darkness beyond.

Did I just imagine the knuckle-dragging mongrel spoke to me?

He looked over, his eyes illumed with a perplexing intensity. "This trip, was it your choice?"

Teetering hours-on-end near the precipice of an abysmal hell, Alma released a boorish snort. "I told you. Though I'd planned my wedding for August when Lord Green returned, Father insisted I marry as soon as possible. It's loathsome, to say the least." She was languishing from sheer boredom -- the only logical reason for her to make such a candid disclosure. Not to mention the distressful fact that her father had ushered her out of Boston beneath the cloak of darkness. Her nerves still jangled from his odd behavior.

The scout traced the metal framework where glass met steel. "Why not just tell him you didn't want to leave?"

"Mister Reed…" Alma exhaled, straightening in her seat. "…one does not tell Charles Talmadge anything. He tells you. When he met the earl through business dealings, my fate was sealed. Besides…I completely approve of his choice."

"Do you love him?"

"My father? Of course, I love him."

"No." His gaze penetrated...unsettling in its pull. "Your fiancé. Do you love him?"

She tightened her jaw, uneasy with their conversation's sudden twist. "Now that is surely none of your business."

"So, I take it you don't." He refolded his arms over his chest. "And you're probably marrying him because of his supposed importance -- Lord Half-wit being titled and all."

She chafed at his satiric disrespect for Lord Green. "I am uncomfortable with all this prying." Another detestable bead of perspiration trickled down behind her ear. She raised a shoulder to swipe away the moisture, mentally counting the days until she could submerge herself inside the rose-infused depths of another bath.

"Are you now?" He chuckled. "We're talking. You should be tickled pink."

Her chin shot up. "Well, I'm not." At what point had this man decided to mock her on her choice of husband? *The nerve of this pompous ass.*

"Look, I'm not here to judge you--"

"But you are. And you don't even know me." She shoved back a limp curl. "Why do you insist on being so...uncouth?"

He stared at her with dark eyes narrowed. "It's who you are, Miss Talmadge. Your type."

The oppressive warmth of the train's compartment was nowhere near as suffocating as the heat now pulsing her veins. "And what type might that be...exactly?"

They glared at one another, the muffled *clackety-clack* of the train's wheels matching them breath for breath.

"Forget it," he growled, trailing his gaze back to the window.

Outrage slammed through her. "Oh, but I insist you tell me, Mister Reed. What type of woman offends you so much you would utter such an insulting tone?"

His head whipped around, his days-old beard—a sable swath across the lower half of his face—delineating a rigid jaw. "Alright then, I'll tell you. The type whose wealth and beauty only emphasize her rapacious nature."

"Perhaps you feel so strongly because you're ignorant of society's ways."

He gave a brittle laugh. "I learned all I need to know from my mother."

"Your mother?" Alma heaved an exaggerated sigh, thrusting back against the leather seat. "I'm shocked someone as coarse as you would even have one." The ache in her heart blossomed at the utterance of mother; she missed her own so much. "Besides, what does your mother have to do with your abhorrent lack of manners? Other than obviously not teaching you any of your own." Shame filled her at her comment as she fought back an imbecilic need to weep. She knew better than to be so rude, knew the impact of how words hurt, but the cad prodded her when normally she'd never utter such spiteful comments.

Dillon placed his hands on his knees and leaned forward, his elbows splayed. His nose nearly touched hers. "Her people were just like you, Princess. All sharp-clawed and demanding." His gravelly whisper spiraled through the shadows to brush her face. A shiver prickled through her. "Those same socialized sonsofbitches pushed her out the door...and straight out of their lives. And because of that, I was left to pick up the miserable pieces of what became of *my* family."

Alma's face blazed. "What? I'm unable to respond when you mumble in such riddles." She clutched gloved hands together in her lap, trying to ignore the damning resentment in his eyes.

He stood and loomed above her, his gaze locked with hers. A mere heartbeat elapsed before his lips crooked into a deprecating grin. "Then I shall remember to keep you confused throughout this entire journey."

He brushed passed her.

Alma twisted in her seat, scowling at his retreating form.

The low-lit oil lamps hanging from their polished brackets flickered, sending gamboling shadows up all four walls as Dillon stalked to the end of the aisle. He jerked open the door.

Clackety. Clackety. Clackety.

The cacophony of the train's wheels rattled through the chamber, waking the sleeping passengers. The baby resumed the same high-pitched wail he'd been sharing all afternoon.

Her escort stepped outside and shoved the portal closed, muffling the grinding sound of metal against metal.

Alma stared through the door's single-paned window as Dillon Reed's broad-shouldered form entered the attached gaming car, then disappeared from view. In all her years, no one had ever stormed away from her like that -- *no one*. She curled her hands over the back of the seat, her fingers pressing against cool brass studs anchoring leather.

But...h-he's supposed to stay with me.

Faster than she could blink them away, tears welled in her eyes. As frightening as this unknown land stretching mile after endless mile before her, now an unbalanced sense of abandonment encompassed her.

Chapter Four

Boston, that same evening

Charles Talmadge exhaled a thin stream of smoke into the air. The fragrant cloud mingled with the pleasing aromas of liquor and leather appointments in the parlor. *Ah, yes. I shall sorely miss this place.*

Settling deeper into the overstuffed wingback, he stretched his legs and rested his booted feet atop a stool. He relished his hard-won position as president of the Eastern Yacht Club. And among the many changes he'd initiated, last year's renovation of this room had been his most aggressive. Elegance now encompassed every inch of the once-dowdy gentleman's establishment. Floor-to-ceiling draperies hugged the windows, and cranberry-colored velvet trimmed with gold-corded fringe held back Boston's inclement weather, as well as the tawdry simpletons who toiled on the docks beyond.

The very same docks where I once labored.

He shook off the remembrance and continued his perusal. Expensive paneling lined the walls, a twelve-foot high palisade of unadulterated Massachusetts timber cut from the dense walnut forest on his estate. He rested his head against the chair's brocaded back as a seldom-used smile tugged at his lips.

Charles lifted his cheroot, then tightened his mouth around the fine Virginia tobacco, pulling in another blistering bite. Smoke burned the back of his throat as he savored the first-rate Dunnington. He glanced to the sideboard. Smack-dab in the middle sat a small chest of quartersawn oak. Last month he'd purchased the stylish humidor once owned by Thomas Jefferson.

A fact that only added to his extreme pleasure.

If only Margaret could see me now. He shoved aside the pang of sorrow at the memory of his wife. Her absence remained as raw as her sudden passing had been a dozen years before, and no amount of whoring could ever replace her. Thank God their baby girl, now fully grown ... and a striking beauty like her mother ... was out of harm's way and traveling westward to the English nobleman who would keep her shielded from life's brutalities.

A brutality I created.

The shocking warning he'd received last week, via a hastily-scribbled note had given him ample time to set his plans into motion. Again he offered thanks for the skilled escort his brother had provided on such short notice. An army scout. Dillon Reed. The gun-slinging bastard had damn-well better keep Alma safe, or Charles would shoot the man himself.

Clinking glasses lured his gaze back to his companions. Some read newspapers. Others chatted in hushed voices, but everyone in this room, as well as in the attached gaming hall, were counted among the important men of America.

And every one of you bore the living hell out of me.

An old crony, the owner of a well-traveled rail line in Massachusetts, lifted a decanter and motioned in Charles's direction.

Charles nodded. "But make it a small one, Ernest. I'm bound for England at dawn. Don't want to miss the boat." He restacked his expensive Wellingtons into a more comfortable position on the tufted footstool, then leaned back and took another long draw. Curling his mouth to form an O, he exhaled wispy rings. The smoke defused the lamplight's shine, then faded. Charles smiled as once more the gilded glow illuminated the grandeur of the hammered gold ceiling tiles above his head. *Another one of my additions.* The subtle sounds of splashing cognac and low laughter ebbing from the gaming salon drew his attention.

"It's unlike you to mingle with the help," said a nearby companion, the owner of several shopping pavilions along the eastern seaboard. The man set his drink on a mahogany side table next to the divan. "Do they even know you're coming?"

"No, but the captain'll clear out his quarters soon enough. After all, I own the damn shipping line."

Their laughter blended as Charles propped his cigar in a nearby ashtray. He accepted the proffered drink and squelched the urge to hide his hands, calloused and arthritic from years of pulling rigging and rope. How he hated the unsightly reminder of his early years.

From its lofty roost above the mantle, a Thomas Eakins painting—his most recent gift to the club—glowed in the lamplight. Flickering shadows breathed into life a fully-rigged Dutch schooner, its sleek bow cutting through the waves as foamy sea spray billowed into a glorious white arch across the canvas.

The siren's sweet call echoed through Charles's mind.

The click of billiard balls in the adjoining room drifted through the wide-arched opening to emphasize the masculine nuances of...his club. Sighing, Charles raised his glass and took an appreciative sip. If only White's, in London, possessed the same comfortable complexities as this place, rather than the stick-up-their-asses stuffiness insisted upon by the Brits.

The railroad baron who'd poured their liquor settled into the chair opposite him. "Why in the hell are you sailing to London, anyway? Rather short notice, isn't it?"

Charles stared at the nosy sonofabitch. *To stay alive ... as if it's any of your damn business.* Instead, he offered, "I've got urgent matters at the shipping office over there."

"Christ Almighty, Talmadge, send an assistant. That's why we hire them." The blunderbuss tipped his head back and swallowed the expensive 1858 Cuvée Leonie in one quick gulp.

Charles stifled the urge to pommel the oaf, and instead swirled his cognac, pleased with the way the amber liquid draped its velvety 'fingers' with each determined revolution. He took pride in delivering only the best libations to his membership. And this particular 16-year-old elixir should be sipped with deep appreciation, not chugged as though it were fuel for some wheezing locomotive.

An hour later Charles rose, straightening the hem of his brocade vest over his massive girth. He traversed the room, shaking hands with those still present at the late hour. He didn't care one flying fig about most of them; nonetheless, he performed the cordialities as if he did.

At the front entrance, he bowed. "Well, gentlemen, I shall be gone for three months, perhaps longer. While I'm away, do try to keep things together."

Without waiting for their replies, he turned the doorknob and exited the club.

The footman leaning against the black-lacquered equipage peered through the darkness as he approached, then straightened. Charles glanced to the team of horses. Moonlight spilled across the two magnificent Bretons he'd just acquired from Scotland…a stalwart team to pull his newest cradle-sprung Brougham down Boston's bricked streets.

His steps faltered as his gaze swept back to the vehicle.

Bloody damnation! My coach lamps aren't lit!

Never had his staff disobeyed a direct order; both knew he needed the extra illumination to enter the vehicle safely, more so after a night of drinking.

Charles scanned the servant holding open the door.

Strange…when did Abner grow so tall?

His gaze cut to the man sitting atop the rig. With hunched shoulders, a rumpled coat and a half-empty bottle resting beside him, the driver sure as hell wasn't Clarence, either. In fact, neither man was one of his trusted employees.

The skin at the base of his neck prickled. Charles raked his gaze over the doorman swathed in a heavy cape from head to toe.

Their gazes met.

Shock slammed through the apprehension of moments before.

Dear God. Simon Bell!

Charles staggered backward several steps. "Y-You!" He glanced toward the Yacht Club, praying others had exited and were making their way along the cobbled path.

The walkway remained empty.

Sweat beaded his brow. If he tried to run, he'd be overtaken in a heartbeat. Nonetheless, he had to try. Charles turned and bolted toward the clubhouse door.

Footsteps pounded behind him.

A hand clamped around Charles' upper arm, jerking him back around. Charles wheezed and gulped for air as he glared into the cold eyes of his attacker. With the cape's hood fallen back, moonlight drenched well-defined features.

"You can't outrun me, old man." Simon's eyes were raw with hate. And a heartbeat later, he angled a dagger against the rapid rise and fall of Charles's chest. Moonlight glinted off etched steel. Charles groaned when the thin blade pressed where brocade pulled taut across his pounding heart. "You've a debt to settle that is long past due."

Terror welled within as the stench of cheap whiskey wafted over Charles, evoking memories of a wharf tavern, the wench who lived upstairs, and a tow-headed toddler darting among buoys and ropes and lobster traps scattered along a wooden pier. But a whore was a whore, and held no place in his swift rise to the top.

Now, that toddler stood before him fully grown.

"W-What do you want? " Charles stammered, sweat slicking his brow. "I-I've paid your mother for years. Her deathbed letter last week warned me of your anger. But, you needn't worry…I'll continue to pay."

"You'll pay?" The mocking question oozed into the night. "By God yes, you'll pay." The dagger pressed deeper, and Charles swallowed back another moan as the tip bit into his skin. A scream locked in his chest. "I've waited this long only because of her. Now, my mother is dead; a long, torturous demise wracked with pain, heartbreak and disease. Unlike yours, which shall be swift and well-deserved." He pulled Charles forward.

"And nothing is going to stop me," he hissed with unhinged vengeance. "Not you. Not your daughter, whom I shall kill next. Not even your goddamned money, Father."

Simon's teeth gleamed in the moonlight around his smile, and then, with a strong thrust, his bastard son drove the blade deep into Charles's heart.

CHAPTER FIVE

St. Louis reigned supreme as a major trading hub since the completion of their imposing railroad bridge over the Mississippi. Indeed, the world's longest railed connection arched over one of the world's longest rivers with enough height to allow the tallest steamboat passage beneath without leaving a single soot stain on the triple-spanned beams. The pier and abutment caissons, the deepest ever sunk, stood firm in the stalwart Missouri granite which anchored the colossal structure into earth. America's expansion westward ignited here as progress now bulged the seams of the once-quaint river town.

With a firm grip on Miss Talmadge's elbow, Dillon guided his companion away from the passenger car and down the platform leading to the depot. Crossing the threshold, they entered the dimly lit building. Small by eastern standards and nowhere near prepared to receive such a flow of humanity, the shadow-filled depot could scarcely contain the influx of travelers. He scanned the room looking for anything amiss. Habits were hard to break, even in the middle of civilization.

As he started to relax, a man bumped against his charge, pitching her against him. Dillon glanced at the culprit, the same man he'd caught staring at Alma on the train.

To warn the man Miss Talmadge was beneath his protection, Dillon wrapped his arm around her shoulder and glanced at her.

A moment later, she slipped her right arm through the crook of his left one. Dillon nodded – surprised at how well they fit together. Obviously, she'd forgiven him for his earlier crassness last evening of momentarily leaving her alone in favor of the gaming car. He shoved aside the bewildering thought, plowed into the bustling throng, and made a beeline for the front door. She stuck to his side like a burr against wool, allowing them to move at an even faster clip.

Halfway across the congestion, his audacious little minx even had the good sense to wrap her gloved-fingers around his upper arm. Dillon chuckled. And increased his stride.

After side-stepping porters and locals waiting on new arrivals, Dillon finally flattened his palm against the walnut panel and gave the main door a shove. He had half-a-mind to thank Miss Talmadge for her quick thinking--and even quicker steps--but the rough-hewed panel leading to the metropolis beyond swung wide and stole away his thoughts.

Despite the late hour, they emerged into a bustling city.

Flickering gas lights perched atop ornate cast-iron poles illuminated the area in a golden wash, and numerous aromas battered Dillon. The scent of fresh-baked bread and grilled onions rose above those of the trains. He dismissed the growling ache in his empty belly and led his bedraggled companion around rain puddles from a recent shower. With arms interlocked, they crossed the cobbled road, stepped over embedded steel tracks used by horse drawn streetcars, and headed for the closest dining emporium. Two blocks away, the Southern Hotel loomed in the distance, light and shadows dancing across its elegant façade.

A few passengers from the train trailed behind him. From their conversations he knew they were also eager to enjoy the finest cuisine west of Pittsburgh. The hotel also boasted the cleanest linens in St. Louis for those willing to pay the extravagant cost, which Dillon never elected to do. The madness of the city made him avoid even the luxury of bed sheets for fear of becoming entangled in them. Every time he came through here, the insanity of the city impaled him like a knife to the chest, a potent reminder that wide open spaces would always be his draw.

The red brick sidewalk fell away beneath his boots as he headed toward the six-story establishment. To his right, pounding hammers and shouting voices radiated from the emerging Grand Avenue Water Tower soaring a hundred feet above the buildings. Construction neared completion on the Corinthian-columned structure. Then, with but a turn of a silver handle, these fancified city folks would have water delivered right from a spigot in their homes.

God spare me from the contraptions of the wealthy.

Moments later, he reached the gilded entrance of The Southern. Miss Talmadge dropped her hold around his arm when an attentive doorman nodded at them with a grin. Dillon placed his hand on her upper back, ushered her over the threshold and toward a maître d'.

Dillon lifted two fingers in the man's direction. "Two please."

The attendant smiled, then escorted them toward the closest empty table. He pulled out their chairs and waited while Alma fussed with her bustled contraption before settling into place. She stowed her parasol beneath her chair.

Dillon lowered onto the ornately-carved spindle-back opposite his charge.

The maître d motioned for a waiter before resuming his place near the front of the restaurant.

The thought of thanking Miss Talmadge for her good sense to hang on to him back in the train depot again flashed in Dillon's mind. As he opened his mouth to mention so, she tossed her reticule atop the linen tablecloth and leaned forward.

"I have been sleeping bolt upright for the past three nights," she rasped. "Why can't we secure lodgings for the evening? I have plenty of money to pay for our rooms."

He had adeptly ignored her earlier request when the train had entered the station, but as she ramped up the tone of her appeal, ignoring her now seemed imprudent. With a sigh, Dillon dropped his hat on the floor beneath his chair, and then straightened, running a hand through his hair. "We're only changing lines here."

"Can't we change lines tomorrow?" she asked, her question shifting into a more annoying modulation.

"No. We're taking the Kansas Pacific across the plains. From there we're catching the southbound stage at Fort Hays."

Her pert mouth tightened. "I must insist we wait for the next train."

Dillon squelched the urge to sprint for the nearest exit. "We've only got an hour while they take on supplies, Miss Talmadge. Then we're pulling out for Jefferson City." A waiter moved past him balancing a tray of libations. Dillon fought the urge to swipe a glass of whiskey off the silver platter.

"Mister Reed," she huffed, "a one-day delay will not matter in the least."

It does to me. His stare locked with hers as he finger-tapped the linen tabletop. "We're not staying in St. Louis any longer than necessary. The stage out of the fort isn't always reliable, so I want to get there as quickly as possible."

And it can't come a minute too soon as far as I'm concerned.

Her expression pinched as she rammed back against her chair. She made a grand display of placing her napkin across her lap. "What supplies does the rail line need, anyway?"

Dillon stifled his surprise at having won this particular sparing match. "For the train?"

She answered with a quick nod as she fussed with removing her gloves, then laid them to the side of her reticule.

"Well…" He drew his own linen cloth across his lap. "Aside from refilling the food stuffs, we're changing to a train whose locomotive has a bonnet smokestack, which tells me it uses wood for fuel. They're stocking with split timber and water, as well."

Blinking, she stared at him. "Trains have different smoke stacks?"

Her question seemed genuine. "There are many kinds," Dillon replied, "but for the most part, straight-stack engines, like the one that brought you from Boston to Washington, uses coal for fuel." He readjusted his holstered revolver, aligning the Colt along his thigh, careful to avoid brushing his dirty boots against her dress. She was so high-strung right now that if he smudged her hem, she might have a conniption fit right here in the middle of the great metropolis. "The locomotives with bowled stacks like the one we'll be taking next, use wood for fuel and are covered by metal screens to catch the embers. Wouldn't do to accidently ignite the wood. A stray spark in the tinder could spell disaster for the whole train."

"I see." She scanned the other diners in the room, then her gaze respeared his. "Why does an army scout know so much about trains?" She leaned back a few inches when a short Chinese waiter arrived.

Dillon nodded to the man, who smiled and handed them each water-filled glasses before moving on to the next table of diners. "I've come this way several times since 'sixty-eight, delivering correspondence for the colonel and such. Watched them build the majority of the line we'll be on. If observant, a person learns many things."

"I'm quite observant too. Yet, all I know about you is that you scout for the army, you know about locomotive smokestacks, and you detest the wealthy." She swept an imaginary speck of dust from the linen cloth near her elbow. "Is there anything else I should know about Dillon Reed?"

He held back a chuckle. This saucy coquette could change her tune in mid-song. "When I think of something else, I'll let you know." Her gaze lingered and a surprising rush of pleasure tugged at him.

"I'm sure you will." She offered back a quick smile, then sipped from her water glass. A moment later, the waiter returned with menus. She settled the crystal on the tabletop and took the elegantly inked bill of fare from his hand. After glancing down the list of available dishes, she spoke first. "I will have the pheasant. And your oysters in crème sauce sounds delectable, so I will indulge in a small serving of those. And, oh my, the steamed---"

"We leave in an hour, Miss Talmadge," Dillon interjected.

She lowered the menu and glared over the parchment's crisp edge. "I'm tired of eating like a vagabond. A person could starve to death in your company."

"When you're with your duke, you may dine in high style. Right now, however—" he glanced to the waiter "—bring us both your house special. We're short on time." The servant nodded, gathered their menus, and scurried off to the kitchen.

"How dare you! I am not a child." She lowered her head, her emotion-choked voice cascading into a tattered whisper. "Can you not see I am careworn here, Mister Reed? You may well be accustomed to 'life in the saddle,' so to speak, but I find this entire episode quite distressing."

Dillon exhaled. "As I mentioned would happen, remember?" But, saying *I told you so* in such a gloating manner didn't feel as satisfying as he'd hoped. He shoved aside the troublesome thought. "What I see is someone who's inconvenienced. Nothing more."

Another sigh slipped from between her pouting lips. "Why should I bother to explain anything? You are not even listening."

"Look." He narrowed his eyes. "I've a job to do here, and dawdling isn't part of the agenda. Getting you, unharmed, to Tucson as fast as possible is my top priority."

She shifted in her seat, piercing him with a blue-eyed glare. "The only danger I've met so far is the very likelihood of death from tedium -- or quite possibly starvation. Not to mention the fact I'm travelling in near-silence with a brooding troll." As if she'd already said too much, she fell silent. Light from a twelve-armed crystal gasolier suspended from the ceiling directly above draped gossamer shadows across her bent head.

Dillon lifted his glass and gulped the liquid, trying to wash away her truthful words. *Sonofabitch.* This was exactly what he didn't need. He thumped the empty vessel to the table, the sound lost beneath the swirling music from a quartet of violinists near the back of the room.

He scanned the diners, stopping on the man who'd bumped into Miss Talmadge back at the depot. Seated with him were the two other men he'd seen on the train.

At his blatant stare, all three dropped their gazes.

Yes. You're watching us.

But why?

Dillon swiped his mouth with the back of his hand, then looked at his impertinent young charge. Her once-elegant chignon lay in a tangled clump across one shoulder, her previously pert little hat listing to one side. The obnoxious ribbons were limp and entwined with her light tresses. The rosy glow had vanished from her cheeks, and the sparkle he'd noticed earlier in her eyes had now somewhat dimmed. Two weeks of hard travel still awaited them, along with the worst terrain yet to cross. He took a deep breath and closed his eyes. If he didn't start handling her differently, she would break. So, keeping Miss High and Mighty happy, might be in his best interest, after all. Though he refused to slow their pace to Tucson, he'd consider taking a softer approach.

The fleeting link he'd experienced with her back at the train depot when she'd slipped her arm through his seeped once more into Dillon's brain. The irksome truth that they fit together well pricked at his nerves. He opened his eyes and their gazes reconnected.

Christ Almighty, why do they have to be so damned blue?

Dillon fought to unclench his jaw. "You're right, Miss Talmadge. I apologize for my...ungentlemanly behavior. We've a long way yet to travel, but I'll do my best to make things a bit easier on you. As long as you understand I make all the decisions."

She nodded. And he smiled, then waved the waiter back over to them to inquire, "Do those oysters in crème sauce take longer than ten minutes to prepare?"

"No sir, they're simmering in their rich broth even as we speak."

"And the pheasant? How long?"

"Not long at all. It's fully cooked and kept in the warming ovens for our patrons."

"Well, in that case, scratch the lady's original order. Instead, she'll have those two items."

"Very well, sir." The waiter smiled at a now-beaming Miss Talmadge. "We'll get both your orders out straightaway."

Dillon slid his gaze back to Alma's. *Checkmate.* He nodded. "That's fine."

He glanced to the nearby table with the trio of suspicious men. *But, you three better damn-well keep your distance. I'm itchin' to shoot something, and I don't mind if it's you shifty bastards, or not.*

CHAPTER SIX

Fort Riley, Kansas
Early Afternoon, two days later...

Defying the bleakness of the plains, and providing protection to the new rail lines crisscrossing the state, the stalwart fort hugged both sides of the track like an indomitable fist. The fast-growing military outpost, built from timber and native limestone, consisted of barracks, stables, a hospital, and private residences, providing a much-welcomed oasis among infinite grassland.

Sunshine drifted through the branches of a cottonwood, laying hazy designs across a wooden bench near the corner of the telegraph office. Dillon had heard the spot marked the geographical center of the United States. However interesting that fact, the only thing this meant to him was they still had a long way to travel.

He pointed to the bench. "This'll only take a few minutes, Miss Talmadge. Please wait for me here." His much-too-quiet charge nodded, then settled onto the weathered wood. Her parasol remained aloft, the silk-edged trim tousled in the ever-present wind.

Dillon stepped onto the boardwalk. "And don't move," he added with a growl to ensure he meant business. Her gaze remained focused on the two-story Rale House hotel and eatery nestled among a line of buildings across from her.

Damn stubborn woman.

He scanned the street. Kicked up by the perpetual wind, dust devils purled before the livery. Despite the barrenness of the Kansas plains, progress had arrived full force at the post. On the southern end of town, the train depot and huffing smokestacks of several locomotives filled his view. And on the northern end, a line of clapboard homes known as Officer's Row proclaimed civilization at its best. Green painted picket fences and matching shutters adorned the front of each residence.

Dillon tucked a smile into the corner of his mouth as he reached for the brass knob of the telegraph office door. All these charming touches belied a grisly truth. Over the distant hills, out of sight but never out of mind, the Cheyenne Nation waited for its moment to avenge the sacred lands the steel-beamed, chugging beasts defiled. Along with a handful of other plains tribes, the *Tsitsistas* renegades refused to be contained on reservations. And he'd bet a shiny ten dollar gold piece they were even now plotting revenge against the *ve'ho'e*. The ugly sounding word was a fitting name for their hated enemy the white eyes. Before such an event occurred, Dillon wanted to be long gone. He had enough to worry about with the damn Apaches back home.

The smell of burnt coffee drifted over him as he stepped into the hazy room. He headed toward the telegrapher, who sat at a counter near the back.

Dillon settled his saddlebags on the polished wood between them. "Mornin' Frank."

The old man raised his head, pushed wire-rimmed spectacles higher up the bridge of his nose, then glanced at the nearby wall clock. The brass pendulum of the fancy Seth Thomas ticked off two seconds before the grizzled old veteran shot him a smile. "More like mid-afternoon, Reed. How's Washington?"

Dillon chuckled, appreciating the man's always-blunt manner. "Still sweltering, as usual. I heard President Grant just appointed a governor to the District to begin bricking over the dirt roads, adding basic sanitation, and generally modernizing the capitol to match the rest of the big cities back east. They've got nearly 150,000 residents now." He removed his hat, swiped an arm across his forehead, and resettled the Stetson. "Oh, and the powers to be are also building yet another cathedral as a monument to peace and reconciliation."

"Yep. Read 'bout all that right here." Frank laughed, shuffling the newspaper aside. "Congress wants to move the capitol further west, but Grant won't hear of it. Progress in action, I'd say." He laughed again, and tapped the article. "They're callin' the cathedral you mentioned the Memorial Evangelical Lutheran Church, after a monk named Martin Luther." The man snorted. "If you ask me, it's gonna take a hell of a lot more than another sainted church to bring about a damned reconciliation in this country."

Dillon stifled a laugh and nodded. "I couldn't agree more."

"Hey, you want a cup of coffee?" The man waved to where a battered pot hung within a small fireplace at the back of the room. "Brewed it fresh near an hour ago."

The old timer may have been a fine sergeant during the war, but his liquefied muck could strip even the turf from a Kansas soddy. "No thanks. Haven't got time this visit. Catching the next westbound train. You got anything for me from Fort Lowell?"

"As a matter of fact, I do. Came in a couple o' days ago." The clerk leaned sideways and pulled a slip of paper from a slot in the bank of wooden cubbyholes. He handed over the message.

Dillon reached for his saddlebags as he scanned the missive from Talmadge. At the colonel's urgent warning, he pulled up short:

My niece might be in grave danger. Not sure from whom. Stay on the lookout. ~ Col. T. Talmadge.

"Damnit!" He jammed the telegraph into his back pocket.

"Problems?"

Dillon banked his unease. "Nah. Nothin' I can't handle. See you next time I'm through here, Frank." Shifting his saddlebags across his shoulder, he brushed past a couple of soldiers entering the office on his way out.

Sonofabitch. The prickly sensation riding his shoulders now made sense. The three men from the train. Dillon glanced toward the bench.

Empty.

What the hell? Boots grated pebbles as he surged into the middle of Main Street. Pulse racing, Dillon scanned in a full circle for any sign of the woman. Soldiers milled everywhere. Wagons rattled past him, whirling up thick clouds of dust.

But Alma Talmadge was nowhere to be seen.

Chapter Seven

A hollow ache unfurled in Dillon's gut...*And I left her sitting there, all alone just ripe for the damn picking.*

A horse and rider cantered passed.

With a curse, Dillon stepped back. Dust settled around him in a fine haze as the colonel's telegram burned a hole in his pocket. *I should've been warned about this before I even laid eyes on the woman.*

Across the way, the Rale House Hotel door opened. A man sauntered out. Lean. With wavy, light-colored hair.

Their gazes locked.

Eyes narrowing, the stranger left the boardwalk and strode straight toward him. "Bet you're looking for someone, aren't you?" he asked, stopping directly in front of him.

Dillon studied the man from the top of a neatly-groomed head, where cinnamon-infused pomade controlled the golden locks, over his dark, well-cut frock coat and trousers, and down to immaculate boots. *This foppish bastard knows something about her?* "As a matter of fact, I am."

The man halted in front of him. "And I bet she's beautiful, too... isn't she?"

Dillon nudged back the side of his jacket, then rested his right palm against the warm butt of his Colt. "Some might think so. And unless you want to ruin your fancy coat with a bullet in your gut, I better start hearin' who you are and where the hell she is."

The stranger raised his hands in mock surrender as a smile touched his lips. "Now settle down, Mister Reed." He chuckled. "There's no need to get all riled up. I'm just joshin' you."

He knows me? Alma's life could be in danger, he didn't have time to waste playing games. "I'm also not in a joshing mood, so you've got less than one second to start talkin'."

The popinjay extended a hand. "Name's George Custer. And your lovely Miss Talmadge is over yonder in the Rale House enjoying petit fours and tea with my wife, Libby. Seems they're old acquaintances."

Relief swamped Dillon. On a rough sigh, he tugged his duster back over his sidearm. "Well, I'm damn glad to hear this." His pulse eased back another notch as the man's name finally registered. "Custer, you said?"

"That's correct. George Custer, at your service."

Dillon slid his palm into the still-outstretched hand. "As in General George Armstrong Custer?"

A shadow crossed the man's features, then just as quickly disappeared. "War's over, Reed. I'm a Colonel with the Regulars now, with the 7th Cavalry." He pumped their hands twice before letting go.

A rush of blood warmed Dillon's cheeks. "I'm sorry, sir. Didn't realize you were military." This infamous man had developed quite a reputation during the late rebellion. On several occasions even Colonel Talmadge had regaled his comrades with the exploits, both good and bad, of the fast-rising legend who many also called Ringlets. Dillon fought to contain a smile.

"Duly noted. Besides, I wouldn't expect you to know, since I'm on leave and out of uniform." Custer sidestepped, and then gestured over his shoulder. "Come on, I've been sent out to fetch you to the ladies."

Dillon nodded, stepped around the officer, and then crossed the dusty street with Custer.

They entered the cool interior of the Rale House Hotel. Now that Alma Talmadge was safe, Dillon itched to wring her damn neck. His fingers flexed. No. He longed to sweep her into his arms and thank God she was safe.

What the hell's wrong with me? She's my job. Nothing more.

The mouth-watering aroma of coffee and roasted meat enveloped him as he crossed the threshold of a well-appointed entry hall. Of the many times he'd been through Fort Riley, he'd never entered this building.

Above his head a fancy gasolier, similar to the one he'd seen in St. Louis, shone light down the corridor that served as a divider between two dining rooms. A red-and-black plaid rug hugged the floor.

To his left a hotel clerk worked behind the high front counter, and near him, a bannister, polished to a fine sheen, complimented the stairway to the hotel's second-floor. Snugged against the back of each riser, thin brass rods held a woolen runner in place. Reflected light from the lamps glinted off each shiny dowel.

Nodding to the hotel concierge, Dillon headed down the corridor, his footfalls muffled in the plush wool. The sound of clanking dishes and muted conversations emanated from the room on his right.

Pausing at the arched entry, the colonel at his side, Dillon squinted against sunlight pouring through the glass panes on a far wall. Colorful curtains, the same design as beneath his feet, dressed the bank of windows. He scanned the patrons and stopped. With her customary apt deportment, Miss Talmadge listened to a woman sitting opposite her.

And then she laughed, humor brightening the incredible blue of her eyes.

Tightness radiated across his chest, forcing the already damnable lump in his throat to swell. Christ Almighty, the colonel *was* right. Even in her travel-worn state, Miss Alma Talmadge was indeed a most beautiful woman.

***

A movement near the doorway drew Alma's gaze. Her breath caught as Dillon's masculine frame filled the opening. The gasoliers in the hallway tossed shadows across his broad shoulders. Embraced by such elegant trappings, he looked flustered and out-of-place. Despite his disheveled appearance, he carried himself with such…purpose. A bewildering glint brightened his dark eyes, sparking an intensity more unsettling than the brooding glances he'd bestowed upon her since first they'd met.

A flutter inside her heart swept her lips upward into a smile.

Stop it. She doused her response. *He deserves no cheer. If not for Libby's miraculous appearance, I'd still be sitting out on the bench.* Alma glanced at her friend's husband. Dillon Reed could learn a thing or two about manners from George Armstrong Custer. *And yet...*Alma's attention drifted back to the scout. The anomalous glint she'd noticed in his eyes had disappeared.

Disappointment festered inside.

Alma skimmed her focus to her dining companion who waved the two men over to join

them. Libby leaned toward her. "Oh my, I had no idea your escort was quite so...*virile.*"

Heat spread across Alma's cheeks as the men approached. She stole a glance at Dillon as she clamped her lower lip between her teeth. *Virile? Well, yes. I suppose if he were clean...*

The soothing tones of Colonel Custer's words leveled the disorder inside her. "Ladies, I have found our missing attendant." He clapped his arm around Dillon's shoulders. "Although I must confess, for a moment there I feared for my life."

Libby's eyebrow arched. "Your life, Autie? Whatever do you mean?"

"Yes," the colonel continued as he and Dillon settled at the table. "My new friend here threatened to shoot me if I didn't share the whereabouts of..." His gaze slid to Alma. "...you. Seems he was in a most worrisome state over your safety."

Alma forced a smile. "Well, I do believe worry is one of his job responsibilities." Heat, nonetheless, continued its sweep down her neck. She avoided Dillon's glare. His exasperated sigh, however, reached over to re-jumble her nerves.

"Perhaps so," Dillon said, a tight smile thinning his lips. "But to save us both further discord, I suggest you advising me of any plan changes before they occur."

Libby placed her hand upon Dillon's arm and patted. "I fear this is all my fault, Mister Reed."

Alma didn't miss her extra squeeze.

"And I apologize for her disappearance." Her old friend gave him a charming smile. "I didn't realize she was waiting for you until after the fact, and I was so surprised to see her sitting there that I practically dragged her inside with me."

Dillon's gaze shifted to the colonel's wife, and his countenance softened. "Of course I understand, Mrs. Custer, and I accept your apology."

"Good heavens!" She swatted his arm. "I insist you call me Libby. Otherwise, I'll think you're addressing Autie's mother." The dimple in her chin deepened.

Several patrons vacated a nearby table, drawing Alma's attention. As soon as they turned the corner, a waiter appeared. He whisked away the dishes, and with a flick of his wrist settled a new cloth into place. A cool breeze brushed her flushed cheeks.

Dillon leaned back in his chair, his action reclaiming Alma's stare. "So tell me, Libby, how are you and Miss Talmadge acquainted?" His markedly charming demeanor irritated Alma. The entire time they'd been traveling, he'd yet to address her in such fawning tones, not when a grunt or clipped nod would suffice. Alma focused on her cut-crystal water glass. She refused the ludicrous urge to gulp the remainder to squelch the dryness in her throat.

"Well, I attended finishing school with her cousin, Pamela," Libby explained, "and spent several seasons at the Talmadges' summer retreat in Rhode Island. Of course, our Alma, here, was but a youngster back then, all ribbons and curls and so full of curiosity."

Libby's accounting nudged sweet memories from Alma's youth. She smiled. "Yes. And I felt so grown-up spending time with you both. Why, I even begged to tag along to every soiree and social occasion. My nanny, however, kept me safely ensconced at home." She glanced at Dillon. "You see, every summer for years, Father sent us to Newport. 'Twas away from the scalawags of Boston."

Libby sighed. "Oh how I loved those parties in the parlor."

Though Alma had been too young to participate in the revelry, she well-remembered watching from the upstairs landing as the events unfolded below. She, too, sighed. "But then, Father sold the estate, and soon thereafter our country became embroiled in the horrid unpleasantness of war."

"Horrid is a fitting word," George added, a fleeting sadness darkening his eyes. "Those years changed many things. Some good. Others not so good."

Dillon nodded. "War's insanity reached all the way out west. There was even a fight with the Rebs in the Picacho Mountains near Tucson. But, now we're just fighting Apache."

Alma edged aside her empty luncheon plate. Sunlight bounced off the gold-limed fleur-de-lis gracing the border of the Limoges china. She focused on the pattern. If only the symbolic lilies could aid her in her emotions regarding the scout as fully as they had Joan of Arc when the flower emblem graced the banner she'd held as she led her troops into battle.

"Goodness gracious, enough about war and fighting," Libby said, breaking through Alma's solemn musings. "I'd much rather converse about the pleasantries of parties." She glanced at Alma and then Dillon. "So, please allow me to extend an invitation to you both to attend one this very evening."

Alma leaned forward. "A...party?"

"Yes. One of George's former commanders is hosting a soiree in honor of our visit. We would love for you to join us."

Alma could barely contain her glee. "Why, that would almost be like old times." Her gaze leveled on Dillon. "And I am checking in with you, Mister Reed...to keep the harmony, I mean. Oh, we must attend."

She knew she had struck a disagreeable chord when his jaw retightened. "Unfortunately, Miss Talmadge, our train leaves in a few hours."

"Schedules can be adjusted, Reed," Custer cut in. "In fact, a westbound train leaves daily from the fort." He reached for his wife's hand and smiled. "One thing I've learned with marriage: Keeping a lady happy makes a man's life more peaceful."

Libby smiled and squeezed his hand, then her gaze shifted to Dillon's. "That's exactly right, Mister Reed. Plus, a break from travelling will do wonders for Alma's wellbeing. We ladies do not do well when we are ruffled."

The scout remained silent. With deliberate slowness, he bent his elbows and settled them on the arms of his chair. Staring at Alma, he clasped his hands before him and steepled his fingers. She tried to swallow, tried to look away, tried to calm her pounding pulse. But, that odd glimmer she'd seen in his eyes had returned.

How she longed for a battle banner to wave in front of him now.

Instead, she settled for the next best thing and tossed out her own challenging gauntlet. "I would dearly love to attend, Libby, but I'm afraid I have nothing to wear. You see, Mister Reed freighted all my gowns and accessories westward. I've only this traveling outfit, which, of course, is inappropriate for evening wear."

Alma narrowed her eyes.

Dillon smiled.

Libby dropped her napkin beside the plate. "Not a problem at all, my darling. I've a dozen dresses with me. And with a tuck or two, we'll find the right one to fit your slender frame." She patted Alma's hand. "In fact, let's spend the remainder of the afternoon preparing in my hotel room upstairs. Mister Reed can rejoin us at the party."

The thrill of socializing again, of dancing, of the gaiety and the excitement of conversing with others sparked through Alma. "I would absolutely love that. How very kind of you to offer."

On a discontented sigh, Dillon released her from the heat of his stare. He straightened in his chair.

"Might as well agree, Reed," Custer said with a chuckle. "It'll be a long trip to Fort Hays if you don't."

A full ten seconds passed, the ire in Dillon's eyes fading into frustration. "Fine. We'll stay for the evening. I'll make the necessary arrangements."

"Excellent," Libby said. "The affair begins promptly at seven at the post commander's residence on Officers Row."

With a victorious smile, Alma reached for her water glass. As she sipped, she pretended she waved a battle banner.

***

Two hours later, Dillon strode from the mercantile with a brand new shirt, frockcoat and trousers folded inside his saddlebags. He refused to consider his reasons for the impulsive purchase of a small, cobalt-blue glass bottle filled with rose oil which now nestled in the bottom of his bag. All he knew was the fragrance had been riding his awareness ever since he'd picked up the damned socialite back in Washington.

He stepped into the street, then glanced down. The square-toed cavalry boots had seen better days. At the top of one, the thin, mule-ear pull-on hung lopsided and flapped as he walked. *Damnit!* There wasn't time to get his footwear mended. He sighed, knowing he'd have to buy a new pair of boots, too. A damn waste of money as far as he was concerned, but at least he could wear the outfit for marryings and buryings when he got back home.

The only good thing about all this godforsaken falderal was that maybe now that uppity prude would quit making her sarcastic comments about his appearance. He'd bathe and shave, but he'd nix the Macassar oil. He wasn't a damn bit interested in slicking back his hair with that greasy, coconut-smelling shit. Besides, he wasn't doing this for her anyway. He knew it wouldn't do to rub elbows smelling like a cow paddy around the officers at the party.

An image of Alma's eyes as flashing blue as the bonnie blue flag rippled through him. Comparing his spoiled charge to the flag of the traitorous Confederacy was an odd parallel.

Regardless, he began humming a snappy melody he'd heard the soldiers back at Fort Lowell singing.

Long-legged strides kept beat with the tune.

Halfway to the station house, he stopped when he realized the pep in his *what-should've-been irritated* step. With a muffled groan, he shoved away the perplexing imprint of Alma's eyes and stalked in silence the remainder of the way to the depot.

The hissing of a nearby locomotive intensified as Dillon approached. He moved into line for service in front of the caged window. Three women, two soldiers, and an old miner stood before him.

While he waited for them to make their ticket purchases, Dillon closed his hand around the two Rale House Hotel keys in his pocket. Getting a room directly across from Miss La-di-da had required an extra Seated Liberty, but the half-dollar was a necessary expenditure in order to keep a closer vigilance on his charge.

"Next," the man bellowed from behind the iron bars.

Dillon pushed his tickets across the counter. "I'll need to exchange these for tomorrow's train to Fort Hays."

The clerk flipped through the cross-country packets, then reached for a nearby ledger, scanning the docket. "Not a problem, sir," he stated. "There's still plenty of seats available." A scribbled notation was followed by a quick thump from his rubber stamp. The worker slid the adjusted receipts back through the opening.

Dillon shoved the tickets into his jacket. "Same time, right?"

"Yes, sir. The train headin' west pulls out at four. Same time every day." The clerk looked over Dillon's shoulder. "Next."

Dillon stepped around the woman with her crying infant in line behind him. He touched the brim of his hat. "Ma'am."

She nodded, then moved before the iron bars as he headed toward the street.

Dillon stopped short when the three men he'd noticed on the trip westward pushed through the crowd. On edge, he slipped behind a post, out of their view. With large bundles slung over their backs, the three ruffians rushed toward the train, bumping into a passenger or two on their way. Without apologies, they pushed to the front of the line and boarded the railcar.

The train's bell clanged several times, announcing the westbound's immediate departure. Moments later, smoke from engine's bonneted stack billowed into the air, then steel scraped as the wheels began to turn. With a shudder the locomotive lunged forward, then settled into a steady rhythm.

Dillon scowled as he watched the train depart. He'd bet a month's wages those sonsofbitches were up to no good. With the unexpected delay, at least the ruffians were no longer following them, if they ever had been. Still, his gut assured him he was better off with those men gone. Regardless, Alma might well be in danger. Until he delivered her to her destination, he'd have to keep her under close guard.

He retrieved his pocket watch, flipped open the cover, and glanced at the time. *Perfect.* He'd have a solid half-hour to snag a supportive glass or two of whiskey before visiting that smoke-filled bastion known as the Gentleman's Grooming Emporium.

Anything to get me through this night.

A half-block later, Dillon pushed through the saloon's swinging doors and headed toward the bar, the notes of the snappy little tune once again slipping past his lips in a soft whistle.

Chapter Eight

Champagne flowed like water as crystal goblets sparkled in the party-goers' hands. Tapers and glass-globed oil lamps cast an elegant glow across the bustled silks and satins worn by the ladies, the soldiers decked out in blue wool, and the few men dressed in civilian attire. Glasses of whiskey and wine were raised high as oft-told tales were once again shared. In the far corner, the musicians struck up another melodious tune. And like moths to a flame, the ebullient couples fluttered out onto the dance floor.

Peering over the shoulder of her first dance partner, Alma scanned the hallway teaming with guests.

Still no sign of Dillon Reed.

The nerve of the man.

Her companion, a scrawny lieutenant, cleared his throat. "May I say you dance quite well, Miss Talmadge?"

She smiled, ignoring the cow-eyed adoration he'd bestowed upon her since the moment she'd accepted his invitation. "Why, thank you..." *Oh dear, I've already forgotten his name.* "I love to waltz and if given the chance would do so from dusk until dawn."

A commotion sounded near the entry, and a newly-arriving couple sashayed into the party.

Alma thinned her lips, glancing at the mahogany case clock anchored near the stairway in the hall.

Fifteen minutes late. He'd been told precisely seven o'clock.

The front door opened, and the oil lamp in the entry hall flickered once more.

A tall, well-built man entered the room, ambling straight into Alma's view. His back toward her, she admired his dark hair, the pleasing shade of brown falling to his shoulders. Individual strands caught the lamplight.

She stifled a grin. *Maybe Libby knows him.* Regardless, he wasn't wearing a uniform. She liked his black, well-cut frockcoat pulled taut over broad shoulders. Matching pants tapered to an expensive pair of Wellingtons. Even his fingernails were trimmed. Perhaps he was a government buyer from back east? *No. His hair is too long, and no mutton chops.*

Excitement slid through her veins.

Now this *virile* man she approved.

And yet, from his confident stance, he seemed out of place in this group of dandified men. The foppish face of her fiancé flitted through her mind. Alma shuddered and shoved away the image of Lord Green.

Then this Johnny-come-lately turned to face the crowded parlor.

Alma gasped – *Holy Mother! It's Dillon Reed!*

"I'm sorry, Miss Talmadge," the lieutenant said. "Did you say something?"

Stunned, she tore her gaze from the handsome features of her unwanted escort, and back to the officer whose arm wrapped her waist. "N-No," she stammered, struggling to calm her thudding pulse. "But I do believe I must stop dancing now. I'm feeling rather…faint."

Worry creased the young officer's brow. "Of course." He guided her over to Libby. "Would you like me to bring you a glass of water?"

"No." Alma gave him a reassuring smile. "I am certain after a moment's rest, I shall be fine."

He nodded. "Well, thank you for the first dance, Miss Talmadge." He drifted back into the crowd.

"Are you ill, my pet?" Libby inquired.

"No. I just need to…catch my breath." She shuddered at the lie that slipped past her lips. Unsettled by the turn of events, Alma dropped open the slats of her ivory fan and moved air over her burning face.

She refused to look. Refused to confirm her upheaval. Refused to admit the shock of seeing Dillon Reed in such fine form. He looked incredible. And would turn any woman's head. Worse, he'd deliberately hidden this specific detail from her!

Alma spun on the heel of her satin slipper.

She swept her gaze across the ever-growing crowd and spotted Dillon with a group of men. He loomed above them all, shaking hands with Custer, then several others. His cordial nods intrigued her. His pleasantries sanguine and relaxed. Then, he tipped back his head and laughed. The impact of his boyish charm rescrambled Alma's comportment.

She thrummed the blades of ivory faster.

How dare he hide such…such…cleanliness beneath an odious layer of grime. I had every right to know…

She stilled the fan. From his actions, how could she have known her sullen traveling companion exuded a virility other men could only dream of possessing?

Control yourself, you dolt! He's just a man.

"I see Mister Reed has arrived." Libby motioned toward him. "See? Right over there. And goodness me, how remarkably handsome he looks."

"He's here?" Alma resumed her fanning. "I really hadn't noticed."

Libby smiled. "I'll wave them over."

"No."

"But, he came to be with you tonight. 'Twould be impolite to leave him standing alone."

Looking so…approachable, he won't be alone long. Not that she cared a whit. He could dance with every woman at Fort Riley. Mattered little to her.

Custer nodded in their direction, then moved through the crowd toward them, Dillon on his heels.

Alma fought to steady her composure.

"A wonderful gathering, isn't it Autie?" Libby said as her husband sidled up next to her.

"Indeed it is. Why, I've talked with chaps I haven't seen in years," Custer replied.

Libby's attention glided to the scout. "And Mister Reed, how nice to see you again. I must say you do look dashing."

Dashing? Alma nearly snorted.

Dillon issued a smart bow before Libby, then turned. "Good evening, Miss Talmadge."

She continued to stare at the twirling revelers on the dance floor. "Good evening, Mister Reed. I see you've...tidied up."

Good heavens, I actually mentioned it.

He chuckled as George reached for Libby's hand. "Would you do me the honor of this waltz, my love?"

"Why, I thought you would never ask." She smiled and moved past Alma, whispering behind her fan, "And you both ought to join us out there, too."

***

One song came and went. The musicians struck up a second tune. Alma's obvious snub rubbed Dillon raw. And she called him stubborn? This woman had him beat in spades. "The Custers sure are nice folks, aren't they?"

Her gaze remained on the dancers, but the breeze from her ceaseless fanning skimmed his face. "Yes." Her reply almost became lost amid the noise. "They're very nice."

Another couple glided past them toward the dance floor.

Dillon again glanced at Alma. "May I get you something to drink?"

"No, thank you. I'm fine."

Bloody hell. She demanded they attend this cockamamie gathering and now she refused to even look at him. Dillon's jaw tightened. If he had his druthers, he'd saddle a horse, choose a trail, and blow for home faster than a plains tornado.

A perturbed huff reached his ears.

"Do you even know how to waltz?" Alma blurted.

Her clipped question caught him by surprise. She'd been stewing on that one a while. "I don't dance."

"You don't? Or you don't know how? There is a difference, you know."

His heart ramped into a hellish beat. "As I mentioned before, tracking for the army doesn't leave me much time for niceties."

"So you say, but you are obviously educated. And I noticed you can carry on a conversation." The flapping of her fan ceased, and she collapsed the ivory blades into her palm. A burgundy ribbon secured the flimsy gadget to her wrist.

The side-swept cluster of curls draped her bare shoulder as Alma lifted her gaze to his. "I believe dancing would be an excellent addition to your scouting arsenal."

His mouth dried into a wad of cotton as his stomach knotted.

A servant holding a tray of drinks brushed past.

Dillon snagged the closest glass.

"I could teach you, Mister Reed, to dance, I mean. The steps of a waltz are quite simple."

He swirled the amber liquid, then lifted the whiskey, pausing before the tumbler touched his lips. "Thanks, but I'll pass." He downed the shot. The generous swallow blistered the back of his throat and joined the half a bottle he'd drank earlier.

Dillon refocused on the twirling couples. Soft lights illuminating the dancers. Women clad in satin, their breasts threatening to spill from low-cut gowns. Women so full of their guises.

"And, by the way, from here on out, I insist you call me Alma." A thin laugh trickled from her lips. "After all, we are traveling together, so we mustn't remain strangers."

The scent of her rose-infused essence drifted over him, straining his already taut nerves. Her form materialized in his mind. *Alma. Small breasts. Rail-thin.* Dillon blew out a long breath, then lifted the tumbler and pulled in another swallow.

Before the burn on his tongue had even dissipated, Alma stepped before him and whispered, "Come with me."

A moment later, she skirted the room. With each determined footstep, the bustle on her back end bobbed at Dillon as if to underscore her demand he follow. She headed straight toward the rear of the house.

What the hell? He deposited the empty tumbler on a side table, then pushed through the crowd after her. Hadn't she wanted to dance? He shook his head, his chest hurting. This damned woman changed directions in mid-stream faster than a trout swimming up Angel Creek.

Dillon followed her down a hallway and through the summer kitchen. A second later, she disappeared out the back, the side-spring, wood-framed door whapping shut behind her tolling her exit.

Sonofabitch. Where's she headin' now?

The cool breeze brushed his face as Dillon stepped onto the bricked courtyard. Moonlight entwined with oil lamps to lay a gossamer cloud across the terrace. An array of empty white-iron chairs and tables served as silent witnesses to his search. He spotted Alma on the far side of the patio. She stood beneath the branches of a colossal cottonwood, the tree so ancient it probably welcomed the territory's first inhabitants.

She turned to face him, her gloved hands primly clasped before her. The evening gown she wore, a deep shade of burgundy, shimmered around her like a fine bottle of port.

He ambled up to her, refusing to let her see she'd thrown him off kilter--*again*. Blue eyes widened as he dwarfed her in his shadow. "What new trick are you pulling on me now, Princess?"

She raised her arms into a dance position. "No trick, Mister Reed. I am going to teach you how to waltz."

Her chin lifted in that way he was beginning to know all too well.

"I thought you would feel more comfortable out here away from the crowd," she added with a smile.

Her words, bright and bewitching, wove through Dillon, destroying his every reserve. Did she now? The combinations of too much whiskey, too little food, and a too-good-to-be-true breeze joined forces to discombobulate his logic. He'd dallied with women his entire life, mostly whores and a favored squaw or two, but this female tangled up his well-guarded defenses and drove a spear through his best laid plans. *What the hell. One quick dance won't matter.*

With his next breath, Dillon swept his arm around her corseted waistline. His other hand seized her outstretched palm.

An easy pull crushed her against him.

She gasped.

His gaze burned deep into hers. "I already know how to waltz thank you very much." His breath moved the golden wisps of hair against her cheek.

In the past thirty minutes, her trivial annoyances somehow had breathed into life, immersing him within an urgent need to...*prove*. Why it mattered, Dillon couldn't quite grasp. But, lurking in the back of his mind where he'd obviously shoved his sanity, he knew touching Alma Talmadge with such intimacy was wrong on so many levels.

And not a damned bit part of the job.

And yet, that flash in her eyes had scrambled him up six ways from Sunday ever since he'd met her.

She shot him a withering look. "My intention is only to teach you dance steps, Mister Reed. I assure you, coming out here meant nothing more."

Her words brushed hot against his neck. *Damn her spunk.* "I think you're safe with me."

He moved her into an easy waltz.

Nearly two decades had passed since his dancing days as a growing lad in Texas, yet the flexibility in his steps returned. The remembrance of his family's parlor. The plucking thrum of his father's guitar. His mother's instructive steps as she patiently taught him how to waltz. He hadn't thought about those happier times in years. Life had a hellish way of slinking on through the pain.

Alma's sweet giggle nudged him to the present. Her lips parted on a sigh. "You do dance divinely, Mister Reed. And certainly in no need of instructions."

A chuckle rolled from him. "I aim to please."

He relished their unexpected harmony. Satisfied he'd surprised her, he twirled her around the patio as the muted strains of a melody bound them with invisible threads. Each spin more comfortable than the last. Each lilting laugh she offered, more rousing. Each heartbeat swamping Dillon's resolution to finish what he'd begun. *One more turn, and I'll stop.* And then, he gazed into her blue eyes illuminated by moonlight; they twinkled so bright he was reminded of stardust.

The rhythm of their steps slowed.

The redolence of roses bedeviling.

Driven by too much whiskey and too little sleep, he tightened his hold and drew her even closer, molding her curves against him. *My God, woman, you feel so good.*

He slowed his steps, his hand pressing against the small of her back. This frustrating and feisty little minx drove him mad with anger, and yet his hold on her involuntarily tightened. He searched the softness of her half-opened mouth, tasted her sweet breath mingling in raspy puffs around his.

God help him, he wanted more. Before he could stop himself, Dillon dipped down. And a heartbeat later, he captured her lips…the press of his mouth a growing demand against hers. He'd kissed more women than he could remember, and yet the heat of her mouth blistered through him in an unchecked aching wave. Desire for her flashed hot in his veins as deep inside his arousal grew.

A ragged sigh of frustration rattled from him as he finally broke apart their kiss. His breath escaped in a long hiss. He peered down at her. Her breath caught as her cheeks flushed an even deeper red. Her eyes, framed by long, inky lashes, widened. Wrapped around her splendor and the stardust in her eyes, Dillon realized he had completely lost his mind. *What the hell am I doing? She belongs to another.*

He sucked in a breath and instantly sobered, the muscle in his jaw jerking taut. His heart pounded with enough ferocity to disperse the stardust entrapping them into a vaporous web of frustration.

Son of a damn bitch.

Shock at his body's traitorous response wrenched logic and reason into place. He released her and pushed back, yet the throbbing ache in his groin demanded more. His words growled out with all the weight of a sledge-hammer. "Lesson's over."

He did not belong in the moonlight with this woman, not here and not like this, and he certainly didn't have any right to kiss her. The only thing that kept Dillon from bolting for the door was the strength of her glare...sharp enough now to chisel through the luminance shimmering around them. He flexed his hands, the ache to touch her still burning hot.

A single, sharp oath fell from his mouth.

He wrapped his hand around her upper arm, his fingers holding tight to prevent her escape. Turning, he pulled her with him, his boot heels grating against bricks. Three strides plowed them past a decorative table. His hip grazed the iron as he surged past, knocking the closest chair to the ground.

The heavy clatter only underscored his asinine...response.

Don't touch her again.

Not ever again.

He hoped he had the strength to follow his own advice.

***

Dillon's firm grip around her upper arm shoved Alma's temper up another blistering notch. Corseted so tightly, she could scarcely catch her breath under his fast-paced strides. He swung wide the door and the music and gaiety smacked them full-on. Surging across the threshold, he pulled her along behind him. The closing door slapped into her bustle, pushing her into him.

Like an unbending oak, the scout remained ramrod straight.

Alma shuffled several steps to keep her balance. *He...kissed me!* Her mind reeled. What had begun as a simple plan to teach him dancing had somehow spiraled into a clash with ... *What?* She struggled to identify the emotion coursing through her veins.

This...manhandling baboon.

Calling him names at least made her feel better.

How dare he keep secret the fact that he could waltz. Worse, just as she was enjoying the flowing turns around the patio, he kissed her and responded in...*that* manner. And then, to drag her into the house as if she were a miscreant. *The rutting beast.* She should ignore him and his maddening, vulgar ways. What did she care anyway? She was engaged, had many admirers.

So why did this man's kiss...or his *response* agitate her to such a degree?

The unspoken truth screamed volumes about something she'd rather not contemplate. She came to an abrupt stop between the back door and the arched opening into the parlor.

"Unhand me this instant!"

His hold lessened.

Alma jerked from his grasp, then stumbled backward, bumping up to a kitchen table stacked with delicacies. Cast in the wavering light from an overhead lamp, several glass jars of pickles wobbled like marionettes, then toppled. With horror, she watched them roll around the center of the wooden plane, thunking into one another. She shuffled around the table and stopped the jars from moving, placing a barrier between herself and Dillon.

He kissed me! Without permission! The breadth of his shoulders, his build, all screamed of stamina and persistence. He loomed well over six feet, yet his body moved with a panther's grace. She swallowed, but the lump in her throat refused to move.

Turning to face her, his expression hard, Dillon stopped at the table's edge. Nothing about him reflected idle time. The fleeting tenderness revealed earlier in his eyes while they'd danced in the coolness belied the burning coldness etched there now.

Alma closed her fingers around the closest jar of pickles. Raising it, she snarled, "If you take one step closer...I swear, I'll...I'll throw this at you."

The thunderstorm across his face whipped at her sanity. She glared at the sharp angle of his jaw. The straight slant of his nose. The full lips that had captured hers. But she'd seen his earlier vulnerability. It was there somewhere beneath his anger.

She'd...*felt* it.

He extended his hand over the tabletop. "Let's go. Now."

Beyond the kitchen, the musicians struck up another tune. Laughter and jollity spun around them, the resonance a pulsing witness to her plight. And yet, she didn't scream for help.

Why?

Inhaling deeply, Alma resettled the pickle jar upon the table. Exhaling, she straightened, now more in control of herself. Her gaze locked on his as she tamped back a shudder. "I am not some common trollop you can ravage and then drag through the streets."

His lips pulled thin as he flicked his fingers. "Come on."

He's not even listening.

With her heartbeat pounding in her ears, she lifted her chin. "I am most serious, Mister Reed. You will not treat me in such a loutish manner."

Seconds strained into ten as the rapid rise and fall of his chest matched hers. Finally, he released a deep sigh, and lowered his hand. By unbearably slow degrees, the irritation across his face receded. "I'm sorry if I was... rough with you." That much-too-boyish grin reappeared, twisting away at her insides and turning her into knots. "I admit it. I'm a bad man."

Alma stared at him, her ire melting away. How quickly he could turn her righteous fury into a bemusing little burn.

Pretending otherwise made no sense. She couldn't help herself. She giggled. "Yes, you are."

That wicked spark in his eyes returned. Laugh lines deepened around his eyes, further heightening his appeal. Never had she been around anyone quite like Dillon Reed, whose raw virility terrified even as it thrilled.

A servant rushed into the kitchen to refill an empty platter from the nearby spread of *hors d'oeuvres*.

Alma nodded at her, then stepped aside.

The young girl placed her tray on a sideboard, picked up the jar of pickles, then added more savories to the salver. "I-I didn't mean to interrupt, ma'am."

"No. You didn't," Alma whispered, staring at Dillon. "We were just leaving."

Extending his hand, he shot her another breath-stealing grin. "Shall we?"

She swept her gaze over him, then quivered -- the warmth of the kitchen air, the lilting notes of the music, and the unshakable power of this man while they'd danced enveloped her in a chaotic whirlwind. But, more than those was the truth of his kiss and what she'd imagined of his...*anatomy* that now burned in Alma's blood with all the driving force of Sherman through Georgia.

Enough of this! She moved around the table and slipped her arm into the proffered crook of his. Tingles scurried up her spine as she struggled for control.

Dillon leaned down, his breath brushing the curve of her ear. "And this time, I'll *try* to be a gentleman."

Much to Alma's vexation, a biting disappointment nipped at her heels all the way back through the crowd.

CHAPTER NINE

More than a million volunteer soldiers mustered out of the army after Appomattox. The ones who elected to remain were organized into a smaller, yet equally competent, fighting force. Many of these battle-seasoned veterans were ordered westward, and the routes they traveled became clogged with merchants and other civilians who serviced their non-military needs.

Forts and outposts positioned *en route* also were strengthened to increase security for a rapidly expanding nation. Once tracks were laid, trains began replacing the stagecoaches crisscrossing the territories west of Saint Louis.

Amid a flurry of activities, Alma boarded the four o'clock train to Fort Hays. She put on a brave face as she settled onto a bench across from Dillon. A breath later, she slid to the window and pressed her cheek against the cool glass pane. The railcar lurched forward. The clack of train wheels upon the tracks increased. The station house fell away, and she waved at Libby and George until they were mere specks upon the horizon.

A sigh fell from her lips as she turned to face the scout. He'd already leaned against the bench cushions, his slouch hat pulled over his face. The message he sent was loud and clear.

Don't bother me.

That suited her as well. A dance with him in the moonlight and his stolen kiss changed nothing. *Liar!* Fine. Not that he would ever know.

She crossed her arms and slumped against her seat to settle in for the twenty-hour ride to Fort Hays.

Late-afternoon the following day, with her parasol held aloft to block the blazing plains sun and muscles stiff from sitting too long, Alma followed Dillon as they transferred to the stage line. Onboard the rolling monstrosity, the stench of the two passengers travelling with them and the jostling of her body as the wheels bounced along the rutted road tested her endurance.

Crushed against the corner of the small stagecoach, Alma wrapped her gloved hand around a leather strap dangling from the side of the window.

Across from her, the scout scowled.

Her fingers fumbled with her hankie, and she shifted her gaze. She refused to give him the satisfaction of knowing how wretched her misery during this trip had become.

Errant dust cast from the wagon's wheels filled the stagecoach. Fighting back a cough, Alma shoved her hat into place with her free hand, then mumbled a hasty apology for elbowing the wild-haired ruffian crammed onto the seat beside her. In malodourous waves, the stench of his unwashed body drifted over her.

Alma stifled another retch and focused on the withering clutter of knobby pines across the sunbaked land.

As they travelled from one swing station to the next, a continuous and jagged purple scar on the western horizon dominated her view.

The Rockies.

She'd read about them, but words on paper were a poor substitute for the soaring mountain range in the far distance. No written descriptions could ever convey the majesty spanning before her. Clouds dared to scrape the rocky tops, while the deepest blue haunted the sky above in a sweeping azure crown.

She felt so small beneath such magnificence.

The roll of scarred plains dotted with thick grass collided with the rush of stone screaming heavenward. For years this land had lain untouched, inhabited only by Indians who'd lived a quiet existence…until the influx of the white man.

Alma bit her lip to stop the tremble. Somewhere on the opposite side of the towering peaks in the deepest bowels of the Arizona Territory waited Fort Lowell.

My destiny.

***

As the afternoon sun scorched the land, the stagecoach descended a steep plateau, then forded a river three times the width of any she'd seen back east. Terrified, Alma peered from the window as water crept up the wheels, passed the hubs and lapped against the bottom of the coach. She shuddered at the bellowing curses of the driver and the coach guard sitting atop the lurching box. The whistling snap of the whip and the mules' pitiful braying collided with Alma's fear as the team plowed their way through the daunting current.

A half-hour later, the Concord clambered up the opposite bank and continued its hellish run southward.

Tears scalded Alma's eyelids, and Libby's words before their departure returned to haunt her mind.

Be strong.

She clung to her friend's advice as the hours rolled past.

Their stops, spaced about fifteen miles apart to change the mules —"'tis the distance a team can travel before gettin' tuckered out," the old man beside her had mumbled—were much too brief. On one stop, the layover was in a dugout carved into the side of a river bank, the station operator a man whose thick German accent mangled his attempt at English.

One day turned into two, and while the others slept inside a rickety wayside station where they had stopped to change the team and allow the driver and guard to rest, Alma refused to leave the coach. Too overwhelmed and frightened even to sleep, she sat bolt upright in her corner, her hand wrapped around the leather strap.

By the third night, this stop at a wayside station in a grassy valley, mind-wrenching exhaustion overwhelmed Alma. Hand trembling, she tugged out the hatpin and let the velvet *fanchon* tumble to the coach floor. The faint rattle of metal followed the half-bonnet as she dropped the ivory-capped hat pin. Alma stretched across the leather seat, the thick, motionless air a smothering silence unlike anything she'd ever experienced.

Every part of her battered body ached.

She stared at Dillon Reed.

On the bench across from her, he lay flat on his back, his slouch hat again hiding his face, his long legs out the window. Tonight, like the previous two nights, he'd remained with her inside the coach.

Moonlight illuminated the design of his spurs and the dark leather that buckled them into place.

Her gaze trailed over the impressive length of his body, pausing at the worn wooden handle of his gun. His holstered revolver, always at the ready, brought her comfort.

He so perfectly personified this wild country. Vast. Raw. Untamed. Neither had talked again about his stolen kiss, nor of that destined dance in the moonlight. And yet, with him by her side she felt...*safe*.

Alma closed her eyes and tried to forget the softness reflected in his dark gaze at the party. The demanding pressure of his lips against hers. Of the few times she'd been kissed, never had she been kissed with such...*fervor*. Only a week had passed since that brief exchange, and yet that evening seemed a lifetime ago. Never had she dreamed she'd be in the middle of nowhere, and never with a man who barely acknowledged her existence.

A forceful ache burrowed into her heart.

She tried to shove back the tears gathering behind her lashes, tried to concentrate on each breath, but the slow suffocation of the past week destroyed her last defense. Tears ran in a cool path over her cheek, the dampness blending with the sweat stains that had been scoured into the leather seat by so many who'd come before her.

Alma pressed her lips together, so dry that the pain forced another rush of tears. She swallowed, but her throat closed up.

And then…in all its ugly form, panic gripped her.

Shallow breaths burned her lungs.

Please God, don't let me fall apart out here all alone

Faster and faster, the tears fell. Her shoulders shook as wracking sobs dug in with teeth and claws. She clenched her eyes tight against the truth of her insufferable weakness.

As another sob shook her, strong arms slid around her shoulders and pulled her against a solid chest.

Dillon's days-old beard scraped her cheek. "Hold on, Princess."

His words gruff, yet soft, against her tangled hair offered hope. He tightened his hold and Alma buried her face into the warm curve of his neck and wept. Her tears fell unheeded, yet he neither moved nor stopped her.

Stolen kiss or not, she *needed* this man's strength.

And he gave it…whispering against her ear, "You've done well under these extremes, Alma." A slight intake caught his breath as the huskiness of his voice deepened. "Don't give up now."

He was offering her comfort…this scout who was built like a fortress and stole kisses in the moonlight. The emotional weight of his words, the compliment of her perseverance Dillon offered was nothing short of astonishing, and given at a time when she so desperately needed his acknowledgment.

Courage stirred.

Alma opened her mouth to speak, but no words emerged. She kept her head bent, her eyes closed. She'd found her safe haven, and latched on to his consoling words. Resonant. Encouraging. Her sobs lessened to sniffles. With her heart pounding, she conjured a weak smile, her lamentations evaporating into the Colorado night.

And still Dillon Reed rocked her.

By slow degrees, her rigidity unraveled against him. Easing the ache from her muscles, from her heart, she inhaled and smelled the wear of the trail on his shirt along with a lingering trace of soap. He'd had his clothes cleaned at Fort Riley. She pressed her lips together and tasted him again, then she imagined something more, that fragrance stirred up in the cool breeze while they'd danced.

A seductive scent only he possessed.

The rise and fall of his chest lulled Alma into quiet. A rattling, ragged sigh fell from her lips.

Warmth flooded her cheeks, and she was grateful for the shield of darkness.

Until now, this man had delivered mostly misery. She should push from his arms, deny herself the need for his comfort, *be strong* as Libby's words had commanded of her days before. And yet, the scout's gentle rocking cocooned her, easing back her desperation.

I've obviously lost my mind.

Alma stared at a button on his shirt. The threading that anchored the pewter disc to the cotton was frayed and worn.

Like my nerves.

Moonlight burrowed into the coach and fell across them. Beneath the V-shaped opening of his shirt, where the material met his skin, his chest bore a dusting of dark hair.

She yearned to sweep her fingers across the coarse curls.

Instead, the knuckle cracked as she clenched her hand. She snuggled deeper. He was a stranger. And yet...surprisingly, now her protector.

For a moment longer, I'll rest against him.

Another broken sigh slipped past her lips.

Her eyelids fluttered closed.

A heartbeat later, Alma surrendered to the realms of an exhausted slumber.

***

Her soft breath against his neck assured Dillon that Alma had fallen asleep. Outside the coach, the soothing chirp of crickets accompanied her tender inhalations.

Dillon leaned against the leather seat, loosening but not relinquishing his hold on her. Though he'd vowed never to touch her again, here he sat with Alma in his arms. His heavy sigh mingled with the night sounds cocooning him.

What the hell was he supposed to do, ignore her?

Duty demanded his attention. She'd been crying, for Christ's sake. Any man worth his salt would behave likewise if put in the same situation. He shoved aside the uncomfortable rationalizing. Her moment of histrionics had prompted his toleration.

Only a bastard ignored a weeping woman.

In the past five years, he'd crossed this land a half-dozen times and had avoided all emotional entanglements. Once she'd pulled herself together, he'd step back. Nothing would have changed. She had her destination, and he had his. A few tears and a consoling embrace meant little in the bigger scheme of life.

She stirred, then snuggled closer, sending his heartbeat into another disconcerting hitch. Cursing, Dillon stared into the night.

This was his job, nothing more.

Bullshit.

No job required him to comfort a distraught debutante. And he'd never pulled a woman into his embrace like this -- overwrought or not -- in any task he'd undertaken. Well...except for a few drunken whores in Fort Lowell, but those didn't count one damn bit.

So what if she smells like every man's dream?

Mattered jack-squat to him. Besides, he didn't need a wooden plank slammed over his head to tell him Alma Talmadge was an innocent soul. There wasn't a damned thing wrong with him showing her a bit of kindness.

Fine. Maybe she's not so annoying, after all.

The rise and fall of her chest, the soft curve of her waist, the weight of her body against him...*there*. Heat mounted. His body stiffened. Dillon set his jaw. All he had to do was get her back to Tucson and hand her over to her all-too-perfect fiancé.

Done.

Finished.

Good blasted riddance.

An empty ache slammed his gut as the taste of her lips returned. So damned soft against his. With a scowl, Dillon scanned the distant timberline, illuminated beneath a full moon's silvery spill. Silhouettes of colossal Ponderosa scraped across the ebony canvas of night.

In the swath of open meadow, a large buck sporting an impressive rack of antlers grazed on Junegrass. Food must've been plentiful this past winter. During the upcoming rut, the beast would need all his strength to stake a claim for a doe.

Stake a claim? Rut?

Damnit.

He should be home by now, not stealing kisses like a school boy or playing nursemaid to some other man's woman. Dillon flexed his fingers once more against the brocade at her corseted waist.

His body tightened. Again.

Stop this shit.

He prayed for the oblivion of sleep to remove him from his self-inflicted torment. This woman was nothing but trouble. And engaged for Christ's sake. He pressed his eyes tighter. The sooner he rode away from her, the better.

Sleep, however, eluded him, as did the reasons he still held Alma.

Wind whispered through the towering pines in a taunting hiss. He lifted his eyelids in time to see the buck raise its head, then sprint into the shelter of the trees.

Lucky bastard.

The shelter of his own damned world couldn't come soon enough. Besides, his best friends, Jackson and Callie Neale, were expected at Fort Lowell in a few months as they delivered another herd of horses to the military. He always enjoyed their company. They were the rare exception to the no-happiness-in-marriage rule…Well, their ranching neighbors, Roberto and Carlotta Eschevon also seemed quite happy. With both couples immense track of land, who wouldn't be happy?

Regardless, marriage sure as shit wasn't for him. Look what that soul-sucking mess had done to his parents. He liked living alone, liked having the ability to up and go whenever he wanted, liked feeling the wind at his back and answering to no one.

Except the colonel. Somehow, Colonel Talmadge kept him on the straight and narrow. Dillon gave a slow exhale. It was only natural he should comfort the man's niece.

Confident he'd resolved the nagging bullshit regarding Alma and his feelings toward her, he started to pull away, put much needed distance between them. Then, she shifted closer.

Dillon tightened his hold, and made the mistake of glancing down.

Moonlight slid over the woman, sending shimmers into the wisps of hair that framed her face, lingering in a silent beckon upon her lips. He stared at her as the truth of her beauty burned the breath from his lungs.

Against his better judgment, he leaned closer, inhaling her woman-soft essence. Christ, he loved her scent. *Roses.* A strained smile pulled at the corner of his lips. He inhaled again…*one more time*…knowing she would never know.

Dillon leaned back, his muscles relaxing. His eyes drifted closed again. He was damn well going to have to find someone to help blow off the steam when he returned to Fort Lowell.

If even for a short while. On an unsteady breath, he shoved the need to touch her tresses into the black hole he called his heart, alongside the other unrequited desires that would never see the light of day.

CHAPTER TEN

Noon the following day, the Concord rolled to a stop. Alma peered out the window, pleased they were in a meadow surrounded by pines. A clear-running creek cut through the middle.

"Water break," the guard yelled, doffing his hat. He smiled at Alma. "You've got fifteen minutes to stretch your legs, ma'am." He propped the butt of his weapon on his hip, then ambled toward the team to help the driver. Alma sent a silent prayer heavenward, thankful for the break from the bone-rattling ride. God only knew what the driver and guard endured seated on the wooden bench above.

After studying her a moment, Dillon shoved the door open and stepped down. Turning, he extended his left hand toward Alma. She scanned his face. His features were tense, his eyes exhausted. Again, she wished things had started out differently between them. She tucked her closed parasol under her arm, smiled, and then slipped her palm into his.

He squeezed her fingers, and a tingle of awareness shimmied up her arm.

The closest passenger behind her stirred, while the other man awoke from his nap and stretched.

On a steadying breath, Alma nodded at them, then with Dillon's help exited the coach. "Thank you."

"I'll be right back." He headed toward the creek. Disappointment laced through her at how quickly he'd rushed off. They'd yet to say a word about her crying episode last night, or the fact that he'd held her all night in his arms while she slumbered. Thank goodness the other passengers had slept outside.

Alma studied her escort as he strode away, his lean hips moving with steady purpose. Dillon Reed was a man who knew where he was headed, and that certainly wasn't to her. Nor could it be. Kiss or no kiss, she was engaged. Why should she even ponder his thoughts when her own life was so well planned? She was happy, wasn't she? Of course she was. The man she was to wed awaited her. A man who had never yet stolen a kiss in the moonlight with her. She sighed. No, thank goodness Lord Green was nothing like Dillon Reed who possessed irritating hard-set ways and a living off the land mentality.

Silly thoughts. Be gone.

Refusing to dwell on Dillon or the conflicted sensations he made her feel, she swooshed opened her parasol and took in her surroundings. A large stand of cottonwoods spread a silver-leafed canopy over the creek, the rush of wind casting their leaves into a vibrant flutter.

Alma inhaled deeply. A hint of rain tainted the high mountain air. She frowned at the rain-swollen clouds as the sun fought a losing battle to penetrate their churning fury…paltry streams of light played hit or miss with the towering peaks.

In the distance, Dillon dropped to a knee beside the boulder-strewn creek. He withdrew a tin cup from beneath his shirt, then leaned forward and scooped water into his mug. His jacket strained across his shoulders. Another sigh slipped from Alma. Her noticing of his build, his body, seemingly continuous now. And then, the scout straightened, sauntered back to her and held out the cup. "Here, Princess. This'll chase away the dust."

Warmth swept Alma's cheeks at his rough and tumble kindness. She smiled and slipped her fingers around the battered metal.

Princess.

She rather liked his lofty moniker.

"I appreciate your thoughtfulness." And she really did appreciate him. More with each passing day. The kiss withstanding, somehow their animosity upon first meeting had shifted into a tolerating kind of friendship.

Suddenly, gunshots shattered the stillness.

Birds perched in a row of scrub pines twenty yards away scattered. Behind her, the driver and the guard crumpled to the ground, and the stagecoach jerked as the team of mules panicked and lunged.

A scream built in Alma's throat as she stared in disbelief at their blood oozing onto the sun-bleached soil. Air whooshed from her chest as Dillon slammed her to the ground, and then shielded his body atop hers.

The click of his chambering a round echoed in her ear. "Don't move," he growled.

She trembled. "Wh-What's happening?"

"Bandits." He scrambled to his knees, caught her upper arms, and shoved her beneath the belly of the coach.

The lower edge of the Concord knocked her hat askew, pulling her hair as she landed hard on her hip. Alma's head banged against the under beam as she rolled to a stop. Tears flooded her eyes from the pain.

"Stay down," Dillon snarled as he dove in beside her, a hail of bullets pelting the ground in his wake.

A bullet sunk a hand's length from her head.

Alma screamed.

Dillon climbed between her and the shooters.

Lead ricocheted against the tin cup near the wheel. Above her, more bullets slammed into the stagecoach, sending a sunburst of bright yellow splinters raining to the ground. With a shriek, she curled against Dillon. From the corner of her eye, she spied the lifeless forms of the men beneath the mules. Terror swept her, and she fought to breath.

Shots thumped above her.

Two separate, pain-filled gasps echoed from within the Concord. Silence. *Oh God...the wild-haired traveler and the sleeping ruffian! Don't scream. Don't scream. Don't scream.*

Thunder rumbled. Wind, cold and raw with the scent of rain, whipped dirt against her face. With a snap, her distant parasol tipped end-over-end across the clearing and then disappeared into the forest.

Alma squinted, trying to block out the nightmare unfolding around her.

Additional gunfire shattered the air.

Mules snorted, tugging harder against their leather traces. Wheels groaned as the stagecoach creaked forward several more inches.

No. No. No.

Alma wrapped her hands around a spoke of the closest wheel in a futile attempt to stop the movement. The mules lunged again, jerking the wood from her grasp. *God, no!* Her entire body shaking, Alma pressed herself closer to the scout. "D-Dillon!"

"Don't move! There's more than one of them hiding in the trees across the creek."

Through blurred eyes, she stared across the field. "Ho-How do you know?"

"Different sound for each shot."

Another spew of bullets sent puffs of dust around them. She yelped.

Dillon laid his revolver across his bent arm and stared down the barrel.

"Wh-What are you doing?"

"Aiming. Got only six shots, and these bastards are at least thirty yards out. I can't see them, so I need to see their weapons discharge. Cover your ears."

Another round of bullets ripped into the ground before Dillon. Dirt sprayed his face. He didn't flinch. Alma bit her lip to stifle another scream and obeyed, lifting her hands to palm her ears.

Dillon squeezed the trigger. A hard blast shattered the air. He fired again.

From the scrubby pines, Alma heard a faint cry.

Dillon fired another round.

Another man yelled.

The stench of gunpowder melded with her fear. Heart pounding, Alma scoured the sunbaked land and the brush beyond. Empty.

Where are they?

Cocking his head several degrees, Dillon fired twice.

Seconds ticked past before additional shots erupted from the tree line.

Again, Dillon fired. Yet, this time only a click sounded. "Goddamnit. I'm empty, and my other cylinders are in my saddlebags in the coach." He shot a frantic glance around the area, then looked toward the mules. The guard's rifle lay on the ground near the man's body. "I've got to get to that weapon," Dillon rasped.

Fear tore through her. "Y-you can't go out there. You'll be killed."

He shifted, then slid over the top of her, pausing as his full weight pressed down upon her. He leaned closer, his breath hot against the back of her neck. "It's the only chance I've got to save you."

Tears burned her eyes as his weight eased off. Using his elbows, Dillon shuffled on his belly to the front of the coach, and then climbed to his feet between the mules.

The animals brayed and shifted, sidestepping and kicking up more dust.

Heart pounding, Alma stared at Dillon's boots as he moved between the terrified beasts. With each step, his spurs chinked against the stony ground. She dared not blink for fear of losing sight of him.

Two paces.

Four.

Dillon closed his hand around the wooden stock of the weapon.

Elation flooded through her. *Oh, my God. Yes! Now, come back. Come back!*

He started to retrace his steps.

Shots erupted from the tree line. With a high-pitched squeal, the mule standing between Dillon and the bandits buckled to the ground.

Another shot.

And Dillon grunted, collapsing to his knees.

Shock coalesced into a hard twist inside her chest. "D-Dillon?"

His eyes filled with pain and regret riveted on her. "I'm so s-sorry, Princess." He crumpled into the dirt.

Nooooooo! Scalding tears blurred her eyes as hysteria welled in her throat. "Do-Don't…you dare leave me." Sobbing, she reached out, her fingers tugging the edge of his black duster. "Get up!" she pleaded in a frantic whisper. "Pl-Please. Don't leave me."

He lay unmoving as his blood oozed beneath him, turning the ground into a sickening scarlet smear.

A snapping sound in the distance grabbed her attention.

Alma whirled to peer between the wheel spokes.

Clutching rifles, two men stepped from the brush. They splashed through the shallow creek and headed straight toward her. Blood seeped down one's shirtfront.

"No. Oh god. No!" She scoured the meadow and the trees with rising panic. There was nowhere she could run. Bile rose to her throat. She knew how to sew, how to dance, how to read and write in four languages, and she knew how to maintain the most beautiful rose garden in all of Boston. But she didn't know how to survive one single minute in the wilds of Colorado without Dillon Reed.

Alma glared at the approaching men, then gasped. She'd seen these murderers before.

On the train!

"We'll toss the bodies into the coach, then push everything down the mountainside," the taller man said to his partner, his gaze never leaving hers as they neared. "No one will ever find a trace."

The other nodded. "Simon's expected at Fort Hays any day now. We'll need to let 'im know."

Another hard kick of adrenalin raced through Alma. *Simon? Who's Simon?*

"After we get settled in," the first man continued, "one of us will have to go telegraph him where we're holed up. And tell him to bring our money."

They halted paces away.

She stared at their boots, at the drops of blood plopping across the scuffed leather of the smaller man's. He stepped over the dead mule and kicked the side of Dillon's body. "You bastard. Thought you could kill me, did you?"

His partner laughed. "Well, he got pretty damn close with you, and he did kill Sam sight unseen." He squatted on the opposite side of the wheel hub. A patch of filthy black hair lay in hanks over his thin shoulders, and a thin, wiry beard covered his face. He leveled his gaze on Alma. Weather-beaten features split open to reveal a tattered grin. "Now, you come on out from under that carriage, Miss Talmadge. We've got bigger plans for you."

CHAPTER ELEVEN

Pain rolled through Dillon as he struggled against the torment that sunk in with unrelenting persistence. Finally, his mind acquiesced. Consciousness returned. He gasped for breath. He'd been shot. That much he remembered.

Alma!

He lifted his head. Agony slammed him. *Hell*. Gritting his teeth, he scanned his surroundings. He lay at a cockeyed angle on the side of a ravine, his body lodged against a boulder. To his left, the stagecoach driver and the guard lay in a twisted heap. Beyond that, the shattered remains of the Concord and the two lifeless bodies of the male passengers were draped over the rock-strewn incline.

No sign of Alma.

He grimaced. The bastards thought to hide the bodies, and then ride off with her. *They should've made sure I was dead.*

Gritting his teeth, Dillon shoved himself up. He remained conscious, barely.

Just breathe.

In. And out.

Much needed strength poured through his veins as he battled the damning call of Satan.

I'm not dead yet, you diabolical sonofabitch.

He pushed to his knees. The rapid thump of his heartbeat echoed in his ears. On an unsteady breath, he eased back to sit on his heels, then peered down at his shirtfront. The entire left side of blue cambric was stiff with blood from collar to cuff. He frowned. From the amount lost, the wound was serious.

If he didn't move soon, he'd die.

If he went to find her, he'd probably die.

Hell. My destiny's all carved out for me.

Dillon grabbed for the jagged edge of the Concord and staggered to his feet. Wood creaked, and the door fell from his grasp. He wobbled. Through sheer will, he kept his balance.

A deep roll of thunder echoed in the distance.

He glanced up. Storm clouds swirled above the canopy of pines. Rain would wash away any hope he'd have of tracking Alma's captors. He must find her while he still had his wits. Sucking another breath through clenched teeth, he leaned over, and jammed his hand beneath the broken wood of the stagecoach seat.

His saddlebags were gone.

Another rumble of thunder echoed…this time closer. Again, he scanned the debris around him. Alma's traveling case was also gone.

Sonofabitch!

His jaw tightened as he stared at the empty harnesses trailing from the coach's broken brace. The bandits had turned the team loose before pushing the stagecoach, filled with bodies, over the edge. *Guess I'm the lucky one.*

He cut his gaze upward. *Or not.* He still had to get up there.

Legs trembling, Dillon straightened, steadying himself. He waited while another wave of blackness passed, then he pursed his lips and whistled.

Another ten seconds ticked into oblivion.

A rustling noise sounded near the top of the rim. A pewter-grey head with long ears poking straight up peered over the side. Nostrils flared as the mule brayed.

Thank God!

The beast had been born to serve the coach line -- he would not have wandered far. The witless bastards who'd turned the team loose were obviously ignorant of that fact, or believing everyone dead, hadn't cared. *Their stupidity is my redemption.* And he'd be sure to tell them so just before he killed them.

His gaze narrowed on the ravine's rock-strewn slope.

But first, he had to climb out of this damn pit.

Chapter Twelve

Dillon shook his head to clear the dizziness, and flexed his fingers, numb now. The hardest part of the last hour hadn't been climbing out of the ravine or even working his way atop the mule. The biggest challenge was staying astride the bulky beast without a saddle or reins as he tracked his way back to the where the stagecoach had been attacked.

Clues of Alma's abduction were everywhere. They'd headed north. Into the mountains. He slid from the mule, his eyes narrowing. Her knitted purse and ribboned hat lay on the stream bank. An ache bloomed in his chest. He jammed the pieces into his coat pocket, wafting the illusive smell of roses upward. *Her scent.*

Wooziness returned as did the taste of her soft, sweet lips. Damn his weakness.

Move it…you're running out of time.

He scanned the edge of the meadow. No sign of Alma's silly parasol. She must've insisted they get it. His gut tightened as rage burned through his blood. *If they've harmed a single hair on her head…*

They were dead men regardless.

Dillon turned and stumbled to the mule, both his body and his heart in torment. Remounting, he turned the beast and headed north across the ridgeline. Signs indicated the riders were climbing higher into the mountains. He settled his gaze on a fifteen-foot, cut-leaf mahogany a few yards ahead. Taping the mule's flank, he angled toward the tree.

Leaves rustled as Dillon pulled the closest limb to his nose. A slight break at the end emitted a pungent, earthy smell. Too high for a mule deer to reach, the splinter likely due to a rider's shoulder brushing past.

He searched the ground around the tree. This specific wood was used to make arrow shafts, but the damage wasn't caused by Indians. Their signs of passing were never this easy to follow. Nor were the sneaky bastards ever this reckless. No, the damage had been made by an unconcerned rider who left behind a clear path of travel with little thought to anyone tracking him.

A half-hearted smile lifted his lips as he released the branch. And from the freshness of the tracks, each depression still crumbling around the edges, they'd passed not too long ago. Another roll of thunder echoed to his south. Careless or not, he must hurry.

He scanned the rock-strewn corridor for signs of riders. Bruised blades of grass. Dislodged sticks. Overturned leaves. The impressions in the earth indicated several horses. That much he already knew. He glanced over his shoulder. The fast-approaching storm clouds smothered the sun. Damn, he needed to see the shadow across the depressions to discover which direction they'd ridden.

An upended rock near a cluster of evergreens caught his eye. A fresh gash in a north-to-south pattern had been caused by metal scraping the moss-covered stone.

Shod horses.

Relief swamped him. He rewove his fingers through the mule's stiff mane. Tapping the animal's flanks, he turned to the right. The colonel's only niece waited for him to save her. And save her he would, if it was the last damn thing he did.

Thirty minutes later, a whisper of words swirled in the wind.

Voices?

Hope igniting, he halted the mule and listened.

The rustle of junipers and hawkweed filled the void. Spots swam before his eyes. Maybe he was hallucinating. His shoulder hurt like hell, and with the amount of blood staining his shirt, he was surprised he had any life left in him. He started to turn, then the skin on the back of his neck tightened.

"I said—"

A howl of wind severed the murmurings.

There! Definitely voices.

Dillon slid from the mule, and stumbled behind the closest boulder. Pulse racing, he scanned the hillock, his gaze pausing on a small opening just behind a cluster of Lodgepole pines.

A cave.

Shivers inundated him, but he ignored his body's trembling. Easing around an outcropping of rocks, he splashed into a stream. His gaze never left the opening as he took a knee and scooped a handful of water into his mouth.

Focus on the task at hand.

Refreshed by the cold slide of water down his throat, he edged closer.

***

Alma tried to move, but rope twisted around her wrists cut into her skin and held her tight. The angle at which her arms were tied behind her made her shoulders ache. All ten fingers tingled. Worse, the pounding headache from a blow to the back of her skull still throbbed. She lay on her side on a dirt floor in what looked like a small cave. With a sob building in her throat, she shifted her shoulder to try and relieve the discomfort. Refusing to give in to her fears, she pressed her lips together.

Flickering flames from a nearby campfire cast an orange glow over the area. Her eyes adjusted to the fading light. She glared at the two men deep in conversation near a pile of supplies. One man taller, the other small-framed.

Why have they abducted me?

She'd not yet been molested, so perhaps that wasn't their intention.

Then for money.

That made sense. These hooligans and their Simon want to blackmail father. In his line of business, no doubt he has many enemies.

Thoughts of ransom demands, days spent with these monsters, and father's fear for her safety raced through Alma's mind as she noticed several packsaddles, blankets, and canned goods stacked against the far rock wall. Shadows played hide and seek with the supplies, but she could make out the word *peaches* on a few cans near the top of the heap. She swallowed hard, fighting back her fear. There was enough food to settle in for a long duration…unless they intended to kill her. She tamped back another rush of tears.

Be strong.

She squeezed her eyes tight as sorrow drove deep into her heart.

He died trying to save me.

Memories of Dillon's embrace, his masculine scent, the scintillating desire born after his illicit kiss, all brought another rush of pain. The scuff of boots echoed from across the cave floor.

Alma feigned sleep.

"Looks like she's still out cold," a man's voice nearby stated.

She struggled hard to suppress another shudder.

"I told you not to hit her so hard."

"She'll be all right," he drawled with a brogue. "Didn't hurt her looks none." She'd heard just such Irish accents many times while visiting father at his Boston wharf. "You know, Zeke…we can have our way with the wench and no one'll be the wiser."

God no!

"I said we ain't touching 'er 'til we get our money, you got that?"

"How the hell will he know if we poke her a time or two?" His coarse laugh settled over Alma and sent another terrified hitch to her heartbeat. "'Sides, how do we even know he'll come all the way out here, anyway?"

"He'll be here. And if you go near her, I'll kill you myself. You got that? Simon wants her alive and untouched. You heard what he told us in Washington."

As they moved away from her, Alma released a slow breath.

"Now go get the rest of the gear off the horses," one of the men said. "And grab some more wood for the fire."

Simon? Whoever he was, he was behind her abduction. As hard as she tried, no one she knew bore that name.

***

With shuffling footsteps, Dillon crept near the cave's entrance. Four horses stood tied to a makeshift picket line. The bandits had Alma inside. He cursed beneath his breath.

The odds were against him.

Another wave of blackness nearly drove him to his knees. He fought back a groan as he inched toward the horses. Hope rose as he spotted his saddlebags slung over the closest gelding. *Thank God.* Several steps later, he sagged against the animal, resting his forehead against cool leather. Exhausted, he shook, chills gripping him.

Move or Alma's dead!

On an unsteady inhale, he shoved aside his weakness and rummaged inside his saddlebags. His fingers closed around the Bowie knife, his wicked companion during all those hellish years before Colonel Talmadge.

My odds just improved.

Hunkering down near a large juniper, he unsheathed the knife. He'd greet these cold-blooded killers on their own terms, and let his ten-inch blade do the talking.

Seconds later, crunching footsteps resonated over rocky soil. A man stepped into view, favoring a wounded arm, his shirt bloodstained.

A wry grin twisted Dillon's lips. He'd hit one of the sonsofbitches after all. Gripping the Bowie's handle, he angled himself behind the man. As the bandit turned, Dillon wrapped his arm around the bastard's neck and squeezed.

"You should've checked the dead," he hissed. A split-second later, he pulled his knife across the man's throat as he released his grip. The bandit gasped, then went limp. Dillon dropped the dead-weight to the ground.

One down.

He wobbled to a knee and caught several breaths. As he straightened, the click of a cocking revolver echoed behind him.

Bloody Hell.

"Stop right there, mister," a gruff voice ordered.

Dillon pulled his lips thin. Slowly, he turned to face the new arrival. Pointing a Colt, the man held the advantage, but one he immediately lost for having failed to shoot when he had his chance. With nimble precision, Dillon flipped the Bowie through the air.

The blade buried to the hilt in the center of the man's chest.

Shock widened the bandit's eyes. And then, on a groan, he fell face-forward to the ground. Dillon's vision blurred as he retrieved his knife. With a curse, he swiped the blade across the dead man's shirt, then slipped the Bowie into his boot. A quick glance assured him no one else followed them. He tugged the Colt from the dead man's grip, and spun the cylinder to check the ammunition. *Fully loaded. Good.* Dillon eased up to the rocky entrance and peered inside.

A quick sweep told him only one person, hands and feet bound, lay huddled upon the ground near the fire. Anger stormed through his veins. His gaze narrowed. "Alma?"

She pushed to her hands, then shifted upward to her knees.

"D-Dillon?" Shock filled her voice. "But, I thought you…" She twisted around and stared at him full-on, her expression incredulous. Tears pooled in the incredible blue of her eyes as her surprise slowly magnified into joy. A smile lifted her lips, and sent a breath-stealing jolt through Dillon. "Oh my God, y-you're alive!"

"Barely," he said, pushing the word through gritted teeth as he stumbled into the darkened interior.

***

Simon Bell refilled his glass from a bottle near his elbow, then lifted the whiskey to his lips. He paused as the door to Kelly's Saloon swung open. Through the swirling cigar smoke a couple of soldiers from the nearby fort ambled in, heading toward the bar. Behind them, several civilians followed.

He grimaced. None were the men he'd hired.

Four days had passed since he'd reached the end of the rail line at Hays City. But the expected news of Alma's successful abduction had yet to arrive.

No telegram.

No letter.

No men.

His anger built. If he didn't receive word by tomorrow morning, he would head to Tucson to complete the task himself.

The scrape of a fork on a metal plate drew his attention to the whore seated across from him. He'd bought her for the night from the best brothel in town. The train's porter, when asked, had directed Simon to the establishment near the brand new courthouse in the center of town. With a broad smile, the servant had assured him the proprietor, a Mrs. Em Bowen, guaranteed her girls disease-free. Not that it mattered to Simon. He would never sink himself inside one of them, clean or not.

The plinking notes of an out-of-tune piano underscored the irritation building in his veins as he stared at the wench stuffing forkfuls of food into her mouth. In between bites, she wiped her lips with the back of her grimy hand.

Disgust curdled through him. He'd seen this behavior before in a myriad bars back east - whores who'd followed down a doomed path, increasing desperation their only acquaintance. He always chose the small-framed ones. The ones with the darkest hair.

The ones who most resembled his mother.

He bought them a meal and stared at them the entire night, amused he could control the women without a word. And this one in particular, younger than most and more anxious, had dressed up for her evening *trade*. Her well-worn, burgundy corset atop the soiled camisole had seen far better days. Sweat stains dampened her armpits. She'd piled her limp tresses atop her head, and an old bruise graced the side of her face, fading into yellow at her hairline.

The consequences of your ungodly profession.

He smiled, and she offered an apprehensive nod in return, her nervousness churning Simon's gut. The girl's fate was inevitable. He could not let what happened to his beloved mother happen to this wretched little soul.

His purpose in life, to save the creatures from a depraved existence, drove him forward.

From outside, shouting and gunshots met his ears as the miscreants of Hays City rolled onto Main Street. *Right on time.* He chuckled, then took another sip of his whiskey. Though the rowdier crowds had been driven further south to Dodge, the local law would still be busy curtailing their remaining dregs of society.

The cheap-glass earrings dangling from the woman's earlobes caught the light from an overhead oil lamp and glinted toward Simon. At one time, she might've been a comely wench.

Like mother, before disease…and Talmadge…destroyed her.

Oh yes, killing this pathetic whore would be easy.

Chapter Thirteen

"Thank you for coming, Sir." Colonel Talmadge motioned for the two middle-aged Englishmen to enter. Lord Henry Smyth Green, the Earl of Locknor, eased onto the serviceable chair opposite him. Even in the heat of the desert, Alma's betrothed looked cool and collected. Behind him, appearing just the opposite, slumped a profusely sweating, Edgar Clarkson. The earl's steward placed a hand upon the back of the chair and drew in several deep breaths.

Swerving around to face his aide, Lord Green snapped, "For Christ's sake, man. Stand up. You're nothing but a withered mess."

Clarkson rammed his shoulders back, sucked in another gulp of air, and up righted.

"That's more like it," the earl said, nodding. "Remember yourself, and your overall reason for being here."

"Yes, my Lord. My deepest apologies, but the heat wears me down, something fierce."

"I don't want excuses, just do as I say."

As the earl turned back, Thaddeus did not miss the scowl that darkened the servant's face.

The nobleman dropped his riding gloves onto the desk, tugged on his blue-brocaded vest, and spoke in a clipped English tongue that was as crisp as his appearance. "Please accept my apologies for all this, Colonel. And thank you for taking my meeting. Have you heard any news of my fiancée?"

A month had passed since the aristocrat's arrival at the fort, an official government *letter of introduction* in his hand. Other than possessing such an unctuous attitude, Thaddeus still couldn't peg why he loathed the bastard.

"As a matter of fact, I do have an update." Thaddeus straightened in his chair, pushing aside the idiotic feeling of inadequacy that arose each time he found himself around this popinjay. "I received a telegram from my scout several days ago. They'd just reached Fort Hays. And from there, they'd caught a Concord south."

The earl swept imaginary lint from his coat sleeve, his lips pulling taut beneath a wispy moustache. "How long before Miss Talmadge arrives?"

"Well," Thaddeus leaned back in the chair and folded his hands over his midsection. Compared to the pencil-thin man sitting opposite him, he looked like some ponderous, ill-kempt buffalo. "The trip from Fort Hays should take a good two weeks. Baring no complications."

"Complications?" The dark-haired Englishman leaned forward and draped an arm over his knee covered in buff-colored wool. His brows furrowed. "Surely you don't expect them to meet foul play?"

Thaddeus inhaled, his impatience with this blowhard mounting. "They're traveling from fort to fort as they make their way south, but the route is tried and true. There shouldn't be too much of a problem. She'll be uncomfortable, of course, but she'll survive." He neglected to inform the man about the dangerously long stretch between Fort Hays and Santa Fe. "Oh, and bored. She will most assuredly be bored since there's little to see or do for a finely bred lady."

Alma's fiancé had arrived at Fort Lowell by way of San Francisco, so he was unfamiliar with the terrain she now traveled. Wisely, Talmadge left out the travelogue of issues that concerned even a seasoned traveler: raging rivers, grueling weather, mountains, and deadly deserts. Redskins and wildlife alike. Again, he felt a wave of relief knowing Dillon had received his warning about possible trouble.

The nobleman ran his fingers around the brim of his brown-felt top hat. "And you're sure Indians will not be a problem?"

"Well," Talmadge said, "The stage line'll clip the corners of the Mescalero and Coyotero Apache reservations in New Mexico, so there's always a threat. But, the military force in that region has full-control over the renegades, unlike the continued uprisings we're experiencing here." The Colonel shuddered at the thought of what Indians might do to his young niece if they captured her. "Nevertheless, Alma is traveling with my best man. So you can relax. Dillon Reed will see to her safety."

The earl arched a fawn-colored eyebrow. "And you're quite sure of this man?"

"I'm confident of him." Talmadge omitted the part about Dillon being like a son to him after he took the wild lad under his wing years before.

"But he's not military, right? Only a scout."

"Yes. But Dillon Reed is much more than merely a scout…he aids the U.S. Army in many other valuable ways." Thaddeus fought to contain a grimace as their gazes locked. "And I trust him implicitly."

Lord Green's pale-blue eyes narrowed as he gave an impatient huff. "Can he be trusted with my fiancée?" He leaned forward, tapping the desk with his manicured finger. "That is my concern, Colonel. After all, he is a man."

Talmadge contained the laugh that bubbled up in his chest. *What a haughty sonofabitch you are, Lord Green.* "I'd trust my own daughter with Dillon Reed." Thaddeus sighed, curling his fingers through the porcelain handle of his coffee cup. "You needn't worry. Reed is a man of integrity with zero tolerance for anything or anyone that gets in the way of his duty."

"Although I am uncomfortable with these arrangements, I shall trust your judgment."

What an ass.

The shrill call of a bugle blared through the open window. Thaddeus shifted his gaze to the aide, then on to the mantel clock. Time for afternoon review. *Thank God. Anything to get these annoying dolts out of my office.* Chinking bridles echoed beyond the open windows announcing the formations of his cavalry. Kicked up by their many horses, an acrid smell of dust drifted over him. He stood, then leaned forward. "Have no fear. Reed will see that Alma gets here."

The Englishman nodded, rising to his feet. His aide, shoved aside the chair to make an easier exit for the earl. For the time being, Thaddeus decided to keep the troublesome details of his brother's telegram to himself. He saw no good reason to worry them further.

***

Emotion swept Alma as Dillon sliced through the rope, freeing her from her bindings. Until his arrival, moments before, she'd thought herself doomed.

His gaze lifted, melding to hers. "Are you all right?" he asked. The rueful intensity darkening his eyes sent shivers up her arms.

Alma took a breath to steady her pounding heart. Joyful at his sudden reappearance, she rubbed her wrists. "Yes," she said, focusing on the blood that stained his shirtfront. "But...what about you?"

"I've felt better." His curse filled the chamber as he stumbled back and slumped against the cave wall. He gave a sharp hiss.

She scrambled to his side, concern stealing away her prior elation.

With shaking fingers, Dillon unbuttoned his shirt, then shrugged his shoulders and slid out of the garment.

On edge, she stared at his bare chest, the hard plane and muscle, the faded scars. A smattering of hair darkened his skin, traveling downward in a thicker path to disappear beneath the waistband of his denims.

Her heart squeezed, stealing what breath remained in her lungs. Never before had she seen a man's naked torso, and his looked as hard as the rock wall behind him. Then she caught sight of the blood oozing from his shoulder wound. "You're still bleeding!"

"Bullet's in there somewhere." He shifted, spreading his legs wider to brace himself. "It'll have to come out."

"What?" she gasped, blinking fast and lifting her gaze to his.

"I said, you'll have to dig the lead out."

Heart pounding, she stared dumbstruck at the blood drizzling past a dusky nipple. "Di-Dig it out? But...I know nothing about digging anything out." Her whisper quivered on the edge of a squeak as her whole world careened into disorder once more. Between her near-death experiences, this man's miraculous arrival, and the sight of his naked chest, Alma could barely find control of logical thought.

The belief that she could doctor anyone was incomprehensible.

"Then I'll make it simple. You either help remove it, or I bleed out. And," he said on a groan as he slid down the wall, "if I die, you're all alone out here." He settled on his hip, his breath a series of panting rasps. His hair draped in a disheveled, sable curtain in front of his face.

Alma grasped for the closest reaction.

Anger.

Yes. Anger she could hold onto, use to shove aside the fear clawing to break her fragile grip on sanity. She clenched her hands at her sides. "You were paid good money to complete your task, Mister Reed. Don't you dare die now...n-not after you've just found me." She cringed at the harshness in her voice, yet the statement brought back much-needed order.

Dillon shuddered as his mouth shifted into a contrite half-grin. "I'll take that as your willingness to help, then. And no one paid me to bring you back, Princess," he growled. "I was just following orders." He collapsed onto his elbow, struggling for each breath. "Use the knife. But, don't cut off your damn finger. You're no good to me injured."

How dare you mock me! "Well, you're no good to me dead."

Another strained laugh. "Fetch my saddlebags. They're on the big bay tied at the end of the line."

With a shaky nod, she stumbled backward, then turned and hurried out. Terror drove each step. Wind slapped her face as she exited the cave. A minute later, insides churning from the sight of the dead bandits, Alma reentered the dank chamber. She settled the saddlebags near him as she knelt at his side.

He didn't move.

God, no! Fear coalesced into a hard knot inside her throat. "Dillon?"

"Empty 'em," he muttered.

Relief coursed through her and she blinked back the building tears. Hands shaking, she dumped the bag's contents beside the knife. A silver flask and small metal tin clanked to the ground alongside a blanket, the outfit he wore to the Custers' party, a tiny blue bottle, and some kind of round metal cylinder.

He gestured to the flask. "Take a big drink, then pour whiskey over the blade and then my wound. Needle and thread in the tin." He stretched out long legs, his spurs chinking against the ground. Alma stared at the rowels. One spun in silent rhythm with her escalating panic. "Now, I'm just gonna lie down here. And let you get to work."

Furious he could make light of this dire situation, she shot him a cold glare. "If I didn't need you to guide me out of here, I swear, Dillon Reed, I'd kill you myself for getting shot."

A barely audible laugh, muffled and pain-filled, reached her ears. "And after I'm stitched up, dump more whiskey over the site. Then, get rid of the bodies. Push 'em into the ravine. That'll keep the wolves busy for a while."

Wolves?

Her heart banged inside her chest.

She wanted to argue.

To deny.

Deny what? That she cared for this man more than she should? As if emphasizing that disquieting truth, the nearby fire crackled and popped. The logs inside the ring of stones shifted deeper into the flames.

Moisture blurred her eyes. Beyond all reason she wanted him to live. And if he died...

She swallowed hard, refusing to linger on that terrifying thought.

He couldn't die.

He wouldn't.

Dillon gave a rattling cough. "Did you get all that, Princess?"

She nodded, terrified by the pain now reflected in his eyes. Vacant and hollow, they were empty of the spark that'd been the driving force behind everything shared between them up till now.

"Good," he muttered. "You're stronger than you realize…now hold out your hand."

Fingers shaking, she obeyed.

He dropped the flask to her palm, then collapsed onto his side, eyes closing. "You can do this, Alma. I believe in you."

Outside, thunder rumbled.

She stared at him.

The fear of being without his guiding influence, the need to keep him by her side, the joy she'd felt upon seeing him again engulfed her. She scanned his bleeding body, his angular face, his…lips. Her throat tightened nearly strangling her. She would never survive in these mountains without him. And all that stood between *living and dying* for them both was…*her?*

A cold, clammy sweat broke out across her forehead. Her hands shook. Another burst of thunder vibrated the air. And a second later, rain pounded the ground outside the cave's entrance. The scents of earth and pine and smoke reached her. She inhaled, drawing the trio of smells deeper into her lungs as she struggled for calm.

You can do this, Alma. I believe in you.

His remembered words lent her strength. If only she were as sure inside. Uncorking the flask, she took a big swallow.

Whiskey scorched a path down her throat.

She gasped, then coughed as she jammed the cork into place. What he asked of her was nothing like sewing passementarie, and until now, that mundane pastime represented the only reason she'd ever in her life lifted a needle.

Alma laid aside the small container and glanced around the cave. "We'll need bandages, Dillon." *Silence.* The scout was long past hearing, but talking aloud helped her focus. "But, where shall I find those?" She scanned the pile of goods stacked against the wall, her traveling case, and then the gray blanket near his elbow.

No. I'll need that to cover him.

She marveled at her ability to quell her fears. Marveled further that she held her panic at bay. Finally, a thought swam to the surface of her frustrations. "Yes, I do believe that will work."

Alma grabbed his bundle of clothes and pulled out the new shirt. Dillon's fresh scent at the party wafted over her, conjuring up his powerful voice, an arm banding her waist, dark eyes narrowing beneath the moonlight before he kissed her.

She took in his sweat-soaked chest, now veiled in firelight. *Y-You can't die.* A desire to sweep aside his tousled hair tugged at her soul.

Stop this! Responsibility demanded she center her efforts. More so now than ever before in her life.

She wrapped her hand around the Bowie's grip, then whacked apart his linen shirt. In a matter of minutes, a large pile of misshapen bandages lay before her.

She exhaled a shaky breath.

So far, so good.

Alma selected several strips and piled them into a small heap. As he'd instructed, she angled the knife over the cloth and poured whiskey onto the blade. The mound of material beneath caught the excess liquid.

Unbidden, a tear slipped down her cheek, and then another, tracing cool paths to her jaw. She swiped the moisture away and then looked at the scout.

Firelight illuminated the redness rimming the bullet hole. With each precious heartbeat, a stream of blood oozed from the wound. She swabbed away the excess. How much more could he afford to lose?

"Hold on," she whispered. A fortifying breath later, she poured whiskey onto the swelling mess.

Dillon groaned as his body lurched upward.

She gasped, then stiffened back and caught his shoulder. "You must lie still if I'm to do this!"

As if he could hear her. Nonetheless, he mustn't move while she wielded the knife.

With care, she pushed aside her bustled skirt and climbed across the lower half of his body. Pushing with her hands, she centered herself, and finally straddled him. The impropriety of their closeness burned her cheeks. Yet, there was no one here to reprimand her.

Or even care if this man lived or died.

Except me.

The tragic thought frightened her. No one had counted on her before in her entire life, ever.

She had always counted on others.

"Now this ought to hold you." Her taut whisper brushed his face, stirring a lock of hair. She bit back a brittle laugh, realizing if the scout had all his faculties, she would be a mere feather in the wind against his strength.

Leaning forward, she again dribbled the amber liquor into his wound.

He shuddered beneath her.

Thankful she'd kept him from moving, she rested her forearm against his ribs. His weak heartbeat fluttered beneath her hand. "Now, I've never done this before, so I cannot promise perfection."

With a steadying breath, Alma began her probe, the blade widening the bullet hole as the sharp-edged Bowie slipped deeper and deeper into the wound.

Dillon moaned. And she drew another ragged breath.

Blood, warm and sticky, smeared the blade and splattered across Alma's hand, but she kept her focus and worked swiftly. With the rain pounding at the cavern's entrance and the fire crackling nearby, she continued her exploration. One minute turned into five as she searched for the deadly bullet.

"Where are you?" she snarled as the rip in his puckered flesh widened. An eternity later, the tip of the knife scraped a hard surface.

Relief swept through her. "I-I think I've found something." She stared at his pale face, engulfed in the shadows.

No comment.

Nothing. His face was as bleak as an Eastern winter. His eyes closed. Oh how she longed for the glint she'd seen in his dark gaze back in the corridor of the Rale House Hotel when he'd spotted her. An unreadable message full of...something.

The bittersweet pang deepened.

Swallowing hard, she refocused on her ungodly task. Using the knife tip, she pried the slug upward until the glob of misshapen metal popped out of the wound and slid across his chest. The bullet came to a stop against the hemline of her skirt. "I did it!"

She scooped up the piece of lead. How could such a tiny object fell this hulking man?

Thankful the ordeal was over, Alma dropped the bullet. Taking the flask, she poured the whiskey into the raw, mangled opening.

As before, he didn't move. Not even a groan.

Her gaze slid from her task, settling on his features. Masculine. Intimidating. His hair lay in a dark swath beneath his head, his nose as straight as an arrow, his jaw firm and steady and strong. Again, Alma felt the conflicted stirrings she'd first known when he'd stepped into the hallway at the dance...two-hundred pounds of unwavering stubbornness relentlessly drawing her to him.

To lose this man now was unthinkable.

"P-Please, don't die," she begged, the hollow void inside her heart widening into a cavern as pronounced as the one in which they now huddled. Another roll of thunder shook the cave as the rain intensified, forming puddles at the entrance like the pooling of her own insistent tears.

She rested her head on his chest, her words a wracking whisper, "I-I did the best I could for you, I promise. Now p-please come back to me."

From the moment they'd met, she'd been transfixed by this man's brashness, his complete and utter indifference...toward her, her position in society, and everything else she deemed important. He was a mystery, the wrong man for her tears, and yet, she could not tamp back her grief. She sobbed out her fear, her anxiety, and her uselessness. He needed her to be so much more. He was a mountain to her meadow, a hawk to sparrow, a lion to her weak little lamb.

Their worlds and lifestyles -- *so opposite.*

And yet, from somewhere deep inside, a startling, never-used strength, a forte he'd mumbled earlier that she possessed, breathed fully into life. Determination to save him bore with immense force into Alma. She swiped her hand across her face, firm in her resolve to at least finish the task he'd asked of her. She shoved aside the truth of her perplexing feelings for this man -- too frightening, too complicated to face.

Outside, the storm intensified as another roll of thunder pulled her back to this moment. Rain dumped in torrents, but all her secrets were safely locked behind the veil of water that now curtained the entrance.

Shaking, she slid off Dillon and reached for the sewing tin. Nothing else mattered right except saving this man's life.

Threading the needle took three tries.

She leaned forward. With firelight illuminating Dillon's shoulder, she pierced the flesh. The needle met only slight resistance, then the thread skimmed through. She compressed her lips and drew the ragged edges of his wound together. This kind of sewing really wasn't that different from needlecraft after all. Ten minutes and twenty impeccable stitches later, her handiwork was complete. Alma poured whiskey over the jagged line of black, and then covered the site with the bandages.

"You know, don't you," she said, tucking in the final piece, "I thought you were a knuckle-dragging mongrel when first we met. And rightly so..." She paused, then with a sigh, she retrieved the bullet and stared at it. "Now I know nothing could be further from the truth."

She wanted to say so many more things to this fearless beast of a man, but didn't quite know where to begin. She rolled the lead between her forefinger and thumb and swallowed hard.

Her gaze shifted back to Dillon, his face as pale as moonlight. "Thank you for finding me." The whispered words seemed paltry for the price he'd paid to save her.

She would properly thank him tomorrow...

...if he still lived.

Chapter Fourteen

Alma awoke with a start as thunder rumbled in wicked fury. Sometime during the night, she'd fallen asleep while resting her head upon the saddlebags. Through tired eyes, she glanced toward the cave's exit. Rain still pummeled the earth as flashes of lightning illumined the rocky walls. Dank smells and endless dripping accentuated her misery. She opened her palm, and more closely studied the blue bottle that had slipped from her makeshift pillow during the night. Even in the low light, the silver-topped vial looked familiar.

She brought the bottle closer. *House of Guerlain Parfumeurs* lay scrawled in an elegant font across the label. More specifically, their expensive Parisian brand *Voleur de Roses*.

Stunned, her gaze cut to Dillon.

My scent.

Alma's heart sank beneath the weight of sadness. Was there someone waiting for him in Tucson after all? Regardless the scout's bravery, the risks he'd taken to save her, or the way he made Alma feel…he wasn't hers to claim.

As if it mattered. She was en route to meet her betrothed.

More confused than ever, she returned the vial to his saddlebags, and then straightened her legs to banish the cramps. She leaned over and laid her finger along the curve of his mouth, resting her knuckle beneath his nostrils. His mustache was so soft to the touch.

When she felt the damp passage of air, she sent a silent *thank you* heavenward. He was alive, but still gripped in the throes of a fever. For hours she'd swabbed his body with freshly-caught rainwater as incoherent words spilled from his mouth. And as she moved the cloth, she memorized every crease, every mark, every single scar abrading his hard-edged body. A time or two she even had to lay across him to contain his thrashing.

Her gaze once more drifted to his prone form.

Other than the swift, back-and-forth darts of his eyes beneath his closed lids, Dillon now lay still. The shallow rise and fall of his chest had become her lifeline, the only indicator that he lived.

When he breathed in…she breathed out.

She closed her eyes and lifted another prayer.

Please, live, I. . .

What?

Frustrated, she glanced toward the fire. During her fitful slumber, the flames had died, leaving only an orangish glimmer to taunt her. Alma scooted to the fieldstone ring and her ever-dwindling stack of firewood.

Carefully, she laid fresh logs across the embers, leaned closer, and blew soft puffs of air against the coals. An bright glow warmed her face and then wisps of smoke swirled upward seconds before flames danced into life. Soon, the pop and crackle of the dry tinder echoed as the fire grew.

Satisfied, she shifted to alleviate the pinch of her corset. The measure of her discomfort loomed large as green material wrapped her frame in a damp constriction. And yet, no matter how uncomfortable she felt, she would not cast aside her comportment. If she gave up who *she* was, she might as well be lying lost and helpless on the ground beside the scout.

Before her harrowing trip westward, tidiness ruled supreme in her world…and one day, it would again. Slowly, she drew up the hemline of her dress and nearly sobbed at the mud staining the bottom of her underslip. The hand-stitched pattern of hollyhocks she'd spent weeks completing last fall now wallowed in a filthy garden all their own.

Her white cuffs were equally soiled…with dirt and muck and Dillon's blood.

Alma raised a hand to the nape of her neck, smoothing back tendrils that lay in wild disarray. She couldn't even imagine the sight that would greet her if she chanced a glance into a looking glass. Nonetheless, a quick twist piled her unruly tresses into a chignon atop her head, and a few well-placed hair pins returned order to her coiffure. If only they could do the same for her world.

A sigh slipped past her lips, and she rolled her shoulders to work out the kinks.

From the far side of the cave, the horse and mule snorted, drawing her gaze. "Quit complaining over there and be grateful I brought you both inside." Late yesterday afternoon, after pushing the bandits over the side of the ravine as Dillon had requested, she'd spent additional time in the pouring rain coercing the stubborn mule and a horse into the cave. Her body still ached from the ordeal. "I'm just thankful neither of you ran away from me like your other three friends."

Alma pressed her back against the cool rock wall and stared at the scout. Other than the rise and fall of his chest from each ragged breath, the man hadn't moved a muscle. She shivered again, blaming the chill on the drafts.

Her eyes slipped closed.

And she waited. And waited.

And waited...

One day turned into two, the rain pounding the earth with a fury matched only by the loneliness hammering inside Alma. On the morning of the third day, she stood at the cave's entrance and watched as the sun slowly rose above the treetops.

She inhaled, drawing cool mountain air into her lungs. Freshness and renewal wafted on the breeze. She peered upward at the wide expanse of blue.

Not a cloud in the periwinkle sky.

Her stomach growled, and she frowned. Breakfast today had consisted of canned peaches, and opening the tin had proved a daunting task. She flexed her hand, her palm sore from smashing a rock against the knife's end to pierce the metal. Prying the blade around the edge took nearly an hour and also gave her with an annoying blister. Although the fruit was edible, it nowhere resembled her favorite peach dish from Boston's Union Oyster House, the flavor of that butter-enriched *pâte brisée* tart was the finest peach dish she'd ever eaten.

A mocking laugh spilled into the rain-washed morning. "Alma Talmadge," she whispered, "I'm afraid you are losing your mind."

She upended the tin and swallowed the remaining peach juice, then tossed the empty container over the side. As metal rattled on rock, movement in the valley caught her eye. A horse grazed along the bottom near the creek. At dawn, he and the mule had wandered from the cave much to her distress. But, they had to have water and food, too. How would she ever get them back inside?

Frustrated at no immediate solution, she reentered the cave. Her newest challenge had been keeping the fire alive, and the stack of wood near their supplies was dwindling fast. She lifted the ax, weighing the implement in her hands.

I've no idea how to use this.

Her mind skimmed back to the myriad times the staff in Boston had brought kindling into her bedroom. Never had she known a cold morning as she'd completed her daily toilette. And yet, in all those years, not once had she thanked her maids. Irritation at her selfish ways pricked inside Alma. Never again would she be so thoughtless.

A soft groan met her ears.

She dropped the ax and whirled toward Dillon.

Firelight traced his flushed face and cascaded over his torso. The fresh bandages she'd added earlier were still as white as snow. *No blood. Surely that's good.* Inch by inch, her gaze traveled down his body.

Ever so faint, his muscles flexed…but this time not in the throes of a fever. She pressed her lips together, waiting.

Did I imagine hearing you?

Another low moan filled the chamber.

Relief propelled hope through her veins. She dashed to his side, and dropped to her knees.

"Come on," she urged. "Wake up now." Scooting closer, Alma pulled the canteen by its strap. Slipping her arm beneath his head, she raised him, and angling the metal spout to his lips, she poured. Moisture collected near the corners of his mouth, then ran past his jawline, soaking the ends of his hair as well as her sleeve.

At the slide of water, his mouth worked, and he managed to down a swallow, though not enough to satisfy her. Alma coaxed again, knowing a wet rag upon his lips wouldn't keep him alive for long. "Please, Dillon. You need more." As he made to take another sip, his breath came, hoarse and rasping, followed by a rattling cough that shook him. "I-I'm so sorry, but you must keep drinking."

Again, Alma held the canteen to his lips.

This time he took a deeper swig. Then his whole body relaxed. She smoothed the crest of his cheek with soft strokes. Slowly, the tension that had twisted tight inside her eased back, and for the first time since he'd found her, hope grew. When she'd changed his dressing earlier, his wound still looked angry, but at least blood no longer seeped out.

She cradled him in her arms, thrilled he still lived. He took another swallow. "That's good. Very good."

Though his face was pale beneath the week-old stumble, his skin no looker resembled the putrid color of tallow. A fine sheen of sweat covered him from his forehead down to the tattered blanket pushed to the waistband of his pants.

Again her gaze swept across his sinewy arms, the whorls of dark hair, and his hands the size of dinner plates. Even his fingertips were callused. She swept back to his face, her own flooding with heat as her heart pummeled her ribs. The image of him laughing with a group of men at the party for the Custers anchored in the center of her frazzled mind. She so desperately wanted to hear him laugh again.

Dillon Reed resembled no man she'd ever known.

So different from Lord Green.

Images of her fiancé tumbled across her mind. Alma sobered at once. Getting to Fort Lowell must take center stage in her thoughts. Her mouth puckered and with a tremble, she shook away the remorse.

She turned on her hip and then stretched her aching body alongside Dillon. Ever-so-carefully, she pressed her fingers against his brow.

His fever, while still there, was lower.

Breathe in.

Breathe out.

He seemed to be rousing, returning to the world of the living. A miracle, indeed. And whatever measure of comfort she could give him, she would.

A log settled deeper into the flames with a soft thud, and sparks shot up in a haphazard burst. For a moment, the floating embers glowed red, then with an erratic flicker, faded to black.

She rubbed her hand up and down his bare arm. Offering comfort. Lifting prayers. She knew most every indentation and swell of his upper body…and yet, she knew nothing more about the man.

You know he'll protect you to his dying breath.

Yes…a blush heated her cheeks…that much she already knew.

The distant howl of a wild animal deep in the Colorado Mountains reminded her of their isolation. Her hand stilled as she stared at his handsome profile. *Another kiss…another kiss…another kiss…*

A shudder rippled through her, and she slowly closed her eyes against the truth weighing upon her soul.

Never.

She must keep a tight rein on her spiraling emotions. Injured or not, he tangled up her feelings. On an unsteady breath, she reopened her eyes. Her breath caught.

In taut silence, Dillon stared back. His gaze intense…a dark, indescribable entreaty that held her spellbound.

***

Pain slammed through Dillon, shaking him to the core, a burn so raw it was as if he lay on a hot bed of coals. Surely the torment was the damned Devil dancing upon his soul.

I'm dead...and burning in Hell's embrace.

Dillon struggled to open his mouth, to beg forgiveness for the horrible wrongs he'd committed over the years, for the men he'd killed with his Bowie in fights he'd deem important at the time. And then, from the edges of his mind, a soothing sensation doused the pain.

An angel's soft touch.

So gentle on his fiery flesh.

He slowly opened his eyes. This time, his administering seraph acquired a face as the beautiful features of Alma Talmadge swirled into view.

Chapter Fifteen

The following afternoon Alma handed Dillon a half-filled cup of coffee, aware he was more comfortable since he'd propped against a saddle. "Here, drink this. I can't promise its good, but at least it's warm."

"Thanks," he said, sliding his fingers around the cup's handle. "I'm sure it's no worse than others I've drank over the years. Some of them made the hairs on the back of my neck strand straight up."

Alma smiled. "Well, I'm thankful you're feeling better."

He tossed her a quick grin between slurps. "This is the best coffee I've had all week."

His subtle attempt at humor. Oh Dillon Reed, what a charmer you are.

"Well, it's been your only cup for the past four days," Alma said, nodding. Preferring a cup of cinnamon infused tea, she nonetheless took a tentative sip from her own mug and swallowed.

Not bad for my first attempt at making the vile brew. Of course, you helped by telling me how.

Concentrating on keeping her hands steady, she sipped again…all the while marveling at Dillon's quick recovery. With each passing hour his strength grew, and Alma had to force herself to stop doting on him. Through this whole ordeal, she'd come to realize how much she enjoyed the *ministering to another* role that had been thrust upon her unbidden. The bloody parts of nursing, of course, not so much, but the other aspects, the *fetching and doing* routine she'd settled into, Alma found now brought her great joy.

Sighing, she tucked her voluminous skirt beneath her crossed legs. "I was wondering…back on the train…what did you really mean when you said you'd learned about the wickedness of society from your mother? I'm guessing she had dealings with that, right?" Her bold questions surprised even her.

"You could say that…." Another swallow took away the rest of his mumbled words, but those she understood carried sarcasm along with a touch of sadness.

Her curiosity grew. And she pushed to know more. "We've plenty of time, so you may as well share with me."

Dillon's gaze across the cup sent another sizzle up her spine. "Why?"

"I want to understand you better, that's all." She craved to know more about him, and his childhood and family seemed as good a place as any to start. "How was she involved in society, I mean? Was she a housekeeper or a maid inside a manor?"

His lips shifted into a half-smirk. "Neither."

He was evading her question, which made the truth all the more intriguing. As far as she was concerned, this guessing game could continue all day. Anything to converse. "All right, then. Was she a cook or a laundress? Or perhaps a nanny?" Alma inhaled the steam rising from her cup, enjoying the fragrant aroma of the steeped coffee beans.

He glanced out the cave's entrance.

And she followed his gaze. Trees rustled in the golden sunrays filtering through the pines. Above them, clouds slid past, stranding from mountain peak to mountain peak in a wispy grid. Void of storms and peril, early summer in the Rockies was peaceful. Aware Dillon was out of danger now helped her frame of mind a great deal. Regardless, her questions went unanswered.

"I'm waiting," Alma said as she glanced back at her brooding companion. "What did she do that exposed you to the horridness of society and turned you against us all with such a burning vengeance?" She tamped back a mocking grin when his gaze locked on hers.

"She lived it."

Another veiled reply. Frustrated, Alma snatched up a stick and poked at the coals glowing beneath the fire's flames. Recuperating, or not, for a moment, she even considered poking him.

"So you're saying your family *was* part of society?"

Several seconds passed as she sensed him weighing his reply. Another habit that only deepened his quirky charm.

With a grimace, his gaze focused upon hers. "If one could describe the people who disowned her by the idiom of *family* . . . well . . . then, yes, my mother was indeed cut from Charleston's upper crust."

So...you're from southern aristocracy. No wonder you know how to waltz.

Dillon's family history was none of her business. And yet, Alma pushed on, blaming her pressing queries on her exhaustive state, not on any matters of her heart.

"Cut?" she repeated in a shallow whisper. The accounting of his mother's ill-fated destiny grew more intriguing by the minute. "W-What happened to separate her from her family?"

"She fell in love with the wrong man."

Alma stared at him. With each passing day in this man's presence she fought to remember who she was...who *he* was. They, too, were so completely different by society's standards.

She fell in love with the wrong man?

He continued on a deep growl. "Since pa was in the army, my folks moved to Texas after they'd married. I was born shortly thereafter." He sipped his coffee again, his gaze fixed on the campfire between them. "Years past. Mother kept writing her Charleston clan, praying they'd open their hearts, but they never responded. And then, Caleb came along."

"Caleb?" she asked.

"My brother." His sigh slipped around Alma and she stared at his forlorn face. "Then, a year later, Mother died from some kind of fever. And Pa? Well, he became a drunk and died a broken man a few years after that...leaving me to raise my three year old brother."

Her heart broke. "Oh, Dillon...how tragic. You were so young."

He issued his breath on a tight exhale. "Fourteen, to be exact." He swirled the coffee in his cup. "I even wrote a few letters to those highbrowed sonsofbitches in their fancy mansions to let 'em know about…everything. They never replied. Not once…but, we did all right, me'n Caleb, though schoolin' was hit'n miss." He shrugged. "Learned to survive the hard way. Stealing. Easiest thing I could do, since I could run fast. Money. Food. Never once got caught." He inhaled, but his gaze shifted again, settling upon the flames. "Then, early one day, outside El Paso, I made the godawful mistake of taking Caleb with me on a simple scavenging hunt for food. He'd just turned ten." A long pause followed as his lips tightened. "He tripped over a damned milk bucket and some sonofabitch farmer shot him dead on the spot. Clean through the head."

She gasped. "How horrible."

"It should've been me to die that night 'stead of my brother. Hell, after all the shit I've done, I should've died now from this…" he shrugged his wounded shoulder, then winced. "But life has a wicked way of keeping me going with the guilt."

She dredged her mind for a response as her fingers tightened around her cup. "B-But…if you'd died from your wound it wouldn't change a single thing that has happened in your past."

He snorted. "True…but our actions are what set things in motion, right? After I lost Caleb, I didn't much give a damn about nothing. I ripped through my life with a death wish."

Their gazes connected and held and the momentary pain etched so clearly across his features stole away her breath.

Emotions tumbled through Alma…grief for the boy too young to have to face the challenge of raising his brother alone, fury for the family that discarded Dillon and his brother as if waste, and compassion for a man blinded by pain until he'd wished for death. "I'm so sorry for all of your losses," she whispered, dropping her gaze.

"My tow-headed lil' brother got the bad end of the deal. And me? Well, I had a knack for tracking. So…long story short, one day while attempting to rob an army pay wagon, I slammed into Colonel Talmadge, literally. Seemed he and my pa had been good friends during the Mexican War." Dillon offered a sharp laugh, lifting his gaze to hers. "Let's just say he jerked me up by the collar."

Your wealthy Charleston family abandoned you in your hour of greatest need. No wonder you despise the privileged.

Her heart ached for him, the sensation so intense it vibrated through her veins. Alma closed her eyes against the sorrow as sadness doused her like a rainstorm. Her breath stalled in her throat. Society's rigid rules. So cruel. So heartbreaking.

So incredibly unfair. And yet, it explained why he preferred his distance. Everyone he'd ever loved, he'd lost. For so long, he'd known only violence. A chill stronger than any known before seized her as a heavy silence stretched between them. Alma studied his profile, defined so clearly in the fire's glow. She'd known handsome men in her life. Polished gentlemen who possessed both grace and charm.

But no one had captured her devotion quite like Dillon Reed…in all ways of society's standards, *this* man was her exact opposite.

And yet…

He shifted against the saddlebags. "But…enough about me," he quipped, swallowing another gulp of coffee. "What does one do after marrying a duke?"

Alma sighed, knowing he'd closed down and she'd get nothing more in regards to his past. Truth be told, though, she knew plenty already.… from every hard, masculine body angle to the grief that made him the man he was today. "Well, if you're referring to my fiancé, he's an earl. And titles, by the way, are usually hereditary and are bestowed by the royals."

"Sounds rather stuffy to me."

"It is…and I'm still learning their ranking system. First, of course, there's Queen Victoria. Then comes her first-born son, the prince. And, in order of importance after him is a duke, then a marquis, and then an earl. The other titles below Lord Green are a viscount and a baron, I believe. Maybe a few more, but I'm not sure. Father told me to marry the earl, so that's why I'm here." She clasped her hands in her lap and glanced around the cave. "Well, not here, exactly, but you know what I mean." She smiled at him and chuckled. "And that's probably way more than you ever wanted to know about England's peerage, too."

Senses on full alert, Dillon narrowed his eyes and strove to deny her smile's powerful impact. Why in the hell had he shared so much about his pain-filled past with her? An unbidden craving pulsed through him as he skimmed her lips. Beneath his perusal, her tongue slipped out to moisten them, and his body hardened like a rock.

Hell and damnation!

He jerked his gaze to the orange flames crackling between them. Drawing in a deep breath to rid him of his asinine need, he cracked a strained smile. "God help me…I think I'm beginning to enjoy these little *chats*."

This time she laughed out loud as she again stirred the coals. "Then I'd say we've come a far piece from those stilted *tête-à-têtes* back on the train, wouldn't you?"

Smoke spiraled before him in thickened tendrils, a fitting framework for his discomfort.

He nodded and wished he were healed. Wished he were anywhere but in the presence of her smile. The longer he confined himself in this cave with this minx, the more he wanted her, which blasted helped nothing. His job was to deliver her to the fort, unharmed – bedding her didn't play into the plan.

"Upon my marriage, I shall become a peer of the English realm and assume the title of countess. I shall assist the earl in the running of his estate, plus aid the Dowager Countess in whatever way I can."

He shifted his gaze back to her. "Dowager Countess? What is that? Some kind of a pet?"

Alma smiled. "No, you silly man. A dowager is an honorary title bestowed upon the earl's mother after he takes a wife. She still lives, but his father died several years ago. As the only child and a son, Lord Green inherited his title, the holdings, and the estate bestowed upon his lineage years before by the royalty."

Her intended may be a noble, but could the well-titled bastard do a better job at protecting her than him? He doubted it. Dillon's stomach tightened at the thought. "Sounds complicated as well as stuffy. Just give me a few acres and some horses and I'll be a happy man." Marriage, an English title, and a swift-sailing schooner bound for England waited upon this woman's arrival at the fort, but after everything they'd endured, how could he so easily let her go?

Her eyes flashed at him from the opposite side of the fire, their intense brightness squeezing his heart.

He moistened his lips and again tasted hers.

The pinch inside his gut tightened. Dillon cleared his throat. Her tenderness and caring for him these past few days...Hell's fire, even her curiosity about his past made everything inside him ache. He'd disclosed way too much about himself and his wicked ways. Hell's fire, coming from such a mollycoddled world he'd been surprised she hadn't gone screaming from the cave in fear.

Regardless of his begrudging admiration of her, she belonged to another...and he had a job to do. Besides, he figured he'd live now, so they would strike out for Tucson in a few days.

Dillon took another swig of coffee and glanced out the entrance.

In the far distance, mountain peaks shimmered in the light.

The Sangre de Cristo Range.

Which meant they were holed up somewhere in Dikes Mountain south of Pueblo. If he could sit a horse, he could damn well track his way through *La Veta* Pass, and head south through Colorado to Fort Garland.

He grimaced as he thought of the events over the past week and a half. Things weren't adding up. Too many years of looking at signs and finding trouble told him something different.

Why did the bandits keep her alive, yet not defile her? A striking woman like this innocent beauty? Only one thing made sense.

For money...yes. But why? And whose?

***

The next day, Alma placed the empty coffee pot by the pile of supplies, then settled onto the ground beside Dillon.

"What do you mean, shoot it?" She followed his gaze out the cave. Nothing moved except the flickers of sunlight upon the water and the frilly evergreen boughs that swayed in the afternoon breeze. "Shoot what?"

Dillon angled onto one elbow and shoved the weapon in front of her. "Here," he ordered, still staring outside. "Take the rifle."

Fear tore through her and she shifted back. "Absolutely not. I want nothing to do with guns."

He scraped his gaze from the entrance and locked on her wide-eyed glare. "Damnit, Alma...there's no time to argue. If I could do this myself, I would." She cringed at the hard snap in his voice. "Unless you want to keep eatin' beans, which is mostly what's left of our supplies."

A lump rose in her throat. The gritty floor dug into her palms as she scooted sideways another few inches. "I'll choose the beans."

With a curse, Dillon leaned higher onto his hip and shoved the weapon into her right hand. "Take it."

Heart pounding, her fingers curled around the cool steel barrel. Unprepared for the Henry's weight, she nearly toppled forward.

Panic roughened her words. "But...I don't want to shoot anything."

"I'll shoot," he snapped. "Now scoot over here. And quietly...don't want her scared away."

Her? Alma pressed her lips together and shot him a pleading glance. "Please don't ask me to do this."

"You just hold the rifle steady. I'll do the rest."

She shook her head, shuffling further away. With a surprising burst of strength, Dillon rolled forward, grabbed her wrist, and stopped her in mid-shift. An easy jerk tumbled her toward him.

Alma gasped as she landed face-first against his hip. Rolling sideways, she hissed, "How dare you maltreat me in such an uncouth--"

"Stop it," he growled, his words searing her already flushed cheeks. "We don't have time for this foolishness." He twisted her around and resettled her in front of him, his belt buckle pressing against her lower back. The heat from his chest radiated through the fabric of her bodice and sent a mind-numbing tingle over her skin, intensifying their intimate alliance.

With a mumbled oath, he propped the rifle before her, then placed her hands to hold the weapon. Leaning down, Dillon pressed his temple against hers, his mouth resting near the curve of her ear. "See that cluster of boulders near the stream?" he whispered, pointing down the steel-blue barrel.

He smelled like the great outdoors and leather and the teasing tang of man. She swallowed, striving to ignore her heartbeat drumming in maddening thumps against her ribs.

"Do you?" he repeated, the pithiness in his voice causing her to jump. Alma nodded, "Y-Yes. I see them."

"Good. Now angle the Henry toward 'em while I sight down on the animal."

With shaking hands, she raised the weapon, moving the muzzle as he'd directed. She drew air into her lungs and blinked back an onrush of tears. Without warning, Dillon slid his arm around her waist.

A tight squeeze, and he hauled her even closer, rasping, "Okay, Princess, now brace yourself."

Brace myself? Oh dear...no. The thought of killing any innocent creature severed her heartstrings. She blinked fast to tamp back the tears

His head dipped lower. Another whisper branded her ears, "And don't regret this kill. Though small, the doe will feed us for days."

She strengthened her fingers on the barrel as the truth of his words speared through her. He was right. They weren't in the dining room of her palatial Boston estate where food was provided in bounty with a mere snap of her finger. He was injured. Had almost died saving her. They needed this meat to survive.

"That's my girl. Now real slow, I need you to lift the weapon. Yes, that's it." She focused on his calm words. "Now even out your breath," he whispered. "And keep the muzzle steady when I fire."

She squeezed her eyes closed, and nodded. *Inhale. Exhale.* In pace and intensity, their breathing matched, as did the *thumpa thumpa* beating of their hearts. Tensed seconds passed.

Then, an ear-splitting blast shattered the stillness.

Propelled by the weapon's recoil, Alma slammed into Dillon's injured shoulder, the acrid stench of gunpowder filling her breath.

He gave a muffled grunt, "Well done, Princess...well done."

Her ears rang from the rifle's sharp report, but his satisfaction with her performance overrode any discomfort. Alma opened her eyes. The expression seemingly imprinted across his face spoke of approval and admiration and relief. Her gaze fell to his lips. A smile kicked his mouth sideways, etching the sun-carved crinkles at the corners of his eyes. Disconcerted, she broke their connection, skimming her attention to his shoulder.

Fresh blood darkened the cloth and slammed sanity back in a rush. Horrified, Alma set aside the rifle and laid her palm atop his broad shoulder. "Oh no...you're bleeding again."

"It'll stop," he rasped. "Right now, we need to haul the carcass back to the cave before the wolves scent the kill." A weak smile touched his mouth. "Don't want 'em stealing dinner after we've worked so hard to get it...now do we?"

"We?" She snorted. "You can't go down there. You can barely walk."

"I never planned too. You'll go."

She was afraid of that. "How am I supposed to haul that poor creature up here?"

He gestured to the line-tied horse on the opposite side of the cave. The animal had wandered into the clearing earlier this morning, and Dillon had promptly ordered her out to retrieve it. "Take a rope and the bay. Once you reach the doe, tie her back legs together and then secure the other end of the rope to the saddle. The horse will do the heavy work." With a sigh, he rolled onto his back and rested an arm across his forehead. "And when you return, you'll need to butcher the doe and then smoke and dry the meat. I'll talk you through all that, too."

Butcher the doe?

The detestable act had Alma nearly gagging as she shoved to her feet. He locked an apathetic gaze upon hers and arched a brow. *The barbarian!* She'd had just about enough. Pursing her lips, she glared down at him. "I'll have you know I don't like this whole skinning and drying thing one wretched bit. It's…it's purely disgusting."

"Oh, you don't mind eating the food, you just don't want to see where it comes from. Is that it?"

She glared at him, then turned and skirted the fire in three strong strides. Head high, back ramrod straight, she stormed toward the horse.

Two steps more, with temper flaring, she whirled back and jammed her fists upon her hips. "And let me also add that I can only *try* to do your bidding"

Dillon held her glower, the humor of moments before fading. His features slid into a frown. "As long as you're with me in *my* world, Princess, simply *trying* is not enough. You'll learn quickly how to do things right… the first time I tell you. Understand?"

Her mouth gaped open. Deafening silence followed. The nerve of the insufferable pig.

And after everything I've done for you, too!

"If I had a choice, *Mister* Reed, I'd rather not be in *your* world at all."

Chapter Sixteen

Her back ached. Her arms ached. Even the muscles in her face ached. In her entire life, Alma had never worked as hard as she had during these past three hours. Once she'd tied the deer to the horse, it'd taken nearly an hour to drag the carcass up the hill.

Revulsion swept her.

Yet, instead of a kind word about her achievement, instead of encouraging her to sit down and rest a bit, Dillon had demanded she pick up the knife and begin the task of skinning and gutting the doe. He denied her any weakness. No clemency. No understanding of her delicate womanhood or her social standing. His words held an undertone of control, tinged with methodical patience. Never had she seen so much blood. Even as she screamed at him vulgar words she'd never dared utter before, even as she proclaimed him a vile monster, that she'd had enough of this butchery… even as she struggled to hold back her need to wretch, he remained resolute in his purpose. Time and again, he guided her back to the loathsome task. Until finally, after removing a bucketful of entrails and gore and tossing them outside the cave, Alma completed the job.

Exhausted, every muscle in her body screaming its outrage, she shoved to her feet. With uneven steps, she stumbled from the cave and into the waning light.

A cool breeze brushed her face.

Her fingers aching from holding the knife for so long, she curled them into fists at her sides, and then strode down the incline toward the creek, tired, disgusted, and needing to wash away the blood-spattered evidence of carnage.

At the water's edge, she unlaced her boots, and then tugged them off. Next, she reached under each leg of her pantalets, yanked free the pink ribbons that secured her stockings. With the grosgrain clasped in her hand, she stripped each legging away. Barefoot, she lifted her skirt to her chin and jerked hard on the string around her waist. In an irreverent swish of cotton, the steel-ringed bustle collapsed into a heap at her feet. Wasting little time, she unbuttoned the pearl discs on her bodice as she stared at water. With a shrug, Alma sent her top to the ground behind her, and then released the waistband of her skirt, shoving yards of billowing brocade downward.

Her corset followed, and in a whoosh of pale-blue satin, the constricting piece tumbled to the pile.

A heavy sigh fell from her lips.

Clothed in the camisole, crotchless pantalets, and her underslip, the hem now stained red with blood, Alma stepped her way over boulders and around fallen logs until she sank straight down into the cool rush of water.

Shivers climbed her arms and back and sucked away her breath. As the current surged around her, she pressed her hands to her trembling lips. Moisture welled behind her lashes and her eyes squeezed tight against the sting.

If only she could wash away this nightmare. If only she could wake up back home in her bed. If only she hadn't killed that innocent creature.

A sob broke free followed by a hiccupping flood of tears. *I will most likely go to hell for what I've done.* She stared at her hands stained with blood. Its throat and chin were so soft, the insides of the ears as white as snow. And its eyes black with death. Another shuddering sob tore through her, and she splashed her face to wash away the doe's image.

Needing to clean every last ounce of her body, Alma tore free dark-green clumps of moss, then set about scrubbing her skin until all traces of the gory butchering was gone. Next, she tugged the pile of garments into the stream, repeating the scouring process on every single piece.

Once she'd cleaned and draped her clothing across the closest fallen tree, Alma pulled out her treasured hairpins and piled them atop her skirt. With a gulp of air, she dipped backward into the water, raked her hands through her tangled tresses, and scrubbed the strands until they, too, were clean.

As she lifted her arms and reached back to squeeze the excess moisture from her hair a prickling awareness swept through her. Slowly she turned, scanned past tree trunks, then over the clearing.

Nothing.

A movement near the cave caught her attention.

Her gaze scrambled upward. Arms crossed, Dillon leaned against the stony entrance. Shadows from the nearby trees spilled over him in mottled patterns of darkness and light. He'd donned his shirt, but the careworn cambric hung open to reveal his chest and the white bandage that peeked from beneath one side.

Alma blinked, unable to look away from him. If he's able to stand then why didn't he help her skin and gut the deer? Tension coiled deep inside, a slow anger that left her floundering. She knew why…*he wanted me to do it.*

She refused to acknowledge him.

Refused to search deeper her acrimony. Instead, Alma sank back into the water, the current slapping hard against her cotton-covered breasts. Her nipples hardened. He didn't turn away. The truth excited even as it terrified, sending a jolt of pleasure through her veins.

His dark eyes narrowed, then he turned and slipped back into the cave.

How could she face him now? When he'd surely seen her…*what?* Nothing. He'd been much too far away to even comprehend her conflicting anger or her response to the mere presence of him.

She would ignore him. The plan give her comfort.

An hour later, still clothed in her undergarments but with her now-dry hair twisted into a knot once again atop her head, Alma stood near the campfire, staring into the flames. Being clean had calmed her nerves, as did listening to the crackling of the burning wood.

Memories of Dillon watching her, however, still left her unsettled.

A lump formed in her throat as she recalled her return to the cave. When she entered, he scanned her still half-dressed body in a much-too-intimate way. How dare the oaf pass judgement on her without uttering one single word? The flood of emotions she'd felt in the creek returned to swamp her: anger and confusion and…a conflicting pleasure she refused to explore.

The logs popped, sending sparks upward, drawing Alma's thoughts back to the present.

She glanced toward the horse and a crudely strung clothesline between the gelding and their supplies. Draped over the limp line, her skirt and bodice glistened in the firelight. Still damp, the brocade shimmered in different shades of green.

They'll be dry come morning.

She glanced at the scout. His eyes were closed, which suited her fine. The last thing she wanted to do was converse with him anyway. Near her feet rested a bucket, part of the kidnappers gear, which she'd filled with creek water earlier this morning. She'd use the liquid as base for the stew the scout wanted her to make for their dinner.

Venison, that's what he'd called the deer meat.

She headed toward their supplies. Anything was preferable to gutting a wild animal. Rummaging through the sacks, she found myriad dried vegetables and beans. These would make a good addition to the stew. How she wished for the skills of her three cooks back home.

If only they could see me now.

The humor she found in the moment surprised Alma as did the eagerness with which she gathered the foodstuffs. Working quickly, she concocted the meal, and then suspended her filled-to-the-brim stewpot from the S-hook on the parallel bar. Pleased with her effort, she stood and dusted her hands. If only there were some crusty bread to serve with her repast.

With a sigh, she glanced to the remaining pile of deer meat. The chore of smoking the venison remained. Tamping back another shudder, she tossed a fresh log onto the fire beneath the stew. With a sizzling hiss, copious flames shot upward, licking the bottom of the pot.

"Too much wood," Dillon said in a thick voice, startling her. "Lower heat cooks the meal and prevents the grub inside from sticking."

Makes sense.

So, he wasn't asleep after all. Feeling a bit foolish, she nodded. Using another log, Alma pushed the just-added piece from the fire. "And what about...those?" She angled her head toward the raw meat.

"Need to hang 'em over the fire. Your goal is to dry out the strips."

She drew her brows together. "There's too much to remember."

He chuckled. "Welcome to life in the wilderness."

A sense of affinity passed between them as warmth climbed over her cheeks.

He motioned to the three extra iron rods leaning against the cave wall near the supplies.

"Add another stand to smoke the venison."

"But why smoke venison? Why not just cook it *in* the stew, like the other pieces?"

"Smoke preserves the meat so we can eat it later...since we'll be heading out soon."

She blinked at him. "How soon?"

"A few days, maybe less." Now that he deemed himself healed enough to travel, an odd melancholy about leaving swept her. As quickly, her sadness disappeared. If nothing else, by the time this *traveling westward* nightmare ended, she'd be proficient at several things besides dancing, social entertaining, and rose gardening. Would Lord Green be pleased about how well she'd learned these survival skills? She chewed on her lower lip and doubted the Earl would find any amount of pleasure in her acquiring knowledge about how to gut a deer.

A half-hour later, with her stew bubbling in the pot and the delicious aroma wafting within the cave, she settled onto her heels and surveyed her work. Glistening, ruby-red strips of raw venison draped the additional bar.

"You know," Dillon said, tucking his arms behind his head, "With a bit more practice, you'd make a fine mountain woman one day."

An unexpected pride skimmed through her. Then she chuckled. "I shall learn to be the finest pioneer woman possible *only* for the length of time needed to survive in these mountains." She rose and checked her skirt. *Still damp. A few more hours ought to do.* "But I shall most certainly return to the niceties of life that make me happiest, have no worry about that, sir." She pivoted on her heel to face him. "And there's nothing wrong with doing so, I might add."

His laughter filled the cave. "Happiness is fleeting when you bind your pleasure to society's ways."

"Don't preach to me." She scoffed, waggling her finger at him. "Remember, you're the one who can't deal with progressiveness in any form." She lowered her hand, burying her fist inside the linen folds of her underslip. "Life is changing. You should learn to appreciate society's conducts instead of scorning those who understand and embrace its proper ways." His gaze narrowed, and she smiled. "I-I could help you try if you'd let me."

Like I helped him with his waltz? With the unwanted thought, the moment shifted. Need slammed through her with a bewildering burn. Shaken, she forced herself to hold his gaze, praying he'd not witnessed her desire and shame.

"Nope. I'm happy the way I am."

She dropped to her knees and stirred the stew. "But why? I mean, look at you. Unkempt. Unapproachable. Will living in this manner bring your brother back?"

His jaw tightened. "Let's just leave Caleb out of this, all right?"

"But he's why you're here isn't he? I mean, not *here* here, but rather why you're at your present station in life. Isolated and all alone." Another stir of the tantalizing broth settled her tightening nerves. "If you relaxed a bit and allowed yourself, you might actually enjoy society's culture. A little of it, at least."

"You're telling *me* to relax?" Dillon gave a cold laugh. "In my world there is no relaxing, Princess. I'm a hard man. And untamable. And I like it that way." He flipped back the flap on his saddlebags and pulled out his flask. He lifted the small metal vessel in her direction and smiled. "If you had any sense in that pretty little head of yours, you'd stop stirring up things with that society stick you're leanin' on."

Society stick? She swallowed, staring at him.

A howl from beyond the cave, much closer than those she'd heard before, shattered her baffling thoughts. She surged onto her knees. The extra wood chips in her hand drifted to the floor like so many falling leaves.

The yowls grew in volume, drawing closer.

Trembling, Alma stared out the entrance.

Blackness of night loomed.

My imaginings are getting the best of me.

Nonetheless, she scooted backward several more feet, halting beside the pile of meat. Her nerves on edge, Alma worked quickly, draping strip after strip into place until the bar glistened like shards of blood-red Christmas tinsel…minus the Nativity scene.

"*Estincele,*" she proclaimed, catching Dillon's gaze as she waved toward her creation. At his perplexed expression, she added. "I'm afraid that French for sparkle does not hold true for venison." She moved to add the last piece of meat in her hand, when a deep growl rumbled from the cave's entrance.

Alma whirled.

At the edge of the light, two enormous yellow eyes stared back at her.

Behind her, the horse snorted, then whinnied, stomping his hooves into the dirt as the bay shuffled closer to the pile of supplies.

Fear tore through her.

"Don't move," Dillon whispered, capping the flask as he edged toward his saddle bags.

The wolf at the entrance stood three-feet tall and well-over five feet long. A grizzled, gray back, light cream under parts, and a broad, bushy tail dappled in the shadowy light.

Beneath the piercing glare Alma's courage wavered. A scream bubbled upward as the wolf edged closer into the cave. Firelight fell over its mottled coat. The horse in the shadows behind her snorted even louder, then squealed.

Her heart pounded hard against her breastbone. Never in her life had she seen anything so terrifying.

"Stay still. And don't look at it," Dillon said, his tone much too calm.

Alma tried to obey, but hypnotized in her fear, her gaze locked with narrowing yellow slits. The wolf laid its long ears against the sides of its head. Another growl rumbled through the cavern. The animal then lifted a black nose high, sniffing the air. With a deep snarl, it lowered its muzzle, revealing a row of razor-sharp teeth. Twenty feet separated her from certain death. Panicking, Alma heaved the strip of meat clenched in her hand toward the animal. Dust puffed up as the venison plopped in the dirt inches from the beast.

The creature snatched up her offering and swallowed the strip in one gulp. Another snarl rumbled in the wolf's throat as he crept forward. She closed her eyes just as a deafening blast erupted. She lifted her eyelids in time to see the ground spray into an arc of dirt across the wolf's face.

With a yelp, the animal turned and bolted into the darkness.

An eerie silence fell within the cave as gunsmoke mingled with the pungent stink of the animal and the rich and hearty bounty of Alma's stew. Catastrophe averted, she drew in ragged breaths to calm her pounding heart.

Her ears still rung from the sharp report of gunfire.

"You can rest easy now. I've scared him off," Dillon said with a chuckle as he spun the chamber of his revolver to check his ammunition. "Won't be back, knowing what awaits him."

"Good," she whispered, staring out of the cave into the darkness. An odd sense of victory smothered her earlier terror. She shifted onto her knees. "And stay away too, you mangy beast." Unsure of what Dillon had made of her unladylike bellow, she glanced at him.

Surprise had creased his face, then a deep laugh rumbled from him.

With hands on hips, she glared. "And if I may ask, what is so blasted amusing?"

"You, Princess," he said, shoving his pistol into the holster. "As daring as that was, you feeding predatory wildlife doesn't fit into our survival plans."

CHAPTER SEVENTEEN

One horse.

And two of them.

Alma sighed. How was he going to make that work? Only five days had passed since Dillon's fever broke. Was he certain he could travel? She turned from the now-cold fire pit.

Surely, the man knew best.

A sudden stab of reluctance pushed through her at leaving the makeshift quarters. She squelched her silly foot-dragging, and turned to shove the tinware and remaining supplies into a bag. With a heaving grunt, Alma slung the canvas across her shoulder and headed toward the gelding. The items inside the cumbersome sack clanked together, whacking hard against the back of each brocade-covered leg.

In her other hand, she clutched her travelling valise.

Dillon stood near the cave's opening, his uninjured shoulder angled closest to her. "Here, I'll take those," he said, relieving her of the bags. "Thanks for gathering up the gear." He draped the bundles across the horse, then set to tying them into place.

As he bent his head, several errant strands of too-long hair slid over his face. She stared, her fingers tickling at the remembered softness of his disheveled locks.

His gaze caught hers and she flushed; a tiny curl lifted his mouth.

For one maddening moment, she wanted to stand on tippy toes and kiss him. Frustration shimmied through her, and her heart rattled inside her chest.

"We're wastin' time." He jammed a gloved hand through his hair, then settled his hat into place. A quick tug leveled the brim. "I'm gonna need every bit of daylight to find my way off this mountain."

"And back to another stagecoach, right?"

His smile faded into a guarded scowl. "There's no more stagecoaches for us, Princess."

"What?" She followed him out to the ledge. He led the horse around and Alma sidestepped out of their way. "I thought we were going to find the closest swing station. And from there catch another stage south."

He sighed and draped an arm across the saddle, his gaze drilling into hers. "The bandits took you for a reason. There might be others waiting to pick up where those bastards failed." He straightened, and then reached below the gelding's belly, pulling the saddle's girth tight. "I'm not taking any more chances with your safety. From now on, we're traveling *my* way."

Her brows drew down as she let out a shaky breath. "And what does that mean...exactly?"

"Light and fast, sweetheart." His gaze slid back to hers. "We're heading for Fort Garland."

"I see." Her mouth tightened. Regardless what she thought, when push came to shove, Dillon Reed would always win. Time and again he'd proven that to her. "Which is on the other side of the Rocky Mountains, correct?"

"Sort of. We're actually going to skirt through the lower range on a continuous southwest heading. And to get there, we're passin' through *Ute* territory.

"*Ute*? What type of animal is that? Nothing like a wolf, I hope."

He chuckled. "Utes are Indians. More specifically, the Caputa band, near the headwater of the Rio Grande. They've welcomed me into their camps before."

Indians! Oh no. No...No.

All the stories she'd heard about the murdering savages out west tumbled into recall. She swallowed hard. "But…d-don't Indians scalp people?"

A flash of ire appeared in his eyes. "Yes, some do, like the Chiricahua Apache's outside Tucson. But, most don't, not much anymore at least, including the *Utes*." He stepped closer. Towering over her, he cupped her chin. "You need to trust me."

She dared not blink. Nor breathe. Yet, his gaze never altered, nor did his hold loosen as he awaited her response. His demand that she *believe in him* melded with the kick of excitement, exhaustion, and fear already swirling inside her. Where he touched, her skin burned, her lips quivering on the edge of a frown.

And still he waited.

Her belly fluttered.

On an unsteady breath, Alma nodded.

He gave her chin a gentle squeeze, and then his hand slid away. Leaning sideways, he retrieved the rifle resting against a rock. "They're the oldest inhabitants in the region, by the way, and call themselves, *Nuu-ci*…the people." He slipped the Henry into a leather holder resting alongside the saddle. "And a few months ago, President Grant signed a peace treaty with their primary leader, Chief Ouray, so they're much more accepting of the white man now." The admiration in his voice reflected his respect for these people. "But, as everywhere else, more of us are moving onto lands set aside for them despite the agreements."

Alma gave him a level look. "If you think it's safe to cross their land, then I'm ready." She pointed south, regaining her composure as she plastered an uncertain smile on her face. "After all, we are burning daylight."

"That's the spirit," he said with a laugh. He then pointed to her skirt. "Now, drop the bustle."

She blinked in surprise. "What?"

"You heard me. We're sharing a horse, and I'm not ridin' all the way to Tucson with that damned gadget poking me in my gut."

"But…" She stepped backward, her hands sweeping around to clutch the swell of her recently donned travelling ensemble. "I cannot leave this particular apparatus behind, Dillon. It is an important part of my trousseau."

"I don't care. Drop it." He stepped closer. "Or I will."

Shock slid through her. "Y-You wouldn't dare." She retreated another step.

And he followed. "I would."

First, no stagecoach.

Then the threat of Indians.

And now…now he demands this of me? Her manner of dress, her comportment? She glared at him. Her gown and accessories gave her hope as she wallowed through this miserable nightmare. Did the tyrant not understand this fact?

Resentment smothered any remaining logic. She'd had enough! Alma straightened and rammed her chin higher, her words rumbling out with indisputable rebuke. "Must I remind you, *again*, that I am not one of your tavern wenches, you…you toad? Nor will I *ever* be. This bustle *will* come with me, and *you* will somehow make that work."

His eyes narrowed.

She swallowed, yet held her ground.

Morning sunlight streamed across his hat brim, casting his features into shadows. He took another step closer.

Don't give in. Stay strong.

With hands still covering her brocade-covered derrière swelling in fashionable glory behind her, Alma took one more step backward. Pebbles beneath her foot shifted, sending dirt and debris pattering down the incline.

And then…horror crashed through her as she felt her body tip.

She released the steel bands and arced her arms forward, grasping out for air as she struggled to right herself. Despite her best efforts, her body fell back. With a scream building in her throat, she closed her eyes and awaited the bone-breaking tumble down the ravine.

"Alma!" Debris crunched beneath Dillon's footfalls. Prickles of awareness returned as his strong hands slid around her waist. A quick tug brought her back from disaster and up against his chest. *"Jeezus,* you almost fell."

She couldn't breathe. Shaken by the near-mishap and his closeness, drawn for a reason she refused to acknowledge, Alma wrapped her arms around his shoulders and pulled herself deeper into his embrace. Her eyes widened, her gaze locking with his, its dark depths soft and luminous. A tremor flounced through her, then another. "Y-You saved me."

***

The heat of her perfect body fused Dillon to her.

His breathing quickened, matching hers, as she stared up at him, her eyes a damnable mix of innocence and need. Hunger flashed through him in a scorching rush. He cursed himself, damned her, and tipped his head closer. As his mouth paused over hers, she closed her eyes, her chin lifting, waiting for…for…

What the hell am I doing?

With a sharp oath, Dillon pushed backward.

Her eyelids flew open, and she stared at him in confusion. Then, red crept up her face, and she looked away. *Damn it.* He turned on his boot heel and strode back to the horse. "Let's get moving."

***

Need spiraled through Alma, and she resigned herself to the truth. She wanted this man…this army scout who lived a hard, uncouth life on the ragged edge of civilization. A man who did not fit at all into her well-cast, society-filled life.

She fell in love with the wrong man. Did the same fate that had befallen his mother now rule her heart? Alma stared at Dillon as he reshifted the packs behind the saddlebags. *I am such a fool.*

He swung to face her, and she caught her breath. "If you'll just remove the bustle so we can ride together, I'll tie the damned thing behind the saddle."

She stifled her unrequited yearning, focusing on his surprising offer. "Y-You promise?"

The muscle clenched in his jaw.

Stubborn troll. She arched an eyebrow, and added, "I'm not moving a step 'til you do."

"Good God, woman." His eyes narrowed on an edgy huff. "*Fine.* I promise."

Victory! With her gaze locked on his, she yanked up yards of emerald brocade, and made short work of untying the bustle. The piece rattled to the ground and she stepped from the cotton circlet. "You may take this now."

He stalked over and swept up the crinolette. Another oath followed as he squashed together the flexible bands and headed for the horse. He secured her apparatus to the back of the saddle...where it promptly sprang back open over the gelding's rump presenting a distinct image of a fashionably bustled horse.

Alma giggled.

And Dillon's mouth flattened into a hard line. He smacked the seat of the saddle. "Get the hell over here right now," he snapped, his voice ice, "before I decide to leave this contraption *and* you behind."

Laughter welled in her throat, but she smothered the urge. She'd pushed him and had won. With a nod, she walked over.

***

The ride downhill was covered in complete silence.

Nestled in front of Dillon on the horse, Alma held herself rigid in the saddle, aware of each brush of their elbows, every tap of their knees, and his countless commands to the horse as he worked to take them safely down the mountain.

She kept her focus on her ire at the impropriety of straddling the horse, but she wouldn't push her luck by demanding other seating arrangements. Her victory over the *battle of the bustle* had served to stoke his temper, one she refused to push further. She did however regret the lack of her parasol, currently folded and stowed away in her traveling bag, to block the intermittent sun.

She gritted her teeth at the thought of her stylish riding habits jolted about in some crate heading westward. When her cargo arrived at Fort Lowell without her in tow would Lord Green send forth a search party? Would he demand answers to her whereabouts?

Do I even care?

For an inkling she wished she might be a free spirit -- not duty-bound by her father's oppressive controls. But then, guilt recoiled through Alma in colossal waves, reminding her of exactly *who* she was and that she had no business gallivanting around the countryside...or entertaining such truculent, misbehaving thoughts. And yet, for all her chastising, something akin to pride flickered again inside Alma, and she knew the six-foot-plus, hard-angled cowboy pressing against her backside right now provided much of the glimmer behind her pretention. The way he looked at her. The timber of his voice. The strong and solid purpose that drove him onward.

Every one of his moods jumbled up her insides.

On an exhale, Alma suppressed the thoughts.

Hooves clattered on rock as they rounded a boulder, and then the ground began to flatten out. An hour of riding turned into two. Wordless, Dillon plodded southward. By the third hour, surrounded by such vast wilderness and her eyes heavy from sheer exhaustion, she eased back against his chest. Her small trivialities seemed unimportant.

Without warning, his hands slid around her waist. She gasped.

"Simmer down," he whispered, his warm breath caressing her ear. "I'm just rearrangin' things." He shifted her into a more comfortable position before him. An easy pull brought her back against his chest.

She should protest his boldness...*the beast*! And yet, lulled by the horse's rhythmic gait as well as the security she felt inside his embrace, she relaxed...just a bit, knowing that the only burn she felt right now was the tiny little flame for this *oh-so-wrong for her* man flickering deep inside her heart. Alma sighed, staring down at his gloved hand resting before her on the saddle, the reins threading through cream-colored, leather-encased fingers. The scout's other hand rested much too intimately on her brocade-covered belly. *I could get used to being in his arms.* Her eyes slipped closed upon the truth and to her confounded disquiet, all thoughts hazed as she at last succumbed to sleep.

***

The military post on the outskirts of a growing Tucson was a million miles away from his problems back in England and the reason Lord Henry Smyth Green, the Earl of Locknor, had selected this location.

His servant, Edgar Clarkson handed him his gloves.

Henry nodded, then slid his hands inside the expensive calfskin, working the leather down each finger. For as far back as he could remember, his aide had been in his life. His nanny had been Edgar's mother and his own mum's most trusted confidant. Because of their childhood bond, he overlooked his servant's misbehaviors, while Henry would never have tolerated such ill deportment in others.

He presented an open palm toward his servant, his fingers flipping inward. Edgar laid a riding quirt across Henry's hand. Cold appreciation slid home as he lifted the braided shark-skin handle, slapping the forked end of the short stock whip against his hand.

Perfect.

He then settled the lightweight Planter's hat atop his head; the wide-brimmed, round crowned chapeau a perfect match to the ebony shade of the quirt. The tantalizing aromas of fried onions and other mouthwatering complexities of the Mexican fare he'd savored for breakfast in the hotel's eatery behind him, still filled the morning air.

He gazed across the compound, scanning past officers' quarters, sandstone barracks, and a gleaming white clapboard headquarters centered before a parade ground. The ingenious layout was impressive and vastly different from the landlocked army posts inside ancient walls in England.

With a pleasurable exhale, he glanced toward Edgar. "Sometime this afternoon, I need you to check with the colonel on the whereabouts of Miss Talmadge."

"Yes sir. I shall."

"Good." Henry crossed the boardwalk, stepped to the dusty road and into the spill of sunlight. He appreciated this enchanting land. So different from the repressive dregs and shadows back home. If only he could escape his ongoing peerage problems as easily as he could ride into the wilds of America.

At his approach to the railing, a bay gelding bearing a white blaze down his forehead snorted. Earlier this morning, as Henry had requested, his aide had brought the animal around. He smoothed a gloved hand down the high-quality steed's ebony coat near the shoulder. Nearly sixteen hands high and muscular, the horse was the finest at Fort Lowell.

And Henry liked only the finest of things.

Eager for a hard ride to help him forget the political upheaval of his mother country, he shoved his high-polished boot into the stirrup and mounted, securing his quirt on the side with a hard shove. Those far-too-liberal Whigs with their asinine social reforms had thrown aside the old dominion and now guided the queen in all matters of her sovereignty.

Henry grimaced as he recalled the first change had been that damnable political decree stating noblemen, such as himself, could no longer purchase their commissions. Advancement in the military, even for British nobility, must now be earned by merit, rather than from a position of peerage. *Appalling.* Fortunately, he still had enough influence to garner this lucrative assignment, in spite of the changes being passed by Parliament. Still, he somewhat reveled in the social instability, which kept the focus off his own growing aristocracy problems.

He settled deeper into the saddle. "And when you visit the colonel, remember not to slouch. I promised mother you'd be a good representative on my behalf."

With a grumble, the servant stepped farther into the shade beneath the overhang.

"Edgar!" Henry snapped. "You're muttering again. You know I detest that behavior. Speak up, man. What's your problem now?"

The aide slumped against the closest post. "It might look better if you checked on your fiancée's whereabouts rather than me. As we both know, your uncaring attitude toward women has caused you problems in the past."

Henry grimaced at the man's continual refusal to address him in the proper social tones when they were alone. And those times were rapidly growing. Regardless, the colonel had assured Henry that Miss Talmadge would arrive safely. In spite of the last-minute change of his nuptial location from Boston to the fort, the bans had finally been posted in England, and his upcoming marriage to the wealthy debutante would go off as planned.

That was all that mattered to Henry.

He cleared his throat. "Since I'm riding with the company into the Dragoon Mountains on an Apache raid today, I don't have time to clutter my afternoon with issues regarding my fiancée's."

"Like when you didn't have time to care about Hillary?"

Hillary? Henry stared at Edgar. The remembered face of an upstairs chambermaid who favored them both during their childhood, zipped through his mind. He shoved aside the image, then tightened his lips. Friendships only went so far, and his patience with this nonsense was wearing thin. "I am required by the crown to learn everything I can of the American soldiers and their tactics in battle." He backed the horse from the railing. "I don't have time to, *again*, discuss Hillary's misfortune."

Edgar's brow crimped. "I understand your position and agree, but she cared for you, and would've done anything for you."

A heavy sighed rolled from Henry's lips. "I couldn't marry her even if I wanted to, a fact you well know. She provided me no financial gain." The stomp of hooves and errant whinnies echoed from the stables. Henry squinted against the sun. The horsemen were preparing to ride. He narrowed his gaze upon Edgar once more. "Hillary's death was...as we agreed by her own hand. Indeed, an unfortunate, but unavoidable, tragedy, yet one that's long past."

"Unfortunate?" Edgar shook his head and snorted. "She was pregnant with *your* babe."

"Lower your voice, you imbecile," he hissed, ignoring the black scowl that crumpled Edgar's face. "Do you want the entire fort to hear us?" He leaned closer, his words a stabbing whisper. "We shall nevermore discuss this nonsense. You just find out what has caused Miss Talmadge's delay."

Assured his aide would comply, Henry jerked the leather reins sideways and dug his heels into the horse's flanks. Dirt flew from beneath the mount's hooves as he galloped toward the soldiers.

***

The sun's warmth roused Alma.

She slowly opened her eyes. A wide, high valley replaced the enormous evergreens of this morning. Impressed, she scanned the smooth wash of rocks. While she'd slept, they must've traveled a great distance.

"You're awake," Dillon said. "Been sleeping for several hours."

Contrition bounced through her. "I'm so sorry for dozing."

"Don't be sorry...you've worked hard these past few days. 'Specially since you're not used to my kind of life."

At his sympathy, she smiled, the enmity she'd felt earlier fading. "I'm such a fish out of water, that's for sure."

Her eyes slipped closed again, but her continued reverie was interrupted by his deep voice.

"See those peaks in the distance?" Somewhat surprised he wanted to converse, Alma nodded. "They're called *Sangre de Cristo* Mountains. Spanish for Blood of Christ."

"That's a strange name for mountains. What makes them bloody?"

"At sunrise and sunset, during the winter months, blood-red bands hover right above the horizon."

Alma tried to envision the image he so eloquently painted with his words. "How is that possible?"

"Well, I'm not sure of all the scientific details, but my guess is when the sun's rays reflect off the snow, the illusion is somehow created. Seen it myself a time or two, and it's quite impressive. Same as this territory's name. Colorado means ruddy in Spanish, from all the red silt carried down from the mountains by the spring thaw." He loosened his hold around her waist and pointed left. "And over there, all along the foot of that mountain range, hot springs bubble up like magic. With all these natural oddities, I understand why the Utes consider this area sacred."

"That's fascinating," she said in awed tones. She skimmed her gaze over the distant peaks, touched that he wanted to share, intrigued that the picture of ruthless savages she'd heard so many stories of back East didn't quite match the dynamic people Dillon now painted. Above her head, a hawk shrieked, coasting on the currents with wings spread wide. Suddenly, the bird streaked through the sky and disappeared behind a boulder on the far side of the valley.

"He's found dinner, I'm guessing," Dillon said, laughing.

Her empty stomach reminded Alma she hadn't eaten since this morning.

"And see that narrow gap in the mountain straight ahead?" She nodded. "That's *La Veta* Pass. We'll cut through the southern range of the Rockies there. Means *mineral vein* in Spanish, 'cause of all the silver mined from there eons ago. But, last spring, prospectors found another rich vein over yonder in the San Juan Mountains. That's where things are really heatin' up now between the Indians and the white man."

"Why didn't you get in on the search for silver…you being the adventurous type and all?"

His laugh warmed the curve of her neck. "All that panning and digging never much interested me. Before you know it, the damned vein goes dry, and the miner is left with only unrequited dreams to show for all his hard work. I like what I do for the army. Plus, I'm able to work with horses."

She let out an answering chuckle, then leaned even deeper into the strength of this man.

"Holbrook Creek lies just beyond the pass," he said, and Alma nearly shuddered as another brush of air skimmed past her ear. "We'll stop there for the night."

The night? Her stomach tightened as she tried to accept their sleeping beneath the stars. It may be normal to him, but to her it left them exposed to any predator — man or beast.

He pointed over her shoulder, his breath wafting across the top of her head. "See how that tallest summit scrapes the sky?" Upon her hesitant nod, he added, "That's *Blanca* Peak, highest point in this region, and a landmark I use on my rides back to Tucson."

"Why *blanca*?" she asked, her voice shaking as she gulped back her reactions. He'd protected her thus far…but a safe day's travel guaranteed nothing for the overnight hours.

"*Blanca* means white," he replied, seemingly unaware of her escalating anxiety. "The Indians believe the peak is fastened to the ground by bolts of lightning." He slid his hand around her waist again. And squeezed. "I'm boring you with my jabbering, aren't I?"

With honesty, she replied, "Not at all. In fact, it's beautiful out here." She enjoyed every single one of the stories he'd thus far shared.

"Just you wait, Princess…you ain't seen nothing yet."

And that was the problem.

In regards to her escalating feelings for him or the challenges they faced ahead, she wasn't sure she wanted to see either one.

Chapter Eighteen

Hours in the saddle had done little to dissolve the starch stiffening the socialite's spine. In fact, Miss Alma Talmadge, sitting so proper on a boulder near the creek, looked as regal as any queen seated on a throne.

Her pomposity was as staunch as the stubborn tilt of her chin.

Dillon's jaw tightened. More than once on this journey she'd tried his patience, but she'd also saved his life.

With a mumbled oath, he pulled his gaze away from the colonel's niece and set to unbuckling the saddle's girth. A quick yank hauled the McClellan off the horse. Leather creaked as he slid the sturdy piece to the ground.

Dillon gritted his teeth against the aching throb in his shoulder.

He needed another full week of rest before his infirmity became more tolerable – time he didn't have. Her kidnapping and his subsequent injury had forced him into survival mode. And he was determined to deliver this woman to the fort without any further delays. Not for her sake, or the promise he gave the colonel, but for his own damned peace of mind now.

Against his better judgement, his gaze drifted back to his charge.

His mouth went dry as Alma smoothed her hands over the sides of her hair, tucking back a pale-as-spun-gold strand. She was beautiful and smart, yet even in the wilderness, this high-browed chit held fast to her pretentious ways. Ways that guided most women's decisions of dress and other fancy manners toward that of common sense.

Most women.

Hell, as if with her stubborn attitude she'd consider any advice he might suggest. Dillon scraped a hand over his mouth. *Jeezus*, did every single one of his thoughts have to revolve back to her? Things pertaining to this girl were rapidly slipping out of control. Regardless how he felt, he was involved with her up to his damned neck.

So stop lookin' at her, fool.

The knot in his chest grew. He stepped around the saddle, guided the bay to the nearest tree, and slapped the reins around a low-hanging limb. With the horse already grazed and watered, it was high time Dillon got to work. He surveyed the area beneath the canopy of trees, and then up and down the creek. The recent rain had left the Holbrook running deeper than usual, otherwise everything looked normal.

Just the way I like things.

Dillon squinted against the dappled light sparkling the water's surface. The restive gurgle of the rippling current around rocks and fallen logs merged with the images of mountain ferns and white-barked aspens, easing back his nerves. More relaxed, he once again glanced at Alma.

And found her watching him, a pretty blush pinking her cheeks. For a long moment she held his gaze, then broke the connection and faced the creek.

Pulse racing, he took a deep breath and slowly pushed the air past clenched teeth. Why couldn't he have been burdened with some withered old crone instead of this sassy-mouthed temptress?

The muscles in his arm tightened as he jerked the blanket off the horse. Hell, the only reason they were even getting along was because Miss High and Mighty needed him to guide her back to civilization. Once there, no doubt, her highfalutin ways would resurface, and she'd be the same obnoxious brat he'd first met in Washington. She glanced back and raised her chin in a pretentious manner, underscoring that all-too-obvious truth.

Dillon nailed her with a stern glare as he tossed the woolen pad beside the saddle.

Wind whooshed around the aspens, rattling their coin-like leaves and flattening Alma's dress against her legs. The ample exposure of her slender curves kicked another gaping hole in his heart.

Sonofabitch!

Heat climbed his neck and he closed his eyes, furious he'd noticed, more so at how he'd hardened inside his denims in response to her perfect form. He tipped his head back and scowled at the darkening sky as if it played in league with his body's betrayal.

With a spiked pulse, he pushed away from the horse. Night would be upon them in less than an hour. The sooner he got their fire started, the better off he'd be.

Anything to get his mind off bedding the damned wench.

***

Alma scanned the clearing Dillon had chosen for their evening's stop.

They were tucked behind a cluster of trees whose roots spread across the ground in a twisted heap, resembling the backs of mythical forest beasts. Her gaze lifted to the creek, a rippling mirror that gurgled past a jumbled array of boulders, wavelets nibbling away the bank's edge. Where endless water splashed on stone, pillows of blue-green moss clung in silent resilience.

Lured by the beauty, she scanned further, narrowing her gaze on the kiss of wood sorrel flecking soft blue petals through the tall grass in the meadow beyond. She'd learned many things along this journey, but like the horrors already witnessed, she also knew catastrophe loomed large without notice and could oh-so-easily shatter the peace.

A twinge of stiffness tightened her muscles, and Alma twisted sideways, working out the kinks from the long hours in the saddle. Who would have thought she'd be trekking through such remote stretches of land? She frowned. By now, her father, Uncle Thaddeus and Lord Green must be worried sick about her. She was out of her element, struggling hard to be brave…and the sheer fact that she hadn't gone stark raving mad was in no small thanks to Dillon. On a sigh, she peered at the broad-shouldered scout hunkered over the beginnings of a small campfire.

I'm safe…as long as I'm with you.

With her ignorance of living on the range, he, however, must think her useless. And she was. In all ways that mattered to him. Still, she wasn't a total failure. She'd saved his life, under his direction gutted a deer, and had even made her first pot of coffee. Through it all, he'd taken every risk to keep her safe, including taking a bullet. Humbled at his bravery, she swallowed hard. Never, in her wildest thoughts, had she imagined such a fierce protector.

What would her cousin think of this silly worriment over a man? Oh, to rejoin womankind again – to gossip and giggle and chat about nonsensical things that only ladies enjoyed.

No deer disemboweling. No bandits. No blood.

Anticipation fizzed through Alma as the image of Pamela materialized. She hadn't seen her cousin in years. How much had she changed since moving to this wild and reckless land?

At the crackling snap of fire, Alma turned. Smoke twisted upward from the pile of wood in a makeshift fire ring as flames danced near its center. "How long 'til we reach Tucson?"

Dillon kept rummaging inside his saddlebags without looking over. "Another week or two. Longer if we run into more trouble." He withdrew a canvas bag, then held out a generous portion of the dried venison, waggling dinner in her direction. "Come get this."

A niggling of unease filled her as she scooted from the rock and headed toward him. She took his proffered gift, then bit off a small section of the cured meat, the salty-sweet taste surprising her. "I'm so tired of trouble."

"Everything's trouble out here." He glanced at her. "Get used to it."

"That's asking a lot, I'm afraid."

"And another reason why we're taking things one day at a time."

One day at a time? Good grief, *every second* spent in this man's presence spelled trouble. Her escalating heartbeat solidified her conflicted reactions regarding this man.

Frustrated, she wrestled her features into bland indifference and took another bite of venison. The sun low on the horizon winked at her from between the layers of clouds blanketing a far-away mountain peak. She sighed as the long, lazy rays spilled an orange-red glow across the clearing. "Nice evening," she said...more for her own validation than for his.

Dillon nodded, and the jangle of his spurs blended with the crackling flames as he drew up a leg. Draping his arm atop the knee, he leaned back on the opposite heel. "We're heading into the best part soon."

"We are?"

He nodded. "You'll see."

Alma sank down beside him. Even under perfect conditions, forging any kind of real relationship with him was unthinkable. The awkward, intimate pairing which had been forced upon them reminded her of that truth. They were as different as day and night, water and oil, and every other timeworn comparison she'd ever known.

Stifling a sigh, Alma took another miniscule bite of meat. As if her father would even sanction such a union between his only daughter and an uneducated army scout? He'd probably have a heart attack at the mere thought. Not that she was thinking such foolish thoughts. The drone of crickets melded with the water's soft churn, and the remaining bit of jerky she held disappeared in her mouth. If only she had a libation to finish off her meal and help her forget about her current situation. *Sparkling wine. That would be nice.* She glanced at Dillon...as if he'd even have some.

A giggle escaped her lips.

And his tightened. "What's so damn funny?" he asked. "Don't you like this time of night?"

"It wasn't that. I rather do love dusk."

"But you laughed. Just now. I heard it."

She drew her knees to her chest and leaned forward, tucking her voluminous skirt around her before wrapping her arms around her legs. "I was simply contemplating the joys of sipping on a cool glass of sparkling wine and the unlikelihood of such an expensive bottle being stowed in your saddlebags." Already knowing of the contents within, she tipped her head to peer at him. "You don't have any...do you?"

His lips lifted into a grin. "Sorry."

"Have you ever sipped? Sparkling wine?" She bit back another laugh, doubting this tall drink of cowboy had even seen anything as sophisticated as that, let alone imbibed.

"Can't say that I have." He swallowed, then glanced at her. "Heard about it a time or two, though."

She smiled. "Well, the best I've ever had is made by the Pleasant Valley Company in upstate New York. They began harvesting their Isabella grapes just before the war. A couple of years ago, they branched out into effervescent wines."

A scowl touched his mouth as he tossed a handful of sticks onto the fire. "How the hell do you know so much about spirits?"

She leaned sideways, lightly bumping her shoulder against his. "I probably should've mentioned Father has a vested interest in Pleasant Valley. But, the winery's so popular now they've even earned the moniker *Reims* of America. Father's quite happy about that, too, I might add."

"Why's that?"

"Why is my father happy?"

"No, the other. That reims thing." He shoved a second piece of venison into his mouth, and reached in the bag for a third.

His interest seemed genuine, so Alma indulged, eager to share what she'd learned from her father. Though she'd never visited the vineyard, he'd told her so many stories over the years. "Reims is world-renowned for their spirits. They're the only champagne-producing region in the world. Well, at least of all the *les grandes marques*." She pressed her fingertips against her lips. With a flourish, she tossed an imaginary kiss into the air. "Champagne is *si délicieux*, so delicious, and since Roman times, it's been created right there in the caves and tunnels beneath Reims...which is an ancient town near Paris." She paused and glanced at him, their gazes connecting. "Which is in France."

His eyes narrowed as he handed her another strip of meat. "Interesting. And for the record, I know where Paris is, Princess."

Guilt slid through her as she bit off another small piece of meat, chewed, and then swallowed. "I'm sorry, I wasn't sure."

He shrugged.

As she finished her second piece of venison, Alma stared into the fire. "I've enjoyed champagne at social gatherings up and down the East Coast, but don't dare indulge too often."

"Why?" He tossed another handful of twigs onto the logs, then stoked the flames with a longer stick.

She propped her chin on her knees, and sighed. "Palliatives and I don't agree. I, um, tend to get twitter-pated."

He settled onto his heel and glanced at her. "How?"

A light laugh trickled out. "More than one glassful makes me tipsy."

He softly chuckled, then reached into his saddlebags and rummaged around. A moment later, he withdrew the silver flask. Shaking it, he frowned. "Damnit, half gone." He lifted the flagon before the fire in a saluting gesture. "You can keep your champagne, darlin'…I'll just take the whiskey." He hoisted the metal to his lips. After two long pulls, he gave a satisfied sigh. Humor touched his brows as he glanced her way. "I'd offer a sip, but now knowing you can't hold your liquor, I guess I'm gonna have to say no." He recapped the container, and then shoved it in the saddlebags.

The crackling campfire and soothing babble of the nearby stream filled the stillness. Dillon handed her the canteen. She smiled and took several deep swallows. The water was no wine, but the tepid liquid quenched her thirst.

As he stared into the flickering flames, she studied the scout's handsome profile. Dillon Reed was the worst kind of trouble for any woman. Too big and controlling. Too ill-mannered. And absolutely too disheveled. She'd already memorized her list of reasons why she must keep her distance. Alma frowned as she handed back the canteen. And yet…two more weeks in this man's company and she'd be crazy with wan…

Dillon surged to his feet, shattering her thoughts. "Let's get our bedrolls," he announced, heading toward the gelding.

An hour later, Alma had stretched out across the blanket beside Dillon. On her back, she stared at the emerging night sky. With the creek's distinctive minuet burbling in the background, one by one the luminous stars materialized.

Nighttime crept in, and sheeted the world inside a silver mystery. The hard days of travel, the dangers they'd faced, and the unknown challenges ahead all pressed with a crushing weight across her chest. "Oh, Dillon," she said in an unsteady whisper. "Everything is just so overwhelming."

"For you, probably yes. But, for me, it's my favorite time of all. Out in the open. No cave. No house. Just staring up at all...this."

Her heart thudded against her ribs as Alma fought back her worries. She forced herself to peruse the slowly evolving display above her as he might see it. With each inward breath, her pulse slowed, and with each exhale she took in the ever-darkening sky. "Look, the stars are beginning to emerge."

"From horizon to horizon and all points in between. Give it a few more minutes."

Silence fell between them.

After a moment, she slid a glance toward him. Was he assessing her? Thinking her foolish in her fear of so many unknowns? How could he expect otherwise? Until this journey, never had she been exposed to such elements. She clenched her eyes closed. All around her, the forest beckoned with croaking frogs and chirping crickets and other unknown animal calls that the night now magnified.

With her senses enhanced, the tang of the composting forest filled her every breath. Trees rustled against the soft breeze and nearby a leaf fell, swishing to the ground in a gentle whisper. The fluty piping of a far-away bird echoed in the blackness. *What a pathetic coward I am.*

"It's all right to be afraid, Princess," Dillon whispered. "This is another new moment for you. When you're ready, reopen your eyes and just behold."

Would she ever be ready for his world? She realized now how desperately she wanted to be.

Alma forced her lids up.

And gasped at the majestic canopy overhead.

Darkness had fallen completely and wispy, translucent clouds framed a crescent moon. Other celestial constellations, known and unknown, real and imagined, shimmered before her in silvery harmony, every single thing pinned into place upon an infinite, blue-black canvas.

Dillon chuckled, then pointed to the brightest cluster of stars overhead. "See that? Each diamond light is a million miles away."

Tears slipped from her eyes, tracking into her hair. "It's all so incredibly...beautiful."

"That it is." Then he continued, his whispered words almost rueful. "And there they stand, the innumerable stars, shining in order like a living hymn, all written in bright light upon the heavens." He gave a soft laugh. "Guess I got a soft spot for the poet N.P. Willis. Many an evening, father read his work to me...and Caleb."

In all her life, Alma had never been more surprised -- this hardened man quoting a gifted bard.

Amazing.

Unsure why, but needing his touch, she released her pent-up breath, then slowly edged her hand over and bumped his, her palm sliding atop. "I feel so small beneath such unimaginable...vastness."

"Remember, Princess, everything's not what it seems." A softness she'd never heard before filled his voice, and a heartbeat later, he turned his palm up and folded strong, callused fingers over hers.

Warmth flowed up her arm and settled into every anxious corner of her heart.

Finally, Alma relaxed.

"And don't be afraid of the night sounds either. Just listen to what they have to say."

She nodded again and swallowed, knowing that as long as he held her hand, she would listen for the remainder of the night. And yet, the clock of despair began ticking. Would her fiancé keep her this safe?

The doubt inside her heart crept ever closer.

***

The following morning after a repeat meal of dried venison, Dillon helped Alma mount the horse. The ten-minute argument preceding resulted in him handing over her parasol. With a well-honed skill, she whooshed open the gadget, then shot him a haughty look. "I am now ready to begin another day."

"Well, I'm so glad to hear it," he growled. The scout pulled up into the saddle and settled into place behind her. With a grumble, he snapped, "Just keep that damned thing out of my face."

Alma promptly tipped the tiny canopy out of his line of vision. "My apologies, sir."

Another guttural groan followed as Dillon tapped his spurs against the gelding's flank, and headed southward, paralleling the Culebra mountain range.

By noon, they'd crossed the shin-deep Costilla Creek, and turned westward. Fort Garland lay a full day's ride ahead, cowering somewhere in the shadows of the distant mountain peak.

Throughout the morning as they'd travelled, her parasol held aloft to block the sun, Alma enjoyed watching the land transform from highlands to plateaus, evergreens to prairie grass, and now into a tranquil meadow strewn with flowers. Tilting her sunshade against the rays of the perfect June day, she scanned the area. As far as the eye could see, white-petaled blossoms arched over ferny foliage and bobbed in the afternoon breeze.

"Yarrow," Dillon said, nodding toward the snow-colored blooms. His chuckle held a smile. "Figured you'd want to know."

Her lips turned upward. "They're so beautiful."

"And a potent medicine in these parts, too. Every bit of the plant is used -- for teas, poultices, even tinctures. An effective painkiller, too. Mexicans call it *plumajillo*...for little feather, 'cause the leaf's shape resemble one."

Glancing at the closest cluster of flowers, she nodded. "Yes, I can see that now."

"If you grind up yarrow and shove it into a wound, it'll staunch the flow of blood. Even Homer's Iliad had the warrior Achilles using this plant to treat his fallen comrades."

Alma turned to face him, her eyes widening. "You've read Homer?" During her schooling she'd studied in depths the works of the epic Greek poet.

Dillon settled his hand atop the parasol, pushing the canopy from his line of site. "Been a while. I wanted Caleb to know the classics."

This man never ceased to surprise her. Slowly, she turned forward and tipped the parasol to her right to block the sun. As the horse slogged onward through the field, crushing blossoms beneath its hooves, she drew in a deep breath.

The pungent scent of the flowers made her cough.

Dillon snickered. "Suppose I should've warned you yarrow looks way better than it smells."

He glanced sideways upon the blooms. "The cavalry even uses these plants when medicines run low on a battlefield. They call it soldier's woundwort."

Ah, Dillon. Such astounding things you know. She shifted again, peering at him over her shoulder. The brim of his hat shadowed his face, but he tipped his head and his gaze pierced hers, clear and intense. His lips slid into a lopsided grin. "What?" he asked, his eyes alight and crinkling at the corners. "It's all true."

Her heart melted. Shaken, she faced forward and fought to squash her reaction to his rugged charm. "You sound like a teacher."

"Education the hard way, Princess...living on the run, and avoidin' other people along the way. The land's many gifts, I learned from the Indians."

She recalled his shared story of stealing food to keep his brother fed, so determined to preserve his beleaguered little family. Sadness over Dillon's lost youth rose inside her. "Well, had I been given some of this miraculous yarrow back at the cave, I would've packed you full of flowers."

He chuckled and tightened his hold around her waist. "Of that, I have no doubt."

Alma nodded and again settled against him, glancing down. The parasol's minuscule shade spilled a hazy, peach-colored shadow across his hands. Stretched across her belly, his strong fingers flexed, then skimmed the fabric of her dress leaving a trail of awareness wherever he touched.

On an unsteady breath, she dragged her mind from dangerous thoughts, and instead focused on him and the hardships he'd obviously known. She stared at his bare hands, so unlike her fiancé's manicured fingers. The years had not been easy on the scout, the weathering and calluses a strong testament to the challenges he must have faced.

After the horrors she'd encountered in the few weeks she'd been on the trail, a pittance really, what must he have experienced over all his years? Her throat tightened as she struggled to ponder such an existence, a way of life so foreign, so out of touch with her reality, she wondered if she ever could understand or accept all that he'd endured.

At times when his guard was lowered, she saw the angst he worked to hide. Whatever bothered him left him far from peace. Dillon Reed wielded his stern countenance as did the warrior Achilles a shield, to protect, to preserve the man inside, one whose very lifestyle had been cast for him during a childhood without choices. Unable to move past his own troubled past...had he chosen the life of an army scout to be of service to others?

Compassion melted the last of her reserve, and the moment shifted. As if a breath in time, the walls around her heart crumbled. She now journeyed to meet her fiancé. Everything about her life was set, and this man who protected her so well had absolutely no place in it.

Tears burned her eyes as she struggled to accept her mind's roiling.

Without a word, she collapsed the sunshade, and drew closed her parasol. A quick release on the handle's center slide, bent the ivory shaft in half. She tucked the piece before her across the saddle.

Frustrated, exhausted, since she'd first met Dillon, her carefully crafted world had been thrown upside down and stripped away piece by piece. Slowly, Alma's eyes drifted closed and she listened to the plodding rustle of horse through *plumajillo*. Eventually, her breathing matched the scout's.

Steady and relaxed.

In and out…

In and out…

In and out…

And then somewhere in the murky churning of her brain, she succumbed to sleep.

***

An hour later, Dillon's voice penetrated her dreams. "Don't be alarmed," he whispered, "but we've got company."

Company?

The words blurred in her sleep-hazed mind, jangled, and then became clear. Alma pried her eyelids open as her meager survival instincts kicked in. She stiffened and sat up, glancing at him. "What do you mean?"

With unsettling intensity, Dillon's gaze penetrated hers. "Three riders. They've been following us for the past twenty minutes or so."

"Wher--"

"On the ridgeline to our right. Do *not* look over."

With her heart beating double time, she searched his eyes. "Who are they?"

"Utes." His gaze shifted to the trail.

"Utes." The single word hissed out. Her right hand gripped the parasol's now-folded handle while her left tightened on his upper thigh. "A-Are they going to attack us?"

"Probably not. They're a small, foraging group. Most likely stumbled across us. Just stay calm. "

"Stay calm?" she rasped. "Dillon, they're…Indians!" As she twisted forward, a wisp of hair loosened from her chignon snagged in his stubble, then released. Her scalp tingled from the slight pull. She tightened her lips against emotions swirling through her -- anger that he could be so nonchalant about such real danger, frantic that she might actually come face to face with red-skinned savages after all, and relief that he was here to protect her.

"They're curious, no doubt wondering what the hell we're up to."

She glared at him again. "Well, do something," she whispered. "Make them go away."

"Doesn't work that way." His gaze sharpened on hers and he let out a long breath, his brows scrunching down in that *don't argue with me* look she knew all too well. "And if they approach us," he warned, his words now frigid with authority, "you just keep your damned trap shut, you got it? I'll do all the talking."

"Y-You speak their language?"

He shrugged. "Some."

On edge, she turned forward, her lower lip quivering. Of course he did…this man knew everything. He was the superior survivor and she was just an *out-of-her-element* shipping heiress he was saddled with protecting.

"That ice you've built up around your *so-called heart*," she hissed, "Well, I strongly suggest you melt that. It's ungentlemanly." Her eyes burned with the ludicrous urge to cry. "I cannot wait for the moment I'm well rid of you and this unending horror."

In a hot rush, his breathe scoured the back of her neck, "I'm not a gentlemen, I don't have a heart, and, trust me, I can't wait for *that* moment's arrival either."

Indignation blistered her cheeks as her breath caught in her chest. Regardless what she had snapped at him, Alma wasn't sure whether she was angry at his clipped response…or hurt.

But, he kissed me. And held my hand last night.

She scrunched her eyes closed, mortification flooding her. *What a fool I am.* A heavy sigh slipped out, ebbing into the late-afternoon breeze.

As they continued to travel, her anxiety built. Despite the tangled mess her world had become, vicious redskins still followed them somewhere nearby. Danger mounted from all sides, and even after everything they'd been through, this brute not only had the audacity to assure her he was more than ready to have her out of his life, but also made her feel as she had when she first met him...lost, terrified, and all alone.

Despite her previous musings about his past, he was the most insufferable man ever to breathe air, yet...she was completely dependent upon the chisel-jawed beast.

May he burn in perdition!

As the horse rounded a bend in the trail, Dillon's body tensed. He drew the gelding to a halt. Surprised, Alma lifted her head.

Her eyes went wide as she sucked a frazzled breath. In the middle of the trail, not more than twenty feet away, a dozen, dark-skinned heathens astride horses stared back at her.

CHAPTER NINETEEN

The Indians remained still, unmoving.

Loose-fitting, shirt-like garments covered the half-naked savages, and she gaped at the long rectangular pieces of deerskin that covered their... private parts. The negligible scraps of hide were looped over some kind of belt knotted around their waists. A shudder raced up Alma's spine and she swallowed, her cheeks burning. Several of them wore beaver pelt head-coverings, and tattoos etched in swirls across at least half of the sun-stained faces.

Heart pounding, Alma scraped her gaze over the closest savage. Two long plaits of braided, raven-black hair fell over thin shoulders. Tube-like, footless buckskins covered his legs, secured onto the same belt that held his deerskin flap. Brightly-colored beaded moccasins covered his feet.

Fear gripped her and she pressed harder against the scout's chest.

Dillon directed guttural words toward the Indian. *"Att-um-bar, Neh-tig-a-gand. Maiku."*

Several redskins chuckled.

"And greetings back to you, my good friend," the closest Indian replied in broken English.

On a hard swallow, Alma widened her eyes and peered up at Dillon. With an unsteady breath, she stammered, "H-He knows you?"

Dillon seared her with a glare, a jaw muscle tightening. "Yes." Exasperation in his voice further deepened the tone. "Now, be still." He scraped his attention back to the obvious leader, the scowl in his voice softening. "I see you've improved on your use of my language since last we met."

"It's good to know the tongue of those who make our unkept treaties." The Indian's gaze slid to hers. "And yes, I know *Eyes of the Army* many seasons." She swallowed, hoping her lifted chin hid her escalating fear at this newest turn of events. The redskin laughed, his attention resettling on Dillon. "*Tooeg-I-ah*...very pretty, your white woman. And brave. This union is new?"

Dillon nodded, his hold ever-so-slowly tightening around her midsection. "Yes. I've claimed her as my woman, and will fight to the death to protect her." She swerved her head, staring up at him. He ignored her, his no-nonsense stare sliding over every man, before reconnecting with their leader. "But, *tog'oiak'*...thank you, I am honored you approve."

A clop of hooves sounded, then several mounted warriors ambled around a thicket to join the group. They were young. Boys, in fact, no older than twelve or so.

Dillon angled a thumb their way. "Couldn't help but notice they've been trailing alongside us on the ridgeline for several miles."

"They are still young and foolish," the Indian said.

"I disagree. You are training them well. Others unfamiliar with your people would not have spotted them."

The leader pointed at the deer carcasses draping a few of the horses' rumps. "We are teaching them the ways of *Nuu-ci,* The People. How to hunt. How to survive." He then spoke over his shoulder in clipped, garbled sentences, before turning back to face Dillon. "You have come at good time. *Senawahv,* The Creator, blesses all *Nuu-ci.* Tonight begins *Mack-onsee-pi.*"

Dillon nodded, stacking his hands atop the saddle's swell. "The Bear Dance is a revered tradition for your tribe."

"You and your woman will join us."

Join them? The urge to insist that Dillon beg off the invitation screamed through Alma's mind.

Instead, he sealed their fate. "We would be honored to attend your celebration of life."

"We go now. To village." As the Indians turned their mounts, the leader motioned Dillon to follow behind them, adding, "Morning Bird is making special food for tonight. She will be happy to see you again."

Morning Bird? Alma stiffened as jealousy sputtered through her. The image of the tiny, cobalt-blue bottle inside Dillon's saddlebags returned. Had he bought the scent for this woman? The thought of his attentiveness focused on any female other than her further tightened Alma's nerves. With a huff, she swished open the miniscule parasol and blocked the late-afternoon sun. Unable to stop herself, she glanced once more at Dillon.

His dark-eyed gaze pierced hers.

Alma shifted an eyebrow, an extra helping of hauteur underscoring her tone. "Morning Bird?"

His smile was slow in coming, but no less unsettling as lines of amusement bracketed his mouth. "Relax, Princess," he said, his voice as smooth as watered silk. "Morning Bird is his woman." Patting her stomach, he leaned lower, his breath brushing warm against her eye. Where he pressed, her muscles tightened. "I've already got mine right here."

Alma flushed, her pulse ratcheting up another notch. Her glare landed upon the rump of the closest horse as heat climbed her neck.

This man drove her crazy with inexplicable...*what?*

"First wolves. Now bears," she muttered on a tattered whisper. "Lord help me survive Dillon Reed."

Behind her, much to her chagrin, her protector issued a low chuckle.

***

Alma scoured the land scruffy with brush, wide stands of evergreens, and chiseled mountains that speared upward from the ground. Earlier, Dillon had shared that the Ute nation inhabiting the plateaus of the southern Rockies now grouped together in large bands upon lands deemed, for the moment, unsuitable for the white man. But, every day the tide of miners and new settlers grew in spite of the government's *Treaty of Peace* which set aside land for the redskins.

The tenuous ride over the foothills to the isolated Indian camp took nearly an hour, and with each mile, the aches in her body screamed. If only she could have a drink of water, anything to stem the growing restlessness inside her.

Their horse crested a knoll and walked into an open meadow.

Alma gasped as a mishmash of structures shimmered into view. She stared in wonderment, studying the objects. Of various sizes, they had broad circular bases created by wooden poles strapped together. Animal hides or white canvas covered every edifice, and the excess timber at the top of each structure remained uncovered, resembling interlocking fingers against the sky. *Are these their homes?*

"Teepees," Dillon said as if reading her thought. "A large one houses thirty people comfortably." He chuckled. "Women rule the inside, while the men rule everything else."

"Queen of her castle," Alma said on a laugh. "They're fascinating."

He nodded. "And they're portable, too. In less than an hour, the whole village can be dismantled. Utes are nomadic and follow their resources."

As they rode closer to the camp, Alma collapsed her parasol and narrowed her gaze. The Indian village lined both sides of a shallow creek for nearly a quarter of a mile. *Prime location. Water always available.*

Moments later, they entered the strangely remarkable village. Dozens of half-naked children raced alongside them, their laughter rising in gleeful waves. Mongrel dogs barked, loping in black and brown and white furry blurs beside the youngsters. With feathers ruffling, chickens darted in madcap melee, their loud squawking accentuating displeasure at this newest disturbance into their lives.

Movement everywhere fought for Alma's attention. She spied women dressed in all manner of colorful cloth and fringed animal hides spilling from the assorted dwellings. In a garbled tongue, they called for the youngsters, sweeping the smallest ones into their arms.

The scent of cooking meat filled the air as the horse galloped past. Though crude, the domesticity of the village unfolded around her. Field-stone fire rings haphazardly dotted the ground between the dwellings. Animal furs draped over boulders and boxes creating cushioned seating. Elderly women occupied several of the makeshift chairs, overseeing the cooking preparations. Near their feet, brown-skinned infants strapped inside cradleboards leaned against the boulders, gourd-shaped water bottles within their caretakers' easy reach. And everywhere Alma looked she saw baskets of potatoes, drying corn, and bars that glistened with strips of drying meat.

She narrowed her gaze on wooden tripods angled over the many fires. Iron or clay pots suspended from every one. Curlicues of steam rose from the vessels, wafting the incredible aromas into the air.

Ignoring her stomach's rumbling, she turned. Near the creek on her right, young boys practiced with their bows, shooting arrows into reed mat targets. Further downstream, several Indian boys perched atop wooden railings, watching over dozens of horses and sheep eating inside a handful of corrals.

The group rode deeper into the compound. At the gate to the closest corral, the Indians halted their horses and then dismounted. Dillon rode on toward the largest teepee at the end of the long row. He pulled back on the gelding's reins and stopped.

Standing before the canvas dwelling, a broad-shouldered man smiled up at them. With a large, well-shaped head and regular features, he exuded an air of dignified authority. Like the others, he wore his hair in two long plaits. Brightly-stained deerskins clothed his stocky frame, and a setting sun splashed golden across the trade beads that ornamented his garment. His left hand, blue-veined and bony, clutched an ebony cane.

A large, gleaming brass medallion suspended from a bright blue ribbon around his neck drew Alma's attention. Even from where she sat atop the horse, she easily read the words *President A. Lincoln's Peace Medal.*

Without any words of explanation or direction to her, Dillon dismounted. His spurs chinked as he hit the ground. In two strides he stood before the Indian. His palm slid against the man's, and they shook hands. "Chief Ouray," he said, his words laced with respect. "I am honored to see you again."

CHAPTER TWENTY

Firelight rippled across the walls of the teepees as women clad in fringed deerskin and brightly colored beads moved to the beat of drums and melodic chants. In accompaniment, dozens of men rubbed long sticks with smaller ones, producing an unusual swishing sound that lent another layer to the hypnotic experience.

Intrigued by the events unfolding before her, Alma sat near the teepee she and Dillon were given to share this night. Never had she witnessed such bizarre steps or heard the creation of such warbling chants. Still, she found herself tapping her fingers against the thick buffalo pelt spread beneath her, keeping beat with the mesmerizing cadence.

"The Bear Dance honors the season of strength and renewal for them," Dillon explained from her right, his attention remaining on the dancers.

She pointed to the notched instruments the men held. "What are those sticks?"

"They're called *moraches*, growlers. Most are made from deer spines. When they're rubbed up and down with a stick, the sound mimics that of a bear emerging from its den in the spring."

Fascinating. "How long do they dance?"

"Until only one squaw is left standing."

He took a swig from a bottle handed to him earlier, then passed the leather-wrapped container to her. "It's called Shrub. Try it."

She stared at him, blinking. "I-Is it…safe?" Though earlier they'd eaten a meal of succulent elk, roasted-in-the-fire sweet potatoes, and ears of corn which had tasted wonderful, Alma held reservations about the drink.

Dillon speared her a warning glance. "They take offense if visitors refuse their hospitality. Have a sip."

She hesitated, then brought the bottle to her lips and swallowed. An explosion of flavors, some sour, others sweet, passed over her tongue. "It's delicious."

Satisfaction filled his gaze. "That's the crushed berries you're tasting."

With the tingle of the drink still on her tongue, she took a big gulp.

"Go easy on that, Princess. It may taste good, but it's full of whiskey."

"Is this called fire-water?"

He chuckled. "Some like to call it that, too."

Shimmers of warmth danced in her head, and more relaxed, Alma shot him back a smile. "Well, this tastes better than any of that vile liquor you men like to consume." Lifting the vessel in a mock toast, she took another swig.

"Do you need a reminder that you tend to get tipsy? Now give it back." He reached over, but laughing, she held the bottle out of his reach. "No. No. I mustn't be inhospitable."

With a snicker, he shook his head. "Suit yourself, but don't say I didn't warn you."

As the music heightened Alma's senses of the star-filled night, the soft warmth of the alcohol lulling her, they talked and shared the ceremonial drink. All the while, half-naked children darted around the festivities, tending to the many fire pits scattered alongside the creek. With the added logs, sparks shot heavenward and the flames licked high, washing an enchanting glow across the encampment.

Alma sighed and relaxed even more. This night contrasted sharply against all she'd ever dreamed of doing, and the fashionable soirees and balls she'd attended back east put this savage event to shame. And yet…no words could explain the enthralling appeal of everything unfolding around her. As the moon edged from behind wispy clouds, the Indian who'd led them into camp earlier walked toward them. At his side, Morning Bird, a woman Alma had met earlier at dinner, wore a beautifully fringed doeskin dress, complimented by a bright red blanket draping her shoulders.

The couple paused before Dillon. For several minutes they conversed in the guttural language of the tribe.

Finally, Dillon smiled and nodded, glancing at her. "Of course she will. You have my blessing."

An odd spark shot through the wondrous haze of her mind. "I will what?"

Mirth sparkled in Dillon's eyes. "Honor his request."

What request? Her gaze shifted to the warrior.

"Come, brave one," the man said. "You must join women in the Bear Dance. Morning Bird will teach you the steps."

Wisps of panic slid through her, but the veil from the Shrug smothered her doubt. She frowned at Dillon. "I don't know the moves." The strange dance looked similar to a Virginia reel's opening steps, but without the reel, and registered somewhere on the extreme opposite range of a waltz.

"It's not hard," he urged with a smile, "you just step forward and back and shuffle around a bit."

It sounded simple enough, and his confidence in her left her further emboldened. She took another fortifying gulp. "A-Are you going to dance?"

"Women go first, so we men can ogle all of you." He winked at her, and the magnificence of his smile sent bubbles of pleasure through Alma.

Must be the Shrug.

For a moment she could envision dancing before him, turning, catching his smile. Her mind shifted from following the movements to something more alluring. Pulse racing, she eyed him for a long moment, then banked the flood of desire. Her courage faded, and she took another gulp of the drink. "I-I think I'll pass."

A shadow crossed his face, and Dillon's gaze narrowed. "Think again." The hard glint in his eyes assured her that he'd not allow her to back out.

The swarthy beast.

Hospitality be damned! As if she had another choice? Fine, she'd dance. Her gaze riveted on his, and she raised the bottle. "Here's to finding courage." She downed several more long pulls, then passed the vessel back to him. The fortifying swirl flowed through her veins as she climbed to her feet.

And swayed.

Morning Bird reached over and steadied her. "*Koon-ah-pah.* Whiskey too strong." She motioned to Alma's dusty traveling gown. "And this too long." Before Alma could step back or protest, the woman bent forward, scooped up a handful of emerald brocade, and shoved the excess fabric into the skirt's waistband.

Startled, Alma glanced down at her cloth-clad limbs, the delicately embroidered bottoms of her pantalets visible for all to see. The thought of impropriety swirled in her mind only to disappear beneath a hazy blur.

With a giggle, she glanced toward Dillon. "Oooh, look. I'm now ready for the ball." Another laugh followed, along with a tiny hiccup. "Oh dear," she whispered, her fingers fluttering across her lips. "I do apologize." She scrunched her nose and blew a wayward strand of hair away from her cheek. Trying to fend off how her thoughts clouded, she inhaled and straightened her shoulders. "All right," she announced, sending Dillon her prettiest smile. "I am ready to sally forth."

He chuckled, his eyes dark, shadowy pools. "Behave yourself out there, Princess."

"I shall surely try," she whispered as she peered deep into his eyes. "But you, my stalwart protector, must promise to ogle me."

Heat burned in his eyes as he slowly scanned her body from head to toe before reconnecting his gaze to hers. "I promise."

His deep, throaty assurance oozed over her, igniting a searing want up Alma's spine. With a skewed nod, she swerved on her heel and faced the woman, her hand motioning forward in pronounced exaggeration. "Lead on, sweet Morning Bird…the Bear Dance awaits."

***

Each step Alma took toward the dancers, lush hips swaying in coquettish rhythm to the beat, further heated Dillon's desire. Lured against what he damned well knew was right, he again raked his gaze over her curves…her perfect breasts just right for cupping, and a waist he could almost encircle to draw her close. He swallowed hard as his gaze dipped to long, coltish legs that went from here to next week.

Dillon cursed, then tipped the bottle and gulped.

Better go easy on this, or I'll forget my duty.

Duty? With a scowl he stared at the saucy minx who made his blood pound hot. A temptress so at odds to the social correctness of the stiff Boston debutante he'd met at the Washington train station; *that* woman he could ignore.

His gaze narrowed on her. Arms high, she swayed in circles to the beat of the drums, her body relaxed. With the amount of Shrug she'd consumed, no doubt any hint of propriety had long since drowned.

The steady beat of the music continued, and with each turn toward him, she rocked her hips and laughed. Repeatedly, Morning Bird interrupted Alma's twirling to demonstrate the correct steps. Moments later, his wayward waif resumed the dancing to her own sensual rhythm.

Unable to look away, held by the pull of attraction he watched, wanted, needed with his every breath. With another mumbled oath, Dillon downed another swig in an attempt to squelch the yearning.

His Indian friend laughed.

Startled to have forgotten his presence, Dillon silently let loose another curse. Served him right. Though he'd only ogled Alma, his mind had traipsed over every damned boundary forbidden to him.

Humor glittered in the warrior's eyes. "I see your woman has taken well to the spirit of the evening. She is causing Morning Bird much frustration, as well as catching the eye of several young braves across the way."

Sonofabitch!

Dillon slowly stood. The rush of the drink temporarily blurred his mind. With a grimace, he planted a hand atop the man's shoulder, steadying himself. "My woman has a spirit all her own that would frustrate even an emerging bear."

"You have spoken the truth, my friend. But we like our women spirited, do we not?"

"Yes," he said, dropping his hold. The corners of his mouth drew down in a frown. "Before she does something foolish, I'll go rein her in." The heels of his boots crunched the ground as he strode toward his dancing sprite.

On her next spin, Alma spied him and brightened her smile. "Did you come to dance with me, my darling?" She gyrated closer and slipped her palms up his chest.

An easy pull on his shoulders brought her up against him.

Dillon gazed down at her. "Don't you think you've had enough dancing for one night, Princess?"

"Never," she purred as her gaze sunk into his. "I'm just getting started." Lost in an inebriated world all her own, her words were carried on a teasing pout. She began to writhe against him.

He unwrapped her arms from his shoulders and clasped his hand in a tight hold over hers, tugging. "Come along, I think you're finished for the night."

"Where are we going?" she whispered as she stumbled along behind him.

"Home." At their teepee, Dillon swept aside the animal pelt covering the entrance.

Alma glanced over her shoulder and with a tipsy grin toward Morning Bird said, "Goodnight, my new friend. My man is taking me to bed."

Smiles wreathed the Indians' faces.

Dillon cursed, his mind not needing to go where her words dragged him. So much for her prudish society standards. This conflicting woman drove him mad.

With another sharp oath, he ducked through the opening, and hauled her inside.

CHAPTER
TWENTY-ONE

The steady flow of music, flickering fires, and chanting outside the teepee infused their humble abode within a muffled cadence of undulating tones and shadows. Dillon swept his gaze across several blankets and buffalo pelts stacked into a pile.

They'd make a nice pallet for her.

"Now you stay put while I make up a bed."

"I promise not to move a muscle, my brave protector," she replied, her attempt at solemnness undermined by another giggle.

Every nerve in Dillon's body tingled. Too aware of her, of how her dress which should be by any man's standard drab and unappealing, flowed across her every curve with mouthwatering appeal. On a mumbled curse, he headed toward the coverlets, unfastening his gun belt in stride. He swung the holstered Colt away from his hips and settled the weapon on the ground.

Determined not to look at her, he dropped to his knees and reached for an animal pelt. Getting Alma away from the ogling Indian braves had been his top-priority.

He snorted, not that she was all too safe with him at the moment.

He wanted her, from her full, pouting lips to her every taste. But that was never going to happen. Once he had her situated, he'd hightail it from the teepee before things shifted into the danger zone for either of them. A cool night under the stars would not alleviate his damnable lust for her, but the distance might do wonders for his self-control. "I think you'll find this more comfortable than the floor of the cave," he said, refusing to look back.

"I'm sure I will."

Pleased he'd resisted her siren's call at the dance, Dillon tugged on the bedding until he'd crafted a berth fit for a queen...or rather, his much-too-tipsy princess. "All right, I think you're ready."

"I know I am."

Relieved, he pushed to his feet. Good. He turned to face her, and his eyes widened. An intense rush of desire ripped through him, playing hell with his resolve.

Paces away, clad only in her half-buttoned chemise and pantalets, her unpinned hair cascading in a flaxen curtain over her shoulders, Alma smiled at him.

Blood rushed straight to his groin. With a hard curse, and knowing he'd be damned come morning, his gaze cut to the flimsy linen outline of her nipples.

J-e-e-z-u-s. He clenched his fists at his sides, terrified if left unchecked, his hands would be on her, all over her, touching her everywhere. Too easily her gasps of pleasure as she writhed against him outside returned to tangle his mind.

He needed to be gone from this teepee...now. "Uh...I s-see you're ready for bed. Excellent idea." Sweat beading his brow, his body pounding with need like a battering ram, he pointed to the pile of clothing beside her. "You'll sleep better without all those trappings."

"My thoughts exactly," she whispered, her fingers continuing their slow skim down her chemise. She tipped her head sideways, and with a provocative smile, slipped free the last pearl button. On a whisper, the garment slid free, leaving her naked from the waist up. The muffled drumbeats vibrated from outside as shadows danced across her flawless skin.

Dillon couldn't move.

He couldn't breathe.

His heart pummeled his ribs in throbbing blows as every part of him begged to reach out and touch her perfection. On a hard swallow, he took in the curve of her shoulders, the slope of her breasts, the silken sweet smoothness of her skin. A tremor shook his body, then another as the hellish need for her burned him where he stood.

Three steps brought her to him, satisfaction darkening her eyes. She leaned forward, pressing her breasts against his chest.

"Don't do this, Alma," he growled.

"Do what?" she whispered, unbuttoning his shirt. "Want you?"

His hands clasped hers. "Come tomorrow, I promise you'll regret this."

"I've given this much thought...and I choose you." With a soft giggle she slid her hands free and reached for his shirt.

Savoring the slide of her fingers against his skin, his muscles bunched as she slipped free his last button. The material parted. Cool air met his heated flesh. Pulling in a rough breath, he fought to quell the fire racing through his veins. Damn the liquor for weakening his discipline, eroding his duty to protect her...even from him.

A quick push on the chambray and Alma shoved his shirt off his shoulders.

A soft giggle followed. "Before you, I'd never wanted to be with a man...like *this*." Her hands skimmed his bare chest, pausing as she flicked her fingertips across his nipples.

He hissed, unable to rip his gaze from hers. Dancing blue eyes held him captive, and a moment later, she yanked the shirt down his arms and tossed the chambray aside. Heat stormed Dillon as desire burned hot and palpable in her eyes.

She swayed against him, her soft breath feathering his lips. "Now... stop talking, and just kiss me again."

Sweet Jeezus... every single part of this was wrong, but he knew he fought a losing battle. The damnable pull across his denims commanded him to take what she offered.

On a guttural groan, Dillon closed his eyes and surrendered, crushing his mouth over hers. His heart pounded, his head spinning. Overcome by the taste of her, the scent of her, control vaporized beneath the lushness of this woman. Like a rush of demons, his hands swept down her sides to the curve of her waist. He dragged her against him.

A soft moan sounded as she responded in kind, climbing his body to get ever closer. Dillon staggered back, dropping to one knee, nipping, suckling, until her taste filled every part of him.

Mother of God...he wanted her beyond all things. Body on fire, his hands slid to her breasts, and palmed them. Soft. Warm. A perfect fit. His thumbs flicked over her nipples.

With a gasp, Alma tore free and arched beneath his touch. "Oh Dillon," she said on a throaty moan, "that feels s-so good."

Like a serenade to this moment, drumbeats echoed their bodies' response, her gasps and cries driving him wild. Passion ran rampant as his need for her nearly burst inside him. He wanted to make love to her. To make her heart sing. To make her his forever...

Forever?

Like an ice-cold bucket of water splashed in his face, reality washed over him. His eyes snapped open. *J-Jeezus. Stop. STOP!*

What was the hell was he doing? This angel belonged to another. She could never be his for even one day.

Get away from her.

His gaze bored into hers.

He wouldn't...couldn't take her innocence this way. Dillon scraped his eyes over each luscious curve, memorizing every precious part of this temptress. His jaw tightened as he surged to his feet, drawing her with him.

A frown tugged at her mouth as she frantically reached for him.

"Damnit...Alma. Stop," he snapped, stumbling backward. He held her away, his grip on her upper arms digging deeper.

"But, I-I don't want to stop," she said, a pout reclaiming her kiss-swollen lips. A sadness smoldered in her striking eyes.

Dillon eased out a shaky sigh. He wasn't as drunk as she...he damned well knew better than to touch her.

Sonofabitch! He'd spent his entire life avoiding such entanglements.

His body still aching with need, before he did something foolish like finish what she started, he settled her upon the buffalo hides, then tossed a blanket atop her nakedness. Out of sight, but forevermore in his mind.

She blinked, her eyes narrowing beneath the hazing effect of the alcohol. "D-Don't you want me?" she asked, her voice beginning to slur as she clutched the blanket to her chin.

"God, yes, Princess," he hissed, "more than you'll ever know. But, what I want

isn't important here." With each passing second she slumped deeper into the blankets.

"B-But…I wanted you to want me…"

"Getting to your fiancée is what you really want."

She wrinkled her nose. "But, h-he's nothing like you." She lowered to her elbows, peering at him. Blessedly, the blanket remained across her body. "You're s-so much stronger…and…virile…and…" her gaze drifted to the side of the teepee, her words fading as she stared at the firelight climbing the canvas wall.

Dillon scrunched his eyes to gain control while the swirling in his head subsided. The ache in his groin was another matter. He let loose a long groan. The only comfort he'd find from this damnable mess was that come morning, she probably wouldn't remember a blasted thing.

The thought protected her, but what the hell did it do for his lost soul?

On a curse, he grabbed his shirt and gun belt, unable to dislodge the boulder that clogged his throat. Three steps took him to the entrance; a glance back proved she was fading fast. "Do not leave the teepee," he rasped. "Do you understand?"

Nodding, she stretched across the animal pelts, and then tucked her hands beneath her head. Flaxen hair tumbled around her face. On a sigh, her eyelids drifted closed.

For a long moment he stared at her, aware her angel-sweet touch was as close as he would ever get to heaven. *My God… you're beautiful.*

The truth burned a hole in his heart.

On another curse Dillon pushed through the opening and strode outside. Inhaling deeply, he shoved his arms into the sleeves. She was safe. For now, but doubts lingered that he would ever outrun his need for her.

CHAPTER TWENTY-TWO

The ten mile ride down Blanca Peak took Dillon and Alma the entire day, the journey toward Fort Garland covered in complete silence.

Dillon frowned at the image of Alma, irritable as hell this morning as she had stumbled from the teepee. Hands clutching her head, she'd squinted at the rising sun before accepting the cup of coffee he'd proffered. As he'd suspected, and to her salvation, she remembered little of the previous night.

He, on the other hand, wasn't to be spared.

Not that he was going to waste time thinking about the softness of her skin, the feel of her perfect body against his, or how easily he could have sated his need in her warmth. As far as he was concerned that subject was more than closed. After a quick breakfast during which his short-tempered charge did little more than nibble at her fare, they'd said their goodbyes and then ridden from the camp.

Dillon shifted in the saddle staring at the army post shimmering on the late-afternoon horizon. Another mile separated him from settling Alma into comfort in the fort's guest quarters, except the thought of taking her to another man now turned his guts inside out. Yet, however much he wanted things to be different, he'd made the right decision in leaving her untouched.

Alma Talmadge spelled trouble in every corner of the word. She irritated him, frustrated him, and had a body that drove him insane. If he remained in her company much longer, he wasn't sure what he'd do.

He needed distance.

And soon.

Two hours later Dillon stood in the front parlor of the post commander's residence, a glass of whiskey in hand. "Thank you for arranging private quarters for Miss Talmadge, sir."

Major Filbert nodded. "My pleasure, Reed. I trust you'll be comfortable in the barracks?"

"I'll be fine. I'm used to sleeping on the ground."

The major laughed. "Ah yes, the life of an army scout." He glanced across the room toward his wife and Alma. "Laundresses aside, Susanna hasn't enjoyed the companionship of a lady in over a year." He sipped his liquor, a frown creasing his brow. "As you know, an army post doesn't offer much of a life for the finer womenfolk."

Dillon narrowed his gaze upon Alma, gut knotting. *Another reason why things wouldn't work between us.* In the subdued light glowing from the oil lamps, she beamed, laughing at something the commander's wife had shared. A moment later, her gaze fixed on his. A small smile brushed her lips...his own mouth tightened beneath the evoking taste of her.

Face tight, he looked away

"I know you've just arrived, Reed, and are probably looking to catch that stage out of Santa Fe, but I've got troopers heading southwest to Fort Defiance tomorrow. I'm sending them to reinforce the garrison that's guarding the Navajo agency. You and Miss Talmadge are welcome to ride along. From there, you can skirt the Mogollon Rim to Camp Apache, and then head on down south through the desert. Route's rather rigorous on the other side of Defiance, but overall a straighter shot to Tucson."

Dillon took a swallow of his whiskey. Two weeks on a crowded Concord winding south through New Mexico, then catching a Butterfield westward at Fort Bayard, the possibility of yet another abduction looming large all along the way? Or...twenty-eight days with fewer distractions on a direct path through a territory he knew well?

His heart squeezed. *Damnit! One's much faster. The other's more controlled.* He shoved a hand through his hair, his jaw tightening. The trail down the rim was daunting, but passable. More important, the days spent with the military would put things back into perspective for him.

Regardless, her safety came first.

I'm sticking with my earlier plan.

"Your offer's too tempting to turn down, Major. 'Sides, I've been that way before. We accept."

"Fine. You'll leave right after reveille. "

He again glanced at Alma and took another deep swig from his glass.

"By the way," the major added. "Lieutenant Vaughn's in charge of the detachment. He's an annoyingly dapper gent who graduated from West Point. Likes to feel important, so I let him."

"We've got a few junior officers like that at Fort Lowell, much to the despair of Colonel Talmadge." Dillon nodded. "Thanks for the warning."

"I'll send a message for Vaughn to join us this evening," Filbert said. "When he arrives, we can iron out the particulars."

They clinked their glasses. "Deal."

An elderly Indian stepped around the parlor's corner and announced dinner.

The major set aside his glass. "Well, ladies," he said, his arm outstretched toward his wife, "our meal awaits us. Shall we four adjourn to the other room?"

Laughing, they agreed and crossed the parlor.

With her bustle re-anchored on her backside and her ivory fan flapping up a breeze, Alma sashayed past Dillon, last evening's tipsiness long gone as she shot him a haughty look.

The memory of her soft breasts against his palm and her sweet taste burned through his mind like a torch. He tipped his glass and drained the remainder of his whiskey.

Good God, if only he could as easily forget.

***

"Thank you for everything, Susanne," Alma said, closing the front door of the commander's quarters behind her.

God bless the woman.

A bath, a light breakfast, and freshly-laundered clothing had done wonders for Alma's spirit. The last-minute dab of rose-scented perfume even returned a whisper of normalcy to her world. With her hair swept into a perfect coiffure and her hat, albeit a bit crumpled from time in her traveling bag, pinned into place atop her curls, she stepped to the edge of the front porch.

Beneath clear skies, the far-away mountain peaks scraped an azure canvas like mammoth ship sails. Alma scanned her surroundings. The rough adobe barracks built for cavalry and infantry were sparse at best and spread out in a long, brownish-pink line. Workrooms, storage facilities and private residences also crafted from adobe housed teamsters and laundresses employed by the army to work with the Indians. To the northeast of the fort, weathered wooden crosses stood like silent sentinels above the remains of those who had perished on duty.

In stark contrast to the beauty of the Rocky Mountains she'd traveled through on horseback with Dillon, austere was an apt description for this remote track of land. She took a deep breath and then slowly exhaled. Chin high, Alma braced herself to face this next phase of her journey.

Commotion across the way had her turning.

Sunlight glinted off cavalry sabers as the detail of soldiers waited for their order to mount.

Her gaze narrowed on Dillon. He stood beside Lieutenant Vaughn, their height similar, but any further likeness ended there. Last evening, she'd met the officer. His well-groomed refinement and flaxen-haired paleness proved the polar opposite of the scout's dark hair and somber mood. A pompous dandy if ever there was one, and yet, the lieutenant's ever-so-doting attention on her seemed to tense Dillon's jaw.

Good. She smiled and swished open her parasol, angling the diminutive canopy to block the rising sun.

Every eye turned her way as she walked toward the men. Her gaze, however, burned only into Dillon's. Glimpses of their passion the night of the Bear Dance twisted around her heart. The searing pressure of his lips upon hers. The warmth of his hands on her breasts.

Alma looked away.

Better to let him believe she remembered nothing than to admit her reckless behavior and embarrassing joy at the moments she'd spent in his arms. The way she'd trembled against him, begging him to kiss her, imploring him to...to...

The woozy rush of blood warmed her face. Nothing in her behavior that night had been acceptable by society's morals. Nothing! She swallowed and blamed the heat across her cheeks upon this newest twist in her journey west. Her slow and steady breathing doused the burn for the scout, and by slow degrees, control returned.

"Ah, Miss Talmadge, how wonderful to see you again," the lieutenant said, stepping around Dillon.

She slid her gloved palm against the officer's extended hand. His oh-so-chaste kiss across her fingertips only forced another grating comparison.

"Thank you, Lieutenant. I am eager to begin our journey to Fort Defiance. I trust I'll be safe under your care."

"It is my honor to escort you." Sky-blue eyes held hers and the squeeze across her fingertips spoke volumes. "Never doubt that I will protect you with my life."

Alma swore she heard Dillon's gritty sigh.

She bit back a smile. Even in these wastelands the laws of society ruled. Alma well-knew the courting signs that the lieutenant shared. She'd played this game for years in a hundred ballrooms back east. Subtle. Predictable.

His cat.

Her mouse.

From the top of his hat to the tips of his boots, Alma itemized the lieutenant's assets. Tall in stature. Slim hipped. Delicate features. When she measured this man against Dillon's raw masculinity, the lieutenant fell leagues short. Worse, the anticipated spark she would've welcomed two weeks earlier had failed to ignite.

And not because of her betrothal to Lord Green, but from the remembered feel of Dillon's callused hands upon her breasts. Her heart tripping even faster, she glanced sideways.

All because of you…

With his hat pulled low, Dillon stood arms crossed, his eyes narrowed upon her with a fierce glare. Without a single word uttered in her direction, he turned and stalked to his horse.

Her heart sank, and she pressed her lips together to ward off a foolish response to his blatant cut.

Lieutenant Vaughn tipped his hat, reclaiming her attention. "I've arranged proper seating for you in the back."

Alma offered a thin smile as he gestured to the closest wagon.

"'Twill be more comfortable for you than sitting atop a hard bench…" he leaned closer and the scent of hair pomade wafted over her. "Or, God forbid, straddling a horse. Had I been with you, my dear, I would've given you the animal and gladly walked the length of America beside you."

She doubted this coxcomb had walked far enough to even scuff the soles of his finely-polished footwear. Nonetheless, at that precise moment she appreciated his aplomb. She dropped open her fan slats and waved the delicate ivory before her. "I'm moved by your kind expression, Lieutenant. But, Mister Reed is still recovering from a grave wound. We did the best we could possibly do considering the circumstances."

"Well, yes…I understand." He tapped his boot heels together and issued a quick bow her way before motioning to the closest soldier. "Kindly assist our honored guest into place."

"Yes, sir," the young private replied.

Minutes later, amidst a collection of canvas-covered crates, blankets and cooking gear, Alma settled upon a chair in the back of the wagon, thankful at least for the added cushions. The rough wooden box was the extreme opposite of the comforts found in her father's elegant, cradle-sprung Brougham. At the clop of an approaching horse, she tipped her parasol, masking her surprise as Dillon drew his gelding alongside the wagon.

"You should be on a horse, but what the hell do I know?" A smirk brushed his mouth as he took in every aspect of her throne-like seating. "The trail's gonna knock you crazy sitting in here."

The wagon rolled forward and lurched, then settled to another stop. Alma cringed. The hours of hard travel ahead promised little except a sore backside. Staring at him, a lump lodged in her throat. As if a rutty track were the worst of her problems. Without him even aware of the complications he'd created, this man had tangled her carefully laid-out marriage plans to Lord Green.

Her breath caught as she stared at Dillon…wanting him…not with the light-hearted, foolish flutters that made a woman swoon, but a soul-deep need that stole her breath. At that moment she wanted nothing more than to climb over the wagon's edge and slip back in front of him on his saddle.

Instead, her words tumbled out in a thin whisper, "I'll be fine, Dillon. Thank you."

His gaze bored into hers. "I'm serious. Grab ahold of something." The order in his voice underscored his disapproval.

Hurt cut through her, and she nodded. For him, nothing had changed. From the moment he'd laid eyes on her he'd seen her as someone he'd been burdened with protecting.

An obligation.

Duty.

Nothing more.

Hand trembling, she clasped her gloved fingers against the side of the rig. "I-I promise I shall hold on tight."

"Good." His saddle creaked as he leaned closer, his expression darkening. "'Cause I don't want a damned thing more happenin' to you until I've delivered you to your dukedom." He tapped his spurs to the gelding's flanks, and cantered toward the front of the column of men.

CHAPTER TWENTY-THREE

The evening of their first stop, Alma crawled from the wagon aching in places she never knew existed. By the arrival of the second night, she could barely walk. At noon the following day, she'd had enough jolting and vacated her throne in the wagon's bed in favor of the wooden seat beside the driver.

Except, through the next day's never-ending battering, the bench proved no better. The watering stops were few and far between, and three nights with little sleep had left her nerves in shreds.

The final night of their trip to Fort Defiance found Alma near tears. She'd seen Dillon only from a distance during the days, and the nights swallowed him into their shadows. Unlike Lieutenant Vaughn who, much to her frustration, was never far from her side.

Now, perched upon a campstool near the fire, she sat within a cluster of blue-coated soldiers as each group took shifts on guard duty.

Alma stared into a bowl of some sort of bean concoction the lieutenant had delivered. He settled onto a seat beside her, dropped his hat upon the ground, and began to eat. Should she tell him she wished to be alone? Would it make any difference? As the muffled conversations melded around her, she absentmindedly stirred her soup. Tired of the soldiers' bland fare, she longed for a lovely Matelot. Alma allowed the savory composition of fish and wine sauce to linger on memory's tongue. Even a bountiful portage, like the stew she'd learned how to make in the cave, would be a welcomed repast.

She spooned up a tiny portion of beans and swallowed. Her stomach roiled against the taste. Memories of the pleasurable night spent beneath the stars by Holbrook Creek in only Dillon's company forced another lengthy sigh from her lips.

With a grimace, Alma set aside the bowl. She stared at the campfire, her gaze following a smoky tendril swirling upward. Thick clouds obscured the majestic canopy that had captured her breath that night.

"Not hungry?" the lieutenant asked.

"No, not really."

"I understand." He scraped his spoon across the tin plate to capture his final few bites, then issued an apology as his bowl rattled to the ground. "Sorry this is not up to Delmonico's standards."

Her eyebrow arched. "You've been to Delmonico's?"

"I'm from Long Island, so yes, I've been there many times. I always order their famous steak." He smiled as he patted his hand over his sticky, matted hair.

"Whenever father and I visit New York," she said with a smile, "We stop in for their Baked Alaska. Their *chef de cuisine* always makes me a special serving." She shifted aside her bowl with her foot.

"Ahh, yes…that is quite delectable." He took a sip from his coffee. "Did you know the dessert was created a half-dozen years ago to celebrate the purchase of Alaska?"

"Imagine that," she said, not wishing to inform him she already knew.

"And how about his other signature dish, Lobster Newburg?" Lieutenant Vaughn asked.

Alma nodded as she readjusted her bustle, attempting to work out the kinks in her aching back. "Absolutely, that butter and sherry sauce is heaven sent."

"True, but there's speculations Ranhofer didn't actually create that recipe. His fight to claim the fame still lingers." He settled his hand on her knee, a smug look crossing his features.

"In actuality, 'twas Chef Fauchere who breathed life into that delicacy."

"The crazy Frenchman?" she asked, dislodging his hold with a much-practiced leg shift. She'd heard of the noted chef, but hadn't known about the squabble over the dish.

"Yes ma'am," Vaughn stated with a glint in his eye. "At the Hotel Fauchere in upstate Pennsylvania." He straightened and stretched his legs. "Had a platter-full in his restaurant many times after hunting in the Poconos while on break from West Point."

Alma offered another tight smile. "Well, it seems we do have a few things in common after all, Lieutenant." The socially unacceptable deed of sitting alone under the stars with a man may have been waved due to her extreme circumstance of traveling to Fort Lowell, but inside Alma struggled to continue her pleasantries.

"Indeed, we do." He leaned toward her, infiltrating her senses with the nauseating stench of hair pomade. "Our love of good food and elegant dining, for one. And please call me Jonathan."

"I don't believe that is necessary. Lieutenant works just fine for me." Alma bit back another groan and inhaled, her gaze skimming over the soldiers engaged in conversations.

"I'm going to pour another mug of coffee, my dear. May I interest you in a fresh cup?"

She shook her head. "I'm planning to retire, so I shall pass." Alma glanced at the back of the uncomfortable monstrosity of a wagon now-boasting its nightly bonnet. Every evening upon making camp, a detail of soldiers diligently added the curved, canvas topper for her privacy. Of course, the rough pallet could never be a substitute for her elegant bedroom back east, but she was glad for the gesture.

Her gaze shifted to the lieutenant. "I appreciate all the kindness everyone has afforded me during this journey."

"I-I enjoy taking care of you and would welcome the opportunity to do so every day…if allowed."

No matter how kind he was, she had no interest in the man. And besides, she was an engaged woman. "That's gallant of you, but if you'll excuse me, I shall say goodnight."

He shifted, leaning toward her again. "B-Before you retire, perhaps you'll consider a stroll with me around the camp?"

Her frustrations with the lieutenant's unwanted advances built. What kind of cads were the army employing these days? Avoiding eye contact, she shook her head and stared across the top of the flickering flames. "No, thank you." Forcing a smile to her lips, she stood, straightening her dress.

He shoved to his feet, knocking over the campstool. "B-But..." he stammered, catching her arm to stop her from turning away.

Alma tried to break free; his grasp remained firm. "This is our final night of the journey. I was...was...hoping we might spend some time together."

Panic threaded through her...*Oh Dillon, where are you?*

***

From the edge of the encampment, Dillon eyed the near-empty flask dangling from his fingers, irritated that even in the shadows, the subtle laughter between Alma and the lieutenant had reached him. Every night since leaving Fort Garland he'd kept his eye on her.

And every night he'd ached for her.

On a curse, he shoved a hand through his long hair and then resettled his hat before draping an arm across his raised knee. She and the man were inseparable. *What the hell does she see in this dandy?*

Dillon leaned back against the tree. Wasn't any one but him concerned about her welfare if her fiancé got wind of all this? And surely word would reach him, with so many officers and men hanging around him.

In a futile attempt to squelch the jealousy sliding through his veins, he closed his eyes and took another swig. What did it matter what he thought? Her laughter at whatever that pompous ass had said proved her acceptance of him.

Another expletive spilled past his lips.

He should've known better than to believe, even for a moment, that she was interested in him. Hadn't she proved her fickle behavior with that drunken Bear Dance escapade? "She wants me, my ass," he mumbled under his breath. High-browed society snobs…cheaters, every damned one of them.

Just like my mother.

The recall of racing into his Texas home and finding her wrapped around a man who wasn't Pa lay seared in his childhood memories forever. Worse, he well-knew Caleb was the end result of that tryst, but Dillon never told his father. Or his brother.

No, that dirty little secret would die with him.

Dillon buried the dark thought and slowly opened his eyes. His gaze skimmed across the encampment, then farther out across the desert. Good God, he needed something…anything in a life so lonely a coyote would mourn at the emptiness of it, and in his desperation, he'd obviously created a fantasy out of Alma.

But he'd been wrong to think their link was anything more. Horribly, painfully wrong. And the obvious upcoming tryst now unfolding in agonizing detail near the campfire between her and Lieutenant Vaughn, drove a spike of regret through his gut. Sonofabitch, he should've just taken what she'd offered him in the teepee.

Remembrance of the soft, supple lushness of her breast had him making a fist. He wished he didn't know now what he hadn't known before that night. Another mumbled groan followed, as did another swig of whiskey.

All this worthless ruminating was akin to torture.

He glanced back at Alma and the lieutenant. Except from where he sat, he could see they didn't look quite so friendly now.

His heart issued an extra thump when she speared the officer with a hot look that scoured him from head to toe. And then, the bastard snagged a tight hold on her forearm.

Dillon straightened, his leg lowering.

He stashed the flask and climbed to his feet, concern shifting to anger. *To hell with keepin' my distance.* His gaze peeled off Alma and resettled on

Vaughn. Before he could take his first step, however, the lieutenant released his grip, then grabbed up his plumed hat. A second later, he stalked away.

Head high, Alma swept across the clearing, stepped up onto an overturned crate, and disappeared into the back of the now-covered wagon. She was safe, unlike that bastard who'd dared touch her.

Fury pounding each step, Dillon strode down the hill and cut off Vaughn.

Surprise flickered on the lieutenant's face, and he pulled up short when Dillon blocked his path. "Reed, I-I didn't see you out here."

"Need to have a word with you," he growled.

Smile dimming, the man stiffened. "You've been short on words this whole trip."

Dillon stepped between the campfire's light and Vaughn, leaving the bastard in his shadow. His lips smirked upward. "But I've noticed you haven't."

"W-What are you talking about?"

"Your nightly interludes with Miss Talmadge."

The man gave a nervous chuckle. "Ahh yes…that…Well, I think she's quite a lovely lady."

"What you think is irrelevant." Dillon took a menacing step closer. "She's Colonel Talmadge's niece, and she's been assigned to me. That means I've got a vested interest in her welfare."

Vaughn stepped backward. "Her welfare is being well taken care of now -- you needn't worry."

"Oh, I'm not worried," he said, his voice ice. "I'm just letting you know your days of sniffing around her like a rutting hound are finished."

"I-I beg your pardon?"

Even in the firelight Dillon saw his face flush.

"And in case she failed to mention this, I will. She's to marry an English earl upon our arrival at Fort Lowell, so that puny *two of a kind* you've been dealing out every night for her around the campfire is no match to his *royal flush*."

The lieutenant's eyes narrowed. "I am merely being sociable and treating her like the lady she is, which is far better than how I've seen you treat her."

Dillon's jaw tightened. Hell yes, he'd let his own jealousies claim the better of his judgement, but he was knee deep in this shit now. He shifted again, his boot tip bumping against the lieutenant's fancy footwear. "Here's my advice," he said between clenched teeth. "And, if you have half the brains of a jackass, I suggest you take it. Until we reach the fort tomorrow, steer clear of her. Got it?"

Thunder rumbled overhead.

"Now see here. I don't like your tone…."

Dillon drilled his finger into Vaughn's chest, pushing him back another step. "Then I'll make this crystal clear. I don't need some West Point turkey-cock like you causing her any more grief than she's already endured on this trip. Understand?"

For a fleeting moment the man puffed up, then as quickly he frowned. "Calm down, Reed. I didn't realize you'd staked your claim on the woman. I-I'll back off."

Staked a claim? Hell's fire, he'd vaulted clear over the boundary line in defending her honor. He nearly laughed out loud. His thoughts as to what he'd like to do to Alma now ran the glacial opposite of pure. He wanted his hands on her body, wanted his name falling from her lips when she lost her innocence.

Furious she'd driven him to this madness, he poured out his frustrations over the inept half-wit fool enough to still be within easy reach. "Just make sure you do…or the next time, I'll make sure for you." With a crunch of his boot heels, Dillon stormed past the man and into the night.

The next morning, Dillon drained the last murky brown drop from his cup, and then handed the mug to the private. "Thanks, Johnson. You make damn good coffee."

"I've had lots of practice," the grizzled soldier replied as he finished stowing the tinware.

"Your brew keeps me going. That's what counts." Dillon pulled on his gloves and settled his gaze on Chuska Peak hugging the horizon. The fort waited on the other side of the pass that sliced through the red-rocked behemoth. He glanced up at the darkening clouds. Streams of sunlight leaked through the billows like slivered strands of gold. They'd probably be chasing rain most of the day. As it was, thunder had kept him awake half the night.

Who am I trying to fool?

On a mumbled curse, he swung into the saddle. Flaxen hair and a perfect body had more to do with his restlessness then the weather.

He rolled his shoulders, then glanced toward the wagon. Though the canvas bonnet had been stowed, Alma's seat remained empty. Her bustle, on the other hand, lay secured to a side pole, and the snow white layers ruffled like a lopsided bell in the dawn's warm breeze.

Dillon scanned the soldiers maneuvering their mounts into position, then skimmed along the plateaus and red-rock mesas. Saltbush and sagebrush rustled in the high desert breeze.

Where the hell are you? Her morning ablutions shouldn't take this long. A movement caught his eye and his breath eased out.

The top of the peach-colored parasol bobbed along between the lines of horsemen.

Seconds later, Alma limped into view and headed straight toward him. He studied her through narrowed eyes, her usual "get-up-and-go" demeanor long gone. She shuffled around to face him, her gloved fingers fidgeting with the ivory handle. "Good morning, Dillon."

"Morning." A beguiling scent of roses filled his lungs. There wasn't a damned hole deep enough for him to crawl in to get away from his want of her. He breathed in sharply, fixing his gaze on the pale, purple mountains hugging the landscape before him. "We're getting ready to head out. Shouldn't you be back on your throne?"

"Well, yes. About that…" Warm, rain-scented air ruffled the silky wisps that had escaped her chignon as she stepped closer. Alma rested her hand upon his leg.

With a hard ache, his arousal strained behind his denims.

"You were right regarding my seating arrangements, Dillon," she continued, ignorant of his less than proper…condition. "I am purely miserable."

In a pathetic effort to find relief, he shifted in his saddle. "Be thankful, then," he said, his voice graveled. He glared at the sun streaks jumping the desert buttes. "We'll be at the fort by dinnertime."

"I'm so sorry, but I don't t-think I can stand another moment in that wagon." He glanced down. The spark in her eyes had dulled, replaced by a sliver of vulnerability. "May I ride with you?" she whispered, more like a plea than a request.

This woman spelled danger to every scrap of sanity he had left. Dillon searched his mind for a million reasons to say no. Not a blasted one appeared. *Sonofabitch.* He tugged his hat's brim lower, and yet, God help him, the corner of his mouth kicked up. "I'm thinking Lieutenant Vaughn might not be pleased."

"I don't give a flying fig what that dolt thinks. I'm just glad he kept his distance this morning."

That made two of them. If the bastard touched her again, he'd find himself picking his ass up out of the dirt. And if he was lucky, Dillon would stop there.

Brows puckering, she clenched the folds of her skirt between nervous fingers. "Now don't make me beg, you ruthless troll. Need I remind you it isn't gentlemanly?"

"Gentlemanly?" He snorted, his heart tripping faster. Another grin twitched his lips. "I'm a stranger to chivalry, and you damn-well know it."

He caught a flash of her straight, white teeth before she nipped back her smile. She snapped her parasol closed and held up a gloved hand. "Well?"

"You're a bossy little thing." Ignoring the subtle throb in his shoulder, Dillon swept her up and settled her into place in front of him.

Several nearby soldiers laughed. "Keep a firm hold on her this time, Reed," the closest one said. Others nodded in agreement. "She'd be hard to replace out here."

He nodded. *Replace?* Dillon swallowed hard, doubtful such a feat could be achieved. He'd met many women in his lifetime, but none had irritated or tangled him up with such expertise. This exasperating woman would set a priest to drinking.

From the front of the column, the command to move out sounded. Dillon slid his arms around Alma's corseted waist with an all-too-familiar ease. He wove the reins through his gloved fingers.

Horses snorted. Brass bridle rings chinked. A bugle's sharp trill punctuated the cloud-covered morning. The uniformed riders trekked forward, and Dillon fell into line behind the wagon. On a sigh, Alma laid her folded sunshade across her lap, then burrowed closer against him.

He'd missed her soft, sweet curves. "What took you so damned long?"

"Now don't be vulgar, Mister Reed."

He chuckled…and fifteen minutes later his stubborn little debutante fell fast asleep in his arms.

CHAPTER
TWENTY-FOUR

Henry wiped his mouth with a napkin, then laid aside the elegant dinner cloth. Even in Tucson, some enjoyed the finer things. A most-redeeming aspect. With his finger tapping the side of his half-filled whiskey glass, he leaned back in the chair.

Beyond the front window of the hotel, the stage from El Paso blocked the street, dust from its arrival settling in the half-dried mud. From atop the coach, the sweat-drenched driver tossed down valises, cases, and portmanteaus. Several additional boxes lay stacked across the boardwalk near the passengers.

Anger thrummed through Henry. Again, his fiancée had failed to show.

Ill-mannered wench.

Four days before when her shipping trunks arrived without Alma Talmadge in tow, his anxiety increased tenfold. Every evening since, he'd waited for his betrothed to step from the daily stage.

And every evening failed to bring him his soon-to-be bride.

He grimaced as each tick of the nearby hall clock further closed his window of opportunity. As the days slipped by, his financial situation deteriorated. In a month, his mountain of gambling debts owed in London would come due.

A shadow fell across him, drawing his attention. His eyes widened and he smothered a gasp. Fury, nonetheless, ignited. He surged to his feet. "What in the hell are you doing here?"

Simon Bell smiled and reached for the glass of whiskey. "Relax, my friend." He lifted the tumbler. "The job you hired me to do is complete." He tossed back the liquor, gave a sharp inhale, and then returned the empty glass to the table...upside down. Another smile tipped his lips as he leaned forward. "Talmadge now rests on the bottom of Boston Harbor."

***

An hour later...

At the creak of his door opening, Colonel Talmadge glanced up from his paperwork. His breath caught. With a smile, he shoved to his feet as his daughter sashayed into the room. "Good God, Pamela, I'd no idea you'd be arriving this afternoon. I could've met you at the stage."

"Nonsense," she said, laughing. "The walk to the fort wasn't long a'tall, Papa. Besides, San Francisco was purely delightful. I'm still floating on clouds." With a well-practiced spin, she asked, "What do you think of one of my new gowns? 'Tis a wine-colored silk dupioni and feels absolutely luscious." As Pamela slowly turned, she tapped her gloved-fingers on the ivory-colored trim at her wrist. "There's even Venice lace. I was beyond thrilled the dressmakers could finish this in time for me to travel." She gave him a smile, then settled back on the heels of her leather slippers. "And Papa..." She pulled out a small, elongated package from her reticule. "Here." She lay the paper-wrapped item atop his afternoon work. "I brought you a gift. They call this delicacy Ghirardelli Chocolate."

"Chocolate?" His eyebrows rose. "I've heard about this, but never tasted any."

"Well now you can. In the city, chocolate is all the rage." She patted her bulging reticule. "I've even brought back a bar for Albert. I do believe my husband will approve." Another lilting laugh followed as she swept around the desk and laid a kiss atop his balding head.

He chuckled. "Thank you, my dearest. I shall relish every bite."

"Enjoy it with your evening whiskey, Papa. The chocolatiers say the treat goes best with finer spirits." Her expression warmed as she peered at him square in the face. "And would you look at this. You've got new spectacles."

"Yes." Thaddeus readjusted the specs. "Finally broke down and ordered me a pair out of El Paso."

"Well, they look quite dignified. I'm glad you stopped being stubborn, especially since you were blind as a bat." She moved to the long window and peered outside. "Speaking of husbands, have you seen Albert? I'd love to let him know I'm home."

Talmadge shook his head. "His patrol rode out this morning. Chasin' the damned renegades again." He leaned back in the chair. "So, you might as well come for dinner tonight. You can share the details of your shopping trip."

She spun to face him. "I'll be delighted. I had a wonderful time in San Francisco, but Rosa's endless chatter all the home has given me a splitting headache. It's been seven years since I've been here, and I still don't understand my housekeeper's Mexican gibberish."

"I'm glad you at least had her as a companion on this trip. By the way," Thaddeus said, his gaze following his daughter as she eased into the chair opposite his desk. "Your cousin should be here in a couple of weeks to marry her earl."

"What?" Pamela edged to the rim of the chair, her caged underthings rustling beneath her bright dress.

"Oh, that's right..." Thaddeus dropped the message to the desk. "You'd left for San Francisco before her plans changed."

"But, I-I thought we were going to Boston this fall for their wedding?"

"That was the original idea, but your uncle has made different arrangements for Alma. Now, she's to be married in Tucson."

Her lower lip curled into a pout. "But...why? I was so looking forward to the trip back East."

"I'm sorry, sweet pea. You know your Uncle Charles. He likes to change things up at the last moment." Thaddeus tapped the paper he'd received an hour earlier via courier. "Just got this message from up north at Fort Garland, though." He peered at his daughter over his wire-rimmed glasses. "Dillon says he's rerouting them--"

"Dillon?" Her eyes widened. "W-Why is Dillon with Alma?"

"Well, since Dillon was back east delivering a legislative packet for the governor, I assigned him the job of escorting her to the fort."

"I see." She leaned back and reached for her fan, dropping open the tortoiseshell slats. "I can just imagine the enjoyment they both must be having right about now. He with his cool and distant detachment of life... and Alma, so out of place in those austere surroundings." Her fanning lifted the wisps of hair around her face. "Well, if nothing else, at least she's in capable hands."

"My thoughts, exactly." He tapped the paper. "His message was dated last week, but Dillon decided to take a longer route home."

"Longer?" She blinked. "Why?"

"He didn't say." Thaddeus tightened his lips. Telling Pamela about the threats to her cousin's safety would do nothing but cause her to worry. "Whatever his reasons, I'm sure the change was necessary. Regardless, he expects them to arrive near the end of June, give or take a few days."

"Does Lord Green know of this change in plans?"

Talmadge smiled. "The earl is none-too-keen on Dillon's involvement to begin with, I'm afraid." He chuckled. "I'll let him know in the morning. No harm done 'til then."

In a swish of dupioni silk, Pamela rose to her feet, another smile wreathing her face. "Oh Papa, I can't wait to see Alma again. Imagine how difficult this must all be for her. She's so fragile and helpless."

"She's not like you, my dearest, that's for sure."

"We must have a soiree for her when she arrives. I know Albert will not object."

"That'll be just fine ..."

"And we'll hold the gala at the hotel. Why, I'll even create the invitations this evening. I do so hope Callie and Jackson...and Gus...can attend, too. If I remember correctly, they're delivering horses here soon. Oh, and we mustn't forget the Eschevons." She tapped her lips with the pad of her fingertip. "Although Roberto has been feeling rather poorly of late." Shaking off her concern, she smiled. "Regardless, Dillon can come, too. I mean, since he's been Alma's escort and all."

Thaddeus frowned at the prospect of sharing the sad update involving the wealthy Eschevons, one of the first settlers in the territory whose vast track of land bumped up next to Jackson and Callie's spread. "I'm so sorry, my dear. Roberto passed away while you were gone. I went to his funeral in your absence."

Grief darkened her gaze, and she set her hand upon the edge of the chair. "Oh no! I must pay Carlotta a visit. What will she do now with all that acreage and no husband?"

"She still has family in Mexico, but you go pay her a visit and comfort her. She'll like that, I know." He stood, walked to her side and slipped his arm around her corseted waistline, leading her to the door. "Go make all the plans, my dear...I, however, must get back to work. I'll see you tonight at dinner."

"Of course, Papa. I have so much to do now. I shall see you soon." With a kiss to his cheek, Pamela disappeared into the hallway.

***

Alma's introduction to Fort Defiance arrived without fanfare. They rounded a bend at the base of a soaring butte and emerged onto a flat land the color of sandalwood. The stronghold spread out before her and blended into the high desert, little contrast existing between the dry earth, the mountains, and the military outpost nestled on the edge of nowhere.

According to Dillon, on the long side of the L-shaped compound lay a line of low barracks, kitchens, and latrines. On the short side emerged simple one-story log and sod buildings. Behind those dwellings, an assortment of small tents sat like snowflakes against a brown canvas.

She'd expected anything but this desolation.

An open field claimed the center of the garrison, a tall, wooden staff dominating one end. At the top flew the American flag. To the right, livestock filled stables and corrals.

Everywhere Alma looked she saw Indians. Young, old, all dressed in colorful garb, their dark hair worn loose or in braids.

"They call themselves *Diné*," Dillon explained, "but the white man refers to them as the Navajo. After years of fighting, this tribe has finally accepted life on the reservation."

"Why are they here...at the fort?"

"The post has been converted into the Indian Agency and supports the government's Navajo treaty signed several years ago. Fort Defiance now provides schooling and supplies to the *Diné*."

"I will never understand these Indian issues."

"Treaties are complicated," he agreed. "Because of that, I'm afraid the Indians will always struggle."

The troops on the post greeted them as they rode in. Near the quartermaster's office, orders to halt the column rang out. Everyone stopped, and the men dismounted.

As he walked past, the lieutenant barely gave Alma a passing glance. *I'm so relieved.*

After saying goodbye to their escorts, Dillon ushered her into a single-room adobe dwelling.

"What is this?"

"Set aside for visitors," he explained. "You'll sleep here tonight." After a thorough security check of the musty chambers, he headed for the door. "I'll make sure your meal is sent over."

"Y-You're leaving?"

"Don't worry, I won't be far."

On a sigh, Alma nodded, then settled in for the night...a small, rickety-built bed and lopsided-table with a single chair her only companions. Ten minutes later, a knock on the cabin door found a private holding out her dinner tray. With a mumbled thank you, she accepted the offering, relocked the rough, weathered panel, and dined alone.

Staring down at her half-eaten meal, Alma sighed. The cabin was sparsely furnished, yet she felt suffocated. She missed her usual evening banter over dinner, missed the clean, freshness of the great outdoors, the breathtaking canopy of stars, the crackling sounds and smells of a well-built campfire. But most of all, she missed Dillon. A restless night followed, and at dawn, Alma arose, hurriedly dressed, and headed for the stable as planned.

Dillon stood beside two horses, a full sack of supplies draped behind his bedroll. Near his now-scuffed boots, another saddle waited. He made short work of hoisting the leather across the closest animal. A flutter of excitement skimmed her breasts. This man personified heat and hardness and she was so happy to see him again. She drew nearer and he lifted his head, dark eyes locking on her. A grin pulled crooked across his lips. "Mornin', Princess."

She tossed back a tiny smile. "Hello."

Sweet poison sluiced through her veins. *Oh how I craved his smile.* Alma squelched the rush of warmth, and yet the intimate areas she kept hidden beneath layers of cloth blazed with a reminder of their night in the teepee. She gulped again. His breathing, on the other hand, remained steady.

Her social repute where he was concerned lay in tatters, but Alma didn't care one whit. *Shocking. Insatiable. Unquenchable.*

Forbidden words that never before held meaning now clouded her mind this morning. Puzzlement tightened her features as she tucked her parasol beneath her arm. "Am I not riding on the same horse with you?"

Her question hung thick in the air.

A long pause later, Dillon bent and checked the saddle cinch. "You'll be riding this horse over the Mogollon." His shirt clung tight against his form, outlining solid muscles.

Muscles she well-remembered caressing.

Alma tamped down a smile. "What's a Mogollon?"

He peered from beneath his hat, scanning her from head to foot. "Part of the Colorado Plateau. The mountain range." He readjusted the stirrups on her saddle to adapt their length to her smaller size. "Two-hundred miles of limestone escarpment cuts east to west straight through the heart of the territory." He walked around, lifting the horse's front legs one at a time, examined the iron nailed onto the animal's hooves to ensure no rocks or other objects that could lame the horse were embedded beneath. "There's no going around the rim…or I would."

"I'm not that good a rider."

"You've endured worse. Crossing the Rockies, facing bandits, taking on a wolf, and after every one, you've come out on the other side smiling." His gaze met hers, and he winked. "'Sides, you're fearless for a Boston debutante, right?"

She lifted her chin. "That I am…and don't you forget it, you unsocialized beast."

A smile kicked up on his all-too-handsome face, and Alma giggled, too aware of her quickening heartbeat. She pulled on her white gloves. At least she was out of that horrific wagon. "How far to our next stop?"

After a final inspection, he lowered the last leg of the horse. "Once we're across the rim, we'll follow the White River 'til we get to Camp Apache." He shrugged. "We should arrive sometime next week."

"Well…riding the Mogollon sounds far different from riding the pastures around father's estate." Nerves jumpy, she patted the gelding on the rump. "So I'd appreciate you checking back every once in a while just to make sure I'm still in the saddle."

Dillon riveted his gaze on hers and stepped closer.

Cast in his shadow, Alma held her breath as his gloved hands slid around her waist. Heat burned in his eyes, igniting another flash of desire.

Not anxiety.

Need.

"I'll check on you, Princess," he drawled, his cool charm enticing. "Count on it."

"I--I…"

His half-grin stole her breath. "Now don't get all flustered, I'm just liftin' you into the saddle." With ease he settled her across sun-warmed leather.

She whooshed open her parasol and counted. One...two...three... four... Control waited at the midway point of ten.

Dillon swung into his saddle and then glanced back over his shoulder. "The mule path we're following over the rim is well-traveled. Still, I'll take things nice and slow...can't have you ruffled before your date with destiny."

My date with destiny. Her throat closed as reality returned, dredging up an unwanted moment with her fiancé amidst the roses in her Boston garden.

"My dearest, I am off to Washington D.C. to discuss my assignment out west," the earl whispered as he offered her a perfect bow. "I will telegraph you as soon as I arrive."

The envy of her unmarried friends since her betrothal to him, Alma's social invitations were never-ending. "But...when will I see you again?"

"August, most likely. Upon my return, I promise we shall wed in your beautiful rose garden." He brushed a kiss upon her hand and departed.

The thudding ache intensified as Alma swirled back to the present. Other memories filled her mind like a smothering fog. The unbridled happiness at being courted by an Englishman, her father's contentment, her horror at being sent off on a train bound westward with an arrogant beast as her only companion.

To her date with destiny. Oh yes, one nearing with every step. Except the flames of desire for the earl seemed a distant flicker now, if the feeling ever even existed between her and Lord Green at all.

Her breathing hitched as her horse plodded behind Dillon. What did she really know about her fiancé?

Nothing.

As for the scout, two things were certain: The high-tension attraction toward him grew deeper, more dangerous, with every breath.

Neither was she in a hurry to become the earl's wife.

Alma's lips thinned. This journey was somehow transforming her from a frightened child afraid to take chances into a woman of confidence. Not from her father's wealth or power, or from her betrothal to an Englishman but from a growing belief in her own self.

She scanned Dillon's broad shoulders, the length of dark hair falling over his collar, his solid, sure presence. His gruff words along the way had only emphasized her own lack of life skills. Cultured talents, she had those down pat…but a competence of life, *that* was where she had floundered. And somehow, he must've known. She'd pushed him in fear. He'd pushed back harder with expectation. He made her stand on her own two feet, and overcome challenges unheard of before in her oh-so-sheltered life.

The gathered-and-tied bustle bumped against her knee with each step the gelding made in her journey. She smiled and resettled the fashionable item, tightening further the rope that held it secure to the saddle. On the outside, she'd changed little, still favoring the role she played in society. A lifestyle that had truly defined her…and still did. Never would she forego her appreciation for fashion, no matter how many times Dillon Reed grumbled.

A flush covered her cheeks and she raised her face, inhaling deeply. She scanned the transforming landscape. Just like the country, changes were happening inside her. No longer did she need a husband to feel important. Rather, she needed a man to love, to care for, to share in the good and the tough times along her journey through life.

Despite the high-desert air brushing her face, lifting her tresses, wrapping her in an ever-evolving clime…a calm and mellow understanding embraced Alma. Decision made, she nudged her mount closer to Dillon's. At her next stop she would telegraph her father and advise him that, for the moment at least, she'd changed her mind about marriage.

CHAPTER
TWENTY-FIVE

With each passing hour, the dust-ridden mesas around them shifted into a sweeping scope of pines. As Dillon led the way over the escarpment, forested peaks soaring thousands of feet above them intermingled with red-rock canyons lush in vegetation, cascades, and emerald pools of water. Along the base, the White River, more a twisting, rock-strewn creek than a wide channel, cut through the Mogollon's limestone via passes and corridors to create a narrow, natural passageway down the rim.

On the evening of the third day, they made camp in a shady pocket near plenty of water and firewood. A herd of white-tailed deer grazed in the distance while Dillon staked their horses in the small meadow, then set about creating a fire.

With only venison and desiccated vegetables to eat as they'd trekked down the steepest part of the rim, tonight, nestled in the shadows of the half-way point, Dillon decided to provide Alma a bounty comparable to society standards. *Maybe, if luck were on his side.* He stepped from the edge of the campfire and smiled at her. "Every so often, toss a log on this."

"That I can do," she replied, scooting closer to the dancing flames.

If nothing else, his little responsibility was no longer being difficult. Now, she seemed eager to help. Stifling a chuckle and doubting he'd ever begin to figure her out, Dillon pulled a wad of string and a small brass hook from his saddlebags.

Near a tree at the edge of the encampment he caught sight of a long stick. After stripping away the excess branches, he tied the string around one end, then placed a tiny piece of jerky onto the hook. "All right," he proudly announced. "I'm off to fish for dinner."

A blush tinted her cheeks. "Look how clever you are, Dillon Reed. You're our very own Samuel Clemens as in his biography, Roughing It."

Dillon lowered his make-shift gear. "Who?"

"Samuel," Alma clarified, "or better known by his journalistic name... *Mark Twain.*"

Dillon had seen that famous name in several periodicals. Good God, first Custer and now Twain. Does this woman know everyone? Nonetheless, he took her comment as a compliment. "From what I've read by Twain, I've found him to be most humorous." He headed toward the river. At least she compared him to a worldly sort of chap.

An unbidden grin creased his mouth.

Streams of brilliant yellows and orange streaked the early evening sky as an hour later Dillon scooped up a still sizzling trout from the pan. He laid the fillet on the tinplate Alma extended, then set a chunk of cornbread and a heaping pile of roasted carrots alongside.

She speared a small portion of the flakey fish. "I am starving, and this smells purely delicious." The bite disappeared between her lips and she savored it, then swallowed. A satisfied sigh followed and she locked her gaze on his. "A dish as scrumptious as any seaside restaurateur could ever hope to make for me."

He wouldn't go quite that far. The little minx. Dillon eased out a long breath, frustrated for having held it, then forked a chunk of fish for himself. "Nothing better than fresh-caught black river trout...and this kind is only found here." Daylight surrendered into night as they ate in companionable silence. An extra cup of coffee finished his meal.

As she sipped on her second cup, their gazes connected over the flames.

Firelight laid a luminous glow across her face. Her hair glimmered as if pure gold. With a silent curse, he forced a smile and looked away.

"You know, Dillon," she said, the crackling wood an intimate backdrop. "I went to the academy with Samuel's wife. Olivia Langdon is such a witty delight. She rejected his first proposal of marriage due to her...

um…society standards." She frowned. "Her father disapproved of Sam's less-than-desirable journalistic position."

"Is that so…" He stared at the fire, a smile pasted on his face. *What angle are you getting at?* She rarely wasted words, and he'd bet that like the bait he'd crafted earlier to catch their fish, Miss Alma Talmadge was angling toward something with this discussion.

"Yes," she continued. "But…Samuel persevered. And two months later he proposed again. This time, true love won out. Olivia said yes, and completely thwarted society with their unexpected marriage. They've been happily united for several years," she added, pausing to toss a small stick into the flames. "So, see? A union between people of different social standings can and does work out."

He nearly choked on his coffee.

What the hell?

Dillon shifted his boots and straightened, staring at her.

"And, in fact," she continued as a surge of hope tangled around his common sense, "they now live next door to Harriet Beecher Stowe."

"The woman who wrote Uncle Tom's Cabin?" he calmly replied, belying the anxiety of where he thought this conversation had been going.

"The very same," she continued, then began another story from her repertoire of tales.

He dutifully nodded, but Dillon heard little else. For a moment, he thought she'd been talking about him and her. He stared into the flames. He was a fool to even think such an asinine thought. As if she'd walk away from her cultured lifestyle for him.

Dillon inhaled and collected his sanity. So what if she'd come through when he was wounded? She'd learned how to handle herself under pressure. And he admired her for that.

But admiration sure as hell wasn't love.

He took a deep breath and centered his thoughts. All he really needed was the silence of wide open spaces. To breathe. To live alone. Without this woman and all her world-renowned connections.

To hell with all these meaningless fancies.

She was betrothed to another and that was all there was to it...

Cutting Alma off in mid-stream, he climbed to his feet and gathered the tinware. He strode toward the river, focused on cleaning-up the dishes.

The scuffing of her footfalls told him she followed. She sat on a log near the water's edge. A sigh fell from her lips as she tipped her head and gazed skyward. "The stars are magnificent tonight, Dillon. I shall always remember this evening."

"It's a nice evening," he said around the tightness in his throat. "No doubt about it."

She swatted at annoying mosquitoes buzzing around her face. "Thank you for the wonderful meal, too. If not for these pesky bugs, the night would be simply magical."

Magical? Dillon snorted. The only magical ending he wanted this night was to toss her skirts and bury himself inside her. He slapped a dish against water in a futile attempt to banish the illicit thought. "Sorry 'bout the 'skeeters," he mumbled after he'd regained control of his idiotic brain. "They weren't as bad the last time I came through here. River's a bit sluggish, though." He angled a fork toward a boggy section. "Lots of low spots now."

She smacked her right palm against her cheek. "Got one!"

For a long moment, Dillon stared at her, his gaze dropping to her sweet lips. He could still taste his mouth against hers.... He shoved to his feet. "Once you're under your bedroll, the mosquitoes won't bother you."

Stumbling to her feet, she patted out the wrinkles from her skirt. "H-How much longer 'til we rejoin civilization?"

"Should be at Camp Apache by Sunday. After that, the final leg of the journey will be much easier."

"I've been through worse," she said, grinning. A skip in her step brought her alongside him to the campfire. "I'm fearless...remember?"

Damn her for turning on her charms. He bit back a laugh. "Yes you are...and you've done a hell of a job staying in the saddle, too."

"Praise?" With all the drama of a seasoned actress, she angled her head and laid the back of her hand upon her brow. "I feel I'm caught in some bizarre dream."

He chuckled. "This ain't no dream, Princess." He shoved the clean tinware into his saddlebags. "And there's no turning back for us now."

The next five days passed without a hitch. Little conversation flowed between them as the miles blended one into the other. Twelve hours from Camp Apache, Alma awoke in a silent mood.

Dillon handed her a cup of coffee, and with a weak smile, she accepted. Something didn't add up...where was her annoying morning perkiness? "What's wrong?"

The smile wilted on her face. "I don't know," she whispered, setting aside the cup. "I'm just so tired, and my...my whole body aches."

He knelt onto one knee before her, a niggling worry rising. Was she fevered? His hands fisted as the need to touch her face burned through him. "Are you ill?"

A sigh followed. "I just want to get off this trail."

"You and me both. We'll be in camp this afternoon. I promise we'll rest up a day or two before heading back out." Dillon frowned at her uneaten breakfast of dried apricots and bread. "Finish up. You need your strength."

She pushed away the dish. "I'm sorry, I-I just can't. I'm so tired."

His concerns grew. The flushed color of her skin. Her lethargy. Good God, this could be something serious. He needed to get moving and find her a doctor. "Stay put, I'm going to get the horses ready."

Minutes later he lifted her into her saddle. Alma swayed. "Whoa there, Princess. I tell you what. Today you're riding with me." He tied her gelding to his saddle, then hoisted himself up behind her, letting the lead rope drape across his leg.

Heat radiated from her fevered body, and she began to shake.

Fear gripped Dillon's soul, and he dug his mount into a canter.

By sundown, he reached Camp Apache. Galloping past gawking soldiers, he made a beeline for the post infirmary. At the entrance of the long, log hospital dominating the north end of the camp, he pulled the lathered gelding up short. With Alma in his arms, Dillon swept from the saddle and pounded across the boardwalk. On a ragged breath, he kicked open the door.

A short, lean captain pushed away from a desk. "What the--"

"You've got to help her, Doc," Dillon rasped, fear rolling through his voice. "She's burning up."

The man resettled his glasses and scraped an assessing gaze over Alma. "What's wrong with her?"

"Shivering. No appetite. She must've picked up something while we were coming over the rim."

The captain indicated the nearest bed as he picked up a journal. "Put her there. I'll take a closer look."

A half-dozen scuffed steps later, Dillon eased Alma onto the mattress. "You're here, Princess," he whispered, pushing away wisps of damp hair stuck to her fevered face. "I promise you'll get better, now."

The doctor pulled a Cammann stethoscope from its tin case and draped the instrument around his neck. "Wait over there while I examine her," he snapped.

With a nod, Dillon obeyed. In a daze, he scanned the empty quarters, damning his decision to cut across this God-forbidden track of land. *I should not have brought her this way.*

We should've just taken the stage. She's fragile. She's not like all the others. He stumbled, and slumped against a support beam. Bile churned in his gut. *My God, what if I...lose her?*

Alma's splash into his life, all of her colorful arrogance, collided with the empty void of his existence.

The truth hit him square in the heart.

His eyes slid closed as a deep, single groan spilled from his mouth.

Sonofabitch...I-I love her ... this magnificent woman so out of his reach that right about now even the moon loomed closer. As if she could ever really want him, a man who'd dragged her through hell, damning society and every part of her world.

They didn't fit.

Nothing about their relationship made sense.

And Twain's life was far different from that of a man on the range, one facing danger at every turn.

A writer could offer a woman stability. He couldn't give her even that.

Dillon inhaled and swiped a leather-gloved hand across his face as the ache inside him expanded.

After a thorough examination, the doctor straightened and reached for another book, skimming the pages. With a deep exhale, he glanced at Dillon. "As I suspected, looks like she's got the shakes. Seen this too many times not to know."

"T-The shakes?" *Jeezus*...Dillon's panic grew. He'd heard of this sickness...entire regiments had fallen ill by ague. "W-What can we do?"

The doctor ignored his question and pushed his chair back to his desk. He picked up a lucifer from an open box. "Based upon what I've been reading, 'the shakes' is now being termed malaria."

The stench of sulfur rose between them as light illumed the man's face. The glass globe rattled as the doctor seated it atop the lantern. "They still don't know what causes the illness, though, which is quite frustrating."

He flipped through another journal, and paused at an entry. "Had a few patients in here last week with the same symptoms. Nothing like the outbreak I dealt with a couple years ago at Camp Goodwin, thank God. The sickness got so bad the army was forced to move the whole compound over here onto higher ground."

The captain closed the textbook with a snap and glanced at Alma. "She sure is a pretty little thing."

The last of his patience snapped and Dillon stepped closer. "Look, Doc, I don't want a damned history lesson or your opinion on her good looks. I just need you to fix her."

Their gazes reconnected and he shook his head. "Only quinine can do that, I'm afraid."

"Fine," Dillon snapped. "Give her some."

"Can't."

Dillon stepped closer, towering over the man. At this point, violence seemed the better option. "And why not?" he growled.

"There's none left." The doctor thinned his lips. "Been waiting on another shipment for days. Might get here tomorrow. Might be next month." He laid aside the book and rubbed his brow.

The hellish pain inside Dillon expanded. "Where are they coming from? I'll ride to intercept, bring the medicine back--"

"I don't know where the army fills my provisions. Wherever the shipment is, they're all weeks away by horseback. Could be the Quartermaster's Depot over at Fort Leavenworth or a half-dozen other locations. Not sure which one 'til my supplies arrive and I sign for them." Fatigue darkened his eyes. "I'm sorry. The only thing we can do is keep her comfortable until they arrive."

Furious, damning his helplessness, damning his poor decisions that had tossed Alma into this dire circumstance, Dillon glared at the man. "I refuse to believe that's all that can be done."

Hard eyes narrowed. "I'm the doctor not you. My diagnosis stands." He reached for another medical tome. "I suggest you prepare yourself, mister. Unless she gets quinine soon, your woman is going to die."

CHAPTER
TWENTY-SIX

The half-day's ride to the Indian reservation gave Dillon something to do instead of pace and worry. Keep her comfortable until the medicine arrived? Like hell! The arrogant *I have a certificate of medicine and you can't argue with me* jackass. His princess needed help, and by God, she was going to get it.

Seated inside a dome-shaped lodge, Dillon narrowed his gaze on the medicine man opposite him. A smoke-filled haze from a small campfire in the center drifted around the enclosure and tainted each breath. Eyes stinging, Dillon rolled his shoulders, trying to work out the tension as he waited, cursing every second.

Alchesay, General Crook's eyes among the White Mountain Apache, sat beside the shaman. A sun-scorched, coppery mass of muscles, the scout wore a muslin loin-cloth. Beading covered his knee-high moccasins, and a hawk feather lay woven into the side of his long, ebony hair.

Flame from the campfire flickered. A glint of light reflected across the recently received Medal of Honor swinging from a lanyard around the nineteen-year-old's neck.

For a moment, Dillon recalled General Crook's crusade against Cochise last winter, a campaign resulting in this Indian's much-deserved tribute. Working alongside him and several other army scouts, Alchesay had played a crucial role in gaining the Chiricahua chief's surrender. During the battle, Dillon had formed a lasting friendship with this wise-beyond-his-years young scout.

Relieved that Alchesay had returned to his home on the newly-created reservation outside Camp Apache, Dillon had shared his worries regarding Alma, thankful his friend now spoke to the revered shaman on his behalf.

Dillon leaned closer. He'd heard enough of the guttural words whispered between the two Indians to piece together the story Alchesay now shared with the wise-old shaman named Toggy: *healing herbs from the spirits...his heart's blood...death has come to visit him.*

Nodding, the old man settled a watery blue gaze upon Dillon and then reached for his leather pouch. *"Ctcimi zdza-I. Bida'a bitsits'in."*

He's unhappy in his eyes and his head. Dillon swallowed the lump in his throat, nodding. Unlike the army doctor, this sagacious old healer had put the truth of Dillon's heartbreak into words. *Wormwood. Other spirit gifts. Doses throughout the night.* The elder poured several powdered mixtures onto a leather hide.

Hope eked through Dillon.

"Shit'sa' ndlaa tah 'nnii," the spirit leader stated as he stirred the powerful medicines together. With care, he slipped them into a smaller pouch. A deep, guttural chant followed as Toggy blessed the concoction.

The shaman's eyes slowly opened. He relocked his gaze with Dillon's.

"She must drink the mixture in clean water each hour," the young scout translated, "and you must bathe her body beneath wet cloth until her fever breaks."

Dillon nodded, and accepted the shaman's gift, his breathing as uneven as his heartbeat. In the tongue of the Apache people, he whispered, *"Ahee-ih-yeh...thank you, wise one. You have given me back my light."*

***

The last shimmers of sunset struggled within the sky when Dillon rode back to Camp Apache. Dismounting, he looped the reins of his horse around a railing, and then skimmed the cavalry compound. Quiet, except for the notes of an ill-tuned piano emanating from the saloon. He glanced at the soaring pines that hugged the edge of the outpost. Fading rays split

around the trees in streaks of gold and white. *Radiant...just like Alma.*
He'd administer the medicine, care for her. That's all that mattered now.

Turning, Dillon hurried down the main road, crunching past the
sutler store and brewery. He caught a glimpse of his cabin as he passed.
A double-eagle had been the shop owner's steep fee to secure a week's
worth of usage for the rickety shack. With a nod, Dillon had flipped
his last twenty-dollar gold piece toward the shyster's outstretched hand.
He didn't quibble the cost. The secluded dwelling was exactly what he'd
needed, and he'd sealed the deal this morning before he'd rode to the
Indian reservation.

An agonizing minute later and terrified of what he might find, Dillon
shoved open the hospital door and made a bee line for Alma. The dozing
doctor, body slumped over his desk, awoke with a start. The chair scraped
back and wobbled as he scrambled to his feet.

"Y-You're back." He straightened his coat. "I'd wondered where you'd
gone this morning in such an all-fired hurry." He angled a thumb toward
the back of the room. "Got you a bed over in the corner made up with
clean sheets."

Dillon glanced at the advancing man before leaning over Alma.

His blood chilled.

Oh my God.

Plum-colored splotches spread across the delicate skin beneath her
closed eyes, her hair lay in damp, matted clumps across the pillow, and
her breath rattled with each sputtering intake. The past few hours had
taken their toll. Since he'd seen her earlier this morning, her condition
had worsened.

He'd give his own life to see her smile again.

The doctor had removed her outer garments. Clad in her unmention-
ables, her chemise was soaked with sweat.

Stomach muscles clenched when he scooped her into his arms. "Come
on, Princess. I've got you now." A throaty groan fell from her lips, and her
head lolled against his chest.

The doctor dug a hand into Dillon's upper arm. "Good God man, y-you can't move her."

A shrug shook loose the captain's grip. "Try and stop me."

Dillon scanned the room for a blanket and grabbed the one that lay folded near the bed. A quick tug, and he draped the thin wool across his shoulder, covering Alma's body from prying eyes. He strode toward the open door.

The doctor hurried around Dillon and blocked the opening, hands raised in a consoling gesture. "Now wait a damn minute, Reed. I realize you're upset."

The truth was he'd never been so shit-scared in his life. "Move."

"Just listen to me for a moment...taking her out like this is not in her best interest. We...we need to wait--"

"We're done waiting. If your quinine arrives, I'll be caring for her in the cabin between the brew house and the mercantile." Dillon shifted sideways around the man. "I've got my own medicines now that'll help--"

The captain's face flushed with outrage. "What medicines?"

Dillon dipped his jaw toward the leather pouch looped around his neck. "A remedy from the shaman on the reservation."

"F-From old Toggy?" he scoffed, eyes widening. "Jesus Christ, Reed, he's a damned redskin! You can't believe all that peyote-induced lunacy he spews. His potion'll probably kill her faster than the damned malaria."

The nerves in Dillon's gut wound tighter. He bumped the brim of his hat against the doctor's forehead. "Can you do anything more for her without your medicines?"

"N-No..."

"Then it's settled. Get the hell out of my way."

The captain hesitated.

With a curse, Dillon shoved past, then maneuvered across the board-walk, a breeze, punctuated with the aroma of brewing beer, swirling in the evening air. He didn't give a damn about the doctor's beliefs. He'd do whatever it took to keep Alma alive.

CHAPTER TWENTY-SEVEN

Firelight flickered across Alma's naked body. For most of the night, her labored rales had vied with the crackling flames. Awash in fatigue, Dillon eased himself onto the chair beside the metal-framed bed and again plunged a rag into the water bucket.

Her nearness. Her scent. Her need for him galvanized his every action.

Water dripped into the bucket as Dillon squeezed out the excess liquid. As the moon rode the night, he'd followed the same routine. He gave her a dose of the shaman's tonic, and then he swabbed her from head to toe. He'd hoped that having stripped her of her undergarments to make her as comfortable as possible would've helped. Thankfully, she hadn't worsened throughout the night.

That, he owed to the shaman's herbs.

Dillon leaned forward and again skimmed the wet rag over her honey-hued shoulders and breasts. "Come back to me, Princess," he whispered. His voice sounded desperate, even to him.

Her words played havoc in his mind. *That ice you've built around your so-called heart...I strongly suggest you melt that.* He sucked a lungful of air, then eased his breath out on a lengthy sigh.

This is all my fault.

The truth burned straight to his soul.

On an unsteady breath, he redipped the cloth, wrung out water, and swabbed her belly, his fingertips flexing against the suppleness. In gentle motions, he smoothed the rag over the swell of her hip, then further down her leg.

Over the past few hours, he'd memorized each precious curve.

Again he dipped and squeezed, then worked his way down her other side. In slow degrees, the anguish of Caleb's death seeped over him. On the heels of that pain flooded his mother's betrayal and his father's downward spiral into drunkenness.

Dillon tightened his jaw.

Though just a child, he'd watched as his family frayed away from him forever. As the years unraveled, all alone, he'd conveniently used their deaths, the loathed deception by his high-society mother, as a means to distance himself from humanity. Safe. Protected. But, hidden behind his wall of ice, there'd still been a gaping void. And all the days spent carousing, killing, and dissention had put little distance between him and that damning truth.

By God...no more.

His eyes misted at the irony and insights of a privileged Boston debutante, full of innocence and sparkle and sass. She'd driven home the bitter pill. And now he'd do all in his power to save Alma. His strength. His purpose. His every breath was now devoted to this woman.

He withdrew the cloth as more words tumbled into recall.

Look at you, Dillon Reed. Unkempt. Unapproachable. Will living in this manner bring your brother back?

Little had Alma known how that statement would transform his world, a fact he hadn't understood until this night. She'd been correct. Life couldn't be viewed as an *all-wrong* or *all-right* affair.

Through her...he saw that now.

The cloth came into focus. He leaned forward and touched his brow to hers. Fear swamped him, and he spilled out in a tattered prayer. "Please God," he whispered, "don't let her die...d-don't take her away from me, too."

Alma gave a shallow moan.

Heart pounding, Dillon dropped the cloth into the water, then grabbed the glass filled with medicine. Wrapping an arm behind her shoulders, he pulled her up. She gave another soft groan.

"I know...you've got a damnable hell burnin' inside you now."

She didn't reply.

He hadn't expected her to. Dillon pressed the glass to her lips. "Swallow for me, baby. Let's wash that bastard away."

As if she'd heard his plea, her lips trembled, and then she took several gulps. "That's good, Alma. So good. Again, baby. Drink for me."

She shuddered, and swallowed once more.

Satisfied with the amount of herbal mixture she'd taken in, Dillon eased her back against the pillow. He scraped his gaze down her flawless form. A spike of heat drove into his loins and tangled around his fears. *Sonofabitch.* With a sharp exhale he pulled the blanket across her naked body, and stood.

Jamming his hands through his hair, he glanced out the window. Purple streams cut through a blackened sky in a glorious arc, much the same as this woman had filled his burning emptiness.

Dawn.

Thank God.

She's lived through the night. However pitiful a benchmark, at this moment he'd take every one he could get. He spat another oath. Never had he felt so helpless. Frustrated that she now suffered, furious the medicine hadn't arrived at the fort, he began to pace.

With each step, his anger built. He couldn't do one damned thing to change this outcome.

He still had nothing to offer her.

And she was still going to marry the earl. Unsure of what to do, but knowing he had to do something to keep from going crazy, Dillon fed a log to the fire.

Flames flared and the wood crackled. He tossed two more pieces on top. Sparks flew up, disintegrating into the chimney.

Much as did the time he had left with Alma.

He glanced at her. She seemed better, more relaxed, and from her even breathing, thankfully, had fallen asleep.

He, on the other hand, needed coffee. Black. Strong. A brew that would keep him awake as long as needed. After filling the pot with water and measuring the grounds, Dillon settled the hammered metal onto the flames. Within minutes, an invigorating smell filled the room to override the pungent tang of the shaman's healing herbs.

He swiped a hand over his face, inhaling, just as a loud knock sounded at the door.

Has the medicine arrived? Praying so, he strode over and jerked open the weathered wood.

Doctor Logan, his face deeply-lined stood a pace away. "I-I just wanted," the captain sputtered. "Or rather...h-how did Miss Talmadge fare the night?"

The hope for the medicine's arrival faded.

Frustration shifted to anger.

Fare the night? She's suffered like hell -- and him, too, with her every broken breath.

Dillon shoved aside his tormented thoughts and focused on the fact the doctor had come to check. Guilt driven, yet he'd come. With a hard glare, he stepped back and gestured toward the bed. "She's still alive, if that's what you're asking."

"She's no worse?" Surprise graveled his voice. "That's amaz—I mean, that's wonderful."

A cool breeze slid past and Dillon's jaw tightened. Damn, the last thing he needed was for Alma to catch a chill.

"Come on in." He closed the door after the captain stepped inside and placed his medical bag upon the table.

"Want some coffee?" Dillon asked. He walked back to the fireplace. "I just made some."

Logan tugged his stethoscope from the black leather case. "I'd like to examine her again." He draped the instrument around his neck. "With your permission, of course."

"Go ahead," Dillon said with a dry voice. "You'll find she's better."

He pulled a mug from his saddlebags near the hearth, squatted before the fire, and poured himself a cup of hot brew.

Several minutes later, Logan straightened and then faced him, a grin plastered across his face. "Well, Reed, if that offer is still open, I believe I'll have that cup of coffee after all."

Hope ignited as Dillon pulled out a second mug and filled the battered tin. He walked to the captain and handed him the full cup. "What's your diagnosis this time, Doc?" he asked, his words curt.

Logan slipped his fingers through the handle, relief illuminating his eyes. "I'm purely mystified. Her lungs are much clearer and…I'm pleased to report her fever has broken." His eyes lowered. "Looks like I owe you an apology."

"You don't owe me a damned thing," he snapped, "but you might want to thank ol' Toggy for sharing a backup remedy with us."

"That I will." He peered at Alma and shook his head in disbelief. "Guess there's something to that redskin's spiritual nonsense, after all."

"Guess there is," Dillon dryly stated.

***

Clothed in her undergarments, Alma brought the thin blanket around her shoulders and slid to the edge of the bed. Her bare feet dangled. The thought of just how close she'd come to death made her heart pound. Without Dillon, she wouldn't have survived. This tall, broad-shouldered beast had blown into her life in all his angry arrogance, and had become her bridge between life and death. Light and Dark. Happiness and heartbreak.

Alma shuddered. She couldn't imagine spending a single moment without this man in her life. Over their journey, however impossible, with each passing mile he'd ruthlessly charmed her, a man who'd yell at her as quick as send her a smile. However much she'd wanted him out of her life on that train platform back in Washington, he'd too, changed all of that.

However much she hadn't prepared herself to become an independent woman who lived by her own rules, he'd also given her a new outlook. In fact, this long-haired desperado now held her every heartbeat in his hand.

Oh the irony of my life.

Alma smoothed her fingers over the tangled mess of hair falling past her shoulders. *I must look a fright.* If only she could reach her hairbrush. The fact Dillon had kissed her on the forehead this morning before he'd left lent hope she didn't look as bad as she suspected.

More confident, her mind turned to the intimacy of the cabin. Alone. Her strength returning. What would the raw kisses they'd shared in the teepee feel like here in this bed, his naked body pressed against hers?

Will I ever know?

She sighed. Whether he felt the same, she wasn't sure. And yet, the way he'd looked at her since the night she'd almost died, the kiss he'd delivered this morning, inspired belief his actions were more than a scout performing a duty. Warmth purled through her body. Would he ever let her close?

Probably not.

Regardless, before she met Lord Green again, her father must know of her change of heart.

Alma spotted her satchel near Dillon's saddlebags, and she pushed against the mattress. A wobbly teeter brought her to her feet. Getting properly coiffured and dressed seemed the first step in achieving her goal.

Shuffling steps took her to the table. *So far. So good.* She must hurry before Dillon returned with their breakfast.

Alma hobbled to her valise and withdrew her boar-hair bristle brush. With steady strokes, she worked through the tangles until her hair lay in a long, silky wave across one shoulder.

The door pushed open and Dillon stepped inside. He glanced toward the bed, then turned and spotted her. Face darkening, he stormed over, shoving the breakfast tray clutched in his hands to the table.

"What in the hell are you doing up?"

"Thank you for asking. I'm feeling so much better, Dillon. Really."

"Three days ago you were almost dead." He wrapped his hands around her waist and guided her to the chair, the anger on his face shifting to relief. "Sit down. Now."

As she sat, she inhaled his scent, coffee and man, fresh and clean. *Powerful.*

He scowled. "You still need your rest."

Alma laughed. "I needed to get the knots out of my hair." She pushed the brush up between them. "See?"

He tugged the piece from her hand and tossed it into her valise. "Damnit, Alma. You could've fallen."

"But I didn't," she replied, pleased beneath his worry. He cared for her, of that she had no doubt. "And I'm much better. You saw to that."

He sighed, and pointed to the rumpled berth where she'd been lying for nearly a week. "Look, you've still got two nights with that bed, and by God, you're going to use it."

"No, Dillon. Right now I'm going to sit in this chair and enjoy the breakfast you've thoughtfully brought me." She pulled the tray closer and removed a dish. "I'll take this one."

The plateful of eggs, bacon, beans, and biscuits looked delicious.

He hesitated, then sighed. "There's obviously nothing wrong with your appetite. All right, you can stay up, but only 'til we've finished eating." He pushed her chair closer to the table, stepped around to the other seat, and dropped into place.

The crackle of flames filled the cabin as they ate.

Unbidden, the memory of Dillon's voice, husky with passion and prayer flooded her mind. Were the words she'd heard in her delirium real or imagined? Had he really whispered such endearments? Or was her mind playing cruel tricks with her heart?

Full, Alma pushed aside her empty plate, then slipped her palm atop his hand. "Thank you for all you've done for me," she whispered, squeezing her fingers in-between his. "I can never repay your kindness."

For a long moment he stared at her, then his eyes softened beneath a near-smile as he turned his palm upward. He interlaced her fingers with his own. "It's what I do, Princess. Another reason why your uncle assigned me this job." He cleared his throat, and the laugh that followed was rough. "He thinks I'm irreplaceable. Now it's time you got back to bed."

"No...no...just a moment longer. How about I walk around the cabin before I lie down?" Again their gazes met and held, and Alma wondered why the beat of her heart didn't echo around the room.

"Fine." He broke their handhold and shoved to his feet. "But, I'm helping you walk."

She could barely contain her smile. "I'd hoped you would."

"We're back on the trail in two days, so you need this time to build up your strength," he stated as they walked around the room. "And our final section goes through the desert."

"When we first met, you said the desert is the most dangerous part."

"It can be, if one's not prepared."

"Well, we're prepared, aren't we? After all, I'm a seasoned frontierswoman now."

He laughed, and they turned away from the fireplace, heading toward the door. "That you are, Princess. But, the weather's also been cooler this spring, so I don't anticipate the heat to be as intense as normal. A stroke of luck I'm thankful for. Considering everything, we should just amble into Tucson with no more problems." Paces from the door, he turned and guided her toward the bed. "All right, you've had enough walking. We'll go again after supper."

She lowered to the edge of the berth and maintained her hold on his arm. "If I promise to rest all afternoon, can we walk to the telegraph office later?"

Surprise darkened his eyes. "What?" he asked, his voice thin.

"I need to send father a message." He started to protest, but she squeezed his arm. "This is so important to me. Please."

He knelt, and studied her for a long moment. Finally, a half-smile crept across his handsome features.

"Look…" He peered deep into her eyes. "I'd probably walk you anywhere you wanted to go, Princess…except to a telegraph office here in camp."

"W-Why?" she breathed, her heart racing.

"'Cause this post doesn't yet have one of those I'm sorry to say. I know you want to let your father know of your sickness, but you'll have to wait until we arrive at Fort Lowell."

My sickness? Telling father *that* hadn't even crossed her mind. "I see."

"But," he said, standing. "We can walk around camp later if we take things slow."

"Yes, I'd like that, thank you." She settled upon the pillow. With a sigh, her eyes slipped closed.

Steps grew quieter as Dillon moved across the room. Dishes clattered. "I'll be right back," he said.

"I'll be here," she answered with a wave.

A moment later the door clicked shut. Silence settled over her, and yet his scent, his remembered kisses, and the intensity he'd brought into her world, now flooded her mind.

Unable to stop the tears gathering in her eyes, she rolled to face the wall.

The absence of a telegraph office changed nothing. Even without her father's blessing, she knew she would never marry the earl.

Not now.

Not ever.

Not when she loved Dillon Reed.

CHAPTER
TWENTY-EIGHT

Five days of travel and near-silence rode with them all the way from Camp Apache. As Dillon sipped his coffee, he celebrated the coolness of the morning. By noon they'd be roasting beneath a hot June sun, baked as dry as pottery in a kiln. Regardless, he'd enjoyed the ever-changing landscapes from cool pine forests to high grasslands to the vast tracks of chaparral. Last evening they'd finally reached the outskirts of the desert's great basin.

My life force.

He didn't much fit-in anywhere, certainly not in this woman's world. But at least here, in the desert, he knew his way.

Dillon tossed the remainder of his coffee, and sighed. By dinnertime, they'd ride into Tucson, and all of this…*whatever the hell this is*…would be over.

After dousing the fire, he helped Alma onto her horse. With her bustle and traveling bag secured behind the cantle, he swung onto his own saddle and headed southward. Hour after hour, as the sun arced across the sky, they trekked through creosote brush and manzanita. Then finally, in the far distance, a broken barrier of rock lurked on the horizon.

The Rincon Mountains.

And home -- *where the fort and the colonel had given a tormented young heathen his purpose.* Yes, home drew ever closer. Relief warred with sorrow and weighed heavy on his heart.

When they arrived, he'd be home…and she'd be gone.

Forever.

The fierce ache swelled. Damn her for sashaying past his defenses, making him waltz again, making him care, making him want her. This whole tortuous mess was her fault. He'd kept her in line on more than one occasion. He'd been a bastard most times, but there'd been no rules of propriety required to do his damned job. Bring her to her fiancé safe and sound. And he was...just so that bastard could marry her and take away the only woman who'd ever gotten past his defenses and made him fall in love with her.

He should just...*what?* He muttered a curse. As if he had any influence to do a damned thing.

Tell her you love her, jackass.

And what the hell good would that do? Other than make him look like a fool when she laughed and walked away. He couldn't compete with an English earl or the security and prestige a royal title presented. Like she'd choose him, a man whose entire life's worth was a pittance compared to a nobleman.

There was no changing this outcome, and he knew it.

Dillon reined his horse to a walk. *Just tell her...* Stop thinking. At least he had her company 'til they arrived at the fort.

A blur of brown on the ground hopped past.

He grinned. Short of taking her to bed and showing her how she'd changed his world, he'd make sure every moment left with her would count.

"Kangaroo rat," he said, pointing to the small creature scurrying from the path of his horse. "They can live their whole lives without a drop of water." He pulled the gelding to a stop. "Unlike us, they get what they need from seeds and insects. Here," he said, handing her his canteen. "Take a swig."

"Thank you." Three gulps later, she handed back the water.

Their fingers touched and her eyes brightened with awareness, forcing his breath to trip end over end out of his mouth.

Just tell her...

She lowered her gaze.

And he tightened his lips on a sigh. Furious with himself, he brought the vessel to his mouth, and tasted her. A gulp pulled the treasure in deeper.

She deserves someone better than me...

Frustrated with the entire situation, he secured the canteen, then scanned the desert. Sunshine streamed in heated waves before him, distorting the vast spread of thornscrub. Undergrowth crept across the ground between palo verde, scrappy Ironwood trees, and the yellow-blooming wands of the Ocotillo.

All types of cactus amassed in the sandy slopes and washes. A grin touched his mouth as he recognized the landscape. Anticipation grew. Like the land he loved, he loved Alma, too, and had waited so long to share this part of the journey with her.

He squelched his melancholy as they crested a hill.

Behind him, she gasped.

And Dillon smiled.

"Saguaros," he said, his voice low. "I wanted you to see this, Princess." The reverence of the moment was staggering. As far as the eye could see the columnar giants filled the dips and swells of land, their spine-covered arms soaring into the turquoise sky. God, how he loved the austerity of these massive sentinels that stood guard over the gates of Hell. "Impressive, aren't they?"

"They're...breathtaking. I had no idea these even existed. Thank you so much for sharing this with me." Her awestruck laugh rippled over him. "Those thick arms reaching upward look just like a million candelabras."

He lifted his hat, tunneled his fingers through his hair, and resettled the slouch. *They did at that -- candelabras.* He chuckled. "Saguaros grow nowhere else but here...in this desert." Dillon nudged his gelding beside the closest giant, pulled the knife from inside his boot, and then glanced back. "Ride up here. Want you to try something."

A broad smile lighting her face, she guided her mount alongside. Time spent in the fresh air this past week had given her back her glow. Keeping his damned hands off her had been sheer torment. Detailed images of her supple breasts, the flair of her perfect hips, every magnificent curve flickered into his mind. As long as he drew breath he'd have the memories of her, of her taste, of how she felt in his arms.

A hard swallow suppressed the relentless image. "See those flowers?" he asked, pointing at the white blooms that covered the tips of the Saguaro. The now-limp feathers on her hat momentarily danced in the breeze as she angled her parasol to shade her eyes, nodding. "Well, they open after sunset and last until mid-afternoon the next day. A twenty-four hour bloom, that's all. Then, they're replaced by that bright red fruit tucked under there."

"They're beautiful."

"And only seen this time of year. They're also lunch." With his feet snug in the stirrups, Dillon eased into a full stand and knocked off one of the red, pear-shaped pieces. "Birds and bats eat the fruit up high," he said, passing her a clump of the rare juicy treat. "When they ripen and drop all other desert critters feast. Won't find anything like this back east."

A tiny half-smile grew as pink blossomed Alma's cheeks. "I'm not sure, Dillon. You well-know I'm more a French cuisine kind of diner."

"After all this time spent with you, I know you pretty well. So let's not forget you're also now a fine frontierswoman, too."

Her gaze melting into his, she leaned forward. "I assure you I shall never forget." She lifted the fruit from his open palm and took a tentative bite. Surprise widened her eyes. "Oh my…it's delicious. So sweet. Like…a big strawberry." She popped the remainder into her mouth.

"Makes great jam on biscuits, too."

"Ooh, I'd love to try some."

But you never will 'cause England doesn't have this. The warmth of her nearness burned through Dillon. Good God he'd miss her moments of discovery, her new-found courage, her laughter, and….

His gaze dropped to her lips.

Her kiss.

On an inhale, he stood and removed two more sections. A quick twist of his knife and he opened the rind-covered fruit, then shoved another glob into his mouth. He swiped away the juices on his shirtsleeve, and then handed her the other tasty clump. "We should be at Fort Lowell by mid-afternoon."

Tears gathering in her eyes, she accepted the treat and stared at him. "S-So soon?"

Tense silence settled between them, and he swallowed hard and cursed every remaining mile. Their breathing matched. Shallow. Strained. The relentless taste and temptation of her body seared his brain.

A tear slipped over the curve of her sunstained cheek.

Jeezus.

His gut twisted.

Just tell her...

Dillon glanced away. With a firm grip, he swiped the Bowie across his pants leg, then slipped the knife inside his boot.

"Let's ride," he snapped, "no sense delaying the inevitable." A quick jab to the gelding's flank and he headed for home.

CHAPTER TWENTY-NINE

In the waning light, Fort Lowell spread alongside the Rillito River on the south side of the territory's capitol city of Tucson. Tangerine tendrils swirled behind the Santa Catalina Mountains as the rocky behemoth swallowed the last of the afternoon light. Dillon scraped his gaze over the majestic site, then rapped his knuckles hard against Captain Palmer's front door.

Pamela better damned-well be home.

Upon their arrival, he'd hoped to find the colonel at headquarters, then he'd simply turn Alma over to the commander. Obligation done. Except, Talmadge's office stood empty. A search of the post had ended in exasperation

Dillon grimaced at the continued delay, his mind wandering.

They're all out on escort duty, Reed...and the colonel took that blasted Englishman with 'im, the clerk at the telegraph office informed him when they stopped in so Alma could send a message to her father. After thanking the man, Dillon took up the suggestion they try her cousin's house next.

A hot breeze swirled around the side of the adobe dwelling, lifting the limp ribbons on Alma's hat. She smoothed out the wrinkles in her dress, and with a quick heel-tap readjusted the bustle she'd insisted on donning before they rode into Fort Lowell.

Across the entire country, this woman refused to lose sight of her propriety. In fact, she'd insisted on following her asinine society standards even in the wilds of America where not one living soul gave a damn.

Despite the truth, a begrudging admiration for his feisty little princess grew.

A line creased Alma's brow. "What if she isn't home?"

"She's here somewhere." He shifted her valise to his other hand, and added a half-hearted smile. "We'll find her."

On a sigh, he rapped again, then scanned the fort. In the three months he'd been gone, nothing had changed.

Three months? God's teeth, the trip seemed an eternity. Yet, his time spent with Alma flew by.

Fort Riley.

The kidnapping.

The cave, the Utes, and Camp Apache.

Sonofabitch, too many places to fall in love.

With a soft creak, the door swung open.

Pamela's eyes widened with pleasure. "Dillon! You're home." She looked past him, and happiness wreathed her face. "And there's my beautiful cousin." Pamela stepped back. "Come in out of this heat, both of you."

Dillon settled the valise on the floor of the entryway, then stepped aside just as crinolines rustled and Pamela swept past him.

She embraced Alma. "It's so wonderful to see you again!"

"I'm delighted, too," Alma whispered, hugging her in return. "There's so much I need to share with you."

More comfortable with a horse beneath him than women talking, Dillon swept off his hat, and paced the foyer.

A smile curved Pamela's lips. "I can't wait to hear everything. Excuse me for just one moment." She glanced down the hallway. "Rosa, my sweet," she said.

An old Mexican woman stepped into view. "*Sí, señora?*"

"Please fill the copper bathtub in my room," Pamela said. "Thank you so much."

The servant nodded and moved toward the back of the house.

Pamela led them to the front parlor where the coolness of the room belied the heat outside. She indicated the closest settee. "Please get comfortable, you must be exhausted from your travels."

Alma drifted down to the cushioned seat.

"No thanks, I'll stand." Dillon toyed with the rim of his hat, looking for the moment he could make his escape.

Pamela nodded, then settled beside Alma on the leather-covered divan. "After father received your telegram from Fort Garland, I scheduled a small get-together for Alma's arrival. Then, we didn't hear another thing, and I was afraid I'd have to cancel." She placed her hand atop Alma's filthy, white-gloved ones. "But you're here now, my darling, so our soirée tomorrow evening can go on as planned."

A becoming blush stained Alma's high cheekbones. "You mustn't go to so much trouble."

"Nonsense," Pamela snapped. "You're family. Of course, we're celebrating." She smiled at Dillon. "Jackson and Gus are expected to arrive tomorrow morning with their herd. They've responded with intentions of attending. Callie won't be joining us." Pamela's face softened as she turned to Alma. "My dearest friend is expecting their third child next month, and her husband forbids her to travel."

"Sounds like Jackson. Forbidding." Dillon chuckled. "I'm just surprised Callie agreed to his orders."

"Indeed," Pamela agreed. "But, you needn't worry, Alma, we'll visit my friends before you leave for England. Right now, however, your fiancé is with father and the troops escorting more savages to the reservation."

"I meant to be back in time to help." Dillon shot a glance to Alma. "We were delayed."

"Yes," she whispered, her lips lifting into an ever-so-soft smile.

Arousal flared deep within Dillon. The accursed thumping of his heart could probably be heard as far away as Yuma.

Pamela studied them for several long moments, then her lips tipped upward. "I see," she said, much too softly. "Regardless, you're here now.

That's all that matters. And our men assured me they'll be back in time for our party on the off chance you'd arrive. They'll be so happy to see you."

"And I them. Did my trunks arrive?" Alma asked, catching Dillon's gaze.

The memory of her standing behind her trunks demanding he bring them along blazed into his mind. The first of many face-offs, and damned if he hadn't started looking forward to the next one.

Yet another thing he'd miss about her.

"I took the liberty of bringing your trunks here," Pamela said. "They're in the back room, but I'm certain Lord Green will order dressmakers to create you the newest fashions upon reaching London."

At the second mention of Alma's fiancé, jealousy pumped through Dillon. She deserved a royal prince, not some jackass named Lord Green.

"Thank you for securing them." Alma pressed her hand to her forehead.

"Are you all right, my dearest?"

"Y-yes …I'm just so tired from the journey. I've been ill, but I'm much better now." She hesitated. "I'll need my things sent over to the hotel. That's where I'll be staying."

"The hotel?" Pamela shook her head. "I will hear of no such nonsense. You must stay with the captain and me. Our home is always open to you."

"I mustn't impose," Alma stated.

"You are not an imposition. You are family." Pamela waggled a finger. "Now, not another word. Besides, Rosa is drawing you a bath as we speak."

"A-a bath?" The determination on Alma's face turned to joy as her hands fluttered across her chest. "Oh my…that sounds purely divine."

"Then you'll stay?" her cousin asked.

"Yes," she replied, "and I cannot thank you enough for your kindness."

Dillon ground his teeth. These women clucked like a pair of hens. *The sooner I make the break, the better off I'll be.* A lie…but one for his sanity he clung to. He damned the fact that he had to leave, more so since he could do little else to change the outcome. "She's been put through the grinder," he said. "That's for sure."

"You needn't worry, Dillon" Pamela stood and reached downward, clasping her cousin's hands in hers. "We'll take extra-special care of her now." She pulled Alma to her feet and a tiny laugh followed as Pamela turned her toward the arched opening. "What do you say we get you out of these filthy traveling things and into something more fitting for your station? After you've rested a bit, we shall discuss dinner plans."

More fitting for her station. A place that didn't include him. "Sounds like everything's all lined up for you," Dillon said, struggling to ignore the bleeding hole in his heart.

Alma whirled around to face him.

The silent longing in her eyes almost had him hauling her to him. *God's teeth. Just say goodbye and go.* "Guess this is where I'll leave you."

Alma darted a frantic look between her cousin and him. "What?" she rasped. As tears filled her eyes, she shook her head so forcefully her chignon tumbled free. Her words rolled across the room and slammed into his heart. "N-no. Dillon, please...not yet."

Her cousin sucked in a startled breath.

Jeezus. Now Pamela realized far more than a cross-country journey had occurred between him and Alma. For her own sake, he had to get the hell out of here before Alma exposed anything more. Yet, everything he'd worked so hard to attain...his chosen isolation, his self-protection, the detachment from others...seemed altered.

Because of her.

Alma gripped the front of his shirt, halting his escape. "Y-you'll come to my party, won't you?"

Silence thickened between them as he held her unwavering gaze.

The clock in the hallway marked the agonizing seconds in a steady *tick-tick-tick.* Every damned one of them felt like an eternity.

Memories of their journey filled him. Her incredible laughter as she sampled the saguaro fruit, how her eyes had sparkled as she peered into the star-filled majesty of the Colorado nights, her antagonistic spark as she confronted a wolf, the sweet pleasure of tasting her body, and the innocence of their kiss in a moon-shrouded courtyard in Kansas. Everything...every single thing...wove around Dillon in vivid, excruciating torment.

Just say goodbye.

Now!

Their eyes locked and his breath seemed insufficient. He drug in another quart full of air to get him through the agony of his next words. "No, Princess. I'll not be attending. You take care of yourself." He lifted her hands from his shirt and set her back, forcing a tight smile.

"But, p-please..." she rushed out. "I can't go on without--"

"Yes, you can" he cut in.

On a huff, Pamela stepped between them, her smile a bit too bright. "Oh for heaven's sake, you two." She shot Dillon a *don't-you-dare-argue* look. "Of course, he's coming to the party." She ushered them into the hallway and stopped near the front door. "This man has accompanied you the entire breadth of the country. He will absolutely walk a few more feet to the hotel. Besides, we can't wait to hear all the details of your exploits."

Our exploits?

His gaze speared Alma's in a silent plea for caution even as he recalled the soft sweet swell of her breasts beneath his fingertips. "I don't think so, but thanks for the invi--"

"Dillon Reed." Pamela glared into his eyes as if she could read what burned inside his mind. He expected to see disappointment or disgust, and was stunned by the flicker of understanding. Her eyebrow arched. "Of course you will be there for her. We shall see you precisely at six o'clock tomorrow evening in the garden courtyard of the Phillips House Hotel."

His jaw knotted as his mind raced with all the reasons why he should not show. *Sonofabitch.*

"Fine," he snapped, the thrumming pulse in his throat squeezing tighter. He'd go, if only to see Alma for a few more precious hours, and prayed he wouldn't put a stranglehold on her fiancé. After the party, he'd mount his horse and ride off into the sunset. His duty done. Half elated, half running scared, he stared into Alma's eyes. "I'll be there."

"I'm so glad," Alma whispered, her sweet voice bathing his wretched soul.

Again, he envisioned her naked beneath him, her legs wrapped in a lover's squeeze around his waist.

Despite the coolness inside the house, a sliver of sweat tracked down his neck.

God help me get through tomorrow night.

With a curt nod, he settled his hat into place and left the house. A bone-deep weariness crawled over him as his boot heels crunched over sandy ground.

***

The following afternoon, Dillon delivered his report to Colonel Talmadge. After they shared a glass of whiskey, he filled the commander in on the details of the kidnapping, Alma saving his life, the selection of a different route to protect her, and her illness and subsequent recovery. Of course, he left out the parts that didn't matter a damned bit to anyone except him.

Two hours later, he stepped from headquarters. A swirl of dust had him glancing toward the range.

In the distance, the herd of horses from the *Dos Caballos* ranch, their colors ranging from browns, bays, chestnuts, and duns, galloped down the wide lane out front.

A half-dozen vaqueros directed the powerful flow of mustangs toward the corrals.

At the rear of the writhing mass of horseflesh rolled a lone wagon. Dillon narrowed his gaze on an aged Gus Gilbert perched upon the wooden seat, reins in hand and cursing a blue streak toward the Percherons that pulled his rig.

Dillon jammed his fingers into his mouth and sent a sharp whistle toward the old man to catch his attention.

On a laugh, Gus lifted his battered hat and waved.

A movement behind the wagon caught Dillon's attention. Visible through the dust rolling across the clearing, Jackson Neale brought up the rear.

Spotting him, his best friend angled the gelding toward headquarters.

Dillon slumped a shoulder against the closest post of the overhang, and waited. A fine row of cottonwoods shaded the wide lane out front.

Hooves clattered on the ground as Jackson drew to a halt, dismounted, and tossed his reins around the post. His spurs chinking against the sandy ground, he headed toward Dillon.

Their palms slid together in a handshake, and Dillon laughed. "Good to see you again."

Jackson chuckled. "I was beginning to wonder if you were just going to stay back east." He tugged off his leather gloves. "You look like hell, my friend."

"Ran into a bit of trouble on the trip back."

"Trouble, huh?" He smacked the side of Dillon's arm as he strode onto the boardwalk. "You mean like in the form of the colonel's niece kind of trouble?"

Nerve endings frayed as Dillon shrugged. "You sound like Callie. How's she doing, anyway?"

"She's pregnant," Jackson said. "I'll let you fill in the rest of that statement."

The image of a beautiful hellion and the love of his friend's life, shone bright in Dillon's mind. "You've got your two boys, Jackson. So this'n will probably be the troublemaking embodiment of her mother."

A full-blown smile cracked his face. "Good Lord, that's all we need."

Dillon pointed to the corrals where dust from the milling horses filled the horizon. "You've got a great lookin' herd this year."

Horses…the one thing I enjoy more than scouting.

Jackson nodded. "Army's buying all I can provide for their forts up north. Hell's bells, I can't even fill the orders I've got now, but they keep offering me more contracts."

"Weren't the Eschevon's selling horses off their ranch, too?"

"They were, but they didn't contribute this year." He scrapped to a stop and slapped his gloves against his thigh. Dust rose from the sewn leather. "We lost Renaldo while you were away."

Sadness filled Dillon. "Sorry to hear that, he was a good man."

"And a damned good neighbor. We're all sad...he ran a nice horse spread."

"That he did...all thirty-thousand acres worth of nice. You gonna buy out his widow?"

"Hell no. I can barely keep up with the fifty-thousand acres I've got now." Jackson moved deeper into the shadows, then jerked his thumb over his shoulder. "Tell you what. Let me square away things with the colonel, and then Gus and I will meet you over at Renaldo's Cantina? You can share the gory details of your little trip."

"Sounds good."

Jackson swept off his hat and ran a hand through his long hair. "See you in about an hour." Turning, he strode across the planked walkway and, with spurs chinking, disappeared inside.

With a sigh, Dillon drew on his gloves.

Just not every detail, my friend.

He slumped against the post, tugging the brim of his hat lower to shadow his eyes. He needed to get his ass back to living alone and scouting, neither of which required one damned ounce of worry or the worthless folderol of falling in love.

With a muttered curse, he walked to his mount, and jerked the reins from around the railing as his gaze shifted to the captain's house.

Where Alma prepared herself to meet her fiancé.

His chest tightened. *Sonofabitch.* Desire, anger, frustration, fear. All four described his feelings toward her.

Tonight the hotel would be alive with gaiety and the talk of the upcoming nuptials. And he, coward that he was, refused to look at the blank landscape of a future without his spoiled debutante. He'd been protecting her, caring for her, living and breathing for her for so long that the *not* doing so now made everything inside him ache.

Fury tore through him at never seeing her again. Worse, there wasn't one damned thing he could do about the pain. Regardless of how he felt, his leaving usually made things better for others, not worse. With a sharp curse, he mounted, sunk his spurs against the gelding's flanks, and headed south. Later, he'd stop at the mercantile to replace the shirt that Alma had used to help save his life.

First, if only for a while, he needed to escape.

A hard ride might help…and yet, as the horse's thrumming hooves pummeled the desert, Dillon knew no amount of miles existed that could remove his little princess from his mind.

CHAPTER THIRTY

A warm breeze sifted through the night as Alma scanned the hotel's garden. True to her cousin's promise, the elegance rivaled many soirées she'd attended back east. Pleasure warmed her as she took in the linen-draped tables filled with myriad servings of dainty cakes, finger sandwiches, and fancy-cut fruits and vegetables.

Beside these delectables stood several silver buckets filled with bottles of chilled champagne. To their left, delicate glassware glistened in the lantern light.

Oh Dillon, you scoundrel...they do have fluted cut-crystal out west.

Soft music wafted, and she smiled at the small stringed orchestra nestled in a far corner. Another recollection from Dillon's descriptions of the wild west resurfaced.

The closest thing we have to an orchestra is an odd collection of brass instruments and a few Mexican mariachis.

The ensemble playing up-to-date tunes was a far cry from the ragtag bunch he'd implied. The cozy ambience underscored the intimacy of the bricked terrace, a formal gathering to garner approval from any socialite.

She nodded at the new arrivals, Jackson Neale and Gus Gilbert. Having briefly chatted with both men, she found them to be a pure delight. Her uncle, the colonel, standing beside the two, gave her a quick wink, then returned his attention to the plateful of delicacies in his hand.

Uncle Thaddeus hadn't changed one bit since the last time she'd seen him. She truly loved the old codger, as did her father.

A full moon rode the sky, spilling a silvery, celestial glimmer over urns of coffee and punch, and a small ice sculpture crafted into a flying Pegasus sitting in the center of the table. According to Pamela, the hotel had brought ice down from the White Mountains during the winter months, then stored the blocks in deep pits layered with straw and sawdust awaiting just such occasions.

Her eyes widened as she spotted cupfuls of varied ices and clotted creams tucked around the base of the glorious winged creature. Back east, superfluous decorations were an every-party embellishment, but Alma never expected to see such finery here.

She grimaced at the constricting pressure at her waist and gave a subtle turn to relieve the pinch of her new corset. Unlike the older-styled undergarment she'd worn for nearly two months across country, the rigidity of this particular unmentionable had been crafted in a longer style that hugged her upper hips. The complexity of the newest bustled fashions required the additional steam-formed and boned support, leaving her scarcely able to catch her breath.

Pamela paused at her side. "Does all this meet with your approval, my dear?" she asked, sliding her gloved palm against Alma's.

Again, Alma took in the terrace alive with candlelight, the band playing soft music, and the bountiful array of food. "This is all so wonderful," she whispered, squeezing her cousin's hand. "Thank you for such a warm welcome."

Pamela's magenta silk rustled as she fluttered her fan. "You know me. I love to socialize. Surprisingly, the hotel had everything I needed." She paused. "Well, everything except the demi-spoons to enjoy the ices. But, the management assured me they'd arrive in time from San Francisco." Joy lightened her features as she pointed toward the Pegasus. "And they did. See?" Moonlight danced across delicate dippers laid in a silver-streaked path along the table top. "I do so hope everyone enjoys the evening."

"Well I know I am."

She nodded. "Tucson is, after all, the capitol of the territory so we must welcome you in style." With a smile, she held Alma at arm's length, her gaze sweeping from head to toe. "And just look at you, my darling. You are absolutely ravishing tonight. The earl will not be able to take his eyes off you."

A flush stole across Alma's cheeks at her cousin's statement.

The earl? Oh dear. Her hands trembled as a spike of worry drove through her. She hadn't dressed with the earl in mind at all this evening.

I've only dressed for Dillon. Angst swept her, and she glanced toward the entry. *Will he even show tonight?*

Emotions swamped her and she forced her sadness aside. "I'm just glad to return to the world of finer things. 'Tis what I am accustomed too, I'm afraid." Swathed from head to toe in her favorite House of Worth ball gown, she hoped the salmon-colored ribbed silk with its pearl-like chenille trim would catch the candlelight…as well as Dillon's eye.

Alma gave a subtle heel-tap to settle her bustle. The larger, lobster-shaped piece hugged her entire backend and swept to the floor, adding additional support to the twelve yards of fabric that draped around her and extended into a long train.

With a weak smile, she lifted a hand to her coiffure and patted her tresses. Earlier this evening, with Pamela's help, she'd woven several strands of Boston pearls through her upswept chignon. A sprinkling of pink and yellow rosebuds, picked fresh from her cousin's garden, added just a touch of whimsical adornment. She'd also dabbed her favorite fragrance at her wrists, throat, and temples.

Heat prickled up her spine when she recalled the time she first saw Dillon's cobalt-blue bottle of *Voleur de Roses*. Did he still have the item? Or, had he given the fragrance to someone here in town?

"Well, dearest, looking our best is what we do." Humor crinkled Pamela's eyes. "We brighten the arm of our men." She glanced toward her husband. From across the bricked patio, Captain Palmer lifted his punch glass toward her in a silent toast.

"I absolutely adore that man," Pamela whispered, "Like you do Lord Green, I'm sure."

Alma lowered her gaze. "Well, um…about that…" Her voice broke. She'd thought her whole life had been laid out for her by her father.

Then, she met an uncivilized army scout.

A man who lived hard.

A man who held firm beliefs of right and wrong.

A man who had stolen her affections.

Pamela faced her. "About what, cousin? Has something changed concerning your upcoming wedding to the earl?"

Unbidden tears filled Alma's eyes. Frantic over her change of heart and her new-found love for Dillon, she simply nodded.

"Because of a roguishly charming army scout, perhaps?"

"Y-yes," Alma whispered.

"I knew it!" Pamela exclaimed in a forceful whisper.

Alma peered into her cousin's eyes, surprised to see a smile warming her face. "How?"

"Women who observe know the look of love blossoming before them. Now, tell me true."

What a wise woman you are, cousin.

"Oh, Pamela," she whispered, unable to stop her flow of words. "I…I didn't tell you everything yesterday. He's taught me this whole new world. And when I think about him…his touch. His every breath. H-his…kiss."

Her cousin's eyes widened. "His kiss?"

"Yes," Alma replied, the burning remembrance of Dillon's hands against her bare skin thrumming through her veins. "We've kissed, more than once…and, well…other things…"

"Oh my. Well, I can see how that would affect your feelings for the earl." Her eyes narrowed. "Does Dillon feel the same about you?"

"I t-think he cares for me, but he's so guarded in his thoughts. I know he believes he has nothing to offer anyone."

"Well then, as scandalous as this might sound," she leaned closer, whispering, "you must help him change that sad thought, my darling." She softly laughed, then nodded. "We women hold all the power."

"Change his thinking?" Alma grimaced. "I've no idea how to do that, I'm afraid...that man can ride my last nerve."

Pamela squeezed her hands. "I'm sure you'll think of a way."

"All I know, right now, is that I cannot go through with this marriage to the earl."

"Of course not." Concern darkened her cousin's eyes. "When are you going to tell Lord Green? He's expected to arrive any moment."

"This evening." Alma straightened her shoulders, her chin rising. "I tried to let my father know that I'm calling off the wedding, but his office sent me a telegram this afternoon stating they cannot find him." Tears blurred her vision, and she dabbed at her eyes with her hanky. "He's not in his townhouse in Boston, nor at the mansion outside of town. And he never boarded his ship bound for London."

"Have they checked the clubs?"

"They're searching everywhere he normally frequents now," she replied. "Or so his shipping manager, Mister Johnson, advised me."

"I am sure your father will be found, my darling. Do not fret," Pamela said. "As for Dillon, I have known him for many years. He is a good and honorable man. If this is meant to be, I wholeheartedly approve of you two. In fact, I am thrilled. After you tell the earl of your decision, I'm here if you need me."

Alma nodded.

The side door swung open.

A small-framed, dark-haired man dressed in an expensive silk coat and trousers stepped into the courtyard.

Lord Green.

Though the earl was impeccably dressed, she missed the softness and durable simplicity of Dillon's cambric shirt beneath her fingertips.

Stop comparing!

The sheen on the earl's black leather boots no doubt reflected hours of polishing by his manservant, Edgar, who followed on the heels of her fiancé into the party.

Lord Green scanned the courtyard, then his gaze settled on her. She caught a flicker of relief in his eyes a second before he smiled.

She dropped open her fan and waved the delicate ivory before her face, aware there wasn't any part of her that loved this stranger.

Or ever could.

Dillon had stolen her heart.

Alma nodded her acknowledgment of the earl's appearance.

After whispering to Edgar, who moved off to the side of the garden, Lord Green headed toward her across the bricked patio.

"I see your fiancé has arrived." Pamela gave her hand a gentle squeeze. "Be strong, my darling. You can do this. True love is worth the struggle." Her cousin moved toward her husband.

Bolstered by the additional support, Alma squared her shoulders as the earl drew to a stop before her.

Her fiancé presented a smart bow. "My dearest Miss Talmadge," he said. "You look exquisite this evening. I cannot begin to tell you how relieved I am that you've arrived in good health after the ordeal you must have endured."

Alma's mouth grew dry. Dreading his touch, she extended her hand and received the lightest brush of his lips. Impatience trickled through her as a thin smile lifted her lips. "I am good thank you, my lord. I hope you've fared well these many months since our last visit."

Lord Green leaned close, and the aroma of his spiced hair pomade assaulted Alma's senses. Until this noxious reminder, she'd forgotten his overpowering scent.

"I am most eager for our upcoming nuptials," he whispered.

The invisible noose around Alma's neck tightened. *Oh Dillon, where are you?* Scraping her teeth against her lower lip, she sent a worried glance toward the entrance.

Empty.

With dread she looked at her fiancé. "Yes. Well…in regards to that--"

The side door opened. Dillon stepped into the candlelight.

Joy swept Alma, and her heart did a quick sputter.

The earl followed her gaze.

Hat in hand, Dillon wore the same outfit he'd donned at the Fort Riley gathering. His hair, however, remained long, falling over the collar of his coat in soft, clean waves.

Her desire for the scout intensified.

Dillon perused the gathering until his gaze locked with hers.

Giddy, her lips parted as she breathed his name. He was so tall, so handsome, and every word, every look, every single touch they'd ever shared flowed over Alma.

He nodded at her.

Heat stormed her cheeks. She'd been staring, after all. Thankfully, he couldn't read her thoughts. He'd made things quite clear at Pamela's yesterday that he was eager to *unload* his responsibility of her and depart.

With a huff, the earl stepped before her, blocking Dillon from her view. Face taut, he clasped her arm in a possessive hold. "Allow me to procure for you a spot of refreshments." He steered her toward the tables. "We have much to celebrate tonight."

Annoyance at his dominance severed her intent to wait until later this evening to share her decision about ending the betrothal. Regardless of the situation with Dillon, she refused to continue *this* charade. "Lord Green," she whispered. "I-I've been giving much thought in regards to our upcoming marriage—"

"My dear," he broke in, moving until he was mere inches from her ear. "We've all evening to discuss our plans. Let's enjoy this celebratory feast, shall we? Afterwards, I insist we dance."

He insists?

The arrogant cad. Dancing with him was the last thing on her mind. She scanned the courtyard until she spotted Dillon standing beside her uncle and the two other men.

Dillon met her gaze and raised a curious brow.

Alma faced the earl, then lifted her chin. "We'll talk. Now."

Irritation flickered in his eyes. "Later."

Alma gasped as the earl's white-gloved fingers clutched her upper arm.

The woman who'd begun the journey westward would have been swayed by the domineering tactics of this man. The weeks of hard travel, of fighting for Dillon's life and then hers, had changed Alma. The helpless debutante who'd boarded an evening train two months earlier in Boston no longer existed.

A fact the earl would learn.

She glared at him, snapping, "Unhand me this instant."

Surprise edged with displeasure flickered in his gaze. He dropped his hold and stepped back. "I do apologize, my dear." Clearing his throat, he straightened the hem of his gold-edged, embroidered vest, and gave her a smile. "In my excitement to see you, I allowed my eagerness to overrule my thoughtful common sense. I am impatient to dance with you." He bowed and motioned toward the refreshments. "Please allow me to escort you to the tables? 'Twould be my honor to do so."

For the moment, Alma suppressed her reservations. After the months he'd waited for her, for propriety's sake, she owed him a few moments of her company. After all, it wasn't Lord Green's fault she'd stopped caring.

She glanced over her shoulder toward Dillon.

Despite the conversation flowing around him, the scout continued to stare at her. The tingly feelings she'd tried to squash inside her heart surged to life. She needed to talk to him again and tell him how she felt. Hiding her feelings did nothing except torment her.

On a hard sigh, Alma collapsed her fan into her tight fist. "Fine, Lord Green…but I insist you be respectful."

"I shall, my dear…of course." A desperate glint returned to his eyes as he motioned to the table. With a grimace, Alma prepared for the moment she *could* say goodbye, knowing full-well a part of her wanted to run across the courtyard and into Dillon's arms.

Bowing to convention, she allowed Lord Green to guide her toward the icy, outstretched wings of a slowly melting Pegasus.

CHAPTER
THIRTY-ONE

Dillon's lips thinned as he studied the earl. Small-framed. Foppish. *So this is the jackass that'll provide Alma her happily-ever-after?*

He had his doubts.

A servant brushed past him bearing a trayful of liquor-filled glasses. Dillon snagged the nearest one. Upending the tumbler, he tossed back the whiskey, then hissed at the burn in his throat. Not even the scalding could kill the jealousy that simmered beneath the surface of his calm.

His gaze shifted to Alma as the drone of conversation between Jackson and Gus whirred around him. Candlelight wrapped his princess inside a golden glow...her hair, her gown, her quintessence unrivaled this evening.

Every perfect part of her now beyond his reach.

Another swallow of alcohol burned the back of his throat. He should've just kept ridin' south yesterday. The Mexican army needed help protecting their new railroad at Veracruz. He could begin again. Yes, start over where no society bullshit could remind him of the loves he'd lost. Slipping back into the habituated bitterness at the misfortunes in his life seemed comfortable...and yet, Dillon felt strangely empty. He licked his lips, tasting the whiskey, tasting Alma even more, reliving again the fire of her kiss.

Numerous times, the side door leading into the garden opened. More and more guests poured onto the terrace. Soon the cozy get-together he thought he'd been invited to had ramped up into a full-blown gala. Feeling as out of place here tonight as the good padre, Father Miguel, might at

Miss Lucy's brothel -- which was exactly where Dillon should've been -- he scanned the now-crowded courtyard.

The well-dressed, important folks of the territory had turned out in droves, each person wanting to capture a moment with the guest of honor. With the earl at her side, Alma graciously greeted all who approached her.

Her cousin, the ultimate hostess, lost little time in introducing Alma to the governor and his wife, as well as several other notable dignitaries from across the fast-growing city. His little princess shined in the midst of Tucson's finest.

In spite of this truth, Dillon wanted to sweep her back to the mountains, to their isolation, to those moments only they'd shared. Time spent with her had been precious, a gift he hadn't even realized he'd received until she was gone from his life.

Jackson nudged him. "Did you hear me?"

Good God, what've they been saying? "What?" Dillon snapped, shifting his attention between the two men.

Jackson set aside his empty plate and frowned. "I asked if you're all right."

"Sure," Dillon growled. "I'm just great."

"You don't look so great," Gus said, lifting a tiny cake from his plate. He poked the tidbit into his mouth, then mumbled around the bite, "In fact, you look angry as hell."

"That's bullshit. What do you know anyway?"

Gus swiped a finger over the creamy remains of the frosting on his plate. "I know something's wrong,"

Jackson's eyes narrowed. "New suit?"

Dillon reached for another whiskey from the tray carried by a passing waiter. "I bought it at Fort Riley," he replied in a monotone, his composure eroding faster than his patience. "What of it?" The ache of watching Alma, now wrapped in the arms of the earl on the dance floor, tore through him. His jaw tightened as he raised the tumbler and sipped.

"Nothing," Jackson said. "It's just unlike you to pander to fashion."

"Pander? What the hell does that even mean?" Dillon already knew, and he'd done exactly that at Fort Riley. Regardless, he didn't want his friends to shred apart things that didn't matter one iota now. "Look," he said, his voice even. "We were invited to a party at the fort with a lot of high-ranking officers. I didn't want to embarrass the colonel by appearing disheveled."

Gus laughed. "Oh yes. That sounds just like something you give a shit about."

Dillon downed the rest of his drink, wincing. "The gathering was in honor of Colonel George Custer. Seems Alma and his wife are good friends."

The remembered feel of Alma's body pressed up against him in the teepee burned through Dillon as she again twirled past on the arm of her fiancé. Candlelight caught the ivory sheen of the strand of pearls woven through her hair.

Dillon stared at her.

Her bare shoulders radiated with a glossy elegance beneath the candle-light and his mind relived the silken texture of every inch of her skin.

"Custer, huh?" Gus said. "I've heard interesting stories 'bout him."

"He's quite the character," Jackson added. "Met him shortly before Appomattox. His division was in the same cavalry corps as my regiment. He's a bit dandified for my taste, but Reece liked him."

"Reece – your wife's brother, right?" Dillon absentmindedly asked hoping to steer the conversation into another direction. His gaze narrowed on Alma as she drew Lord Green to the side of the dance floor.

"That's right," Jackson replied, turning to stare at him. "And I was his second-in-command…but, then again, you already know all this, pal." For several long moments, his friend also peered at Alma and the earl before recapturing Dillon's attention. Awareness slowly lifted his lips into a smile. He nodded, a knowing understanding shining bright in his eyes. "Ah, yes…now I know."

Dillon swapped his empty glass for a full one from another waiter. "Just let it go."

"You're gettin' slow, Jackson," Gus said on a laugh. "I had all this between them figured out yesterday."

Colonel Talmadge sauntered up, a plateful of food in his hands. "Have you tasted these little cucumber thingamajigs? They're mighty fine." He swallowed, his gaze shifting between the three men. "What? They are."

Gus smacked the commander on the arm. "Thaddeus, let's you and I head back over to the tables and make up another plateful? These young'uns need to talk about the goin' on's 'tween Dillon and your lovely niece."

"A fine plan." The colonel agreed, and the two men faded into the crowd.

Jackson stepped before Dillon, momentarily blocking Alma from his view. "So, now...why don't you tell me the rest of the story?"

"No." Dillon lifted his glass and swallowed again, sidestepping. The further away from the topic of loving Alma Talmadge he stayed, the better. His gaze narrowed on the earl deep in conversation with her.

She didn't look a damned bit happy.

Glass of whiskey in hand, Jackson shrugged, then leaned his shoulder against the trunk of a nearby cottonwood. Lanterns swung from the lower branches to illuminate the terrace. "All right, then, how 'bout I guess, and you let me know if I'm getting close."

Dillon took another sip. *Jeezus...*he didn't want to talk about this.

Not now.

Not ever.

His friend raised the glass, an index finger pointing toward Lord Green. "Now, I'm guessin' you'd probably like to strangle some English sonofabitch right about now for holding on to your girl. Am I getting warm?"

Jackson's question had nailed him straight in the center of his heart.

Dillon's gaze lifted and he swallowed, his mind spinning, his heartbeat ramping double time. Moonlight washed silver the night sky, but what he saw was the image of Alma lying naked on a bed in a cabin in Camp Apache. "Fine. Goddamnit," he snapped. His hand tightened around the glass. "So you've ciphered things out. Now what?" Never had Dillon been so torn between what he wanted and what he could not have. He shifted his gaze back to Alma just as she raised her head.

Indigo eyes, suddenly serious, locked on his.

Her fan fluttered faster than a jackrabbit chased by a fox.

Something's wrong.

His heart slammed against his ribs. The earl and Alma were arguing. He could see the frustration on her face.

Dillon's gut clenched tighter.

All trace of humor had fled Jackson's voice. "Have you told her how you feel?"

"And what the hell good would that do? I've nothing to offer her, and *that* bastard out there can give her the world." Dillon slammed back the remainder of his whiskey.

The knife of loneliness cleaved deeper. He wanted to hide from the truth, from the past two months with Alma, from his own maddening fears of love and need and desires. He searched the crowded room for a waiter bearing another tray filled with drinks.

"Look," Jackson said, drawing his attention again. "You once told me living a full life with Callie came down to one thing: whether or not I loved her." He jammed a finger in Dillon's shoulder and shoved him back a step. "So, I'm returning the favor now. No matter how much you drink, your answer isn't in the bottom of a whiskey glass. If you love this woman, tell her. Let her make her own decision." He dropped his hand. "The rest of the bullshit isn't important. You also told me that, by the way. And I'm glad I listened. I suggest you do the same." With a grumbled oath, his friend walked toward Gus and the colonel standing near the dessert table.

The lump in Dillon's throat tightened.

Sonofabitch.

His gaze swung back to Alma.

She pulled away from her fiancé and took a step back. Then, took another.

Lord Green advanced on her, his hand grasping her arm.

What the hell?

The earl gave her a hard shake. Once. Twice. Moonlight flashed off the diamonds and rubies dangling from her ears as Alma struggled to break free.

Anger blazed through Dillon. He'd despised this royal piece of shit on sight. He slammed his empty glass on a sidetable, then pushed through the crowd. With each step he took, his rage grew. Hands fisted, he stepped in front of Alma's fiancé. "Let her go. Now."

"Dillon," Alma whispered, a blush riding high on her cheeks. His name falling from her lips eased his rage back a notch, but far from brought the satisfaction driving his fist into the bastard's face would bring. "It's all right," she said. "I'm fine."

Shock decayed to resentment on Lord Green's face. He held her arm a moment longer, then released her. "Ah, how well opportuned," he quipped, a crisp lift to his chin. "Look who has arrived. The raw and tritely predictable Mister Reed. The infamous army scout, are you not?"

Dillon leaned forward, casting him in a shadow. "That's right. I'm *that* army scout."

The band continued to play and dancers swirled past, unaware of their escalating confrontation.

"Well then," Lord Green said with disdain, "I'm afraid that does make you a true nobody."

Dillon shot his hand out, crumpling a fistful of the man's gold-embroidered silk. He dragged the earl closer. "Listen to me, you ignorant lobcock," he snarled, not giving a damn who might hear him. "No one, not even you, will disrespect her."

"Please, Dillon. Turn him loose," Alma beseeched, laying her white-gloved hand upon his arm.

He hesitated, too aware of how good it'd feel to drive this arrogant ass to the floor. A lesson in propriety he needed.

"Please," she repeated. "Don't let him upset you. We were just conversing about…things."

Dillon stared down into the earl's widened eyes. "How fortunate for you she's merciful," he hissed. "Unlike me." On a mumbled curse, Dillon shoved him away, satisfied at the mix of outrage and fear on the man's face.

Lord Green smoothed his crumpled vest, and a quick twist resettled his white satin bowtie. "We've just met, Mister Reed, and yet, I already find you tedious and boring." His grim expression darkened. "And the things Miss Talmadge and I discussed is how she insists on calling off our engagement." One at a time, the earl straightened the cuffs beneath his dress coat's sleeves. "Now, I don't suppose you had anything to do with that, did you?"

Dillon's heart pounded so hard he thought the damned thing might rip from his chest. He glared into the fop's eyes. "If I had, you'd be the first person I'd tell."

A crowd around them grew as couples stopped to gawk.

Moments later, Colonel Talmadge pushed into view. "Hold up there, Dillon," he said, sidling next to Alma. The commander patted her back. "You all right, my dear?"

"Yes, Uncle Thaddeus. We were just having a...discussion."

"A discussion, huh?" The commander looked Dillon square in the eyes. "Why don't you go cool down, son? I'm sure what needs saying can be accomplished in a far better and more discreet manner at some later time."

Pamela arrived and shot Dillon an understanding look, then slipped her arm around Alma's waist.

A firm hand pressed hard on Dillon's shoulder.

"Colonel's right, my friend," Jackson said. "Come along with me, and we'll let these fine folks get back to their dancing. There's a bottle of whiskey at Renaldo's that's waiting for you. My treat."

"Thank you, Jackson," Pamela whispered.

"No. Wait." Alma pleaded. "H-he doesn't need to leave."

"Yes, he does," Jackson stated. He glanced over his shoulder. "Gus? You coming with us or staying here with Thaddeus?"

"Think I'll stay awhile longer," Gus said, eyeing the fuming earl. "'Sides, I got me a hankerin' for some more of that clotted cream over yonder once this is all settled."

Dillon shrugged free from his friend's hold and stared into Alma's eyes, drawn to her like a restless sigh pulled into a hot, swirling wind.

Her indigo gaze intensified. "We'll talk soon," she whispered. "I promise."

"For you, Princess." Nerves taut, temper guiding him, Dillon shoved past the earl, crossed the terrace, and jerked open the side door.

He glanced back.

Alma still watched him.

With a sharp oath, he left the hotel and headed straight for the cantina.

***

As Alma moved off with her cousin, Lord Henry stepped to the side of the courtyard and cursed under his breath.

Two peas in a pod those two.

Across the bricked terrace the dancing and frivolity of the evening resumed.

Henry glared at the belligerent wench. How dare she humiliate him with her whispered endearments to that condescending scout? Gone was the colorless woman who'd stared up at him with adoration in her rose garden several months earlier. *That* Miss Talmadge would never have called off their wedding a week before the occasion. An idea no doubt planted in her mind by Reed.

What else had that low-class scout planted inside his fiancée?

Tension knotted in his gut as the time to save himself from a debtor's prison ticked away. He'd spent months finding the perfect bride in this insipid Boston beauty. All his hard work, all his well-thought-out plans, all his deliverance quashed by some insignificant dullard.

A waiter moved past with a tray of refreshments. Henry snatched the closest glass of wine. He inhaled, forcing a look of calm upon his face as he nodded at several passing guests. With a thin smile, he sipped the aperitif.

"Ah…an aromatic Bordeaux," he stated to his manservant, Edgar, standing beside him in the shadows. As the claret flowed through his veins so did much-needed control. Henry raised the stemware and swirled the magenta liquid, perusing the *tears* that draped the side of the goblet.

"A strong alcohol, indeed." He smiled. "Though not as perfect as a fine Portuguese spirit…I'm impressed."

Henry sipped again, then removed a handkerchief from the inside breast pocket of his coat. He dabbed his lips as his gaze settled on Miss Talmadge, standing near the colonel and his daughter.

Henry's gaze met Alma's

He smiled.

Salvaging her affections should prove little trouble as long as that lone wolf scout could no longer influence her.

A problem easily resolved.

"Edgar?" he whispered.

His loyal servant nodded, leaning closer. "Yes, m'lord?"

"Find Simon Bell. Tell him to come to my cottage at first light."

"Yes, sir."

Henry drained the remainder of the Bordeaux, then dabbed at his lips once more. With another smile, he handed the empty glass to his servant. "Let him know I have another job for him."

CHAPTER THIRTY-TWO

With the *Welcome to the Arizona Territory* gala over, Alma settled in the guest bedroom at her cousin's home. According to Pamela, the evening had been a huge success. Exactly what determined the declaration, Alma was unsure. As far as she was concerned, after Dillon had been forced to leave, she couldn't wait for the festivities to end.

"*¿Algo más, señorita?*" The servant mumbled in Spanish.

"I'm so sorry, Rosa," Alma replied, lowering into a nearby rocker. *I must learn this language.* "I don't understand your words."

"*Lo siento…*I sorry, *Mees* Talmadge. I ask if you need anything more."

Alma shook her head, offering a soft smile. "No, I'm fine. Thank you. I appreciate all your help tonight."

"*De nada, señorita.*" With a nod, Rosa departed, pulling the door closed behind her.

At last.

Alone.

Alma scanned the small room, pausing on the jewelry glittering the top of the dresser. Lamplight spilled in an unrestrained glow across the diamond and ruby earrings, the only visual left to affirm this evening. All the clothing, toiletries, and accessories had either been hung up in the wardrobe or stowed inside her trunks.

As if tonight had never happened.

On a sigh, she leaned back in the rocker and clasped her hands in her lap. Despite the exhaustion, bliss bubbled through her. With the marriage called off, she could make whatever decisions she wanted in her life.

A warm pulse thumped at the base of her throat as Dillon's image resurfaced. She leaned forward and drew her fingers through her disheveled locks. Free of pins and pearls, her long tresses spilled across her shoulders in a silky wave. Unrestricted. *Wanton.* She shuddered, feeling each nerve ending inside her breathe into life.

Her heartbeat fluttered as her anticipation grew. Every single part of her decision screamed impropriety. Yet, she cared for Dillon more than the rules that had structured her life.

He'd not deserved the embarrassment Lord Green had spewed at him this evening. At the very least, he warranted an apology for the earl's chastisement in front of half the population of Tucson.

A tremor coursed through Alma. She loathed the earl for his rude behavior, anger she'd shown by publicly cutting him in response to his mistreatment. Instead of acting like a gentleman and accepting her decision to call off their engagement, he'd caught her arm with anger.

Her heart ached for Dillon.

Willingly, he'd taken the blame for his transgressions in response to the earl's ill-mannered behavior and left the party. His intervention on her behalf had been driven by concern, his protective actions that of a gallant cavalier.

Her frustrations escalated.

Stop seeing him?

The earl might as well ask her to stop breathing.

Alma leaned back and closed her eyes again. As the chair rocked upon the wood, a pang of longing enveloped her, raw and crushing. Her time with Dillon was unforgettable. From the first moment they'd met up through this very night, he'd protected her, kept her safe, cared for her like no other man ever had, except her father.

The slow and steady sway of the chair calmed her. There was so much more to Dillon Reed, to them, than the protector role he'd claimed.

Still rocking, Alma closed her eyes. No matter how much he might deny his feelings for her or fight the truth, Dillon could not call back the longing burning in his eyes when he'd looked at her this evening. That same raging desire now driven by an equal and undeniable need that sang through her own veins.

Joy purled through her. For a second, his possessive kisses, his touch during their journey and their time in the teepee, how his mouth had captured hers, his teeth nipped her skin, and his hands cupped her breasts, the acts made even more enticing by their very wickedness.

Her confidence soared, and she opened her eyes.

Yes. I can do this.

She stood and walked to the wardrobe, pulling open the mahogany doors. A light *whish-whish* echoed in the room as she scraped the array of expensive garments along the metal bar.

Looking...searching...focusing on just the right one.

Her fingers paused on a simple, sheer ecru cotton-and-linen frock. She smiled at the limitless tiny rose buds, the billowy sleeves, and the bodice drawn into soft gathers at the waist.

Soft...like his cambric shirt.

So perfect.

Alma withdrew the garment and laid the modest dress upon the bed. A tug loosened the satin belt around her waist.

With a whisper-thin promise to her heart, she slid off the robe.

Lamplight illuminated her nakedness as excitement sizzled through her. Staring at herself in the mirror, recalling his bold touch, she ran her hands over her bare flesh. Her skin tingled. She wished Dillon were touching her, and determined that before this night ended, he would be.

A siren's smile reflected in the mirror.

Never in her life had she been so shameless, but time spent with Dillon had changed her. She wanted him, yearned for his touch. She'd left Boston to marry for propriety, but she was now a woman with desires for a man.

Not any man, but Dillon. And he, an unlikely hero, deserved her at her most vulnerable.

She must tell him...*everything.*

Alma donned the dress. The material settled around her nakedness like a cloud of softness caught on a summer sigh. Understanding that this night must be perfect for her planned seduction, she secured the four buttons to shield her neckline.

After donning leather-soled slippers and running a brush through her hair, Alma paused once more before the mirror.

Go.

Now.

She settled a full-length Kinsale cloak across her shoulders.

You need nothing more.

A quick tug, pulled up the hood.

Whisper soft steps and the voice inside her head, her heart, propelled her through the darkened house and out into the night.

Like a beacon of determination, moonlight spilled in silver streaks around her.

Alma raised her chin as her unwavering footsteps crunched over the ground. The frightened girl who'd quivered at the changes unfolding inside her no longer existed. Tonight her purpose waited in a rundown adobe cabin clinging to the shadowy edges of life. And ultimately, the rugged army scout inside who'd deemed himself unworthy of love would succumb.

Tonight, and every one of her nights forthcoming, belonged to Dillon Reed.

CHAPTER
THIRTY-THREE

Dillon paced his one-room shack, an oil lamp in the center of the table flickering each time he passed. Twenty minutes earlier, Jackson had shoved him inside and told him to sleep things off.

He grunted. *Yeah…right. Like that's going to happen.*

The bottle of whiskey he'd consumed hadn't even touched the frustrating *things* still boiling inside him. He muttered a curse. In scouting, in life, for every problem he'd ever faced, he'd worked out a resolution… bedamned the unpleasant consequences.

Except, there was no resolution for loving Alma.

Names anyone could cast at him far from matched those he called himself. This was the stupidest *thing* he'd ever done.

He'd been ordered to escort her, nothing more.

Escort? Another snort fell from his mouth. Like any sane man could've spent time with her without falling for those indigo eyes he wanted to drown in. Hell's fire, however irritating, he'd even come to appreciate her defiance.

In the end, that spunk had saved his life and stolen his heart.

Hell. A scowl pulled tight as Dillon reached for his gun belt. A hard jerk freed the buckle. The Colt swung free of his hips and he settled the weaponry onto the seat of his rickety chair. She wasn't some cherry he could poke and then walk away with a flip of a coin, bollocks emptied. A sharp huff shucked his jacket and shirt. With another curse, he tossed them into the corner, quickly followed by each boot.

The entire bottle of whiskey. *Shit*, he was half-rats, surprised he could even think. His head spun. There'd be hell to pay come morning. Another grate filled the room. He'd done what he had to do, he'd left her damned party…but there was no way in hell he could ever sleep off the *things* he burned to do with Alma.

Jeezus.

She'd called off her engagement. He struggled to crush the hope-filled trembling that rolled through his veins.

Why?

His heart pounded at her reason: because of him. Hell, as if that were even a thought in her mind. Why would a woman who possessed everything want a man with nothing to give? And yet, if by some miracle he ever made love to her, his life as he knew it would be over. Done. Finished. Did he really want that?

God, yes…in a heartbeat. He'd walked away from her once; if she allowed him into her bed, her heart, he'd never walk away again.

Dillon squelched the asinine thought and plowed his fingers through his hair as he resumed pacing.

Sonofabitch.

She embodied perfection, while his life was riddled with flaws. He found control in hiding his feelings and moving on. Nothing, and no one, had ever broken him.

Until Alma.

Dillon stared at the saddle in the corner, his sparse furnishings, fewer clothes…and the cobalt-blue bottle sitting beside the oil lamp. By choice he had few possessions. He'd always travelled light, wanted no one, allowed himself to care for but a few friends.

The flickering flame tossed shadows and light over the vial.

Like a fool, he'd fallen for a society woman, a woman so far beyond his reach the mere concept of claiming her forever seemed laughable.

The huff of his breath filled the spartan room. He'd built himself into a fortress void of caring.

Until Alma.

She proved his greatest weakness. He gripped the side of the table, narrowing his gaze on the bottle of perfume.

A soft knock sounded at the door.

He cut his glare to the entry and cursed. *Jackson.* No doubt he'd returned with more "sage" advice. His friend wanted to talk?

Fine, Dillon had a few choice words to say, as well.

He shoved from the table and jerked open the door. The cool night air brushed across his bare chest. "I don't know what you…"

A diminutive figure swathed from head to toe in a voluminous cloak stood before him. A hand reached from beneath the ample folds and pushed back the hood. Pale hair glistened in the moonlight as recognition slammed into his heart.

Alma.

"Good evening," she said, a smile dusting her lips.

Too much whiskey and too little control swelled the instant want for her in his denims. He dared not blink, petrified the angel before him might disappear.

As well she should.

"You shouldn't be here," he snapped, wanting nothing else but to pull her into his home.

"May I come in?" she asked, her voice weaving through the frustration and need in his veins.

His grip on the wooden door tightened as he forced himself to meet her eyes.

God, yes.

Hell no…sonofabitch.

Before he could respond, she ducked beneath his arm and entered this sadly sparse side of his life. Dillon scoured the surroundings, cursing beneath his breath. If even one gossip-monger spotted her slipping inside his cabin, her reputation would be in shreds.

He didn't give a shit about himself, but a late-night visit with any man unchaperoned would destroy a woman of her standing. She must leave.

His mind swirled as he turned to face her, adding his heated reminder. "We've already said our goodbyes, Alma."

As if he hadn't spoken, she swept off her cloak and laid the garment across the closest rickety chair. Lamplight spilled over her dress, outlining her curves in a golden radiance.

No corset.

No society restrictions.

Only softness, simplicity…and a staggering hope that bubbled once more into life inside him.

The scent of roses wafted around Dillon. His heart clenched as he closed the door. He leaned his back against the weathered wood.

His jaw tightened as she lifted the blue bottle, weighing the glass in her hands. "For a special woman?" she asked, not turning to face him.

"Yes. For you," he growled, unable to hold back the truth. "In remembrance of our time together."

She faced him. Her chin lifted, and she closed her fingers around the blue glass. "I see," she whispered. "Then I shall treasure your gift always."

Inexplicably, the walls of the room closed in around Dillon. His mind spun with anger…the easiest emotion he could conjure. *What hellish game are you playing now?* He folded his arms across his chest. "Shouldn't you be patching things up with Lord Green?"

She settled the perfume vial back on the table. "I came to apologize for the disrepute that befell you this evening."

Disrepute? He snorted at her nicely spun words. "I'm a big boy, Princess. I can handle that jackass." She couldn't stay. However much he wanted her, she couldn't stay. Not after he'd been drinking to forget her.

For a long moment she studied him. "I know you can. In fact, you've handled everything life has ever thrown at you. Tragedy, betrayal and loss of loved ones, sadness, doesn't matter, you overcame them all." She took a step closer. "But you didn't deserve such ill treatment this evening. You were only protecting me, and I can't thank you enough."

He grunted. "I don't want your thanks, Alma." Unable to stop himself, his gaze dropped to her lips. "I was doing my job, remember?"

She nodded, sending her tresses into a shimmering dance. "Yes. Your job."

The spike of desire for her sharpened, driving into his soul. With a curse, he pushed from the door and stalked to his pile of clothing. A quick shrug pulled on the faded chambray. He whirled, the front of his shirt gaping open. "Let's stop revisiting things I should've left unsaid, all right? I've delivered you to the fort safe and sound. Why are you really here?"

"I'd like to talk about our journey..."

She took another step closer.

And his blood ran hot as Dillon struggled for restraint. He wanted to plunge his fingers into her hair, drag her against him, and devour her with kisses. "The journey we've shared will never be over," he growled, his patience fraying by the second. "You've one more chance to go. I suggest you take it."

"I should," she agreed, "but I'm not leaving." Alma settled her hands upon the first pearl button. A subtle move slipped the opaque disc through the opening. "Not now. Not ever. Not when there's still so much left for you to show me."

Need blurred his mind into a haze of red. He regained control. Barely. "Stop this, Alma," he said between clenched teeth. Three steps took him to her and Dillon caught her upper arms, giving her a soft shake. "You've no idea what you're doing."

"I know exactly what I'm doing." A sultry smile lifted her lips as she undid the second button. "And just like that night in the teepee, which I do remember by the way, I am in full control of this moment, too. I'm unskilled in love's ways, yes, but I trust you will remedy that, as well. You are a hero, Dillon...my hero."

"Hero?" he spat, unable to stop himself from taking in the shadowy tease of her cleavage, the promising heat in her words. His gaze again leveled with hers. "Do you want to know what I really am? I'm selfish, Alma. Selfish because I want you and there's not a goddamned excuse in this world that can cover all the reasons I'm wrong for you."

Instead of taking a step back, she leaned closer.

Dillon mumbled another curse. Loving this woman hurt. "And I don't like sharing you, not with your earl, not with anyone." And trust... *Son of a damn bitch...* trust hurt even more. He scoffed. "You don't know what the hell you want."

"I know I want you," she whispered, her voice confident and filled with a mixture of hope and understanding. "We were brought together for a reason. You know this. I know this. Y-you've shown me the world, made me question everything I've ever known about my life." She smiled again as she slipped free another button.

The exposed flesh drew his gaze. With a scowl, he looked up.

"But, I'm not questioning this choice tonight," Alma continued. "I love you, and I always will. You cannot push me away like you've done everyone else. No matter how hard you try, I'm staying."

S-she...loves me?

His heart banged inside his chest as he struggled for control. Another oath ripped from his throat as he dug his fingers deeper, desperate. "I don't fit in, not in your world. Don't you see that?"

Something intense and riveting and all-consuming brightened in her eyes. "Of course you don't fit in, my love. You were meant to be out front, leading, guiding, protecting others, protecting me."

Good God, did he dare believe her, trust he could be this close to paradise? Had the whiskey blurred his sanity? He released his hold on her, and yet, with every rattling beat of his heart he wanted her to stay. "Go back to Lord Green. He'll give you the world, which is what your father wants for you."

"My father wants me to be happy." Alma slipped the last button from its closure, and the slope of her breasts illuminated beneath the shimmer of lamplight. "And you, Dillon Reed, *you* make me happy."

Sweat broke out on his brow as he imagined the cherished treasure that awaited him beneath the dress. She was heaven on earth to his tortured soul. He'd memorized every curve of this woman whom he loved with a depth that left him frightened. The time they'd spent together, the miles they'd traveled, the dangers they'd faced, had bonded them in a way nothing or no one else ever could. She'd seen the angry man, the unforgiving man, the untrusting sonofabitch inside him that made him run from everyone and everything…except her. She'd broken down every damned wall he'd erected, and had pushed hard, even this night, to claim him.

He was finished with fighting her.

Fighting himself.

On a rough groan, Dillon accepted the turning point; finished with denials, fear of intimacy, the feverish fear of abandonment. Dillon swallowed hard. "I want you, Alma," he growled, the pulsing need for her straining hard to break free from his denims. "Right now, forever, for me nothing else matters in this world but loving you."

He'd crossed the line. He'd said it…there was no going back now.

Tears misted her eyes. "Together, we'll get through anything, Dillon. I promise. You're all that matters to me, too."

With a shrug, she dropped her dress to the floor.

He stared transfixed as lamplight illuminated pure ecstasy. Her hair caressing the top of her breasts. On a ragged breath her name fell from his lips. A scalding tightness pulled across his chest, his groin, and in one raging heartbeat, Dillon drove her back against the wall. "Know this," he rasped. "I'm never saying goodbye to you again. Do you understand?"

She nodded, her indigo eyes wide, filled with adoration, filled with need. "Completely." She slid her hands around his shoulders. "And I will never leave you agai—"

Dillon's mouth found hers. Desperation surged through him as love for this woman flooded his starving soul. Every static heartbeat became Alma's, his breathing frantic, matching hers. Weeks of denial tore a tattered groan from his throat as he skimmed his hands lower, dipping into the small of her waist, slicking over her buttocks.

A rough pull burned her nakedness against his hard length. "You've no idea how much I've wanted you," he grated against her silken flesh. "My beautiful Princess."

"Yes…yours," she rasped. "Forever."

Dillon cupped her breasts, skimmed his thumbs over her nipples, teasing, taunting. Her. Him. He bent and suckled, cherishing the sweet and salty tang of her against his tongue, craving every luscious flavor that spiced this flawless woman.

Their breathing accelerated, matched only by the other's frantic need. He was finished with the wait. He lifted her, and with a throaty gasp, Alma tunneled her fingers into the hair at the nape of his neck.

As if she'd been born for this moment, she curled around him.

In three steps, he took her to his bed.

With infinite possession, he laid Alma across the blanket and leaned over her, staring into her eyes that held his, beckoning, their bewitching blue ablaze. He ran his hands into her hair as further down, his body pulsed for damnable release. "You are my life, Alma. Know that, always and forever."

"I know, and you are min--"

Again, he kissed her, heat burned through his veins. He claimed her, his tongue plundered deeper, teasing, until she gripped his shoulders, groaning beneath his pressure. He shifted, kissing her mouth, her face, dipping lower to nip her collarbone. Months of forbidden now stoked the flame that raged inside him. He cupped her head, drawing her closer. "I'll teach you how your body was born to respond to me," he breathed into her ear. "Tonight and every night that follows."

He released her and on a deep breath stood, never breaking their gaze. With a shrug of his shoulders, he shucked his shirt. A heartbeat later, his denims followed.

Boldly, he stood before her.

Her gaze lowered, her eyes widening. A second passed, and her lips tipped upward in pleasure. "Oh my."

His lips quirked sideways, pleased with her guiltless approval. "I mentioned I was a bad boy, remember?" he chuckled, his tone deep and gravelly. "This right here affirms that, my love."

Her gaze enchanted him.

"I love new discoveries, you beast" she whispered, reaching up for him. "And I'm not one bit afraid with you."

The iron bed creaked as he stretched beside her, drawing her close. *A beast, indeed.* And she a precious innocent. He slicked his hand down her body, then back to cup her breasts. Sensuous. Silky. Pure perfection against his calloused palms.

An easy pull brought her closer.

He bent his head and buried his face in her hair, thrilled to be the one to show her the revelations that awaited. "There'll be pain at first, Princess…but only for a moment. Know this: For the precious gift you give me this night, I will cherish you as long as I draw breath."

He reclaimed her lips and ground his body against hers. Arching her against him, eager in his quest. Dillon suckled her breast, worshipping her, nipping and licking and relishing every second with this angel. Bliss waited. He reclaimed her lips, then angled back, gazing down at her kiss-swollen lips. She slid a fingertip over his cheek, then down his stubbled jaw to his mouth.

His lips tilted up.

Alma continued, her lashes lowering, skimming her hand over his chin and chest, his stomach, and lower.

He hissed, the blistering ache inside him begging for relief.

She paused, her gaze locking on his. "I want to…"

"Yes, God yes…touch me," he pleaded. He guided her hand where he wanted her fingers to go. As she wrapped him in her warm grip, he gave a sharp hiss. His body pulsed against her boldness. "You've claimed me…forever."

Tears of joy misted her eyes. "Now, you claim me and make me yours…forever."

On a coarse moan, Dillon slid his bare leg over hers, and the feel of her silken flesh sent another shiver upward. Her skin pebbled beneath the sweep of his hands. She moaned and he shifted, adjusting his weight. He ran a hand up her thigh, over her breasts, until he found the swollen nipple and flicked his thumb over the hard nub, squeezing, teasing the gateway to heaven.

She gasped and arched against him. "Dillon," she rasped. "Please…"

She beseeched for more, and the thrill of her plea ripped through him. A demanding force consumed him as her sweet essence enveloped him, provocative and beguiling. Dillon obeyed her brazen beckon. Bracing himself above her, nudging her legs wider, her peered into her eyes. "Breathe in my love…" She obeyed and he sank into her slick warmth. At the fragile barrier he paused.

The honor of being her first banished his hesitation. He drove deeper. Her breath caught, followed by a soft, sweet gasp.

And he stilled, treasuring this woman more for her precious and perfect gift. Once her body began to relax, with care he set a smooth, rhythmic pace, slowly building. Dillon guided her legs around him, and their breathing fused.

As he knew they would be, their bodies were a masterpiece of one.

"Move with me, baby," he urged. And she moaned, answering him with each lift and lower. He pivoted each thrust and she followed his lead into the paradise of a perfect love's dance. "Yes…like that. Just like that."

With unwavering rule, Dillon clutched her hips and deepened his strokes—every single part of him complete. Easy sweet circles. Brushing against her most sensitive spot created for this moment, created just for him.

"Yes, you feel that, baby," he ground out, the words ripping from his throat. "I know you do." She matched his rhythm and speed, learning quickly…gasping her pleasure. Wanting more. Imploring, his name a whisper on his heart. And for each stroke he gave her, for each of her answered thrusts, Dillon's control further weakened.

Over and over she moaned his name until, with an indrawn breath, she finally crested, crying out her culmination in deep, unrestrained gasps.

His blood roared in his ears as the pressure inside Dillon ramped, mounting, refusing containment another moment. And then…on a strangled cry, he followed her, transcending into heaven-scent bliss as he released himself deep inside his princess, his Alma…forevermore his home.

CHAPTER
THIRTY-FOUR

A swath of late-morning sunlight streamed through the cabin's window illuminating Alma. She secured the first button on her dress as Dillon stepped behind her.

With a moan, he slid his arms around her waist and pulled her against him. "How 'bout you take this damned thing off again." He nestled his face in her hair. "I'll show you all the reasons why."

Desire tingled along her skin, and Alma drew him tighter against her. His lips nuzzled her.

On a sigh, she closed her eyes, relishing his touch. "You were magnificent last night, my love, and undressed me thrice already this morning. Surely you've grown tired of me?"

"That'll never happen." He cupped her breasts. "I now live for you."

"I shall never forget with reminders like this."

"I've a few more things to teach you." He pulled her with him to the bed.

She giggled and slipped from his hold. "If I let you have your way, Dillon Reed, we shall be undressed all day."

With a chuckle, he stretched across the bed, leaned back and pillowed his head on his arms. "Sounds good to me."

Sunlight fell across his naked body. So masculine. So beautiful. So much of everything she'd dreamed this man might be…and more.

"Well," he said, his smile slipping, "if I can't entice you a fourth time with my instructive prowess, allow me to take you to breakfast. Saturday morning means biscuits and gravy over at the hotel restaurant." A wicked grin lifted his lips. "I'm starvin' near to death, and the meal will replenish us when we return to resume our...lessons."

She laughed, joy cascading through her. "First you think with your..." –her gaze dropped to his impressive length, before lifting— "well...you know. Then your stomach rules your world. I feel keeping up with your ever-shifting whims might drive me crazy."

"Good, 'cause I intend to keep you crazy with want forever."

Alma bent over him, bracing her hands on either side of his body. "I'm already there. Now, get up and cover that beast."

Without warning, he caught her in his arms and pulled her beside him among the rumpled covers. Tenderness reflected from his eyes. "I need this, need you."

A mere breath separated them, brushing warm across her lips. He claimed her mouth, and then...in his skillful way...her lover returned her to paradise. He taught her new things. Lovely things. Things that burned bright as he teased and tasted, savoring every single part of her body...*even there.*

With each beat of her heart, Alma treasured this exciting side of loving him. As she reached her summit and tipped, she cried out in bliss.

Knowing Dillon had brought her hope and new discoveries. A fulfilment she'd never known she needed. With him, she felt free and open. No inhibitions. No stifling society rules.

Alma rolled onto her side and faced him.

His lips curved again in that mischievous, utterly charming and irresistible way. "Might be a good thing if you marry me. What do you think?"

Alma shoved to her knees. *A good thing?* She stared at him, a soul-deep exhilaration winging through her. "M-Marry?"

"Well--" He pushed onto an elbow. "--I can't have you sneakin' around in the shadows of night anymore." He tucked a wayward curl off her cheek. "I mean, you might stumble into the wrong cabin, and we can't have that happening, right?"

He watched.

Waited.

Love for Dillon filled every part of her. Alma was certain he could hear the pounding of her heart. For him, her body heated. Hungered. "We certainly can't," she whispered.

His touch was addictive.

She craved more...of him, of this happiness, of waking every single day with him for the remainder of her life.

He sighed. "Sonofabitch...I've asked too soon. Too fast. I mean, I realize there's not a damn thing I can offer that you don't already have. I wouldn't fault you if you said no, but..."

Alma placed her fingertip on his lips. "Stop talking. You've given me the one thing I'll ever need...you. Dillon, I love you, always and only you."

With a swift move he brought her beneath him, the breadth of his shoulders blocking out the swatch of sunlight. His dark gaze locked on hers.

The same heat she felt registered in his eyes. "I love you, too, Princess. Say you'll marry me. We'll through life together...somehow."

The rough intensity of his words left her trembling. Humbled by his love, looking into his eyes, she saw their past, their present, and every day of their future together. "A thousand times yes," she whispered. "Yes, I'll marry yo--"

He caught her lips with gentle warmth and intimacy, his tongue teasing. Yet, intimacy wasn't only what they'd discovered in this bed... intimacy had also brought them through their arduous journey westward.

Pleasure mixed with pride inside Alma.

And for the next half-hour, her soul linked with Dillon's in complete agreement as her husband-to-be sealed their deal.

***

Two hours later Alma stood in her bedroom at the Palmer's house, bathed and dressed in one of her stylish Worth creations. With care, she pinned a Wedgewood blue cameo bar at the throat of her gown. Smoothing her hands over the cream-colored Brussels lace collar, she assessed her reflection, the skin tone of her face now golden from time spent in the sun.

A proper pioneer woman, indeed.

Having spent the night and early morning being loved by Dillon, she'd expected some outer show of change to match the joy that simmered inside. Yet nothing appeared amiss. She was proper and quite ill-mannered all at the same time.

A giggle followed.

Nonetheless, she approved the way her corset lent an elegant curve to her figure. The cotton and horsehair bustle hidden beneath the draping folds of fabric gave a lovely lift to her backside. After wearing the tattered emerald brocade across country for so long, she appreciated even more the rich detailing of the luscious lavender-colored silk.

Her smile widened.

Life had taken a turn into a new and most exciting direction, and she was more than ready for her afternoon outing with Dillon. A public statement, for sure, and she couldn't wait to proclaim their union to the world.

This was her man and she couldn't be happier.

Alma glanced toward the mahogany Fusee wall clock on the far wall. *He should be here any minute.* As the pendulum tick-tocked alongside her impatience, she added the finishing touches to her upswept chignon, then retrieved her Brussels lace day cap. A tuck of hair pins, and Alma secured the face-framing confection of tufted ribbons, blonde lace, and tiny quail feathers atop her head.

Dainty lace lappets fell across her shoulders. *Perfect.* She added expensive, golden filigree drop earrings to emphasize the risqué shading of her skin.

Refined, yet relaxed.

Just like the new me.

A sharp rap sounded at the front entrance as Alma entered the parlor. Inhaling to settle her pounding heart, she opened the door.

Dread eroded her newfound joy and she frowned. Why had *he* come? After last night's skirmish, God help him if Dillon arrived now.

She had to get him out of here.

"Lord Green," she said, clasping her hands before her. "I hadn't expected you."

"Do forgive my boldness, Miss Talmadge," he said, his thin frame swathed in a pewter-gray frock-coat adored with black velvet collar and cuffs. "I hope I've not arrived at an inopportune moment."

She scanned the entry walk behind him, then further into the dusty lane for any sign of Dillon. A part of her wished he were here, another was thankful for whatever caused his delay. Her gaze reconnected with the earl's. "Well, actually, I am preparing for an outing this afternoon."

Without an invitation, he stepped across the threshold. "I promise I shan't be long."

Anger at his impropriety faded beneath her guilt about how she'd ended their engagement. She allowed him into the entryway. "Well, I suppose I can afford you a few moments. Please, come into the parlor."

With a sigh, he followed, then settled onto a leather chair, the mahogany warming the cool tones of his frockcoat. He laid his top hat aside. "I wanted to apologize for my behavior last night. I'm most ashamed about my rudeness to the scout, as well as making you feel uncomfortable."

She remained standing. "I appreciate your candor, Lord Green, and thank you for your apology." A shadow moved across the front of the parlor window. *Dillon?* Her pulse raced. "I, too, offer my apologies at the abrupt dismissal of my affections."

"A point, my dear that I wish to discuss. Our union was sanctioned by your father. Surely disappointing him with your dismissal is not in your best interest."

The shadow neared the entrance. "My father is only concerned with my happiness," she snapped, impatient with this man's inane persistence.

A rap sounded at the door.

Whatever Lord Green's reasons for trying to win back her favor, she didn't want to hear them. Neither did she appreciate him trying to sway her by mentioning her father. "Last night I made it clear that I refuse to marry you. There is little more to say. Please allow me to show you out."

A disturbing smirk pulled across Lord Green's face. "I am not finished with our conversation."

A threat?

The knock sounded again.

"Unfortunately for you, Lord Green, I am."

Her unwanted suitor rose from the chair and reached for his hat.

"And I do wish you well, sir," she added, her voice cool. A smile wreathed her face as she turned and swung open the door.

Eyes widening, the earl gasped. "W-What are you doing here?" he snapped at the stranger who pushed his way into the house.

Lord Green knows him?

"Sir, you will leave," Alma demanded, stunned by the intruder's arrogance.

"A lovely day for a visit, isn't it?" The man jerked the weathered wood from Alma's grasp, closed the door, and then faced her. Vibrant blue eyes, the same shade as hers, peered back. A foot taller than the earl, every single thing about this man, from his slicked-back hair to his thin, pressed smile screamed danger. "Ahh, Miss Talmadge…at last we meet," he said, impudence underscoring each word. "And may I say how fetching you look in your expensive silk."

A flush of blood purpled Lord Green's face.

Fear, on the other hand, oozed through Alma, at Lord Green's intense resentment toward this stranger. She took a hesitant step backward, narrowing her eyes. "H-how dare you push into this home uninvited, sir?"

"Indignation?" He gave a cold laugh. "Yes…I like your fiery spirit. 'Tis a family trait, I do believe." He swept off his hat, smartly bowed, and then plopped the brown bowler upon the entry table. "Allow me to introduce myself. The name's Simon Bell."

Simon Bell!

The kidnappers. The cave. Dillon's injury. Panic sluiced through Alma as everything collected around this man's name and swirled back into blinding recall.

She must escape.

Warn Dillon.

Alma bolted for the door.

Simon intercepted her, shoving her against the wall. His gaze narrowed on her. "And you, my dearest sister, are going nowhere."

CHAPTER THIRTY-SIX

Dillon secured the thin black tie around his shirt collar, then jammed his arm into his frockcoat. Getting cleaned up this morning didn't seem quite the chore as it had for the damned party last night.

Course, a lot had happened since then.

Get up and cover that beast.

Proud of his prowess, a grin lifted his lips. *For you, Princess.* He envisioned Alma's beautiful eyes alight with excitement and desire, her body...their love.

He'd never been so happy in his life.

Alma changed everything.

Every.

Damn.

Thing.

His smile widened as he buckled his gunbelt, then slipped the Bowie knife into his boot. With a new-found pep in his step, Dillon exited the cabin, pulled the door closed behind him, and headed toward the Palmer's house.

As he neared the mercantile he spotted Pamela's house maid, arms laden with supplies, scurrying across the walkway.

"Mornin', Rosa," he said drawing her attention. He tipped his hat. "Here, let me carry those for you."

Recognition brightened her face. "*Buenos días, Señor* Reed. *Gracias.*"

Dillon scooped up the bundle. "I'm heading your direction anyway. Escorting Miss Talmadge to the hotel for a late breakfast."

"You *de buen humor*…good mood," she said as she fell into step at his side. "*Señora* Palmer told me about big party, last night."

"She did, huh?"

The old woman pushed a thick braid off her shoulder as they passed headquarters, then veered onto the dusty side lane. "*Si, Señora* Palmer share *muchos* before leaving for visit to the *padre* today."

"Why's she visiting Father Miguel?"

She smiled. "Taking new school books to orphanage."

"Ah, yes," Dillon said, nodding. "She and Callie keep that place afloat, that's for sure."

"Follow me, *Señor* Reed. I know a quicker way."

"Lead on, I'm right behind you." Laughing, the old woman cut across the alleyway behind officer's row.

The aroma of horse manure from the private stables filled the air. "*Apestoso*," she said, holding her nose, "but…saves *muchas* steps."

He smiled and a few minutes later, they arrived at the back porch of the house. "Allow me," he said, stepping before her. Dillon turned the knob and then pushed open the door.

Scuffling noises, a muffled gasp, and several sharp curses sounded from within.

What the hell?

Muscles tensing, senses on high alert, Dillon lowered the basket to the floor, then raised his hand to silence the servant. "Wait here," he whispered.

Face pale, Rosa nodded.

He entered the supply room that backed the house, muttered a silent curse, then returned to the porch. "Get Colonel Talmadge," he said in a hushed tone. "He should be in his office. Tell him to bring soldiers. Now, go."

She ran toward headquarters, dust puffing up with each one of her hurried footfalls.

Dillon withdrew his Colt and stepped into the hallway. Scuffling steps and a grunt echoed from the parlor.

He edged closer along the dimly lit passage.

"Thank you, Henry," an unfamiliar voice said. *Henry? Henry who?* A high pitched scrape sounded as something pulled across the floor. "That's good," the stranger continued. "Now, take a seat. I'm going to tie you up like our Miss Talmadge here. And if you don't behave I'll also gag you like I did her."

Dillon crept closer.

Tied and gagged? Alma?

Goddamnit.

Anger collided with the fear in his gut. The urge to rush in stormed over Dillon. He held himself in check. Barely. Now was not the time for recklessness. A wrong move and she could be killed.

Subdued grunts and words of protest elevated. Obviously, the second man hadn't complied fast enough. Terrified for Alma, Dillon inched closer.

How many were inside?

Two?

Three?

He hadn't a damned clue.

"And now, it's time I shared the unpleasant truth of everything with my half-sister," the too-calm voice continued.

Half-sister? Who in the hell was this person? Dillon frowned, and took another step.

"Shut your mouth you imbecile," the second man snarled. *Lord Green.* He'd recognize that cocky bastard's voice anywhere. He should've guessed Alma's ex-betrothed was somehow involved. "Have you lost your bloody min--"

A resounding slap echoed from the parlor. "Oh, how quickly you've changed your tune," the stranger retorted.

A long pause.

Dillon hugged the side of the passageway to avoid squeaking the floorboards.

"Do you mind if I call you Alma, my dear?" the unknown man continued. "After all we are kin?"

A subdued moan, female, met Dillon's ears. *Alma.* His heart stopped, then started again, off beat and jangled.

"Did you know your fiancé hired me to kill our beloved father?" the voice expounded. "Not that I minded…Charles Talmadge was going to die one way or the other, anyway."

More muffled sobs met Dillon's ears.

"I'm sorry you had to hear news of his death this way," her half-brother said without remorse.

"She has no need to hear of any of this, you mongrel," the earl snarled.

Dillon eased forward another step.

"Oh, but she does."

"D-do not listen to him, Alma," Lord Green sputtered. "He's full of lies."

"Ah yes, lies," the smooth voiced speaker mocked. "Like those regarding your intensions with her? In actuality, Lord Green is in debt up to his hocks and wanted to marry you only for your money. Did he not share this bit with you, my dearest?"

"I'm begging you to shut your mouth," the earl pleaded.

"Begging? How pathetic." The man laughed, then continued. "Unaware of my true heritage and with a handful of bills, your betrothed laid out the plan for our father's demise…which I joyfully accomplished. Yes, father now rests at the bottom of the harbor, and you've inherited the Talmadge wealth."

Alma's mournful sobs continued. Where the hell was the colonel? One way or another the madman who'd killed her father would die.

Another mocking laugh sounded. "And Alma, my sweet, you have caused me a great deal of trouble. Especially these last few months. Do you know how hard it was to find three men willing to kidnap you and hide you in the mountains *before* getting paid?" A snort. "And then to have them fail due to some troublesome army scout. That man seems to be a bur beneath Henry's saddle, too…isn't that right, Henry? Why else would you send Edgar to me with instructions to kill this Dillon Reed?"

Lord Green's frustrated groan came from the room. "You double-crossing bastard. My fiancé was not to be harmed in our arrangements."

"Oh Henry…you were merely a pawn in my plans. The money was never my issue. And by the way," the stranger added, "your servant won't be returning to your employ. You should be proud to know he died bravely, unlike the two whores I've recently sent to their maker since being here." The swishing pace of bootsteps followed. "You probably don't know this, dear sister, but our father had an affinity for whores, as well. One being my mother, whom he'd paid for years to keep silent. I am the result of that liaison."

More footfalls.

Dillon worked his way further along the wall.

Steps away from the parlor now.

Hold on, Princess.

"But enough of reminiscing," the lunatic spat. "Henry, I do believe you've reached the end of your usefulness."

"Noooo---" A rasping gurgle faded.

To hell with waiting for reinforcements. Gun at the ready, Dillon took a solid step around the corner. His gaze swept the room as he assessed the situation: Alma sat tied to a chair, a gag in her mouth, her self-proclaimed half-brother crouching behind her, an eight-inch bollock blade pressed to her throat.

Dammit, no clear shot.

A mumbled gasp erupted behind Alma's gag as her sapphire-blue gaze collided with his.

He released a heavy breath and glanced sideways. Lord Green slumped in a chair, his throat slashed from ear-to-ear.

The madman met Dillon's hard glare, then smiled, a cold, withering look rich with malice. "I'm Simon Bell. And who might you be?"

Hatred poured through Dillon and his brows slammed together. "I'm the man who's going to kill you," he said, calmness belying the raw anger that swirled inside him.

Alma's tear-filled eyes met his and she struggled against the ropes. Concern for her safety escalated.

Sit still. Don't provoke him.

The lunatic laughed, then pressed closer to her, his mouth jammed against her ear. "As passé as this sounds, my dearest, I do believe your scout has arrived just in the nick of time." He nodded to Dillon. "Kindly remove your gun belt, Mister Reed."

Stalemate.

Simon pressed the knife harder.

Alma cried out, and several droplets of blood slid down her throat.

Dillon seethed as he shoved the Colt into the holster, his heart thundering. *Don't look at her. Stay focused.* He unbuckled his belt.

The leather thumped to the floor.

"Good," her half-sibling said, his voice cold, his eyes even colder. "Now kick it over to me."

With the tip of his boot, Dillon shoved the gunbelt across the floor... just out of the man's reach. "Hiding behind a woman?" he said on a grizzled half-breath. "How 'bout you let her go and see how you do against me?"

With a smug look, Simon reached toward the Colt. The action caused the knife to move ever-so-slightly away from Alma's neck. In the instant his gaze dropped to the gun, Dillon charged, jerking aside the arm that held the blade.

Recovering, the man swung his knife downward, and pain tore across Dillon's forearm. Blood spread warm, darkening his coatsleeve.

Behind him, Dillon heard Alma's muffled shriek. He sucked air into his tight lungs, then slammed into Simon, driving them both to the floor. They grappled, then rolled upward into a stand six feet apart.

The maniac's eyes brightened. "Weaponless, I like that," he mocked, crouching. He brought the bollock up between them. "First blood goes to me, Mister Reed."

Dillon sidestepped, putting himself between Alma and this twisted devil.

Sunlight glinted across Simon's knife as he gripped higher on the hilt. "Did I mention I'm a master of the blade? Indeed, I grew up on the Boston wharves...this my only friend."

Without blinking, Dillon bent sideways and slowly withdrew his Bowie. "I was born in Texas, you sick sonofabitch, and this was mine."

Simon's chuckle seeped over him. "Excellent. I look forward to this fight between two gentlemen."

Dillon snorted, pacing sideways.

The man followed.

Every step took them farther and farther from Alma.

On a laugh, Simon charged.

Dillon slashed his blade.

A large gash opened across Simon's cheek. "My dear sister," he hissed, "your scout is an impressive foe." He laughed, then lunged.

Dillon deflected him, grabbing his arm and twisting.

Clanging blades echoed within the room.

A quick spin, and Simon nicked Dillon's jaw. Satisfaction glimmered in his eyes as he slashed again.

Knives met. Steel scraped steel.

Simon darted forward.

Dillon ducked, breathing hard. Pivoting on his heel, he brought his blade forward. A fierce thrust sank the Bowie deep in the madman's chest. "For Alma. And her father." He jerked the blade upward, then twisted. "Oh...and I forgot to mention, I'm no gentleman."

Blood gurgled from Simon's throat, then spilled down the side of his mouth. Pain-filled eyes faded to emptiness. With a rattled grunt he collapsed, dead before he hit the floor.

Relief poured through Dillon as he faced Alma.

Tears coursed down her face. On an oath, he stumbled to her and slashed through the ropes binding her to the chair. A quick tug removed her gag.

"Dillon," she sobbed, surging into his embrace.

His heart pounding, he swept her up and buried his face in her tangled tresses. He'd never let her go again. "You're safe now, Princess," he rasped. "You're safe."

The front door crashed open. The colonel and four soldiers charged inside. "Hold!" the Colonel called out.

Dillon turned and nodded, watching as the worry on the commander's face disappeared.

"I see you have the situation in hand," Talmadge said, motioning his men to deal with the bodies.

"I do, Sir," Dillon said. "And I'll fill you in on all this shortly, but first, I'm taking Alma away from here."

CHAPTER
THIRTY-SIX

Three weeks later...

High clouds skirted across the turquoise sky, promising to make Saturday morning a most spectacular day in the territory. Alma dropped the curtain and stepped from the window. Dillon had been gone for nearly ten minutes. *How long does it take to find a newspaper?* She ambled to the table and lifted the packet delivered to her by courier moments before. Heart pounding, she peered inside at the paperwork. *Surely he'll like it.*

Alma hugged the large envelope against her chest as a blissful shiver raced through her. She loved the starkness of the west, the openness, the freedom of choice knowing Dillon had brought her.

Her heart swelled with love for her husband. And on a contented sigh, she smiled at the gold band encircling her finger.

Their wedding yesterday morning...*perfection!*

A turning of the knob sounded, then the door of the hotel suite opened. Dillon stepped inside. "Looks like we've made the front page of *The Arizona Citizen.*" He angled a folded newspaper her way, while in his other hand he carried a mug of steaming coffee. "Sorry I took so long. I stopped to grab another cup, and got waylaid by more well-wishers in the dining room downstairs."

Her slippers swished across the carpet as she walked to her handsome husband and plucked the anticipated weekly edition from his outstretched hand. "I missed you. And thank you for getting this." She kissed him soundly on the lips, then headed toward the table. "Pamela assured me the editor would keep our marriage notice small this morning. I didn't know she'd planned to have the announcement splashed across the first page."

"Tucson's proud of their little shipping heiress, my love," he said with a chuckle, "and so am I." He settled upon the settee, stacked his feet atop the ottoman, and then took a sip of coffee. "Read the article to me."

Laying the packet alongside the newspaper, with reverence, she opened the newsprint, smoothing out the wrinkles:

"The wedding ceremony between Boston socialite Miss Alma Talmadge and renowned military scout and Fort Lowell's own Mister Dillon Reed, drew the largest attendance of any marriage before in Tucson's history. Father Miguel Hernandez performed the nuptials at the Mary Help of Christians Catholic Church before an attendance of more than two-hundred and fifty well-wishers. Mister Jackson Neale, the owner of Dos Caballos (one of the largest horse spreads south of the city), as well as the groom's friend, served as Mister Reed's best man. The bride's matron of honor duties were filled by her cousin, Mrs. Pamela Palmer, wife of Captain Alfred Palmer, officer in charge of Company E at Fort Lowell.

The groom wore a black serge cut-away suit, while the bride wore a spectacular Charles Worth gown of ivory watered silk. Sixteen yards of material completed her wedding ensemble, which had the longest draping train this reporter has ever seen. The bride's matron of honor exclaimed that it took a full day to prepare her cousin for the ceremony at the small church on the edge of town. The bride was given away in marriage by her uncle, Colonel Thaddeus Talmadge, Commander of the troops at Fort Lowell.

The couple will honeymoon later this summer with a trip to Boston, Massachusetts, where the bride will finish settling the estate of her recently-deceased father and shipping magnate, Mister Charles Talmadge. Upon her father's death, Mrs. Reed inherited the largest shipping company on the east coast, the well-renowned Talmadge Shipping Lines. Rumors swirl that she will be selling the company to long-time manager Stephen Smith, though she will continue to own stock in the enterprise.

The couple plan to settle in the Arizona Territory on a ranch just south of Tucson.

Alma lifted her head and saw the questions in his eyes before he even spoke. She smiled at him...waiting.

Confusion blanketing his face, he set his cup aside and leaned forward. "A ranch south of Tucson? Where'd they get that idea?"

"Well...I asked Pamela to include that bit of news in her interview, too." Alma lifted the parchment packet and withdrew the papers. As she walked over, she held out the legal documents. "I wasn't sure when to give you these, but I believe now is the best time. I bought this the day after the knife fight. So, here, my love...'tis my wedding gift to us."

"What's this?" he asked.

She laughed. "Look and see for yourself."

Dillon scanned the first paper. Shock registered in his eyes. "T-The deed to the Eschevon property?"

"I snagged the ranch before Carlotta sold it to someone else, but, you'll need to run the place. I know absolutely nothing about horses, whereas you, well, you know everything. And with our marriage...everything becomes yours anyway."

"Are you serious?" He reread the document. "This is unbelievable?" His lips shifted into a lopsided smile. "I-I married you for love, Alma. Not for your money."

She laughed. "I know that, silly." She waggled her finger toward the documents. "Um...you might also want to look at that next paper."

With trembling hands, Dillon shuffled aside the forms and gasped.

Warmth swept through her. *Good, he's happy.* "'Tis a contract offer from Uncle Thaddeus for us to provide horses to the army. All that's waiting is your signature. I hope you're interested in fulfilling the order, because I know nothing about that, either."

He lifted his stunned gaze to lock on hers. Smile widening, Dillon lowered the papers to the side table. "I-I can't believe this...I mean, oh my God. You, this, everything is a dream come true."

Another grin edged her lips. "We must do something with our money, right? I mean, we can't live forever in a hotel, and I'm afraid your cabin won't hold all my Boston belongings that are being shipped out here." She leaned forward and placed her hands on his broad shoulders. "Since my journey westward and learning of father's death, I've come to realize I never want to live in a big city again. Visit them, yes. But live? No. I want to live in the country, with you, with our children. And, as I plan on us having several, so we can all look up at the stars together each night." She issued a soft laugh, tears gathering in her eyes as she gripped tighter. "Besides, knowing how much you like Jackson and Callie, I thought being neighbors might be for the best." She paused, and a tear spilled down her cheek. "Please tell me you're happy about all this?"

On a loud whoop, Dillon pulled her onto his lap and cupped her face. "Other than the joy of marrying you and loving you for the rest of my life, *this* is the best thing ever. No more scouting. *Jeezus*, Alma...I love you so much." He caught her mouth in a long, heated kiss. On a hum of pleasure, he slid his hand beneath her robe, his callused fingers warm against her skin. His touch stole her breath. "Regardless of ranches," he said against her mouth, "I'm just grateful for the gift of *you* in my life."

Love rushed through her. "I'm the lucky one," she whispered, her voice thick with emotion. The many joys this man had already shown her outnumbered the stars in the glorious night sky. She hugged him. "And I'm so glad you approve." However much she wanted to make love again, she slid from his embrace. "I'll dress and we can go see our new place."

"We'll go in a minute." He held the edge of her robe, and the paisley silk glided from her naked body.

Eyes dark with need, he slipped off his jacket and then pulled his shirt from the waistband of his pants. "For right now, Mrs. Reed, I'm going to thank you good and proper." Dillon scooped her up and she wrapped herself around him. "You beast," she breathed.

"As I recall, you like things this way."

"I do at tha--"

Long and intimate, his kiss cut off her words as they tumbled into bed.

When they finally exited the hotel hours later, the sun blazed high in the sky.

Alma smoothed her hands over the peplum of her black riding habit, the skirt void of a full bustle, much to her husband's delight. A top hat finished her stylish ensemble, the tails of the black bow falling off the back edge of the brim and down her back. Before she'd left their room, she also tucked a folding parasol beneath her arm.

A smile across her face, she nodded at the hotel patrons passing by as she followed her husband out the front door.

He clasped the brim of his Stetson in one hand, his other giving hers a squeeze. "I'll call for a carriage," he said, turning toward the stable.

"Wait. No carriage today."

He glanced at her, a glint in his eyes. A half-smile touched his lips. "You don't mean what I'm thinkin', do you?"

A breeze lifted the wisps of hair falling over his forehead. Another sizzle slipped through her. She cherished this man with all her heart. "Yes, Mister Reed," she said with warm teasing. "I do mean exactly that."

Dillon nodded and stepped into the sunlight, his spurs chinking as he hit the sand. The sun laid a glint across his holstered Colt. "Wait here out of the heat. I'll be right back." Five minutes later, he pulled his gelding to a stop, paces away. "You sure 'bout this, Princess?"

She stepped onto the dusty lane. Shielding her eyes from the glare of the territory sun, she glanced up at her husband. "Absolutely."

With a laugh, he leaned down and slid his arm around her. "Up we go, darlin'." He lifted her onto the saddle and set her before him, then slipped his arm around her cinched waist.

Wrapped within his protective embrace, Alma settled against him, never so happy in her life. "Perfect," she sighed. "Now, I'm ready."

"I'm glad you're here, too," he whispered against her ear. "Within easy reach." He squeezed her tighter against him as tears of joy filled her eyes. They had their whole life ahead of them, and she couldn't wait to get started. She pushed open her tiny sunshade and held the peach-colored parasol aloft in her gloved hand.

Chuckling, Dillon pushed the gadget a smidgen more to the left, then reined his gelding around and headed south.

Anyone who caught a glimpse of the mismatched newlyweds as they rode by didn't really know the full love story between this army scout and the beautiful Boston socialite he'd been assigned to protect on her journey westward.

But…they knew.

And that was all that mattered to them.

The End

ABOUT THE AUTHOR...

Born in Arizona to a family of educators, Cindy Nord moved from the southwestern desert to southwestern Indiana during her teenage years. After the birth of her two sons, she became a stay-at-home mom. When the boys went down for naps, she settled in to read and escape into the world of historical novels. A thousand stories and a divorce later, Cindy pulled out her father's Tower typewriter and decided she would write a saga that contained the elements *SHE* liked best in a hero.

Cindy met her husband, Tom, on a Civil War battlefield, where he was portraying a captain of the 14th Indiana Infantry. Right then and there, she decided to don a corset and become part of a unique little hobby called Civil War Reenacting, something she and her family could enjoy together. The rest, as they say, is history.

A member of numerous writers groups, Cindy's work has finaled or won countless times in chapter competitions, including the prestigious Romance Writers of America National Golden Heart Contest. Her writing is fresh and intense, and conflict keeps the pages turning. A luscious blend of history and romance, her stories meld both genres around fast-paced action and emotionally driven characters.

Indeed, true love awaits you in the writings of Cindy Nord.

Website: www.cindynord.com
Facebook: https://www.facebook.com/cindy.nord.9
Twitter: cnord2@sbcglobal.net

Cindy invites you to enjoy her other passion-driven novels in her bestselling
The Cutteridge Series
NO GREATER GLORY
(Book One & the #1 Civil War Romance at Amazon for over one full year)
https://amzn.com/B008GWOI9S

WITH OPEN ARMS
(Book Two & a #1 Bestselling Western Historical Romance)
https://amzn.com/B00KT23WO0

BY ANY MEANS
(Book Four – Coming the winter of 2017)

Amid the carnage of war, he commandeers far more than just her home

NO GREATER GLORY
©2012 Cindy Nord
(The Cutteridge Family, Book One)
Samhain Publishing
https://www.samhainpublishing.com/book/4282/no-greater-glory

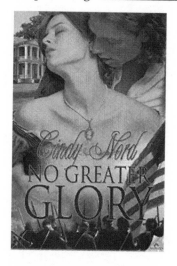

Widowed plantation owner Emaline McDaniels has struggled to hold on to her late husband's dreams. Despite the responsibilities resting on her slender shoulders, she'll not let anyone steal away what's left of her way of life...particularly a Yankee officer who wants to set up winter camp on her land.

With a defiance born of desperation, she defends her home as though it were the child she never had...and no mother gives up her child without a fight!

Despite the brazen wisp of a woman pointing a gun at his head, Colonel Reece Cutteridge has his orders. Requisition Shapinsay—and its valuable livestock—for his regiment's use, and pay her with Union vouchers. He ever expected her fierce determination, then her concern for his wounded, to upend his heart—and possibly his career.

As the armies go dormant for the winter, battle lines are drawn inside the mansion. Yet just as their clash of wills shifts to forbidden passion, the tides of war sweep Reece away. And now their most desperate battle is to survive the war with their lives—and their love—intact.

(Available now in ebook and print from Samhain Publishing and all other booksellers)

** Also available in audiobook -- www.amazon.com/No-Greater-Glory/dp/B009G7VPIO/ref=tmm_aud_swatch_0?_encoding=UTF8&qid=&sr=

A war-weary ex-soldier. An untamable woman. Love doesn't stand a chance in hell...

WITH OPEN ARMS

©2012 Cindy Nord
(The Cutteridge Family, Book Two)
Samhain Publishing
https://www.samhainpublishing.com/book/5115/with-open-arms

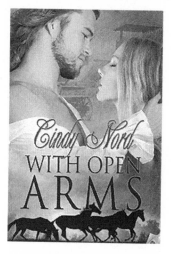

Hardened in childhood by the death of her parents, then left to run the family's southwestern territory ranch when her brother rode off to fight for the Union years before, Callie Cutteridge hides her heartbreak behind a mask of self-sufficiency. Breaking horses for the army proves she's neither delicate nor helpless. When a former cavalry officer shows up claiming to own her brother's half of the Arizona ranch, she steels herself to resist the handsome stranger's intention to govern even one single aspect of her life. After all, loving means losing...to her it always has.

For months, Jackson Neale has looked forward to putting the blood-stained battlefields back east behind him. Callie isn't the agreeable angel her brother led him to believe, but he's damned well not the useless rake this foul-mouthed hellion thinks he is, either. His quest for calm stability contradicts sharply with her need for control, yet still their heartstrings tangle. But how can these mistrusting partners transform their fiery passion into happily-ever-after when all Callie knows how to do is fight...and all Jackson wants is peace?

(Available now in ebook and print from Samhain Publishing and all other booksellers)

Made in the
USA
Lexington, KY